# THE HOUSE ON
# HARBOR HILL

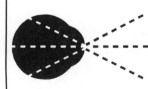

This Large Print Book carries the
Seal of Approval of N.A.V.H.

# THE HOUSE ON HARBOR HILL

# SHELLY STRATTON

**THORNDIKE PRESS**

A part of Gale, a Cengage Company

∴ GALE
A Cengage Company

Farmington Hills, Mich • San Francisco • New York • Waterville, Maine
Meriden, Conn • Mason, Ohio • Chicago

LIBRARY OF CONGRESS CIP DATA ON FILE.
CATALOGUING IN PUBLICATION FOR THIS BOOK
IS AVAILABLE FROM THE LIBRARY OF CONGRESS

978-1-4328-5243-6 (hardcover)

Published in 2018 by arrangement with Dafina Books, an imprint of Kensington Publishing Corp.

Printed in the United States of America
1 2 3 4 5 6 7 22 21 20 19 18

To Chloe and Andrew, thank you for your love, support, and distraction. To Mom and Dad, thanks for being there from day one.

■ ■ ■ ■

# PART I

■ ■ ■ ■

*Camden Beach, Maryland*
*September 2016*

# CHAPTER 1

When Tracey first saw the envelope taped to her front door — a four-by-six-inch yellow square set against blue paint made gray by decades of unrelenting sun — she instantly thought it was an eviction notice.

"Oh, hell," she muttered under her breath, shifting her sobbing thirteenth-month-old farther up her hip.

"What's wrong, Mommy?" her son, Caleb, asked as he swung his Batman backpack back and forth, making it look as if the caped crusader was about to take flight. He wiped his runny nose with the back of a chubby hand already smudged with some drying substance that could be chocolate or mud. Wide, blue eyes gazed up at her innocently. The vulnerability in those eyes almost broke her heart.

*Sorry, sweetheart. Mommy's failed you yet again.*

The boy had been fed a steady diet of

disappointment for the past eleven months.

Tracey painted on a smile and turned to him. "Nothing, honey! Nothing!"

She had to shout to be heard above her daughter's ear-piercing screams. She bounced Maggie up and down, but the screams didn't subside; they only increased in intensity.

"It's all right, honey. It's okay," she whispered against the child's wet, flushed cheek. She then reached for the envelope and yanked it from the front door. There was no address label, so she flipped it over and inspected the back.

"To Tracey Walters," it said in a script so elegant she wondered if it had been written with a calligrapher's pen, "from the woman you met at Chesapeake Cupcakery."

*Who?*

Tracey's brows furrowed as she stared, flummoxed, at those words.

When was the last time she had been at Chesapeake Cupcakery — the little shop on Leonardtown Avenue her friend Jessica owned? And what woman had she met there? Invisible fingers groped into her memory, but latched onto nothing.

"What is it, Mommy?" Caleb asked.

Tracey opened her mouth to answer, but Maggie screamed again, making her wince.

Tracey hastily tucked the envelope into her purse along with the rest of the mail. She dug out her house key, inserted it into the lock, and shoved the front door open.

She was in no mood for cryptic messages, but at least it wasn't an eviction notice — though she would probably get one of those any day now.

Her landlord, Mr. Stapleton, had been harping on her for the past few months about the piecemeal rent payments she would slip through his brass door slot late at night or in the wee hours of the morning. Not checks, because he no longer trusted in the validity of any checks she wrote, and frankly, she didn't blame him. Any check with her signature had more bounce than the red inflatable castle her son liked to play in at Jasper Jumpers — whenever she could afford to take him to Jasper Jumpers, that is. So when Tracey paid her rent, it was either crumpled bills in denominations of twenty and ten that smelled of sweat and peanut oil from the hotel restaurant where she worked or money orders wrapped in a sheet of paper with an apologetic note attached.

*I'm sorry I can't pay more,* the last note had read, scribbled in the purple ink of one of her son's oversized magic markers. *I SWEAR*

*I'll get the rest to you sometime next week!*

His response had been that her rent was eight hundred and fifty dollars a month. "Not six hundred! Not five hundred! And certainly not four hundred and fifty dollars!" He said she should look elsewhere for somewhere to live because he had several potential tenants on a waiting list that wanted to live in the home she was renting.

*Then times must be harder than I had imagined,* she mused, because the two-bedroom, one bath, ramshackle rambler where they lived wasn't exactly a mid-century modern luxury rental in Palm Springs.

The temperature of the water in their only bathroom was so unpredictable that if you turned on the shower faucet, it was a roll of the dice whether the water would come out icy cold or scorching hot. (She had the scalded shoulder to prove it.) The beige carpets were so threadbare she'd started to cover them with a patchwork of throw rugs to mask the holes. The paint along the ceilings had a maze of cracks like a web of veins and capillaries. The electric outlets sometimes worked, sometimes didn't. The cockroaches were so numerous she was on the verge of asking them to chip in for the rent. And no matter how high she turned up the heat during cold months, there seemed to be a blustery draft that made its way from the front door to the back porch, causing goose bumps to sprout on her arms and legs whenever she ventured from her bedroom without wearing a robe.

But the house had a roof, a door, and four walls. It had running water and electricity. Her humble home had the essentials, even if it wasn't perfect. And it was one of the few rentals in this middle-class neighborhood, with its low crime rate and grade-A school district, that she could afford on her meager salary.

Tracey wanted to make more money; she had no romantic illusions about the life of a pauper. She'd applied for other, better paying jobs — even jobs where the hours weren't ideal or the location was so far away from her home she would have developed a stiff neck and a bad back from driving for so long every day. Cashier at Burger King, manning the check-in desk at a seedy motel off Route 4, receptionist at an office building downtown . . . she had applied for them all, but her applications either got lost in the shuffle or she didn't make "the cut," according to whomever was holding the scissors. No one seemed eager to hire a college dropout and former full-time, stay-at-home mom.

Desperate, Tracey had even swallowed her pride and tried to apply for financial assistance three months ago. The county caseworker had handed her a clipboard with a form attached, asking not only for her name, address, and the names of her children, but also for their father's name and address.

"Why do you need this?" Tracey had asked, pointing at the blank space on the page with the tip of her ballpoint pen.

"We need it because the state isn't going to pay to take care of your kids unless their father can't to do it," the woman had answered bluntly as she popped her gum.

Tracey had caught a whiff of spearmint as she spoke.

"Wait. You're going to *contact* him? You're going to make him pay child support?"

The woman had nodded. "Either he pays you or he pays us." She'd inclined her head. "Look, if you don't know for sure who the father is . . ." She had paused to glance at Maggie, who had been sitting on Tracey's lap, sucking her pacifier, and Caleb, who had stood in the corner, making explosion noises as he banged his Incredible Hulk action figure into the wall plaster. "Or if you don't know who the *fathers* are," the caseworker had said, raising her eyebrows meaningfully, "you can always give the names and addresses of your best estimation."

Tracey had lowered her pen, too stunned by the woman's words to be insulted.

"It's no big deal. You wouldn't be the first. Flip it over and write as many names as you have to on the back of the form."

The caseworker had then turned back to face her computer screen. As she clicked away at her QWERTY keys, Tracey had stared at the back of the woman's blond head. She'd silently placed the clipboard back on the woman's desk, risen from her leather chair, and grabbed her purse.

"Caleb, let's go," she'd whispered.

The trio had fled from the welfare office, much like she had fled from her home with the children in tow almost a year ago. They had been at a near run by the time they reached the parking lot.

Tracey still had no intention of returning.

She didn't want child support from her husband — not one single dime. And she certainly didn't want to reveal to him where she and the children now lived. If she did, he'd come for her; he'd come for all of them. He'd try to make her come back, and she was never, *ever* going back.

■ ■ ■ ■

"Homework *before* television!" Tracey shouted half-heartedly over her shoulder as Caleb raced down the short hall to their living room. She veered toward the eat-in kitchen.

As Tracey walked through the kitchen entrance, out of the corner of her eye she saw Caleb beeline for the television, grabbing the remote from their second-hand IKEA coffee table and tossing aside his backpack onto their love seat. He turned on Nickelodeon, ignoring his mother's command. The sound of lasers and explosions suddenly filled the house.

Tracey's lips tightened in frustration. She should order him to turn off the television, but Maggie's screams of agony took precedence over Caleb's blatant disobedience.

"What he needs is a good smack on the rear end," she could hear her mother say. "Spare the rod, spoil the child, Tracey!"

But her mother hadn't done much spanking, let alone disciplining, during Tracey's own childhood. And since leaving her husband, Tracey hadn't had much of a stomach for corporal punishment. The idea of raising her hand to Caleb made her almost nauseated.

Tracey dropped both her purse and the diaper bag onto the kitchenette table before falling back into one of the wooden chairs and setting Maggie on her lap. She fished around in the bag's inner pockets.

"Where is it? Where is it?" she muttered amid the soundtrack of wails and blaring cartoons before finally locating the plastic tube of Orajel. She'd had to buy a spare since Maggie's babysitter kept losing them.

"Does the woman think I'm made out of money?" Tracey mumbled to herself before covering the tip of her index finger with the bubblegum pink gel and swabbing it on her daughter's inflamed gums. Gradually, the screams and tears subsided. The baby thumped her head back against Tracey's collarbone in relief, making her mother wince, then smile.

"All better?"

"Eat! Eat!" Maggie shouted.

Tracey kissed her crown and rose to her feet just as the doorbell rang. She glanced over her shoulder again.

"Eat! Eat!" Maggie chanted as the doorbell rang a second time, followed by a loud knock.

Tracey rushed out of the kitchen and down the hall, perching Maggie on her hip as she did so. She swung open the front door and took a step back in surprise.

Mr. Stapleton stood on the doormat with his fist raised and his hairy knuckles poised to knock again. When he saw Tracey standing in the doorway, he lowered his hand.

He was a short man who resembled a melting candle — his pale, bald head sank into his thick neck, which sagged into his bowed shoulders, which then turned into a doughy frame and finally ended in two stubby feet encased in unremarkable cheap, leather shoes.

"Ms. Walters," he said, shoving his wire-framed glasses up the bridge of his nose, squinting his watery gray eyes at her.

"Mmm-Mr. Stapleton," she stuttered, pushing the door farther open. "Umm, look, I know I told you I'd give you the rest of this month's rent early this week, but I'm going to need a little more time."

He quickly shook his head. "Don't worry about it. I'm not here to collect your rent."

"You aren't?"

He shook his head again. "No. I was hoping you'd be here so I wouldn't have to dig out my key." He held up a key ring and jingled it, showing an assortment of more than a dozen keys of all shapes and sizes. "The damn thing isn't here. I must have left it back at the house. It'd be a pain to have to go back there now. I'd hate to have to postpone the tour."

She frowned. "*Tour?* What . . . what tour?"

Tracey watched as Mr. Stapleton suddenly turned and beckoned a couple she hadn't realized had been standing there the whole time. They were waiting at the end of the driveway near a red hatchback missing one of its hubcaps. The woman had her arms wrapped around her and her head bowed. The man had his hands shoved into his pockets and looked anxious. When Mr. Stapleton waved at them, they immediately shuffled across the yard toward the wooden steps.

"What tour?" Tracey repeated, though she already knew the answer.

Mr. Stapleton turned to her and grinned. "I'm giving a tour to the new tenants." He extended a folded sheet of paper toward her. "This is your one-month notice to vacate."

That night, after the children had gone to bed, Tracey sat alone at the kitchen table, staring at the notice. A chipped glass sat beside her, half filled with a Lodi zinfandel the hotel manager had given to her for Christmas. He'd given a bottle to all the wait staff, a splurge meant to reward them

19

for a stellar year filled with happy tourists who readily opened their wallets and plunked down more than twenty bucks for frozen scallops and overcooked lobster at the hotel's restaurant.

She hadn't opened the bottle when she'd received the gift, deciding to save it for some special occasion, keeping it in its feather-fringed gift bag and tucking both in the cabinet underneath the sink next to the bottles of 409 and Pine Sol. But tonight, she pulled the cork and finished a third of the bottle. She figured losing your home was a rare enough occasion to warrant getting drunk on a decent wine.

Tracey twirled the gift bag around and around her index finger and raised the glass to her lips. As she sipped, she tossed the bag aside and began to write on the blank side of the eviction notice how much money she had left. As soon as she'd begun to dream of her great escape, she had squirreled money away like acorns to last her through the cold, hard winter. Now, less than a year after leaving Paul, Tracey was already at the last of it — a sum total of three hundred and twenty-seven dollars.

She then calculated how much money she would need to move to a new place: first month's rent, deposit, hiring movers, etc.

*There's a big difference between those two numbers,* she thought forlornly.

She reached for her purse. It was still sitting on the kitchenette table. She shoved her hand inside in search of her latest bank statement among the bills that had arrived in her mailbox that day, foolishly hopeful she had more money than she remembered. Instead, she pulled out a yellow envelope. She stared at it in bewilderment, wondering why this was in her purse, and then she remembered.

*The elegant script on the back . . .*

*The woman from Chesapeake Cupcakery . . .*

She examined the envelope, laughing softly to herself. The parchment was thick, and you could spot its woven pattern even with the naked eye. It looked like something you would send to invite someone to a wedding or an induction ceremony. How could she ever have mistaken this for an eviction notice?

She opened it and tugged out the letter inside. As she read it, her smile disappeared.

Dear Ms. Walters,

I saw you and your beautiful children at the Chesapeake Cupcakery. You seem like a warm woman, though — I hope

21

you don't mind me saying this — a bit worried and maybe even a little scared. I want to assure you that you are not alone in this world. Please accept my invitation for help of any kind. My door is always open.

Sincerely,
Delilah Grey of Harbor Hill

# CHAPTER 2

Delilah placed a brown, wrinkled hand over her heart as she watched the men load the suede love seat onto the back of the truck. Instead of feeling her breast under her palm, she felt the soft give of baggy cotton, then her bare chest, as she tried to soothe the ache swelling there, the ache she felt at saying good-bye yet again.

Though this phantom pain probably would never go away, her breasts had disappeared years ago. They hadn't been there since she'd had her double mastectomy in 2009. Delilah didn't wear the prosthetic breasts the doctor had given her after her surgery. They sat abandoned in a box, sealed in the original plastic wrapping, somewhere on a shelf in her walk-in closet. They would remain there because she did not — and would never — care for such things. People mattered; fake breasts did not.

She continued to watch the two movers

slowly walk up the metal ramp as they carried the love seat, one shouting directions she couldn't hear clearly from behind the second-floor bedroom window. Sweat stains were along their backs and armpits, darkening their tan shirts with Vs. Their pants sank low on their hips, as young men's pants often did nowadays, each revealing two to three inches of boxer briefs. After they loaded the sofa onto the truck, they both trudged down the ramp and walked toward a stack of cardboard boxes in the driveway with large labels on them. KITCHEN one box said in big black letters. BEDROOM said another.

Keeping a watchful eye on the movers was a redhead who stood off to the side with her freckled arms crossed over her chest. As if she felt Delilah's eyes on her, she turned and looked toward the bedroom window. She and Delilah momentarily locked gazes. The young woman waved, and Delilah raised her hand from her chest and waved back.

Delilah remembered when she'd first seen Claudia standing on her front porch. It had been raining that night all those many months ago, much as it had rained the night decades before when Delilah had first arrived at Harbor Hill hand in hand with her future husband. But unlike Delilah, who had sauntered up the stairs to her new home, Claudia seemed to hesitate to even ring the doorbell. The poor girl hadn't had a coat or umbrella. She had been soaked from the downpour — from her long, stringy hair to her mud-stained canvas shoes.

Claudia had shouted over the sound of thunder in the distance, above the sound of pelting rain as her thin shoulders had trembled, either from the cold or the fear of lightning. "I'm . . . I'm sorry, ma'am, to just show up like this, but I got your note! I had nowhere else to go!"

That night, Delilah had seen the same desperation in Claudia's eyes that she saw in *all* their eyes — that she had seen reflected in her own eyes decades ago. But that's why she had chosen her, wasn't it? It was why she had sent her the note that she had sent to many others, always ending with the same words: *Please accept my invitation for help of any kind. My door is always open.* She'd done it because of that frightened animal look and because Claudia seemed to believe there was no one in the world to whom she could turn for help.

Seeing her there, Delilah had wordlessly pushed the door open and ushered Claudia inside her home.

But now the aura of desperation was gone. Standing in the driveway, Claudia looked confident, content. She seemed renewed. She wasn't that scared little animal any-more, frantically burrowing into a hole. She was finally ready to leave her four-thousand-square-foot nest on Harbor Hill.

Tears started to well in Delilah's eyes.

"It's always sad to see them go, ain't it?"

Delilah jumped at the sound of the voice behind her, though she shouldn't have. It was a familiar voice — one that had spoken to her for the past several decades. But she didn't remember hearing it quite so clearly before. It was like the voice had been using a tin can and waxed yarn to reach her and suddenly decided to upgrade to an Apple iPhone.

"So, so sad," the voice continued.

She sniffed, blinked back her tears, and looked over her shoulder, though she knew no one would be waiting for her there. Her eyes settled on her ornate oak four-poster bed, where her brown and black tabby lounged, grooming himself with one leg stuck straight up into the air.

"Did you say something, Bruce?" she asked, raising her gray brows.

At her question, Bruce stopped licking the

long hairs on his tummy and narrowed his yellow eyes at her.

"Of course he didn't say anything, you silly girl," the voice drawled. "He's a cat! He didn't say it — I did."

Delilah walked toward the bed and sat down, exhaling as she landed on the mattress. Bruce hopped to his feet and sauntered toward her, his small paws leaving light indentations in the plush velvet duvet. He then climbed onto her ample lap and began to purr as she stroked him.

When she'd brought Bruce home from the local animal shelter six years ago, he had been a scruffy little thing — a mass of dandelion-like fur and oversized ears. Now he was an overweight prima donna who had a penchant for fresh tuna and had declared eminent domain over her bedroom. The bed, carpet, chaise lounge, and every other cloth-covered surface seemed to have a permanent coat of Bruce's cat hair.

"You're one persistent little man," she said as she rubbed Bruce's back, feeling his rib cage vibrate beneath her palm as he purred contentedly. "Can't stand for your mama not to pay attention to you, can you?"

"Can you blame him? Who would want to compete with all the other strays you drag in off the street?"

Delilah's hand stilled.

"Delilah and her strays," the voice continued merrily in a singsong voice. "If it's mangy, dirty, and from the dregs of humanity, she'll offer you a couch, a shower, and a glass of lemonade. Won't you, Dee?"

Bruce raised his head and turned to gaze at her. He nudged her wrist with his brow, urging her to pet him again. She obeyed and resumed stroking the cat's back.

The voice released a deep, throaty chuckle. "You can drag home your tired, your poor, your beaten, and your broken, but it still doesn't change anything, you bitch," the voice said with an icy coldness.

The ghostly voice would usually start off enticing; it had an almost saccharine sweetness that would lull her into thinking it wasn't *that* bad. So what if she'd had a voice whispering in her ear for the past forty and some odd years? It was so charming, so kind. Who wouldn't want its company? And then the voice would grow needlepoint teeth and claws, and she couldn't get away from it fast enough.

"Good morning, beautiful," it would whisper to her when she stood in front of the bathroom mirror in the morning, brushing her teeth. Then she would pause to spit the minty froth into the sink, and it would shout, "Didn't you hear me talking to you, you lying cunt?"

"Isn't it a lovely day today?" it would ask cheerfully as she worked in her garden, patting soil into a clay pot filled with geranium seeds. "Not that you deserve it, bitch."

She had tried to get rid of the voice over the years. She had been blessed by her minister and read the Bible until her vision blurred, seeking guidance from the holy word for some recipe that would make the voice go away.

*Submit yourselves therefore to God. Resist the devil, and he will flee from you.* — Book of James, chapter 4, verse 7.

She had gone to a mystic healer who'd waved burning sage over her and around the rooms of Harbor Hill while mumbling some mumbo jumbo.

The old woman had promised she wouldn't be haunted anymore just before tucking the two hundred dollars Delilah had given her into her bosom.

Delilah had even confided in a doctor, telling him how the voice tried to instigate fights with her, though she refused to take the bait.

*"Really?"* the doctor had asked, furrowing his dark, batwing-like brows as he scribbled on a notepad. "Does the voice tell you to

do things, Delilah?"

She had frowned at his question and the presumption he had taken at calling her by her first name. "What do you mean?"

"I mean does the voice tell you to hurt yourself or hurt others?" the doctor had asked, nibbling on the tip of a pen already covered with gnaw marks. He studied her like she was one of the pages in the many journals on his mahogany office shelf.

"He's told me to go swimming in the Chesapeake Bay and just stay there, if that's what you mean," she answered dryly.

"He?"

"Yep."

"And who is *he*, Delilah?"

She had fallen silent. The tick of the doctor's wall clock and the noise of a garbage truck passing by the building several floors below had been the only sound in the room as they had stared at one another and the doctor had waited for her answer.

"You've got ink all over your face," Delilah had said as she pointed at the doctor, breaking their silence and reaching into her purse to withdraw a Kleenex.

"Oh, oh!" the doctor had said, sitting forward in his chair as he futilely wiped at the large glob of blue ink on his chin. He'd reluctantly accepted the tissue she'd handed him.

Soon after, the doctor had suggested more intensive therapy sessions and a multitude of pills to deal with her "hallucinations." They would then see how she responded to the treatment and "take it from there."

But Delilah didn't come back to therapy or take any fool pills. How could she trust the word of a man who couldn't even keep ink off his face?

The voice wasn't a hallucination. The voice was *real* — as real as the sky above and the ground below. And it wouldn't go away, not with therapy or pills or mystic hullabaloo or intervention from God himself.

She would just have to ignore it, to treat the voice like it was an annoying child acting out, clamoring for attention — treat it like the nuisance that it was. It would shout a few more times and then disappear. She planned to take the same approach today.

"It doesn't mean a thang," the voice continued to sing with a Tom Jones–like bravado as Delilah gazed out the windowpanes, still stroking Bruce. "Doesn't mean a thang! It doesn't change what you did. You hear me, Dee?" it barked.

She flinched and reflexively squeezed the hunk of fur in her hand. Bruce let out a yelp, then nipped her, leaving twin-sized punctures on her knuckles.

"Oww! Damn it!" she shouted, tossing Bruce to the floor and clutching her hand to her chest.

Bruce's ears went flat as he squinted at her. Each gave the other a reproachful look before Bruce fled from the bedroom with his tail whipping behind him.

Delilah stared down at her hand, where two trickles of blood slid over the wrinkled skin and landed on her lap before fading into the yellow-and-blue flower pattern of her sundress.

"That won't come out," she murmured, remembering a similar stain from many, *many* years ago.

At the sound of a metal door being shut, Delilah tore her gaze away from the blood. She looked up and out the window.

The two movers walked back down the ramp, laughing and shouting to one another. They then raised the ramp before shoving it into a slot beneath the moving truck. Claudia walked toward a man who stood off to the side. He was also wearing a sweat-stained T-shirt and sagging jeans like the movers, but he held a pair of garden shears in his hand.

It was Aidan, the landscaper and resident

handyman for Harbor Hill. Aidan had called the expansive cottage his home when he was a teenager, when he and his mother, Rosario, had moved here after living out of their car for months. He had returned four years ago to help Delilah maintain the property.

*And to hide,* Delilah thought. Because Harbor Hill not only seemed to serve as a place for sustenance and healing, but also as a place where one went to bury things, and poor Aidan had more pain, scars, and loss to bury than most.

# CHAPTER 3

Claudia spread her arms, wide and welcoming, and walked toward where Aidan stood in the driveway, and he wasn't sure how to respond. Should he hug her back? Should he kiss her? Should the kiss be chaste or something heated, like the ones they usually shared? What was a proper way to say goodbye to a woman you've slept with more than a dozen times but to whom you've never said, "I love you," let alone "Wanna grab some breakfast in the morning?"

But then Aidan reminded himself this was during the day, not at night. He wasn't slinking out of her bedroom at 2:00 a.m., careful not to wake Delilah, who was fast asleep three doors down the hall. Instead, he and Claudia were standing near her moving truck, and two twenty-something men — one with dreads and another with a faux hawk — were standing only a few feet away, loudly regaling each other with stories about last night's basketball game.

So when Claudia wrapped her arms around him, Aidan responded in kind, keeping the gesture innocuous — simply a hug between friends. Because even though they had been fuck buddies, that still made them buddies. But he wasn't prepared when Claudia whispered, "Thank you for everything, Aidan," before brushing her lips across the beard stubble on his cheek.

"Thank you for what?" he asked, squinting down at her when she released him and took a step back.

"You know what," she said with a knowing smirk and a wink before walking backward toward her car, which was parked next to the moving truck. She then gave him a wave, tossed her reddish-orange locks over her shoulder, and turned away.

He continued to stare at her in confusion, even as he watched her open the door to her Honda Civic.

It was Delilah whom the women usually thanked — not Aidan. She was their Mother Teresa, Florence Nightingale, and Princess Di all rolled into one. She was the one who deserved to be canonized for what she did for these poor, wayward women. He was just the asshole who helped them carry in their bags, pruned the tree branches outside their windows, and screwed them occasionally.

Though he guessed what he did offer them was his own brand of "help." He didn't know how many times he had heard the sundry women confess how ugly they felt, how useless they believed themselves to be, and how no one in the world could possibly love them, let alone *want* them.

Aidan had "helped" Hannah, a twenty-something ex-waitress who had stayed with Delilah two years ago. Hannah's boyfriend had once told her she was a "big fat blob," after she had gained weight after her mother's death from lung cancer. "It was depression, I think," Hannah had confessed to Aidan. "Instead of drinking, I'd just stuff my face with Snoballs and Twinkies. I couldn't stop. I put on forty pounds. He told me I was just gross . . . that I was disgusting."

He had also "helped" Wendy, a former heroin addict from Texas who had briefly stayed with Delilah back in January. Wendy had told him that she knew she wasn't pretty and had never been that hot to begin with "and the drugs messed me up awful bad. Ruined what little I had." She had pulled down the sleeves of her wool sweater to cover the needle tracks on her arms as she said it. "Any decent guy would take one look at me and go runnin'. I wouldn't blame him."

Aidan made them feel beautiful and desirable, and he didn't have to ply them with drinks or compliments. He simply listened to them. He'd smile and nod his head at the right moments and let them unload whatever burdens they wanted — an endless stream of worries, doubts, past trespasses, recriminations, heartaches, and disappointments. He noticed that they rarely, if ever, asked him about himself. They never asked him about his past or what sad or traumatic events had brought a man like him — a high-powered attorney from Chicago — to Harbor Hill, of all places. But that was fine with Aidan. He accepted the confessions; he wasn't the one doing the confessing. He was the receptacle for all their pain; he felt no need to share his own. The only time he would ever speak was when they talked about their dreams and their aspirations for themselves. Getting that GED ten years after dropping out of high school, letting go of that nasty drug habit, regaining custody of your kids . . . nothing was beyond reach, according to Aidan — whether he secretly believed it or not.

37

"Just take it one day at a time," he would say.

Aidan made them feel seen and acknowledged, something his mother had never felt. They weren't one of millions of faceless women on street corners and waiting in line with bowed heads and sunken shoulders, with slack faces and nondescript clothes, looking like shell-shocked refugees. They were special in every sense of the word. It wasn't long before he would hear that soft knock at his bedroom door and see that tentative smile before they asked to come in.

Some, the more broken ones who were looking for love not just friendship or physical companionship, he would turn away. He was here to offer a brief respite, not to break a heart. But the others — the ones who were willing to take only what he could give — he would wave inside his bedroom, and he would spend the night with them.

Aidan wished he had been so attentive, so benevolent and understanding with his own wife, Trish. How many times had she prattled on about her volunteer work at the local library or homeless shelter and his eyes had glazed over with boredom? How many times had she raved about her latest find at the local organic grocer — holding out the grapes, squash, or carrots for him to examine — and he had glanced up from his BlackBerry, done a quick nod, then resumed whatever text or e-mail he was typing.

"Oh, my God, Aidan!" Trish had squealed when she was six months pregnant. She had rushed into his home office. "You won't believe what I found today: the absolute perfect mobile to go over the baby's crib. Look, it has these little sheep made of the softest cashgora! It's so adorable, honey. You have to feel it," she said as she grabbed his hand, pulling it from the laptop where he had been typing notes for the latest court brief. "See! Isn't it soft?"

"Jesus, babe! Can't you see I'm busy?" he had shouted, yanking his hand back. "I've got more important things to do than feel fucking miniature sheep!"

He had then returned his attention to the laptop screen and resumed typing, trying to regain the mental thread he had lost.

Trish had stood silently beside him after that, a looming tower of judgment.

He hadn't had to look up to know what expression was on her face, to see how her shoulders sank at his words. An apology had been on the tip of his tongue, but he didn't offer it. Some stubborn part of him had kept him from uttering those words. Finally, after a minute or two, Trish had left his office, shutting the door quietly behind her.

Aidan had convinced himself he was so neglectful of Trish because his life had been full of things back then that were all clamoring for his attention. Back then, he had pulled fourteen-hour days at the law firm, where he was trying diligently to make partner. Those slivers of time in between were filled with business lunches and networking over golf and tennis, with sleeping and breathing. He had even started to pop caffeine pills to maintain his rapid pace.

*So, fine,* he'd thought that day, staring at his closed office door, *I didn't feel the fucking cashgora sheep like she asked. But what does she think paid for the sheep hanging off that stupid mobile? Does she realize how we got the money for it and that four-thousand-dollar crib and the custom-made curtains and the baby wardrobe that could clothe all the infants in a Brazilian favela?*

They had gotten it through Aidan's hard work, by him keeping his nose to the grindstone. He had been a provider for his wife and child — unlike his father had been for him and his mom. He hadn't had time to gush over mobiles and baby crap when work needed to be done.

But he knew better now; his defensiveness

had been a lie, a shoddy excuse for bad behavior. Running his hand over the sheep would have taken all of five seconds, ten tops. Would it have killed him to pause, to slow down for once? Would it have killed him to show his wife that he was just as excited about the new baby as she was?

Nowadays, Aidan's free time was abundant. His days were filled with changing blown light bulbs, cleaning gutters, pruning rosebushes, and setting mousetraps — nothing emotionally or mentally taxing. Some days, he would have long stretches of time when he would sit near the shed in Delilah's backyard, drinking a beer, staring at nothing but the bay in the distance, trying not to drown in tedium.

Maybe if he had had more time, he could have treated her better. He *should* have treated her better. He had watched his mother be ignored and taken advantage of her entire life, only to repeat the same thing with his own wife. Trish had just wanted to be seen by him, and yet in the painting that was Aidan's life, Trish had forever remained in the background, an indistinguishable piece of scenery. He would always regret that.

Aidan now watched as the movers climbed into their truck. Claudia turned on her car's engine and pulled out in front of them. She then did two quick beeps of the car horn.

He forced a smile and waved back to let her know that he saw her. He then bent down, grabbed his garden sheers, and walked back toward the house.

# CHAPTER 4

*My door is always open.*

Just what exactly did it mean?

It was a question Tracey had been asking herself for the past two days. She did it as she lay awake in bed with the letter from Delilah Grey and the eviction notice on the night table beside her. She considered the question as she served the tables in the dining room of the hotel and resort where she worked, refilling glasses with watered-down iced tea, gathering half-eaten plates of wilted lettuce and shredded carrots. And she thought of it again during her ride home as she ventured a half mile out of her way to drive past the lone house at the end of Harbor Hill Road, where the enigmatic Delilah Grey lived.

The two-story house was at the highest point in Camden Beach, only a quarter of a mile from a steep cliff that led to unforgiving rocks below and the frothy foam of the

Chesapeake Bay. The house — a beach cottage on steroids — was flanked by a series of pine trees and oaks. It had a high-peaked, shingled roof and six dormers. Cheerfully bright geraniums burst from flower boxes along the second-floor windows. Navy blue Adirondack chairs sat on the wraparound porch. A wooden bird feeder dangled from a copper pole in the front yard, facing the circular driveway.

From a distance, despite its massive size, the house looked serene — maybe even inviting, entreating a passerby to stop inside and share a pitcher of lemonade with its inhabitants.

*My door is always open,* Tracey thought again as her minivan slowed almost to a stop while she gazed out the window at the house on the top of the hill. The driver of the Ford Explorer behind her beeped his horn, and she snapped out of her reverie and floored the accelerator. The house on Harbor Hill became smaller and smaller in her rearview mirror and then finally disappeared from view.

Those five words continued to haunt her.

*My door is always open . . .*
*My door is always open . . .*
*My door is always open . . .*

They became a puzzle, a complicated

44

mathematical equation she had yet to solve. With the children in tow, Tracey drove her beat-up minivan not back to Harbor Hill, but to downtown Camden Beach and the Chesapeake Cupcakery to finally solve it.

Though there were several shops along the boardwalk, the Chesapeake Cupcakery was located farther down, along a series of upscale stores on the first floor of a dual-use, eleven-story residential condo and commercial complex near the bay that had opened in Camden Beach two years ago, before Tracey had arrived. The complex was all concrete, stucco, and glass, with palm trees and hibiscus plants in giant clay pots flanking each entrance and garish five-foot-tall sculptures of dolphins, starfish, and whales along brick pavers.

Tracey had heard that several of Camden Beach's longtime residents had protested the building of the complex. It would block the views of residents who owned houses along the waterfront, they'd complained. It wasn't in keeping with the character — architecturally or aesthetically — of the sleepy beach community with its Cape Cods and ramblers built around town in the 1960s and some as far back as the dawn of the twentieth century. It was just god-awful ugly.

Ultimately, the business community ended up silencing the naysayers. They pacified them with wicker baskets full of coupons for free massages left on porch steps, with comped parking at the new parking garage within the complex. Even Jessica Cho, the owner of Chesapeake Cupcakery, had handed out cupcakes and free coffee the first week she'd opened her shop.

"No one alive can say no to my red velvet cupcakes," Jessica later boasted.

There were still mutterings of displeasure in town about the "monstrosity along the waterfront." The discontented wrote the occasional op-ed piece in the local paper or ranted during zoning meetings. But they were murmurs, not shouts. Tracey, who was relatively new to town, got the sense that these blowups happened often in Camden Beach. It was part of the ongoing war between the new and the old. The residents who had lived in town for decades resented the encroachment of the newcomers — those who moved in from D.C. and renovated old, staid houses into the beach version of McMansions, raising property values and clogging the sleepy roadways with their SUVs and luxury sedans. Camden Beach was a town in flux and under an almost palpable tension you could feel as soon as you drove across the border.

Many of the shops in the complex were meant to appeal to the wealthier newcomers. Tracey walked past the Lilly Pulitzer store, where mannequins stood in the window with colorful sundresses and bikinis, permanently waving and smiling at each passerby. She then walked by a wine and cheese bistro where classical music seeped out of the opened doorway. She gazed at the window display, at the bottles of sauvignon blanc and pinot noir stacked in an artful arrangement on open wooden crates.

*Paul would love a place like this,* she thought absently.

Her husband, Paul, was a bit of a wine connoisseur, keeping a collection of his favorite cabernets and merlots in a custom-made wine fridge she had joked glowed blue like an alien spaceship.

Tracey now thought back to that wine fridge. She remembered the last time she had gotten a bottle out of it, the last time she had been *allowed* to remove a bottle from it.

Paul had sent her downstairs to fetch one of the bottles. She had been distracted, talking on the phone with some telemarketer, when she suddenly heard Maggie's infant cries upstairs. She'd rushed to the first floor to answer her daughter, tripped, fell, and dropped a bottle of Buoncristiani Cabernet Sauvignon Napa Valley 2010. As the telemarketer continued to drone, Tracey had watched the bottle roll down the steps before it had shattered on the floor below. The red wine had exploded like a paintball on impact and seeped into the Afghan rug.

Tracey had lowered her phone from her ear, closed her eyes, and said a silent prayer Paul hadn't heard the bottle shatter. Maybe he had been in some other part of the house when it had happened. But when she'd opened her eyes and seen him standing at the top of the staircase, she'd realized her prayers hadn't been answered. She had felt the blow of reprisal even before Paul charged down the steps and slapped her across the face, knocking the phone out of her hand and sending it ricocheting against the stairway wall.

"Where are we going, Mommy?" Caleb now asked, skipping in front of her.

"It's a . . . a surprise," she answered distractedly, turning away from the window display, shuddering at the memory, and feeling the ghostly burn of her husband's year-old slap on her cheek.

After passing a few more shops, they arrived at the glass door of Chesapeake Cupcakery. Tracey eased the stroller back so Caleb could step forward and hold it open for her and Maggie.

He liked to do things like that. He said it made him feel like a grown-up.

"I'm a gentleman, Mommy!" he would say with a smile, revealing one of his missing front teeth. He said it as if he was proclaiming that he was a magician or a superhero.

But today Caleb didn't hold the door open for her. He let the door slam closed along the side of her stroller, making Tracey yelp as she veered to the left to keep it from falling onto Maggie's extended legs. Instead, it landed on Tracey's elbow, making her wince.

"Caleb!" she shouted.

He ignored her, raced inside the shop, and beelined to the sales counter, where Jessica stood, assembling a platter of oversized cupcakes decorated with candied sailboats and life preserver rings.

"Can I have a cupcake?" he shouted before leapfrogging onto one of the old-fashioned, 1950s style swivel stools.

Jessica pushed a lock of dark hair out of her eyes with fingertips that were purple from some cupcake ingredient, likely fresh berries. "I don't know. Did you ask your mom?"

Caleb spun around on the chair to face Tracey, who was still struggling to get through the shop door. "Can I, Mommy? Can I have a cupcake?" He kicked his sandaled feet back and forth, leaning forward eagerly.

"No!" she barked before finally arriving inside and letting the door fall shut behind her.

"But Moooommy," Caleb whined. "Just one cupcake! I promise that I —"

"I said no, Caleb! You let the door fall on Maggie and me. What you did was . . . was rude! It was selfish. It wasn't right! I'm not going to reward you for that!"

Jessica flinched. Caleb lowered his head. His bottom lip poked out and his blond locks — which were long overdue for a haircut — hung limply into his eyes.

Tracey realized she was being harsh, that her words may have had more venom than she intended, but she was forever vigilant with Caleb. She didn't want him to turn out like his father — cruel and thoughtless, violent and vindictive. And Caleb looked so much like his dad. The older he got, the more his baby fat melted away, like butter on a warm bun. Tracey could see it in his face even now with his head hanging down — the features of the man he would one day become. She could see Paul's high cheekbones and his stubborn chin, his cool blue eyes and Roman nose. It was the ghost of a monster superimposed over the face of a six-year-old boy.

"So," Tracey said, painting on a smile, "how goes business, Jess?"

Jessica glanced uneasily between mother and son before returning Tracey's smile.

"Uh, pretty good lately. Better than you'd think, considering how everyone keeps saying gourmet cupcakes are so passé." She added the last cupcake to the platter. "At least I should be able to pay my parents back the money they loaned me by the end of year."

"*Really?* You'll be able to pay them back already?" Tracey asked as she leaned down to unbuckle Maggie's straps. The toddler shoved herself out of her stroller and made her way with an unsteady gait toward her brother. "That's great, Jess!"

"Yeah, I know. Maybe I can finally afford to expand . . . bring in extra staff. Maybe I can finally hire *you* so you don't have to work at that tacky place anymore. Tell them to go choke on their fried clams."

"You're sweet," Tracey said, laughing softly.

She didn't have the heart to tell Jessica that the end of the year may be too late for her . . . that she was getting kicked out of her home by next month and might no longer be able to afford to live in Camden Beach at all. Instead, she changed the subject.

"I bet your parents will be so proud of you, paying them back so soon."

Jessica waved away her compliment and walked behind the counter, where an array of cupcakes, mini cakes, and pastries were on display in the eight-foot glass case. She tightened the strings of the apron around her waist. "Not really. I became a baker when they thought I was going to become a doctor or a software engineer working in Silicon Valley. I may as well have become a ventriloquist!"

Tracey's grin disappeared. "You don't really mean that. They can see how well you're doing . . . how hard you're working!"

"Please," Jessica chuckled. "I'm a *huge* disappointment to them. They constantly compare me to my sister, Amy — the pediatric surgeon who's married to a nice Korean guy and has two kids."

"I'm sorry, Jess."

Jessica shrugged. "Sometimes parents can be hard on their kids." She glanced meaningfully at Caleb, whose eyes were still downcast. He was ignoring Maggie, who was slapping his shins and leaning her chin against his knee, slobbering onto the khaki fabric of his shorts.

Tracey chewed the inside of her cheek.

"I mean it's heartbreaking how some people can put unrealistic standards on their children, isn't it?" Jessica continued with raised brows.

The shop fell silent. Tracey longed to tell Jessica why she was being so harsh with Caleb, why she'd said what she said, but there were still parts of her past she had yet to divulge to her friend — to anyone. Jessica thought she was just a poor, single mom of two trying to make do on a waitress's salary. She didn't know who or what Tracey was running from.

Rather than try to explain the rationalization behind her behavior, to dredge up her past, it was easier just to offer Caleb an olive branch to prove she wasn't a fire-breathing dragon of a mother.

"Look, honey," she began, turning to Caleb, "maybe . . . maybe you can have a cupcake later before we leave, if you behave yourself."

Grudgingly, Caleb raised his eyes.

"And I'll throw in a one-of-a-kind smoothie too, Caleb . . . if you're good!" Jessica quickly added before grabbing a roll of paper towels and a bottle of Windex. She then wrinkled her nose at Tracey. "What brings you guys here anyway? I thought you said you were cutting down on trips to downtown Camden."

Tracey had said that. Coming to the shops along the complex meant too much of a hit to her wallet, and her funds were meager to begin with, but today she'd made an exception.

"I needed to ask you something." Tracey set her purse on one of the stools. She stuck her hand inside and pulled out the yellow envelop, the one she'd found taped to her front door three days ago. She removed the letter and handed it to Jessica. "First, read this."

Jessica frowned as she reached for the letter. She unfolded it and read it. When she finished reading, she handed the letter back to Tracey, chuckling. "Oh, man! So *you're* the next one on her list?"

Now Tracey was the one who was frowning. "What do you mean?"

"Delilah is always handing out those letters! She gives them to women who are down on their luck. Some even come to her with a sob story or tale of woe. She's been doing it for decades, from what I've heard."

"So she didn't ask you for my address? She didn't get it from you?"

"No!" Jessica furiously shook her head. "I would never do anything like that!"

"So where did she get it from?"

"Who knows! I guess Delilah has her ways. Like I said, she's been doing this for decades. She leaves these mystery letters with people and invites them to live in her house. Free room and board, I think. Like she's the friggin' Make a Wish Foundation."

*"Really?"* Tracey gazed down at the letter again. "She lets them live with her for free?"

Maybe this was what Tracey needed; it would help save her little family. The letter from Delilah Grey was the parachute tossed to her just as fate pushed her out of the airplane and she hurled to the earth below.

Jessica, who had been busying herself with wiping down the display counter, abruptly stilled. "You aren't seriously considering taking her up on her offer, are you?"

"I don't know. Why?"

*"Why?* Because she's obviously crazy, Tracey! You don't want to live with a nut like that, let alone owe her something!"

"Why do you think she's crazy?"

"Because she lets random people live with her — homeless people, prostitutes, and crackheads! No sane person would do that!"

"Maybe she's just . . . I don't know . . . kindhearted."

"There's a difference between being kind-hearted and being nutty — or stupid!"

"That's a bit harsh, isn't it?"

"You call it harsh; I call it honest. Besides, there are . . . well . . . other things about her that I'd be wary of."

Tracey narrowed her eyes again. "What other things?"

Jessica pursed her lips and seemed to hesitate. She returned her attention to wiping down the counter.

"What is it?"

She paused mid-swipe. "I've heard rumors about her. Nothing substantiated," Jessica hastily added, "but still . . . rumors. And not good ones."

In small towns, rumors were plentiful, but Jessica wasn't usually one to gossip. Tracey hadn't known her long, but they had developed the sort of relationship other women took years to hone; she knew her friend well enough. If Jessica was saying something like this now — if she chose to share gossip — it had to be important.

"What rumors, Jess?" Tracey persisted.

Jessica let out a loud breath. She glanced at Caleb and Maggie, who were now at the other end of the counter, pointing at the shelves in the glass case, ogling cupcakes. She leaned over the counter and gestured for Tracey to do the same.

"They say she killed someone," Jessica whispered into Tracey's ear.

Tracey leaned back and stared at her, dumbfounded. She barked out a laugh. "You don't . . . you don't really believe that, do you?"

Jessica sat the paper towel and Windex bottle on the counter and shrugged. "I don't know! Part of me says, 'Why would someone lie about something like that?' But then I think about the rumors about me that I've heard . . . that I'm sabotaging the other bakers on Camden Beach . . . that I serve chopped-up dog in my pastries." She rolled her eyes. "And then I think, 'Hey, maybe some people in town make up outrageous lies just to be mean!' Still I'd think twice about living with her, about bringing my kids around her."

"Mommy, can I have a cupcake now?" Caleb interrupted.

Tracey slowly turned to her son, now stunned. "I'm sorry . . . w-what, honey?"

"I said can I have a cupcake now? You said

I could have one."

"Uh, s-sure, honey."

"All right! Pick out which cupcake you want, big guy. It's on me," Jessica said, winking at Tracey and opening the glass display case. "We've gotta get one for your mom and your little sister too."

Tracey watched as Jessica and the children got to the business of the cupcakes, but she felt removed from the scene, lost in her own thoughts.

Of course, when it finally seemed things were changing for the better for her, there was a catch. But there was always a catch, wasn't there? There had been one when she had decided to marry Paul. She had been awed by his good looks and his ambition, by how much he was willing to woo and pursue her. She didn't find out until later — much too late — what came with those looks and polished veneer. When she had finally decided to leave Paul, the decision had come with a catch too. She had to eschew everything from her old life: her home, her friends, and her financial security. Now she was facing yet another conundrum.

"Do you know which one you want?"

Tracey blinked and turned to find Jessica holding out three cupcakes displayed on a platter — three sugary beauties covered in candied pearls and pastel icing. Neither looked more appetizing than the other. They seemed almost identical.

"No," she answered honestly, shaking her head. "No, I don't."

# CHAPTER 5

Delilah shuffled down the hall toward the stairwell. The soft flap of her slippers on the hardwood and the creak of hundred-year-old floorboards beneath her feet were drowned out by the chainsaw-like buzz of the lawnmower. She glanced out one of the second-floor windows to see Aidan riding up and down the front lawn, wiping his sweaty brow with the back of his hand as he created orderly columns of cut grass. He looked to be nearly done; he would probably start on the backyard soon.

She descended the stairs, careful of Bruce, who zigzagged between her legs.

"You're gonna kill me one day with this nonsense," she admonished, though the cat ignored her.

The stairs at Harbor Hill were precarious. She knew this firsthand.

*But there'll be no falls today,* she thought as she descended the last riser and her feet landed safely on the first floor.

It had been almost a week since Claudia had moved out, and that old feeling was starting to sweep over Delilah. The feeling came with the absence of bodies in Harbor Hill's many bedrooms and seeing the numerous empty chairs at her dining room table. It was the feeling that came with the lack of someone to take care of and cater to — since Aidan refused to let her do it. He was like a petulant child some days, shoving her away every time she tried to embrace him and help him heal.

She longed for voices and laughter, for the thump of footsteps on the stairs and even half-eaten bowls of cereal and oatmeal in the kitchen sink that weren't hers. She longed for *people.* She could feel the loneliness expand within her each day the house sat empty.

Since Claudia had left, Delilah had peered eagerly out the front bay windows, on the hunt for an unfamiliar car pulling into her driveway, hoping it might belong to Tracey Walters.

Tracey would be someone she could help. Tracey also had young children — boisterous beings who could keep Delilah amused and busy, bright-eyed innocents who could thrive under Delilah's love and care. But

Tracey hadn't arrived or even responded to Delilah's invitation, and it might take days, perhaps weeks before she did. Or she may not respond at all. Until Delilah found another suitable candidate — one who wouldn't steal her jewelry or hold wild parties — she would continue to wait for Tracey Walters like a hotel manager eagerly awaiting the next incoming guest.

"That's what I feel like some days — like I own a hotel," she mumbled as she made her way into the living room. Bruce glanced up at her as she spoke. "Like I'm a caretaker. It's like it's not even my home."

"Because it isn't your home," the voice replied, making her pause in her steps. "It never was your home — until you tricked me into giving it to you."

That was the other thing about the loneliness. The voice — her ever-present companion — grew bolder and louder. Sometimes it would talk endlessly, babbling to her day and night, interrupting her sleep.

"I didn't *trick* you into doing anything," she whispered as she stepped into her living room, not willing to deal with its nonsense today. "I never asked for this damn place! Remember?"

"All things connivers say," the voice replied dryly.

She sat down in one of the wingback chairs facing the sofa. Her eyes scanned the books on a nearby shelf, held in place by porcelain bookends belonging to one of the house's original owners. She finally settled on one of the leather-bound hardbacks and removed it from its shelf: *The Grapes of Wrath.*

As she settled into the chair, Bruce staked out his ownership of a nearby footstool. He stretched like a sunbather on a nearby beach and closed his eyes. Delilah turned on a table lamp despite the afternoon light filling the space. Her eyes weren't what they used to be and needed all the help they could get.

"She's never gonna come, you know," the voice said just as she opened the book. "You can wait until doomsday, Dee. That woman is going to find out who you are, and she won't be able to get away from you fast enough. I wouldn't be surprised if she hasn't thrown your letter in the trash already. Maybe she burned it."

*Be quiet,* Delilah thought, trying her best to concentrate on Steinbeck's words but failing miserably.

"And you were so excited." The voice chuckled. " 'Oh, look, she's got little children!' And we know how much you like children, don't we? Especially since you didn't have any."

"Be quiet, I said," she whispered, flipping to the next page.

"But, on the bright side, sweetheart, you're lonely, but not dead. But you'll die soon enough. We aren't getting any younger, are we?" It laughed again. "And when that time comes, you and I are gonna tango, Dee. And not like we tangoed in the old days. This will be worse . . . much, *much* worse. I'll make sure you feel everything I felt, you bitch! Every day, for all eternity, I will —"

"Enough!" she shouted, shooting to her feet, dropping the book to the woven rug. Startled, Bruce scrambled off the footstool and ran out of the room.

"Enough," she repeated breathlessly, whipping off her glasses and pressing the tips of her fingers to her eyelids.

She couldn't take it anymore — the menacing voice, the solitude, and the silence of this house.

She walked from the living room into the foyer, leaving the table lamp burning bright. She grabbed her sun hat from the center table and her purse from a hook on the wall adjacent to the front door. Delilah marched down the front steps of the porch to the blacktop of her driveway, pulling the keys to her PT Cruiser from her purse's depths.

Aidan paused from mowing the lawn to stare across the yard at her. He shaded his eyes with his hand.

"Hey!" he shouted over the riding lawnmower's idle engine. "Where you going, Dee?"

She didn't answer him. Instead, she opened her car door and climbed inside. She turned on the engine and turned up the volume of the radio so the walls almost vibrated with the gospel music blasting from the car's speakers.

Delilah threw the car into drive and pulled off.

She was about to do something she loathed almost as much as the voice in her head. She was about to head into downtown Camden Beach.

After driving for less than ten minutes, Delilah slowed to a stop and pulled into one of the open parking spaces in the small shopping center less than half a mile from the waterfront. She looked around warily at the faces of people who sauntered out of the grocery store, pushing shopping carts or carrying plastic bags filled with goods, at the couples and families who sat at the metal bistro tables outside of the Seafood Shack, eating crab legs and shrimp po'boys and curly fries sprinkled with Old Bay seasoning.

Would they narrow their eyes at her or conspicuously shift their gazes when they saw her walking toward them? Would they turn and walk the other way?

Over the years, it happened less and less. The longtime residents of Camden Beach who remembered the Delilah Buford whose bewildered and haggard face had appeared on the cover of local newspapers were starting to die off, taking their judgment and condemnation with them to the grave. The newer residents didn't care enough about her to even bother to do a Google search and were content to give her the anonymity she craved. Still, on occasion, Delilah would step up to a counter at a store in town and be met with aloofness or, worse, outright fright from a salesgirl. Or she'd enter a local deli and the entire shop would fall silent. She'd always wonder, *Do they know? Is that why they're acting like that?*

*Better head inside,* she now told herself as she continued to peer out the car window. If she didn't, she knew the voice would start speaking again. She could practically feel it chomping at the bit to say something to

66

make her shout at it.

Delilah turned off the PT Cruiser's engine and slowly opened the door. She was assailed by the scent of the bay: the brine-like, fishy smell that sometimes came with high tide. She ventured toward the grocery store, removing her sunglasses and keeping her head held high as she walked. She told herself to keep an even pace.

*Don't run like you're in a rush to get away. Just walk.*

Thankfully, no one looked at her or did a double take when she passed.

*They don't recognize me,* she realized with relief. *None of them have heard or read about me.*

She stepped through the automatic doors, from the humid heat of early September to the blustery cold of the air-conditioned supermarket. She squinted under the glare of the overhead track lights.

"Welcome to Milton's Grocer!" the greeter in suspenders shouted, waving at her with a wide grin.

He looked to be no older than eighteen. Shaggy brown hair almost fell into his eyes. A smiley-face pen dangled from one of his suspenders, along with another pen showing the Milton's Grocer emblem.

"H-hello," Delilah stuttered, pulling her

purse close to her side.

"Let us know if you need anything, ma'am!"

She nodded absently before grabbing a plastic basket from a stack near the automatic doors. "I will. Th-thank you."

Delilah then made her way to the produce aisle, scanning a pile of oranges and then a tower of lemons. She headed to a display of grapefruit, thumping one with her forefinger, then placing it in her basket. She turned to grab a second, then stopped.

That's when she felt it — the heavy weight of someone's gaze on her. The hair on the back of her neck stood up. Her stomach muscles clenched. Her pulse began to race. She was seized with the urgent need to set her basket on top of the bin of cantaloupes and flee the supermarket.

*Don't run,* she told herself, even though every part of her rebelled. *Don't you* dare *run*!

"Ms. Grey!" a booming voice called from behind her, jolting her to her core.

She turned to find a man wearing a navy blue visor and matching polo shirt with khakis so immaculate they looked as if they had just come off the sales rack. This was a man who went to the golf course to talk business and rub elbows, rather than play actual golf. He strode down the produce aisle toward her, casually tossing a Granny Smith apple. She squinted at him, momentarily confused as to who he was.

"Ms. Grey, how are you?" he asked.

She continued to stare at him blankly.

"Don't you remember me? It's Teddy!"

"Oh . . . oh, yes. Hello, Teddy."

She did remember him now, though she did not find comfort in the recollection. Instead, her brow wrinkled, and her mouth formed a grim line.

Teddy was a developer who had recently moved to Camden Beach. There were so many these days, all looking to buy vacation homes, renovate them, then flip them for a profit. He had stopped by the house in May.

"Uh, how can I help you, Mr. —"

"Theodore Williams," he had told her the first time she had met him on her front porch. He had held out his hand to her in greeting.

Delilah had glanced down at his hand before reluctantly shaking it. His hands had been soft and clammy, almost like a saturated sponge. She'd immediately drawn her hand back. "Mr. Williams, how —"

"Not Mr. Williams . . . just Theodore." He had shoved his hands in his pockets and offered a smile that was more smug than warm. "Or you can call me Teddy. Actually, I'd prefer if you'd call me Teddy."

"All right," she had said, gazing at him warily. "What can I do for you, Teddy?"

"It's not what you can do for me. It's what I can do for *you,* Ms. Grey. I'd like to buy your home . . . the entire property . . . and I'm willing to pay above market value for it — *top* dollar."

She had turned down his offer without a second thought. She could never sell Harbor Hill, especially to a perfect stranger. For better or for worse, it was her home. It had been for several decades, and it had been standing for almost one hundred years. It was a place that had offered solace to so many others. Harbor Hill was all she knew, and she was too old to move on, to start all over again.

But Teddy didn't seem to accept her answer. Like clockwork, he would call once a month, offering to buy Harbor Hill and raising the price of his offer. The last had been three million dollars.

Delilah was at a loss to understand Teddy's logic. Realtors had been leaving business cards on her door for decades, offering to put the house on the market for her. Developers had called over the years, offering to buy Harbor Hill — some with cash deals.

But all had gone away when she politely but firmly turned them down. Why was Teddy so persistent? Why was he offering so much money? What *was* it about Harbor Hill? It was a nice property and home, but nicer properties and houses could easily be found in neighboring towns.

"It's a property that has history . . . that has *meaning,* Ms. Grey," Teddy had explained. "No price can be put on meaning."

*Meaning?* What possible meaning could Harbor Hill have for him? Was Teddy one of those men with a perverse interest in the macabre? Would he point to the stairs and tell visitors, "You know someone was killed right here?"

But his motivations didn't matter. She still said no. Now, with him standing in front of her, she prepared herself for another onslaught.

He set aside the apple, stepped forward, and embraced her like they were old friends. She tried not to flinch but kept her arms stiffly at her sides.

Teddy stepped back. "Funny running into you here!" he said with a laugh.

"Why is it funny?"

His laughter tapered off. "Well, I guess it isn't funny really." He loudly cleared his throat. "Anyway, did you give any thought to my latest offer? That's quite a nice chunk of change, if I do say so myself."

"I did, and my answer is the same as it was the last time you asked me. I'm sorry to disappoint you, but I'm not gonna sell Harbor Hill."

His grin teetered a little, like a picture on a wall not hung correctly. An invisible finger nudged it back into place.

"Uh, no offense, Ms. Grey," he whispered as he leaned toward her, shifting his visor aside. "But do you really want to continue to live on such a big property, in such a big house, at your age? All those stairs and an acre's worth of lawn that needs to be mowed and raked? The snow removal alone . . ." He let out a low whistle and shook his head. "I know *I* wouldn't want to have to deal with that in my eighties."

"I'm not quite eighty yet, Teddy. And I have a caretaker for all that."

"But wouldn't you rather go to a retirement community where *you* could be taken care of? I heard some are really nice, and with the money I'm willing to give you, you could get into one of the best."

"I don't want to live in a retirement community. I'm happy where I am."

*Most days . . .*

"But you may not always be happy there.

I'm willing to take care of Harbor Hill and treat it like it was my own."

She tiredly looked around her as Teddy prattled on, glancing at shoppers who passed them by as she waited for him to finish so she could politely extricate herself from the conversation. Out of the corner of her eye, she caught sight of a young woman with mousy brown hair in a lanky ponytail, wearing a white shirt and black skirt. The outfit was so bland it had to be a uniform. She was pushing a cart where a baby sat in front, sucking on a foot-shaped teething ring clutched in her pink fist. A boy walked beside the young woman, talking and pointing to a line of cereal boxes on display.

Delilah startled when she realized who the woman was: Tracey Walters.

"I may develop properties for a living, but I wouldn't do a thing to change Harbor Hill," Teddy continued. "Well, maybe a few renovations here and there, but that's about it! I certainly wouldn't knock it down or try to make it into something it's not. I would —"

"Would you excuse me?" Delilah said. "I see someone I need to speak with."

He blinked in surprise. "Oh, yeah. Sure, I'll follow up with you some other time."

She nodded before rushing after Tracey,

who was joining one of the checkout lines. As Tracey began to load groceries onto the conveyor belt, Delilah tapped her on the shoulder. Tracey turned and looked at her quizzically.

"Yes?" she asked.

"Hello, Ms. Walters. It's nice to see you again."

Tracey's look of confusion stayed in place. She tilted her head. "I'm sorry. Do we know each other?"

"Mommy, can I *please* get some Lucky Charms?" her son asked.

"Excuse me," Tracey muttered to Delilah before turning to face her son. "I said no. When I say no, I mean no. So stop asking, okay?" She then turned back to Delilah and gave an apologetic smile. "You were saying, ma'am?"

"I was saying it was nice seeing you again. I've been waiting to hear from you. My name is Delilah. I'm . . . I'm the one who sent you the letter."

Tracey's smile fell. The openness in her big brown eyes was abruptly shut, like a window blind pulled closed. "Oh."

"I didn't mean any offense by that letter," Delilah insisted, her confidence faltering under Tracey's reaction. She hesitated before placing a hand on Tracey's forearm.

"I'm sorry if it . . . it came off that way."

The bearded man in line in front of Tracey grabbed a grocery bag off the counter and walked away with receipt in hand. The cashier looked at Tracey expectantly and leaned forward to remove the yellow plastic divider in front of the groceries on the conveyor belt.

"How're you doing today?" the young woman asked as produce slowly made its way to the scanner.

"Fine," Tracey said, then gently pulled her arm out of Delilah's grasp.

She didn't turn her back to Delilah exactly, but she was no longer looking at her as she loaded her groceries. Her children continued to stare. The baby tore her teething ring from her mouth, letting a thick line of drool slide over her plump chin. The boy looked at Delilah with guileless fascination.

"If you don't mind me askin', do you like where you live now?" Delilah persisted over the beeping from the barcode scanner. "If so, that's fine. That's good. I'm . . . I'm glad that you do."

Delilah didn't want to be too eager, to scare her off, but she was hungry — so hungry to end the loneliness.

Tracey paused as she placed a can of Chef Boyardee on the conveyor belt. An expression crossed her face at Delilah's question, the same one that had been on Tracey's face at the Chesapeake Cupcakery a few weeks ago. It was the frightened, cornered look. Delilah knew it well. She had seen it enough times in her life that she could spot it a mile away.

"No, I don't," Tracey answered honestly, "but I'm moving out soon."

"We got kicked out," the boy piped, leaning against the side of the cart and bouncing on his tiptoes in his mud-plastered tennis shoes. "I don't wanna change schools again, but Mommy said —"

"Caleb!" his mother barked at him, making him lower his eyes, shamefaced.

Tracey continued to load groceries, this time angrily slamming them onto the belt.

"Please . . . at least see the house," Delilah said. "Have a look around to see if you like it. I've got plenty of bedrooms. You can even take one for yourself. You don't have to share it with your children, unless . . . unless you want to. You can have a bedroom next to the room where the kids would stay. It wouldn't be —"

"Thank you, but no thank you."

"I'm not crazy!" Delilah shouted.

In response to her declaration, Tracey stopped unloading groceries from her cart and furrowed her brows.

"I'm not crazy," she repeated in a softer voice.

Tracey glanced down at Delilah's feet. Delilah followed the path of her gaze, embarrassed to realize she was still wearing her fluffy, pink bedroom slippers.

Because of the phantom voice, she had been in such a rush to leave the house she hadn't changed into the black Crocs she kept underneath the bench next to the front door.

"Well, I'm forgetful — but not crazy." She laughed. Tracey didn't join her.

"That will be $114.58, ma'am! Will that be cash or credit?" the cashier asked.

"Credit," Tracey said, pulling out her wallet.

Watching her, Delilah noted that Tracey's purse looked old and worn. Though it was an expensive brand, with the emblem prominently displayed on the front flap, the inside seam was ripped. The strap's thread was unraveling. She then looked at Tracey's face as the younger woman handed a credit card and a discount card to the cashier. She noted that her eyes were puffy and bruised. She looked like she had gone through quite a few sleepless nights.

"You wouldn't have to pay," Delilah

whispered to her. "You could —"

"I said no," Tracey answered firmly, glowering at Delilah. She then pursed her lips and took a deep breath. The glower disappeared, though her gaze was unwavering. "Thank you very much for your offer, Ms. Grey, but I don't need your help. I'm doing fine. Really."

"Uh, ma'am," the cashier interjected, holding up the credit card and waving it back and forth in the air. "I've tried to run this through twice, and it isn't working. Do you have another card?"

Tracey turned and stared at her. "Are you sure?"

"Yep." The cashier turned the computer screen toward her. "The card was declined."

Tracey stood silently for several seconds, as if contemplating what to do next. She finally opened her wallet and dug through it again. "No, that's my only card, but I'll . . . I'll pay for it in cash." She rifled through all the bills in her wallet. Her lips moved as she counted them once, then twice. She looked up. "All I have is eighty-two dollars. Can you . . . can you take some of the stuff off of my bill, please? Sorry."

The cashier's polite veneer disappeared. She grabbed the microphone over her cash register. "I need manager assistance!"

Her high-pitched voice echoed over the supermarket's loud speaker, making several patrons in other lines turn toward their lane and stare at Tracey.

"What do you want to take off?" the cashier said with a loud sigh.

"The juice boxes." Tracey reached for the grocery bags on the counter. Delilah noticed her hands were shaking. "The chicken legs and the ice cream bars."

"No, mommy!" Caleb whined. "Not the ice cream! You said I could —"

"Caleb, *please* . . . not now!"

The boy pouted again.

"You're still short twenty-five bucks," the cashier said, leaning her elbow against the counter and tossing her hair aside.

Tracey stared at the bags of food again and then the conveyor belt. As she did, the young cashier rolled her eyes. "Lady, we don't have all day."

Delilah watched as a flush of red creeped into Tracey's cheeks, as the young woman bit down on her bottom lip.

"This isn't necessary," Delilah said, rushing forward. She reached into her tote bag and pulled out her wallet. "*I'll* pay. Here!" She then held out six crisp twenties to the cashier.

Tracey shook her head. "No! No, I can't

accept —"

"Please, let me do this . . . so that your son can get his ice cream," Delilah said, smiling down at Caleb.

"Please, Mommy! Please?" he cried.

"So is she paying or what?" the cashier asked, pointing to the plastic bags.

Tracey stared at Caleb. Her shoulders slumped before she turned back to the cashier and gave a barely discernable nod.

After the groceries were paid for, Tracey walked out of the line. She paused to whisper "Thank you" to Delilah.

"It's fine, sweetheart," Delilah said, waving at her.

"Ice cream! Ice cream! We got ice cream!" Caleb sang as he danced and twirled behind his mother while they walked toward the automatic doors.

Delilah watched them leave, feeling as if some grand opportunity had eluded her.

"Just the cantaloupe then?" the cashier asked, yanking Delilah's attention.

"Oh!" Delilah turned and looked at the lone cantaloupe in her basket. "Yes, that's . . . that's it."

A few minutes later, Delilah emerged from the grocery store. She pulled out her keys, adjusted the wide brim of her hat, and started to walk toward her car.

"Ms. Grey?" a voice called to her.

Delilah turned to find Tracey standing with her son and daughter near the line of carts gathered several feet away from the supermarket's entrance. The little girl was back to gnawing her teething ring. The boy was sucking on an orange ice cream bar. Some of it was dripping onto his T-shirt.

Delilah smiled, feeling a lightness enter her at the sight of them. "Hello again! I thought you had left."

"I had planned to leave, but" — Tracey lowered her tired eyes — "before . . . before I left, I wanted to apologize to you if I came off as rude or . . . or if I seemed ungrateful about your offer."

Delilah walked toward her. "No apologies needed, honey. Really, I understand."

"You see, the kids and I *do* need a place to stay . . . to live, but . . . but . . ." Her words drifted off.

"Why don't you see the house?" Delilah asked, taking another step toward her, drawing close. "See if you like it. Stop by for dinner tonight. I'll make something nice for you — for *all* of you!"

Tracey hesitated again.

"It's just dinner. Nothing can be lost."

As Delilah held her breath and waited for Tracey's answer, a family of five strolled by them. The mother barked orders to a teenage boy. A gaggle of girls also ran by, giggling and pointing at something in one of the adjacent shop windows.

Finally, ever so slowly, Tracey nodded. "Okay. Why not?"

# CHAPTER 6

Aidan walked into the kitchen, tugging his T-shirt over his head and down his torso. His dark hair was still wet from the shower he had taken minutes earlier. He'd lingered under the shower-head much longer than he'd intended, letting it blast his back and shoulders until the water went from steaming hot to tepid. But he'd needed that shower. He was sore and tired from the hours he'd spent doing yard work today in the hot sun, mowing the lawn and trimming overgrown bushes and the dying remains of hosta plants.

He had come into the kitchen hungry and intending to make himself a roast beef sandwich and maybe crack open a can of soup for dinner, but he was met by clutter of grand proportions — pots and pans, strewn flour and potato rinds, cutting boards and bits of grated cheese. All of it was on the six-foot butcher-block island and granite counters. The smell of fried chicken, cheese and chives, and sweet potato pie filled the air, along with a sweltering heat from the open flames and oven. Stepping into the kitchen, Aidan felt as if he had just strolled into a sauna, minus the towel wrapped around his waist.

Delilah closed the door of her stainless-steel fridge and turned to Aidan. She frowned and looked him up and down, framing her mouth with quotation marks.

"Oh, no!" she said, shaking her head, sending her gray hair swinging. "You march right back upstairs and put on something decent . . . something better than a wrinkled T-shirt and pair of jeans."

He narrowed his eyes at her.

"Go on!" She shooed him off as if he were an annoying fruit fly. "We're having folks over tonight, and you need to be presentable."

He began argue with her, to tell her he was a grown man of thirty-four years and he could wear what he damn well pleased, but then she turned back toward the stove and began to stir a pot of mashed potatoes. She began to hum as she cooked.

Aidan silently stewed like the dark gravy sitting on one of the burners. He glared at the back of Delilah's head, then turned and walked out of the kitchen through the living room and back toward the stairs.

"And put some shoes on while you're at it!" she shouted after him.

Aidan grumbled as he yanked his T-shirt over his head. He headed upstairs and back to his room to change his clothes.

He supposed Delilah's henpecking had something to do with the last time they'd lived together in this house, when he had moved into Harbor Hill at the age of eight. When his mother, Rosario, couldn't be a mom — when she had her "bad days" and refused to eat or come out of her room — Delilah had been his mother.

Before Aidan and Rosario had arrived at Harbor Hill back in 1990 and stayed for almost eight years, they had hopped from place to place.

Their journey began when Rosario was seventeen and he was still floating around in her womb, waiting to make his debut into the world. Rosario's mother wanted her to reveal what boy had knocked her up, but Rosario refused. So her mother sent her packing with a suitcase filled with clothes, her pale pink rosary, and a baby blanket her mother had knitted for her when she was an infant.

"When you're ready to tell the truth *ante tu mamá y Dios,* then you can come back!" her mother proclaimed, before slamming the apartment door in Rosario's face.

But Rosario couldn't tell the truth before her mother and God. She couldn't lie and say the father was what her mother believed him to be — some pimple-faced, seventeen-year-old jock at Rosario's high school or a bad boy in her neighborhood she had given her virginity to in the back seat of a Trans Am. Aidan's father was really Michael "Mike" Aidan Jankowski, the Dominguez family's married landlord. He had seduced Rosario over a period of months with costume jewelry, pepperoni pizza, and a small bottle of Lancôme perfume.

If Rosario had told her mother the truth, Mike could've gone to jail.

"I'm not protecting him," Aidan overheard his mother explain to one of her friends one night when the other woman asked her why she would care if Aidan's father went to prison. He was a grown man who had taken advantage of a teen girl. He should have been locked up, the friend insisted.

"I just didn't want that on my conscience. He has a wife and four kids to take care of, you know," Rosario said.

But that wasn't the reason. Aidan knew

the truth, even as a boy who didn't know much else.

His mother protected his father because she was and would always remain in love with that man. It was why she kept the empty bottle of perfume his father had given her during their "courtship." It was why she made Aidan finally meet his dad, though he had protested and sulked.

They met at an ice cream parlor with laminate countertops spotted with syrup stains and a waitress who had blond hair and black roots.

Aidan thought his father seemed freakishly tall, though this was admittedly from the perspective of a nine-year-old. Mike had eyes as green as the mint chocolate chip ice cream that Aidan ate, and thick hair and a beard that were prematurely gray. It wasn't that cold outside that day, but Mike's cheeks were ruddy, as well as the tip of his nose. He looked like a forty-something Santa Claus.

"So . . . how's it going?" Mike had asked as they sat at one of the corner tables in the shop. He slapped Aidan on his thin shoulder with his wide, heavy hand.

"Fine, I guess," Aidan murmured as he toyed with the single cherry that topped his chocolate sundae. He then tossed the cherry

87

into his mouth, stem and all.

"You like school?"

Aidan shrugged in response as he chewed.

"You like sports? I'm big into baseball. Got season tickets to watch the Orioles. Maybe I could take you someday."

"I don't like baseball."

"Football then?"

Aidan shook his head.

"How about basketball?"

Aidan shook his head again, though that was a lie. He loved the Chicago Bulls with the same passion some boys in his class had for their crushes, and he wore his Michael Jordan jersey religiously. But he wasn't about to tell his father any of that. His father didn't deserve anything from him, including the truth.

Unable to get past Aidan's wall of silence, Mike leaned back in his chair, drummed his fingers on the tabletop, and peered out the ice cream parlor's floor-to-ceiling windows. The awkwardness between them ended only when Rosario arrived a half hour later to pick up Aidan and take him back home.

She hugged Mike good-bye, clinging to him longer than necessary. The hulking man was much bigger than her, so her tiny feet dangled several inches above the floor as she held him tight, looking like a small brown elf to his Santa Claus. She wept as she held him.

Aidan refused to watch their emotional farewell. He mumbled a "Bye" over his shoulder and walked out the parlor's door toward his mother's sedan, slumping against the car as he waited for her on the curb.

After they arrived home at Harbor Hill, for the rest of the afternoon Rosario stayed in her bedroom with the door shut, blasting her music at full volume. Even when Aidan knocked, she didn't answer him. So he left her alone to indulge in her thoughts and her music. But Aidan eventually grew bored with hanging out in the yard and playing rounds of Super Mario Bros. He ventured back upstairs to his mother's room to draw her out. By then, Rosario had switched from mariachi to sixties soul music — a lonely ballad by Sam Cooke. Aidan tried knocking again.

"Ma!" he called over the music. "Ma! I'm hungry. Are you gonna make me dinner? Mami?"

He knocked again, only to get silence in reply.

"Mami! Mami, open up!"

But the door didn't budge.

Aidan stared at the metal knob and the closed wooden door, feeling hot tears sting his eyes.

"Mami," he croaked before knocking again.

"I can cook you dinner, if you'd like."

Aidan jumped at the sound of the voice behind him. He turned to find Delilah standing at the end of the corridor, at the top of the stairs, holding her hand out to him.

"I'll make you whatever you want," she said.

Aidan glanced back at the closed door, waiting to hear his mother's footsteps or the sound of the lock being removed, but he heard neither. Finally, he turned back to face Delilah.

"Okay," he said and walked toward her.

She threw an arm around his shoulders, gave him a squeeze, and guided him downstairs while Sam Cooke continued to wail behind his mother's bedroom door.

Aidan returned to the kitchen ten minutes after Delilah had dismissed him, wearing an outfit he figured she would find more acceptable: a blue-striped dress shirt and chinos. He was even wearing Oxfords.

*There. I changed my clothes. I'm a good little boy,* he thought sarcastically as he glanced down at himself.

He watched through the kitchen opening as Delilah set ceramic plates and long-stemmed glasses on her dining room table. She adjusted a vase of roses at the center of the table, then fussily wiped at the wrinkles on the white tablecloth. She looked like she was preparing for a visit from an ambassador or maybe the president.

*Just who the hell did she invite tonight?*

Midway through adjusting a fork and knife, Delilah's head shot up, quick and alert — like a squirrel hearing a twig snap, signaling the presence of a hunter. But her face didn't crease with alarm or fear. Instead, she smiled and clapped her hands.

"I hear a car pulling up," she said gleefully before darting around the dining room table and scurrying to the front door. She patted at her hair, smoothing her curls into place.

"Whose car?" he called after her.

"Our dinner guest!"

Aidan followed her with a mix of bewilderment and amused interest. She certainly hadn't acted this way when they'd had guests in the past.

Delilah threw open the front door and bounded down the wooden steps as fast as her stiff knees would allow.

"I'm so happy you came, honey!" she

shouted just as a forest green minivan with a rusted bumper and tinted windows came to a stop in the driveway.

The driver's-side door opened, and a woman stepped out. She wore a simple, pale yellow sundress and an equally simple blue sweater and white canvas shoes. In fact, everything about her was simple, from the way she wore her long brown hair pulled into a ponytail at the crown of her head to the lack of any jewelry or makeup on her pale, heart-shaped face. The only thing about her that stood out were her eyes — big dark eyes like a doe's. Audrey Hepburn eyes.

Aidan leaned against the door frame as Delilah opened her arms and embraced the woman, who accepted Delilah's hug clumsily. She laughed and patted Delilah on the back in return.

The woman looked like she may have been beautiful once, but now she could pass for cute, at best, thanks to the waxy sheen of her skin, the frown lines near her mouth, and the weary look about her. But she would be beautiful again. He could see it even now. If she was next in line to stay at Harbor Hill, with time she would go through the same transformation all the women did. And he would be part of the transformation.

Aidan put on a charming smile, happy he had changed clothes and thrown on some cologne. He stepped forward as the woman reached inside her car and pulled out a bouquet of flowers from the passenger seat. He eyed the wilted daises. They looked like they had been purchased in a rush at a gas station.

"Are you going to introduce us, Dee?" he asked, strolling down the stairs.

The woman suddenly looked up at Aidan. She must not have realized he'd been standing on the porch the whole time. Delilah took a step back and gave him a rueful look.

"This is Aidan," she said. "He's my groundskeeper, and he helps fix things around the house. I've known him since he was a boy."

"Hello," he said, pouring caramel into his voice. He walked across the driveway and held his hand out to her. His smile widened, revealing his pearly white teeth; he hadn't bleached them in years, but they still looked nearly perfect. "It's pleasure to meet you, Miss . . ."

"T-T-Tracey . . . Tracey Walters," she stammered, barely shaking his hand before letting it go, giving him only a brief feel of her soft, warm palm. "P-pleasure to meet you too." She then abruptly turned and headed to the rear door of her minivan.

Aidan cocked an eyebrow. She was nervous. He found it rather sweet.

"Do you need any help with . . ."

His words tapered off when Tracey opened the rear door and reached inside. The other rear door flung open, and a little boy leapt out, making Aidan blink in surprise. The boy hopped onto the asphalt, clutching an action figure in his fist. He peered up at Harbor Hill, slack-jawed.

"This place is *big,* Mommy!" the boy yelled. "It's bigger than the White House!"

Aidan then watched as the woman leaned inside again and undid the straps on a car seat in the back where a little girl sat. She couldn't have been much more than a year old. She had a cherubic face and eyes as big as her mother's, but instead of being the color of hot cocoa, they were a shade of blue. It was the same shade as the water off the coast of St. Croix he and Trish had skinny-dipped in during their honeymoon seven years ago. It was a blue so clear you could see all the way down to the coral and fish on the ocean bottom.

When Aidan saw the little girl and those big beautiful eyes, his smile dissolved. He took an unsteady step back.

The boy continued to gush about the house, and Tracey wrestled the little girl out of the car seat. Aidan turned and glared at Delilah, who seemed to be purposely avoiding his gaze.

What was Delilah thinking, bringing kids into this home?

His hands clenched into fists. He shoved them into his pockets.

Yes, children had lived at Harbor Hill before. Hell, he had been one of those children long ago. But why would Delilah do this *now,* while he was still living here. For the past four years, since he had moved in to help her with the property in exchange for free room and board, Delilah hadn't invited any women with children to live with her. He hadn't asked her explicitly not to do it, but she knew . . . she *knew* how he felt about it.

*Goddammit.*

"This is Maggie," Tracey said proudly as she propped the little girl on her hip. Her nervousness had disappeared, and she seemed almost radiant, gazing at her little girl. "Say hi, Maggie!"

"Hi," the little blond girl chirped, closing, then opening her hand before shoving her sippy cup into her mouth.

"And this is Caleb." Tracey reached out

and ruffled the boy's hair, which was a blond several shades darker than his sister's.

"Hey," Caleb said with a bashful wave.

Aidan didn't respond. His mouth was sealed by a tight band of anger.

"Well, you three come on inside," Delilah said, turning and waving them toward the stairs. "Dinner is done, and I warn you, it's a big one. I hope you all brought your appetites!"

Aidan watched helplessly as they made their way toward the house, hand in hand, climbing the stairs and laughing and talking with one another as though they were already at home.

Throughout dinner, the laughing and talking continued, though Aidan remained conspicuously silent. He watched as Delilah did her best to charm her guests, engaging Tracey and coddling the children. All the while, Aidan shoved food around his plate. Occasionally, his eyes would drift from his plate to the little girl with the magnetic blue eyes.

He remembered staring into similar eyes years ago, as he stood in the sunlight of a bay window with the smell of baby powder in the air. He remembered gazing into those eyes in the dark as he wearily rocked back and forth in a white glider that was too small for his tall frame. Those vivid memories haunted him. They stole his appetite.

Aidan had nothing against Tracey Walters and her children, but he wanted them away from the dinner table, this house, and the entire property of Harbor Hill. He hoped they hated Delilah's home and her clawing eagerness to please and entertain them. He hoped they walked out the door and never came back.

Hours later, after they had left and the dinner table was covered with dirty plates and half-empty casserole dishes, Aidan sat silently in his chair, staring into a glass of Merlot.

"Well, that went well, if I do say so myself," Delilah practically sang as she began to gather plates that she would carry to the kitchen and place in the dishwasher. "They all seemed to love dinner. I hope they loved Harbor Hill just as much."

Aidan didn't answer her but instead leaned back in his chair and took another sip from his glass.

"Are you going to help me clean up or just sit there gatherin' dust?" she asked.

When he didn't budge, she paused and squinted at him.

"What's the matter with you? You were quiet all evening . . . barely said a thing during dinner, which isn't like you." She wiggled her brows. "I've never known you to pass up the chance to flirt."

"You aren't seriously considering having her move in here, are you?"

"Sure. Why not? She's a young lady who needs help . . . a place to stay."

"She has *kids,* Dee. You know how I feel about kids, especially young ones."

Delilah loudly sighed and lowered the stack of dishes she held back to the table. "You always liked children, Aidan. Up until a few years ago —"

"You know what happened," he said tightly. "You know what happened, so why would you do this? Are you doing it on purpose? Is that it?"

The dining room fell silent. Delilah walked around the table and placed a gentle hand on his shoulder.

"Aidan, you're still a young man. You've still got plenty of life ahead of you. Trust me when I say that if you keep dragging the past around behind you, the load doesn't get easier to carry with time, honey. It just gets heavier. You've got to . . . you need to just . . ."

She didn't finish, but she didn't have to. He already knew what she was going to say.

*You need to move on.*

Like what he had been through could be slept off as if it were nothing more than a light case of food poisoning or a bad hangover. Like what had happened to him wouldn't be painted into his memory until his dying day.

"Save it. Save it for the women you drag in off the street! I don't need your pseudo-psychology or your half-assed spiritualism, okay?"

"No, I think you need it more than they do. You need it more than most."

He shot out of his chair and rose to his feet, making her jump back. He strode across the room, toward the dining room's entrance, then paused.

"Maybe I'll just leave! You can move them in instead. How about that? Huh, Dee? Let her mow your grass and clean your fucking gutters. Let her remind you to take your pills, set up your cable, and turn off your car lights when you leave them on. Let *her* be your babysitter! I'll just pack up my shit and go!"

"You aren't going to leave, Aidan," she replied tiredly, gathering plates again.

"Why the hell wouldn't I leave? What makes you so sure?" he yelled. "I'm not shackled to this place. Trust me! I can pack up and head out whenever I damn well —"

"Because if you were going to leave, you would've done it by now!" she shouted back. "You would have left a year ago! *Two* years ago! But the truth is you're not ready. You're not ready, boy! And at rate you're going . . ." — she took a deep breath, making her nostrils flare — ". . . you never will be."

He then watched as she stomped out of the dining room and into the kitchen, carrying the burden of heavy dishes alone.

In the wake of Delilah's exit, Aidan's anger seeped out of him, leaving behind the deflated balloon of emptiness. He walked out of the dining room, up the staircase, and down the hall, slamming his bedroom door behind him. He beelined for his stereo system and pressed a few buttons, turning up the volume so he could almost feel the voice coming from the speakers. He slumped back onto his bed and closed his eyes, listening to Otis Redding promise that change would soon come. Aidan listened to it until he drifted off to sleep, hearing the words in his dreams.

# CHAPTER 7

"Caleb, *stop* fidgeting, please?" Tracey beseeched her son as she peered out the shop window at the passersby. She clutched Maggie on her lap and bounced her gently. "Your grandmother will be here at any moment. All right? Just *sit down.* Why don't you color in your book, honey?"

But Caleb didn't want to sit down or color in the Elmo-themed coloring book she had brought to the shop to keep him busy. Instead, he kept hopping on and off his plastic chair, climbing on top of the seat and leaning from side to side, making growling and banging noises with his treasured Hulk action figure, annoying his frazzled mother in the process. Caleb also seemed to be annoying the man sitting at the small table behind them who was typing on his laptop while trying to enjoy a panini and iced coffee. The man kept glaring over his hunched shoulders at Caleb, muttering to

101

himself.

"I don't like this!" Caleb suddenly cried as he pulled at the straps of his overalls. "Can I take it off, please? It's itchy!"

"As soon as we get home, but you have to keep it on for now." She tugged his hands away. "Wear it for just a bit longer. Okay?"

"But why?" he whined, pulling at the straps again.

*Because your grandmother bought it for you,* she thought, though she didn't say the words aloud. She was too embarrassed to admit it.

She was making Caleb wear stiff, denim overalls covered with an appliqué of choo-choo trains better suited for a two-year-old than for a boy of almost seven, because her mother had purchased the outfit. She didn't want her mother to complain or to point out for the umpteenth time, "I buy the children clothes, Tracey, but I never see them wearing them. For someone who constantly asks for money, you'd think you'd be grateful for the things I give you."

And now Tracey was about to ask to borrow money again. At the end of the month, they officially would have no place to live. If she and the kids were going to move to a new home, they needed cash to augment the little she had left in savings — but she couldn't tell her mother this. She knew what her mother would say.

So Tracey had a little white lie prepared. She would tell her mother the money was for Caleb. He *did* have book fees, soccer fees, and field trips coming up.

"I don't want him to feel left out, Mom," she would say. "He shouldn't be forced to sit on the sidelines because his mother's too poor to let him participate."

Finally, Tracey saw her mother gliding down the sidewalk. As usual, Gwendolyn Humphries appeared flawless. Her dark hair was cut in a glossy, chic bob she had probably had dyed and trimmed only days ago. The dark locks blew back with a gust of wind, revealing makeup likely applied by one of the girls at a mall MAC counter. Gwendolyn wore a cream-colored jacket and tanned slacks. A smart leather Chanel handbag dangled from the crook of her arm. When she tugged the door open, she half-heartedly waved at Tracey and the kids, spotting them instantly.

"Well, there you are," she said as she strode toward their table, like she had been looking for them for hours and hadn't only just arrived. "Ninety-five was an absolute nightmare! A four-car pileup near one of the exits, and we had to be rerouted. It took me forever to make my way here!" she rambled. "Why on earth did you have to move so far away?"

"Hi, Grandma!" Caleb yelped, hopping off his chair and galloping across the shop toward his grandmother. He plowed face-first into her, wrapping his arms around her waist, making her stumble back slightly under his weight.

Instead of smiling and eagerly returning his hug, she placed her hands on his shoulders and eased him back. "Oooo, sticky fingers. Sticky fingers! Don't mess up Grandma's St. John, honey."

Tracey grimaced. How could her mother be so formal and awkward around her own grandchild? But then again, her mother had never been very maternal. Even during her years of raising Tracey, she had often differed with the nannies when it came to mothering. Gwendolyn wasn't the type of mom who baked cookies, kissed boo-boos, or ferried a caravan of kids to and from dance practice. But she could tell you what clothes to wear, how to keep your figure trim, and how to make the right social connections.

"Frankly," her mother had confided once, "I've never found children very interesting. I was *so* relieved when you finally grew up!"

Caleb now grinned up at Gwendolyn, who nodded politely down at him like he was a fellow attendee at one of her country club socials. "How are you, Caleb? Being a good boy, I hope."

"Yes!" he said before grabbing her hand and tugging her toward their table. Gwendolyn followed him, though seemingly with great reluctance.

As they walked, the door to the shop swung open again, and another woman stepped through the doorway. She was an old black woman with a warm smile, waving at the young man behind the counter.

When Tracey saw her, she grinned and sat upright in her chair. She raised her hand and almost shouted out, "Ms. Grey!" but stopped herself when the woman drew closer and took one of the nearby tables, placing her canvas tote bag on its metal surface. Tracey's grin fell when she realized it wasn't Delilah Grey. She lowered her hand, dejected.

Unlike Gwendolyn, Delilah hadn't been awkward around Caleb or Maggie. She had joked with Caleb during dinner and played with Maggie, who had gotten fussy midway through the meal. She had given them all a lovely evening, so lovely Tracey had been almost able to ignore the sullen-looking handyman/gardener, Aidan.

She had tried to draw him out once, but he either hadn't heard her or had outright ignored her. He seemed content with his glum silence, and after a while, she had been equally happy to leave him to it. She'd been admittedly caught off guard by how handsome he was, but she knew not to be too overwhelmed by a pretty face. She'd learned that hard lesson long ago.

As Tracey had basked in the warmth of a good meal in what seemed like a beautiful, loving home, she had started to seriously consider accepting Delilah's offer to move into Harbor Hill with the children. But then she remembered Jessica's dire warning. She remembered the rumor.

*They say she killed someone . . .*

But how could Delilah possibly be a killer? Tracey had wondered this as she watched Delilah dole out mashed potatoes and charm those at the table with stories about her childhood, where she'd lived on a farm in Virginia filled with apple trees and surrounded by tobacco fields. Delilah didn't look like she'd lift a hand to swat a fly, let alone murder someone.

But people could wear masks. Paul certainly had. Why would Delilah be any different?

"You look good, Mom," Tracey said with a false cheeriness and a tight smile, turning away from the older black woman sitting on the other side of the sandwich shop.

She watched as her mother pulled out the chair facing her. Her mother wrinkled her nose, removed one of the paper napkins from the dispenser at the center of the table, and wiped at an invisible spot on the chair before taking a seat. Caleb climbed onto the chair beside his grandmother, flipped open his coloring book, and grabbed a blue crayon.

"Thank you," her mother replied as she placed her purse on the table and eyed Tracey. "You look tired — and skinny. Are you eating?"

"When I can. Working in a hotel restaurant kind of puts you off your appetite most days, anyway. All that food . . . all those smells."

Her mother wrinkled her pert nose again. "You're *still* working as a waitress?"

Tracey lowered her eyes and nodded. She bounced Maggie more vigorously as she did it. The toddler looked like she was perched on a pogo stick.

"Why haven't you found another job yet?"

"You don't think I've *tried,* Mom? I have!" To her own ears, she sounded a lot like Caleb; she sounded like she was whining. "But . . . you know . . . most of the better paying jobs want people with . . . well, college degrees and experience and —"

"Which is what you would have if you hadn't have dropped out!"

"You know why I dropped out," Tracey snapped.

"Yes, I know, but that doesn't mean I was happy about it. A mother has a right to be disappointed about something like that."

"I couldn't take the morning sickness!"

"What's morning sicky-ness?" Caleb repeated slowly, looking up from his coloring book at Tracey, but both women ignored him.

"I lost more than fifteen pounds, Mom! Remember, my gyno had to put me on that medication. The same they give to chemo patients. I couldn't make it to my classes. My grades dropped. If I hadn't left Drexel, they probably would've kicked me out anyway."

And she had planned to go back after Caleb was born. She had wanted to go back — but Paul had talked her out of it. He'd said finishing her degree wasn't necessary. She would take care of their child, and he would take care of her.

She now wanted to laugh at the naïveté of

her twenty-one-year-old self.

"Oh, Trace," her mother now lamented, slowly shaking her head. "You're always full of excuses, aren't you?"

"It's not an excuse! It's the truth!"

"Excuse after excuse after excuse," her mother continued, as if she hadn't heard her. "You're making excuses even now. Your situation . . . your life is your own doing, sweetheart. You could go back home and try again with Paul, try to make it work. But you haven't."

"I told you why I left him. I told you what he —"

"Yes! Yes, I know what Paul did," Gwendolyn said, rolling her eyes, "and it wasn't right."

" 'Wasn't right' is putting it lightly!"

"But everyone makes mistakes. *No one* is perfect!"

Tracey's lap felt hot and clammy. She fidgeted in her chair and shifted Maggie, who was squirming in her arms.

"And the thing is, Trace . . . I can't keep giving you money." The older woman pursed her lips and glanced at Caleb, who was back to coloring Elmo's pirate hat. "You do need more money, right? That's why you called me?"

Tracey didn't respond.

"Well, I can't help you — not anymore. I'm all tapped out. Harold cut back my allowance," she said in a stage whisper as she leaned forward.

Harold was Tracey's stepfather, Gwendolyn's third husband. He was the owner of two car dealerships and always smelled vaguely of Bengay and the cigarettes his doctor had banned him from smoking. Harold was one of many men in Tracey's mother's life who had financially supported her in the past thirty or so years. In fact, when Tracey had married Paul, her mother had applauded her decision because he reminded her so much of her own boyfriends.

"It's a shame you dropped out of school, but at least you made a good choice with Paul. If you didn't catch him, someone else definitely would've — like me!" she had said with a laugh.

Even at the time, Tracey had known her mother was only half joking.

"Harold got a look at my credit card bill from last month, and he went ballistic, *absolutely* ballistic!" her mother now continued, rifling through her handbag. She pulled out a small gold compact and flipped it open. She squinted at her reflection and tucked a few wayward strands of hair back into place.

"Harry can be *so* melodramatic sometimes. I think one of his dealerships isn't doing well. I told him he should just hire new staff, but he won't listen to me. And he started a new diet. He always gets cranky when he's on a diet. Well, anyway," she said, dropping her compact back into her purse and waving her hand, "I'm tapped out. I can't give you any more cash."

Tracey nodded, though she could feel her throat tightening and going dry. That was it — no more help. She was officially on her own.

"This is for you, Grandma," Caleb piped before shoving a drawing toward Gwendolyn. Again, she nodded politely.

"I . . . I understand. I appreciate all . . . all that you've done already," Tracey said, staring down at Maggie's head, at the wispy curls swirling at her crown. She startled when her mother suddenly reached across the table and grabbed her hand. Her mother had never done that before.

"Just go back to Paul, dear. You've made your point. Trust me! He's heard it loud and clear. He knows he was wrong and feels horrible for what he's done. He told me himself!"

"He told you himself?" Tracey yanked her hand back. "You *spoke* to him?"

111

"Well, of course, I spoke to him! What a silly question. All you left him was an empty house and a note! He had to look for you. Being your mother, he came to me first."

She squinted at her mother in disbelief.

"He was really concerned. He still is, Trace!"

"What did you tell him?"

"Well, I . . . I told him that you and the children were fine, that you were safe. Like I said . . . he was very concerned."

"But did you tell him where we went? Did you tell him where we live?"

Even before her mother spoke, Tracey knew the answer. She could tell from the way her mother hesitated — how she anxiously licked her lips and averted her brown eyes to the sales counter.

Tracey started to tremble. It was a tremor threatening to turn into a full earthquake.

"Trace," her mother whispered, finally looking at her again, "I didn't have to tell him. He would've figured it out himself — eventually. He could've . . . I don't know . . . hired a detective to look for you. People do that nowadays. I see it on TV all the time!"

*It had all been a waste,* Tracey thought as she dazedly shook her head while her mother prattled on.

She had moved twice in less than a year,

packing her things when she caught a whiff of Paul on her trail. She had changed their last name and started over again. She'd had friends she'd once considered close but hadn't spoken to in almost a year. Tracey had lived like a hermit, like a Luddite, avoiding Facebook and Twitter for fear one day Paul would stumble upon a photo of her or the children and discover where they were. She had drilled into Caleb his new last name, how they should never talk about home and avoid talking about his father.

All her efforts had been pointless.

And what had it taken for her mother to sell her out? Had Paul offered her an expensive gift to coax the secret out of her — or maybe money?

"Let's be honest, honey, if Paul was *really* going to come after you, he would have done it by now! Don't you see? He's not some boogeyman or crazy stalker. You don't have to —"

She stopped when Tracey leapt from her bistro chair, almost dropping Maggie to the tiled floor as she did. The little girl started to cry, but Tracey barely heard her. Instead of her daughter, her focus was on the floor-to-ceiling windows. Her eyes scanned the cars parked along the sidewalk and those in the lot next to the sandwich shop. She searched for a black Mercedes among the pack — her husband's Mercedes.

"Get your things, Caleb!" she ordered, grabbing for his crayons, which were strewn along the tabletop. A few fell and tumbled to her feet, rolling in all directions. She flipped his coloring book closed, making him jump back in surprise. "We have to go! We have to go right now!"

Caleb frowned. "Why do we have to go, Mommy? I thought we —"

"We just have to go! Now pack up!"

Several eyes in the shop shifted toward their table. Heads pivoted in their direction, drawn by Maggie's wails and Tracey's shouting. Tracey reached for her purse, which was draped on the back of her chair, and threw it over her shoulder.

"Trace, what are you doing?" her mother asked, staring up at her uneasily. "Why are you leaving?"

"You *promised* me you wouldn't tell him!" Tracey yelled, making her mother flinch. "You promised!"

"But it's not like I gave your address. *I* don't even know the address! I just told him you were still in the area. He was worried you'd moved to California or Hawaii or something. Please, Trace just . . . just calm down!"

Was her mother telling the truth?

Caleb sat frozen in his chair. He started to sniff.

"*Why* aren't you moving? I said we have to go!" she yelled at him, making him cringe and Maggie scream even louder.

"Trace," her mother whistled through clenched teeth, "you're upsetting the children."

But her mother hadn't seen the kids upset, not really — not like they'd been the moment she'd decided finally to leave Paul. It was the part of the story she hadn't told her mother because it made her queasy to tell it.

If it wasn't for that day, Tracey would have been content to stay locked in her expensive, beautiful prison at the end of the cul-de-sac on Holly Lane for the rest of her life.

*It isn't such a bad prison when you think about it,* she had rationalized for years.

At least she was surrounded by other lovely homes filled with mothers who coordinated carpools and helped with homework, and fathers who coached Little League and held barbeques. It was what she had always wanted in her own childhood — a sense of family and belonging. So what if her husband slapped her for forgetting to buy laundry detergent or shoved her into a wall for leaving the lights on in the basement overnight? It could be worse!

But that morning, Paul had hit Caleb — something he had never done before. He had slapped him over something as trivial as knocking over a coffee cup.

Tracey had been reaching for the paper towels to clean up the mess when it happened. It had caught her off guard, and she had tugged the roll so hard she'd sent the paper towels streaming across the counter. She had almost dropped Maggie, who'd been cradled against her side.

The loud slap had startled a normally talkative Caleb into silence.

"Shit!" Paul had spat as he shoved back from the kitchen table and dabbed the dime-sized spot of coffee on his shirt with a napkin. "Be more careful next time, Cabe!"

He'd tossed the napkin onto the table, complaining that he didn't have time to change, that he had to get to an early office meeting.

While he'd spoken, Tracey had watched, paralyzed, as tears slid over Caleb's reddened cheek.

"What a way to start the day," Paul had mumbled ruefully seconds later as he rose to his feet and walked out of the kitchen.

"It's okay, honey," Tracey had whispered

to her son when the front door slammed shut behind Paul. "It's gonna be okay."

But it wasn't "okay," and Caleb knew it. He had cried silently at first, but then began to hiccup and sob, his thin shoulders shaking as he gulped for air.

Hearing her brother's cries, Maggie had begun to wail. The infant's tiny face had twisted into a tight ball of outrage. She'd sobbed even louder than Caleb.

The slaps, punches, shoves, and hair pulling had been Tracey's and Paul's dirty little secret, hidden beneath long-sleeved shirts, sunglasses, and makeup, buried under painted-on smiles and false laughter. Now the dirty little secret had been whispered into her babies' ears.

Tracey had realized that day it wasn't just about her anymore. She came to the realization again now.

She turned from the shop window and looked down at her children — their frightened, bewildered faces. She told herself to pull it together, to patch herself with glue, gum, tape — *whatever* was necessary to not fall apart right now. Her children needed her to keep it together. If she had done it before, she could damn well do it again.

Tracey took several deep breaths. She

leaned down and scooped Maggie into her arms.

"Shsssh, honey," she whispered into the little girl's ear before kissing her cheek. She then reached over the table toward Caleb. She ruffled his hair. "Mommy's . . . Mommy is sorry she yelled at you," she began in an even voice. "We just . . . we just have to go now, all right? I'll even let you change clothes as soon as we get home."

He smiled a little.

"But I only just got here," her mother protested. "I drove all the way to —"

"I don't have anything else to say to you," Tracey snarled, whipping around and glaring at her mother.

The older woman's mouth clamped shut.

A minute later, Tracey and the children emerged from the sandwich shop. She looked from her left to her right, still on the lookout for Paul's car, waiting for the moment he would call out her name and come charging across the parking lot toward her.

"Mommy, you're squeezing my hand too tight!" Caleb said.

She looked down and realized that his fingers were turning white in her clammy hand. She loosened her grip slightly. "Sorry, honey."

She and the children walked toward the

car and climbed inside. All the while, Tracey told herself not to panic, not to fall apart. But she could feel it loosening — the glue and the tape patching her together. Her hands shook as she fastened the lock on Maggie's car seat and then as she inserted her key into the ignition.

She startled again when she heard a male voice, only to realize it was the sound of the newscaster on her car radio announcing the weather.

*High of 68 with a 30 percent chance of rain . . .*

"Mommy?"

Tracey turned to Caleb, pulled by the worry in his voice.

"Mommy, are you okay?"

She knew he was asking her about more than her current emotional state. He needed reassurance that she was with him, that she could protect him.

"I'm fine. *We're* fine, sweetheart," she lied.

But her lie was sufficient. He slowly nodded, then gazed out the car windshield at the sandwich shop where his grandmother still sat at the bistro table, staring out at them.

"When will we see Grandma again?"

"Probably not for a while."

She threw the minivan into reverse, pulling out of her parking space. When she turned, the image of her mother disappeared behind the glare of the sunlight refracting off the window glass. It was replaced by the reflection of the gas station across the street.

*We might not see her* ever *again,* she thought, but she didn't say it aloud.

If living with Paul had taught her anything, it was to be careful with her words; some thoughts were best kept to yourself.

Caleb nodded thoughtfully again before reaching down to retrieve his Hulk action figure from the car floor. He held it aloft, moving Hulk's arms up and down.

"I don't think Grandma likes seeing us anyway. She always talks about how we're too far away. I don't think she likes driving for a long time."

Tracey didn't comment but instead continued to drive.

"Will we see Miss Delilah again?" He sat upright in his seat. The fear had left his voice. "I like her!"

"I like her too," Tracey whispered, turning onto a roadway.

"So will we?" he persisted, lowering the Hulk to his lap and gazing at Tracey.

"I don't know, honey. Maybe."

He seemed to contemplate her answer.

"I think we will," he said after some seconds, then stared at the sidewalk.

# CHAPTER 8

*Blackberry. Blackberry. Where the hell is the blackberry?*

Delilah stood on the balls of her feet and peered at the kitchen cabinet shelf overhead. Her eyes scanned the line of cans and jars in front of her, skipping from the Cento tomatoes to the boysenberry preserves. She shifted two cans aside, dropped back to her heels, and pursed her lips.

Aidan must have used the last of her blackberry jam. Why hadn't he told her? She kept a chalkboard near the fridge where they could list items she needed to purchase at the grocer every week. He often laughed at her list; he thought it was an anal-retentive nuisance.

"If you need something, I'll just head out and buy it for you, Dee," he had said casually only two weeks ago. "No big deal!"

Well, now she needed blackberry jam, and Aidan wasn't here to get it.

He had disappeared early that morning, driving off in his Toyota pickup without so much as a good-bye. He hadn't said more than a few words to her since their blowup after the dinner with Tracey Walters and her children a week ago.

Had it already been a full week?

*She should have called by now,* Delilah thought.

Tracey and the children seemed to have enjoyed their dinner at Harbor Hill, to love the food and her home, and yet she obviously hadn't won them over. If she had, the young woman would have told her she wanted to move in by now. She would be standing on Delilah's welcome mat, juggling suitcases and boxes. Caleb would come tearing through the doorway and go charging toward the stairs, eager to pick out his room on the second floor.

What had Delilah done wrong?

"When will you get it, Dee?" the voice chided. "She doesn't want to live with you! Honestly, you're like a girl waiting by the phone, hoping that boy you met at the dance is going to call. For the last time — she's *not* coming!"

"Shut up," she whispered fiercely, slamming the cabinet door shut. "Just shut up."

The voice let out a low chuckle. "You

know I'm right."

Perhaps he was.

She would have to let it go, let Tracey and the children go. The recipes she had earmarked in her cookbooks for the large meals she would make for all of them would sit unused. Her fantasies of the sound of little feet clomping along the hardwood floors would have to fade. She had done it before, tucked away her dreams under a blanket of disappointment.

Dee blinked as she looked around her. The kitchen, which had seemed bright and full of warmth only seconds ago, now felt much darker and colder. She peered through one of the windows near the farm sink and saw a shadow drifting across the backyard, turning the vibrant kelly-green lawn to almost a dowdy blue. She shivered and rubbed her shoulders before turning away from the window and the cabinets. She walked to the kitchen's entrance.

*I'll just find someone else,* she resolved as she shuffled down the short hall leading to the staircase. Bruce trailed her, walking near her ankle. His tail flicked back and forth, rubbing her pants leg and grazing the wainscoting.

There was never a shortage of women who needed help and a place to stay. Delilah would find another candidate, one who would appreciate her kindness and banish her loneliness.

"And what will happen when *she* leaves?" the voice asked. "And the one after that and the one after that?"

She slowed her steps down the hall, coming to a halt at those words.

"How will you feel then? Those women are just covering up what's always been there. What will *always* be there. It isn't loneliness that you want to get rid of."

"That's . . . that's e-enough of that," she whispered, fear rather than anger now making her stutter. The truth terrified her.

Oh, how she hated being alone like this. She hoped Aidan would return home soon. Delilah reached for the glass doorknob leading to the small storage pantry underneath the staircase. It was where she kept all her extra goods that wouldn't fit in the kitchen cabinets. If the blackberry jam she couldn't find in the kitchen was anywhere in this house, it would be here.

She turned the knob and tugged twice before the door popped open with a painful squeak. She made a mental note to remind Aidan to squirt some WD-40 on the old hinges, maybe replace them entirely. A small shaft of light from the hall entered the dark, damp space. The pantry smelled vaguely of wet newspapers. Delilah rubbed her shoulders again. She felt even colder now, to the point where she thought a mist might appear in front of her lips.

Delilah blindly reached inside the room, flailing her hand in the air, grasping for the string dangling overhead. The tips of her fingers finally brushed it, and she pulled, filling the pantry with light, revealing shelves on all sides. She stepped inside, stooping slightly to clear the doorway. She squinted as she stared at the jars all lined neatly on the shelf to her right. Within seconds, she noticed a solitary jar of blackberry jam. So Aidan hadn't eaten it all. She smiled a little, almost with relief. As she grabbed the jar, the door to the pantry slammed shut behind her, making her jump in alarm and almost drop the jar to the floor.

Delilah turned and stared in amazement at the closed door. She rushed across the pantry, nearly whacking her head on the low ceiling. She grabbed the doorknob and pushed. The door wouldn't budge. She pushed again and again. It stayed firmly shut.

"Hello?" she called out. "Hello?" She pushed a third time and began to frantically knock against the wooden slab. "Aidan!

Aidan, you out there?"

Only Bruce's muffled purr answered her.

Delilah stared at her hand clasped around the door handle, at the two screws in the gold knob.

"You're stuck, huh?" The voice laughed and her stomach dropped. "Too bad I can't let you out this time."

*This time . . .*

He had done it before — locked her in the pantry. Was he doing it again?

*That's not possible,* she thought. But she could not tamp down the panic. It wrapped its tight hold around her now as it had more than forty years ago.

She pushed against the door again with all her might, shoving with her shoulder. It wouldn't budge.

How had he done it?

Maybe hatred and revenge had empowered him from the grave, allowing him to cross the ether and subject her to the same torture he had when he was alive. That's what he had been promising her for years, a slow agony that would make her regret he had died first.

But she wasn't strong enough to last three days locked in the pantry, like she had been at the age of eighteen. She wouldn't survive this time around. She was old and worn.

She would crumble within hours. She wanted to get out. She *had* to get out of here.

Delilah pushed against the door, pounding her fists against the wooden slab until her hands were sore. She sobbed and yelled. She kicked the door until her toes were sore and damp with her own blood.

"Cee, let me out! Let me out, dammit! You can't do this!" she screamed. "You have to let me out! I can't stay in here! Let me out, Cee, *please!* Let me —"

She slammed herself into the door again, and it suddenly swung open. She bolted toward freedom, only to find her jailer waiting on the other side.

# CHAPTER 9

Aidan heard the screams as soon as he opened the front door, stopping him in his tracks on the wicker welcome mat.

For a second, he had wondered if it was a mistake. Perhaps he had misheard, or maybe it was the television. Delilah was always doing that, leaving on her soaps or the Hallmark Channel on the flat screen in the living room. She'd turn it up to its full volume, like she was hard of hearing, then go wandering off to some other part of the house.

Aidan would come into the living room, annoyed, and turn the volume down or turn the TV off. Delilah would come back to the living room a few hours later, turn on the television, and go wandering off again. He'd sigh and trek back downstairs in search of the remote to lower the volume.

It was a dance they both knew well — a waltz they executed with perfect synchronicity.

But when he listened to the screams more closely, he knew it wasn't the television. It was Delilah.

He dropped the plastic bag he'd brought back from the local hardware store and rushed inside the house, not bothering to close the front door behind him. He ran through the foyer and down the hall, searching for the source of her screams. He paused when he neared the pantry closet.

Bruce paced back and forth in front of the pantry door, twitching his tail nervously. The plump tabby's ears were flat against his head. He stood on his hind legs and pawed at the door frame like he was trying to reach the glass handle two feet above him.

"Dee?" Aidan called, nudging Bruce aside with his foot. "Dee, I'm here! I'll get you out. Don't worry."

But she didn't seem to hear him. She continued to scream and wail. Her voice sounded so supplicatory, she could be on bended knee with hands clasped on the other side of the door for all he knew. She yelled for someone named Cee to let her out. She yelled for God to help her.

Aidan tugged on the door once to no avail. On the second try, he gave a hard yank, and the door popped open with a loud burp, like he was removing a Tupperware lid. He then felt a cool rush of air against his face.

Delilah tumbled out, wild-eyed. She fell into his arms. They both went crashing into the adjacent wall. Aidan hit his shoulder hard and winced. He caught Delilah just before she fell to the floor.

"Let go of me! Let go of me!" she yelled, pounding her fists against his arms and his chest, exhibiting a strength he didn't know she had.

"Oww, dammit, Delilah!" He shoved her away. "Calm down! I was only trying to help!"

"You weren't helping me!" Her brown, wrinkled cheeks glistened with tears. Her gray hair stood at all angles. Some was pasted to her sweaty temples. "You locked me in that place!" She pointed toward the pantry, then turned her bright eyes back toward his. "You locked me in there!"

He shook his head and rubbed his sore shoulder. "No, I didn't! Why the hell would I lock you —"

"Because you're mean. Because you're a hateful, evil son of a bitch!"

Aidan stopped rubbing his shoulder, now taken aback. He'd never heard her curse before.

"You said you would never do it again! You said you wouldn't! You promised me!"

"Dee, what are you talking about? I've never locked you in there. I wasn't even here! I just came home a minute ago."

Delilah fell silent, staring at him as if he was speaking a foreign language. She blinked rapidly and gazed around her. She had the glazed look of someone who was waking up from a dream, like the hallway of her home had morphed into alien terrain and was now fading back to its normal state. She reached up to her hair and looked down in bewilderment at her disheveled clothes.

"Dee, are you all right?"

She nodded and slowly turned to him. "I just . . . I just need to lie down," she said as she walked toward the staircase, dragging her slippered feet as she went.

He guided her up the stairs, holding her elbow and wrapping his arm around her shoulder as she took one shaky step, then the next. They walked down the hall, and he eased her bedroom door open. She shuffled across her room with Aidan at her side and Bruce at her feet. He lowered her to the four-poster bed, and she leaned back against her dozen or so decorative pillows, a mountain of velvet and tassels. Delilah lay with her arms at her sides. She stared at the wall in front of her.

She looked like a corpse in a satin-lined casket.

"I should call a doctor."

That's what he would do when his mother got like this.

When Aidan was fourteen, doctors had finally diagnosed Rosario with clinical depression, explaining that it was of the cause of her black moods that kept her locked in her room for days on end, refusing to eat or wash until the room reeked of her body odor and she could barely hold up her head. She had bounced from doctors to mental health wards for years before her last suicide attempt. Aidan had finally placed her in a facility where she was monitored in a private room by friendly nurses, where she did arts and crafts on Wednesdays and had music therapy on Fridays.

When Rosario was at her worst, she would get the same glassy-eyed, slack-jawed expression Delilah had now. It made him uneasy. It made him scared.

"To hell with this," he muttered, reaching for the cordless phone on her night table.

"Don't call the doctor."

Her voice startled him, almost making him drop the phone. It didn't sound like it came from her mouth; instead, it felt like a ventriloquist with an odd voice had said the words for her.

Aidan looked at her again. She faced him now. Delilah no longer had that faraway look in her eyes. She seemed more alert but weary.

"Can you . . . can you get me a glass of water, honey?"

*"Water?"*

She dipped her chin into her neck in a stiff nod. "That's all I need."

*"That's all you need?* That's all you need?" He lowered the phone back onto its charger. "Dee, I just found you screaming and crying in a pantry closet! You didn't know who the hell I was! You thought I'd locked you in there!"

"And now I know you didn't. I'm better. I just need some water," she whispered hoarsely, shifting slightly so that she sat up higher on her pillows. Bruce leapt onto the bed and took his perch beside her, curling into a ball near her hip. She began to rub his back gently.

The two looked like nothing had happened, like they had always been there. Like the scene Aidan had stumbled upon only minutes ago had been a figment of his imagination.

"Can you hand me my remote?" she asked

casually, gesturing to the remote control. It sat on the night table next to her phone and box of Kleenex. "I want to see if I can catch *All My Children.*"

Aidan's eyes widened. *All My Children?*

He stared at her, then at the remote. He took a deep breath and shoved his fingers through his hair. "Look, we don't have to call 9-1-1 or anything like that. But I really, *really* think we should at least have you —"

"Hello!" someone shouted from the floor below, stopping Aidan. "Hello? Is anyone home?"

He let out a sharp breath and pointed at her. "You stay right here. You hear me? I'm going to see who the hell that is. But please, whatever you do . . . don't move. Okay?"

She nodded, and he headed toward her bedroom door.

"Remote!" she called to him, making him roll his eyes. He snatched the remote off the mahogany tabletop and tossed it onto the bed. It landed on Bruce, and the cat narrowed his yellow eyes at him.

"Hello?" someone shouted again just as Aidan ran out of the bedroom and down the hall. He could hear the opening soundtrack to *All My Children* coming from over his shoulder as he rounded the corner. When he reached the top of the staircase, he could see through the white spindles a man in a pale blue dress shirt and gray slacks standing in the foyer. His hands were on his hips as he peered around him. He leaned in closer to stare at one of the paintings on the wall. He turned, ran his hand over the ornate wood trim along the front bay window, nodding appreciatively.

Watching him, Aidan felt like he was witnessing someone at a car dealership inspecting an Audi he was about to purchase.

"Can I help you?" Aidan asked, now frowning as he walked down the stairs.

The man gazed up at him. "Ha! Someone is home after all!"

Aidan inspected him more closely.

The man couldn't have been more than fifty, judging from the first signs of wrinkles around his mouth, the slight puff to his eyelids, and his receding hairline. But he looked like someone who also went to great lengths to hide his age. That was obvious from his shoe-leather tan, the absence of a single strand of gray hair on his head, and his bleached-white grin.

"I'm sorry!" the man began. "I didn't mean to just barge in here, but the door was open." He gestured to the open front door as evidence, then held out his hand for a shake. "My name is Teddy! Pleased to meet you, Mr. . . . uh . . ."

"Dominguez. Aidan Dominguez, and how can I help you?" Aidan repeated as he shook his hand, but this time there was a firmer edge to his voice.

He did not like this man, though he couldn't say why. The vibe Aidan got from him now wasn't that he was here to buy something, but to sell something — and Aidan was in no mood for a salesman song and dance because of the crisis he was dealing with upstairs. He didn't know when he went back to Delilah's bedroom if he would find the old woman lying on her queen-sized bed watching television or dangling her feet from the second-floor window, ready to jump into the rosebushes below.

"Is Ms. Grey home?" Teddy asked, looking hopeful.

Aidan glanced over his shoulder toward the staircase. Breathy soap-opera dialogue funneled its way to the foyer from the floor above.

"Yes, she's home but she's . . . uh . . . a little occupied right now."

"*Occupied?*"

"Yes, she's a . . . a little under the weather. She's tired and lying down."

Teddy took a step toward him. His blue

eyes squinted with keen interest. "She isn't feeling well? Is it something serious?"

Aidan quickly shook his head. "No! No, nothing like that. Like I said . . . She's just feeling under the weather, that's all."

"Oh."

The two men gazed at one another awkwardly. Aidan cleared his throat.

"Look, I'll tell her that you came to visit when she's feeling better. I'll have her —"

"May I ask . . . Are you Ms. Grey's groundskeeper, Mr. Dominguez?" Teddy drew even closer. "She'd mentioned that she had one."

"Yes, I am, but I haven't *always* been!"

Aidan was quick to correct the assumption. People often saw a guy with the last name Dominguez who did yard work. They'd then assume yard work was all someone like him *could* do. He wouldn't put it past a guy like Teddy to imagine Salvadoran men sprung from the womb with garden shears in one hand and a spade in the other, ready to tend someone's lawn.

"I used to work for a big law firm in Chicago in the banking and financial services division," he clarified, starting the prepared speech he had reiterated those rare times when someone asked him just how he had come to live and work at Harbor Hill.

"But I lived here before . . . when I was a kid. Delilah and my mom stayed in touch. Dee kept inviting me back to visit. I finally did it. I decided to stay and help her take care of Harbor Hill."

"Wait . . . you just decided to pull up stakes like that? You gave up your job at a big city law firm to mow grass and trim hedges?"

"Well, I needed a change of pace after . . ." Aidan's voice drifted off.

"After what?"

Aidan swallowed the lump that had formed in his throat. Four years had passed, and he still couldn't say it aloud. He lowered his eyes, then raised them to look at Teddy again. "After . . . after my wife and I separated and I . . . I got tired of Chicago," he lied.

"Oh. Well, I guess anyone would get tired of all that cold!" Teddy's grin abruptly widened, and he lowered a hand onto Aidan's shoulder, catching him off guard. "It's awful nice of you to come here to help Ms. Grey. I told her a place like this has to get overwhelming for a woman her age. In fact, I even offered to take the house and all the property off her hands so she wouldn't have to deal with the burden anymore. But that old gal keeps turning me down!"

"You want to buy Harbor Hill?"

"I do indeed! I've made her a few offers. She's got me up to three million but keeps telling me no." He leaned toward Aidan's ear. "Truth is, I'm willing to go higher, but don't tell her that." He chuckled.

Aidan stared at him in confusion. Why would someone pay *three million dollars* for Harbor Hill?

Sure, he loved it here — most who lived at Harbor Hill did. Though it had housed literally more than a hundred people in the past three decades, it didn't feel like a bed and breakfast or an impersonal hotel with a revolving door and check-in desk. All you had to do was set down your bags and lower yourself into one of the beds in the guest rooms and you were at home. There was a warmth and sereneness to the house and the surrounding grounds, from the way the sunlight slanted through the second-floor windows at noon, splashing the hardwood floors with their golden rays, to the soft murmur of the Chesapeake Bay one hundred feet below that you could hear from the backyard. But was all that worth seven figures? Aidan would find it hard to make that case.

"Maybe you could speak with her," Teddy ventured. "You know what it means to maintain a place like this. A young man like you won't be here forever. When you're ready to move on, who will take care of it? Who will take care of her?"

Aidan considered Teddy's words. He glanced again at the staircase, listening as the peppy soundtrack of a commercial came from Delilah's television upstairs.

Teddy was right. Though she had told him only a week ago he would never leave this place, he knew he'd have to one day. Where would that leave Delilah? She was getting up in years, and her body was starting to show the signs of those passing decades; she often complained about her creaking knees, and she was on both blood pressure medication and insulin. But he had always described her as hearty.

"I'll die before you do," he'd once joked with her when she mentioned that she might need knee surgery in a year or two, and she wanted to make him her beneficiary if she died on the operating table.

But today he was second-guessing himself. That moment in the pantry was a startling reminder of her age and her mortality. Would Delilah really be fine on her own, all alone in this big house? Would she end up wandering through the rooms, confused about who and where she was — a ghost haunting the halls of Harbor Hill?

Someone had to take care of her. Someone had to watch over her. But Aidan wasn't the man to do it. Not for the long term. But he could be assured of her well-being if she no longer lived here alone and had a million dollars or more at her disposal. She could live anywhere she wanted with that money, in places even better than the place where his mother now stayed.

"Why don't you take my card?" Teddy said as he reached into the pocket of his shirt. He pulled out a laminated card and handed it to Aidan. "I came here to tell her I was willing to up the price by another half million. Maybe you could relay that to her for me." He slapped his shoulder again. "Maybe you could convince her to take the money, since I haven't been able to do it."

Gradually, Aidan nodded, staring at the card, then at the stairs again.

"Glad to have your help, *amigo!*" Teddy said, making Aidan eye him again. Teddy then lowered the aviator sunglasses perched atop his head. "I'll check back in a week."

Teddy stepped through the open front door, jogged down the stairs, and walked toward his BMW parked at the end of the driveway.

Now Aidan realized why he had taken an

instant dislike to this man. Watching Teddy's confident gate and the way he whistled as he walked, Aidan was reminded of the partners at his old law firm in Chicago and the associates who were set to skyrocket their way up the firm's ladder. They all went to the same Ivy League colleges, came from wealthy families with vacation homes off Lake Michigan, and had children coddled by French au pairs. He had once envied those men — had even aspired to be like them.

"Why do you work so hard to impress those blowhards, baby?" his wife, Trish, had asked while they were driving to one of the firm's cocktail parties, where he planned to kiss copious amounts of ass while shamelessly showing off his beautiful wife. "You're so much better than them!"

"Because they are where I want to be," he'd answered without hesitation. "You want to be successful, you find people who already have success. You make sure you're around them, and you soak it up like a sponge."

*What a fool I was,* Aidan now mused, thinking back to that day. He leaned against the door frame and watched as Teddy paused to examine his reflection in the car's tinted window before opening the driver's-side door.

But whether Aidan liked Teddy was irrelevant. This man could hold the key to a secure future for both Delilah and Harbor Hill. Maybe Aidan should hear him out.

Aidan looked down at the card he held, running his thumb over the embossed letters.

"Aidan! Are you still planning to bring me some water, or should I just wait to die from thirst?" Delilah boomed from upstairs, making him sigh in exasperation.

"Comin', Dee!" he said before tucking the business card into his jeans pocket, stepping back into the foyer, and shutting the front door behind him.

# CHAPTER 10

Could someone subsist on panic and desperation? Could they eat it like bread or drink it like water? Could they breathe it like air?

Tracey suspected you could. She certainly felt like she had done it for years while she lived with Paul. She'd treaded so carefully through their life together you'd think their house and yard were littered with land mines that could go off at any moment.

She'd planned every meal in advance, always considering Paul's gluten allergy and his dietary preferences. She'd charted her wardrobe with the precision of a map of the globe, lest she wear a dress that was too short or a top that was too revealing and anger him. She'd kept the house spotless, going over every surface with the same fine eye a craftsman would a concert violin.

If she'd managed to make it to the end of the day without a slap, punch, or shove, she was triumphant. It was a gold star on the mental chart Paul had tacked into her brain, similar to the chart she had tacked on the fridge for Caleb while he was potty training. But she knew the next day would be littered with chances for mistakes and worse, impending reprisals. She knew one day she would mess up again and disappoint him. The anticipation of failure made it hard for her to sleep. It made her heart race as she drove Caleb to school or when she stood in line at the dry-cleaner. The lingering sense of dread had caused her to break into tears one day in the grocery store, though she really had wanted to scream, not cry. She wanted to toss the packages of gluten-free pasta Paul always made her buy to the floor. She wanted to drive her car head-on into a tree just to end it, to make the anguish go away.

It wasn't until she had spent the first night at a motel, the night after she had escaped and left Paul, that she knew what it was like to live without a sense of impending doom. She had sat awake in the motel room's only bed while the children slept beside her, snuggled under the sheets. She stared at the television thinking, "So this is how normal people feel?"

She didn't have to plan out each day in

minute detail to make sure everything was perfect. Of course, there was still the chance Paul wasn't deterred by the photos of bruises she had left on his dresser and the note threatening to call the police if he ever tried to find her or the kids. He could have been in his car at that very minute, driving to their hotel. But for that minute . . . that hour . . . that *entire* night, her life was her own. She could chart her own course, and the knowledge was both freeing and terrifying.

Each day, Tracey got more and more comfortable with her new existence. She had started to covet it, to relish it. But now that her mother may have told Paul where she and the children lived, she knew she ran a real chance of losing her freedom. She couldn't let that happen.

*Should I stay or should I go?*

She wrote the words in big bold letters on a sheet of paper as she sat alone at the kitchen table while Caleb and Maggie slept. She listed the pros and cons of staying in Camden Beach versus packing up all their things in the minivan and heading to another town, maybe to another state.

Reasons to Stay

1) Job in town. Might be hard to find another if I left.
2) Caleb is settled in school, finally making friends.
3) We have some stability in our lives.

She stared at the list for a long time, pursed her lips, then began to write the other.

Reasons to Go

1) Paul may have found us.
2) We're getting kicked out of our home anyway.
3) We're running out of money/could be cheaper to live out of minivan.

Tracey considered the lists side by side, weighing each word. The choices were equal on face value; the risks associated with leaving were just as troublesome as those that came with staying in Camden Beach. If they moved away, would she find another job? If they stayed, would she pull into the driveway one evening only to find Paul standing at her front door, waiting for her?

Tracey closed her weary eyes. She lowered her pen and bowed her head, rubbing at the knot along her neck and shoulder.

She was not equipped for this. She had hoped the longer she was away from Paul, the easier decisions would get. She thought she'd made the hardest decision first — choosing to gather what money she had, pile her kids into a vehicle purchased in cash through a Craigslist ad, and strike out on a path unknown. But she had been wrong. That decision was only the first step on a never-ending tightrope. All it would take was one misstep, one bad decision, and she and the children could go tumbling to the ground below.

Tracey pushed her chair back from the kitchen table and slowly rose to her feet. The house was achingly quiet. Only the drip of the kitchen faucet and the creak of settling wood filled the void. A cold draft seeped through the terrycloth fabric of her robe into her skin. She wrapped her arms around herself. She felt an overwhelming sense of loneliness.

*You are not alone in this world,* a voice whispered to her.

It was Delilah's voice.

Delilah . . . That was the one thing she hadn't considered, the factor she hadn't added to her list.

They wouldn't have to live out of her car

if they moved in with Delilah. She wouldn't have to use what little money she had left because Delilah had offered her a home rent-free. She could save money. She would not feel lonely with Delilah; the old woman's warmth could ward off any chill.

*But the rumor,* Tracey reminded herself. Could she really have her children live with a woman who may have killed someone?

Tracey stood in the center of her kitchen and considered her options. After several seconds, she turned off the kitchen overhead lights. She knew what she had to do. It was time to go to bed since she'd have to have an early start in the morning.

"I want to get a Curious George book," Caleb piped. "No, I want Peppa Pig!"

"Whatever you want, honey," Tracey replied as the automatic doors to the Camden Beach Public Library slid open with a soft hush. She pushed Maggie's stroller through the two-story, glass-ceilinged foyer while Caleb skipped at her side. "But three books max — and don't lose one of them like you did the last time!"

The last thing she needed was to have to pay a lost-book fee.

"I promise I won't lose it, Mommy! I'll —"

She raised a finger to her lips, motioning for him to quiet down as they passed the laminate check-out desk. Behind the counter, a woman peered at them sternly over the top of reading glasses as she typed on her keyboard. Tracey gave her an apologetic smile and waved. The woman nodded back.

"I want you to stay in the children's section over there while Mommy sits over here," she said, dropping her voice to a whisper and pointing at the line of computers along the far wall. "Don't go any farther than that. I want you to stay in my sight, all right?"

"Okay!" Caleb shouted before rushing to the children's reading nook. He ran to a shelf filled with picture books and fell to his knees. She watched as he grabbed one of the books and flipped it open. He then sat his Incredible Hulk action figure beside him and began to quietly read to it.

Tracey turned back toward the computers. She eased the stroller forward, lowering the brakes, before sitting down in one of the leather chairs. Maggie babbled quietly beside her, playing with a cloth doll that was soggy with her drool. Tracey gnawed her lower lip as she clicked the computer mouse a few times, bringing her to the Google search engine. She hesitated only briefly before typing in the words "Delilah Grey."

Tracey had decided last night it was finally time to stop mulling over the rumors about Delilah and find out the truth. She worried over what she might discover. She had almost talked herself out of going to the library to research the answers, but she knew she had no other option at this point. She had to know who this woman really was.

She sighed with defeat when she got more than three thousand results from her initial search. She typed in the name again, this time along with "Camden Beach, Maryland."

That dropped the results down to 286.

She scanned through the links, squinting with concentration as she read them. A few were real estate listings, phone numbers, and even a gardening club announcement. Tracey finally landed on the Chesapeake Estates Homeowners' Association message board. The page showed a post made by Angie Fuhrman of Camden Beach on August 16, 2016 — only last month. The profile picture showed a plump woman with a wrinkled face and a dopey-looking Collie at her feet.

**Angie Fuhrman:** I would like to make it

known that Delilah Grey is not a nice woman!!! She told me that I couldn't walk Ronnie on her property though it's the quickest path to the bay. She CLAIMS he was pooping on her lawn, WHICH ISN'T TRUE!

**Ellen Morris (reply to Fuhrman):** I hate it when neighbors aren't neighborly.

**Pamela Sutton (reply to Fuhrman, Morris):** She's not even part of our community. The woman doesn't pay HOA dues because her home is grandfathered in. It's a travesty, if you ask me. She uses the development's roads just like everyone else, but won't let your dog walk on her precious lawn???

**Angie Fuhrman (reply to Sutton, Morris):** And she shouldn't even OWN that home! I can't believe she's still walking the streets and not in jail!

**Ellen Morris (reply to Fuhrman):** Why jail? What did she do?

**Angie Fuhrman (reply to Morris):** KILLED HER HUSBAND! Can you believe it???? She wouldn't even own that big house if it wasn't for her murdering her husband. I heard she stabbed him in the chest or something. I think she did it back in the 70s.

Tracey started blankly at the computer screen, reading the words over and over again.

*Delilah murdered her husband?*

Just then, Maggie started to babble. Startled out of her stupor, Tracey turned to find the little girl leaning from her perch in the stroller, her fingers fluttering in the air as she reached down for her doll. It had fallen to the floor.

"Daw-wy! Daw-wy!" Maggie cried.

"Oh, I'm sorry, sweetheart. Let me get that for you," Tracey murmured before absently picking up the soggy doll and handing it back to Maggie. She then returned her attention to the computer screen.

"Delilah Grey husband murder," she typed.

Again, she got several links that lead nowhere. She cursed under her breath in frustration, then typed the words again. This time she added "Camden Beach."

A new list of links popped up on her screen. One showed a LexisNexis link to an old *Camden Gazette* article, dated August,

23, 1970. Tracey hesitated only briefly before clicking on it.

On Aug. 22, Delilah Buford of Camden Beach was found guilty of second-degree murder of her husband, Chauncey Buford. The jury deliberated for almost seven hours before reaching its verdict.

The guilty verdict brings an end to a contentious trial that had dragged on for nearly three months and included allegations of affairs and embezzlement against the accused by Mr. Buford's estranged family. The prosecution argued that there was no question of Mrs. Buford's guilt because she had confessed to arresting officers that she had pushed Mr. Buford down the stairs at their estate on Harbor Hill, causing his death. But the defense argued that the push was . . .

The story was abruptly truncated. Tracey squinted at the ellipses.

A knot formed in the pit of her stomach and tightened, making her feel queasy. So the rumors were true. Though the name was different, she could tell from the description that Delilah Buford and Delilah Grey were one and the same. Delilah really had killed someone. That sweet, little old lady who had cooked her dinner, hugged her children, and charmed Tracey with her stories had pushed a man to his death.

Tracey slowly shook her head. There had to be an explanation for this. There is no way . . . *no way* someone like Delilah had taken a life without a valid reason. Tracey had to know more about what happened, what had led to the murder, but the news story had ended so abruptly. Where was the rest of it?

She clicked on several links on the page, trying to find the rest of the story, but gave up when the links led to dead ends. Her shoulders sank. She gnawed her bottom lip again.

*The rest of it has to be somewhere!*

Tracey quickly rose from her chair, gathering her purse and the diaper bag. She raised the brakes on the stroller and eased it away from the line of computers. She glanced over her shoulder at the children's section, where Caleb still sat on the floor, quietly reading among the stacks. She walked back toward the counter where two librarians stood.

"Excuse me," she said as she drew closer.

One of the librarians looked up at her. The woman's plump face brightened with an expectant smile.

"Do you carry old copies of the *Camden Gazette* here?" Tracey asked.

"Why yes, we do! Are you looking for something in particular, ma'am? A specific article?"

"Yes, this article appeared in the 1970s. It was the . . . the August 22nd . . . no 23rd, 1970, edition."

"Oh," the librarian said, pushing her rollaway chair back from the counter, "then that would be in our microfiche collection." She turned slightly to click a few keys on her desktop computer. She stared at the screen. "I'll have to find that in our archives and show you to one of our microfiche readers. Have you ever used one of those before?"

Tracey nodded. "Though not since college."

The librarian grinned. "I'm sure you won't have any problems. Give me a minute, and I'll give you a refresher."

Twenty minutes later, Tracey, the librarian, and the children took the elevator to the basement, to the archival section of the library.

"Here you go," the librarian said as the elevator doors opened. They stepped into a large room where a few tables were arranged in the center and a row of microfiche readers were arranged along the wall. The librarian dropped a stack of boxes filled with microfiches onto a small plastic desk. In addition to pulling the August 23 article, she also looked up others, upon Tracey's request. After a quick search, she pulled several related to Delilah's murder trial. She gave Tracey a brief tutorial on the microfiche reader.

"Let me know if you need anything else. Okay, ma'am?"

Tracey nodded. "Thank you so much," she whispered as the librarian walked away. She removed the lid of the box on top, revealing a plastic canister.

"You're going to read *all* of that?" Caleb asked, watching his mother unspool the microfiche as he hopped into a wooden chair next to her desk. It wobbled slightly, then steadied itself.

"Not the whole thing, Cabe. Just one or two stories."

"Oh," he said before flipping open one of his books. As if accepting her answer, he returned his attention to his dinosaurs. Meanwhile, Tracey shrugged into the sweater she had brought with her, feeling cold all of a sudden. She wasn't sure if it was a chill going up her spine at the prospect of what she would discover in these articles or whether it really was cooler in this part of the building.

While the top floor of the library had been all soaring glass ceilings, stainless steel, and modern couches and sofas, the rooms down here were older and shoddier, with heavy oak bookshelves, orange plastic chairs, and small glass-block windows. Even the lighting was darker. She felt as if they had descended into a poorly lit cave.

Tracey finished loading the microfiche and sat in her chair. She turned the knob on the reader and watched a series of articles and ads flash by, a haze of gray and yellow. Only a few caught her attention: one article showing the photo of a woman screaming and kneeling beside a dead man under the headline "4 Bums Killed at Kent U Following a Riot," another announcing Elvis Presley's death. Finally, she reached the August 23rd issue. Under the banner headline NEGRO CAMDEN WOMAN FOUND GUILTY OF MURDER OF WHITE HUSBAND, she saw a picture that halted her breath.

It was of a young black woman sitting behind a table in what looked to be a crowded courtroom. Two white men bracketed her. One wore those old-fashioned Buddy Holly glasses and had his long hair parted on the side. The other was bald and wore a thick striped tie. The woman's hair was pulled back from her face, and her head was slightly bowed. Her expression was withdrawn. Tears were in her eyes.

*"Delilah?"* Tracey whispered, wanting to reach out to touch the face on the screen. Instead, she read the article, then all of the six others related to the trial. From those bits and pieces and loose strings of narrative, she was able to compose an overall story of what had happened to Delilah.

Delilah Buford had been found guilty of second-degree murder of her husband because the prosecutors couldn't prove premeditation, though Delilah's lawyers argued it should have been involuntary manslaughter, considering that she had accidentally pushed him down the stairs. But they couldn't prove for sure it had been an accident since Delilah admitted she'd woken up after being knocked unconscious, only to find her husband dead at the bottom of the stairs. She'd had no recollection of how he had gotten there but had assumed, based on the evidence, that she had pushed him.

Her lawyers had argued that she must have been trying to escape her angry husband when the accident happened. He had been known to abuse her regularly. Delilah's friend — an Agnes Macy of Charleston, South Carolina, whom Delilah had once worked with — and even the caretaker of Harbor Hill estate admitted to seeing bruises on Delilah's arms and face. But they were all Negroes, so their testimony before an all-white Southern male jury hadn't carried much weight.

Delilah had testified that her husband had systematically terrorized her, beaten her almost daily, and raped her, which the prosecution, many of the jurors, and the reporters covering the trial had considered laughable. How could a husband possibly rape his wife, they asked? She claimed she had been afraid for her life, and she had been running away from him when he grabbed her, likely tripped, and fell down the stairs.

But the jury hadn't believed her story. His family had argued that Chauncey Buford would never have abused his wife. They also claimed Delilah had been eager for her wealthy husband to die because, upon his death, she stood to inherit not only the money his family had given him, but also Harbor Hill. He had changed his will only weeks before the murder, making Delilah his sole beneficiary.

"Delilah didn't do nothin' but fall in love

with the wrong man," Agnes Macy had said while on the stand during the murder trial. "I warned her that she'd pay a price for it, but I didn't think it would be this bad. She didn't mean for this to happen. She ain't no killer."

Three years after Delilah was sentenced to fifteen years in prison for involuntary manslaughter, she was released on appeal, based on evidence that "drew into question the true assailant and nature of the murder, all of which the original judge had deemed inadmissible."

The appellate judge had ruled that the jury's inability to hear evidence that could have possibly exonerated Delilah "was a gross miscarriage of justice."

Tracey read the last line, now at a loss.

*She could have been exonerated?*

So had Delilah murdered him or not? And if she had killed her husband, was it an accident, as her lawyers insisted in court — or had she murdered him in cold blood, as Chauncey Buford's relatives argued? What was the truth?

Tracey loaded the first article again. She stared at Delilah's face in the newspaper photograph, pressing a button on the microfiche reader so she could zoom in and make out every shadow, angle, and plane in the black-and-white image.

The young woman on the screen didn't look like a hardened or conniving killer. She looked lost and scared. She looked like it took every effort just to hold up her head and not drop it on the table. On her face was the expression of a woman giving herself over to fate. Tracey wondered if young Delilah had been crying that day but really felt like screaming.

Had she also felt alone?

Tracey pressed the button to turn off the reader, watching the screen as it went black. She stared at the black screen for a long time.

"Did you find what you were looking for, Mommy?" Caleb asked, looking up from this book.

Tracey turned to her son and nodded. "Yes, I . . . I think I did."

# CHAPTER 11

Delilah was euphoric. She hadn't been this happy in months — maybe even *years*.

Tracey had called her two days ago to tell her she was accepting Delilah's kind offer to move into Harbor Hill. Tracey and the children wanted to live there for the next few months, or at least until Tracey got back on her feet.

As Delilah washed the sheets that would go on no longer vacant beds, as she planned the grocery list for a household that would abruptly expand from two to five, Delilah was filled with a sense of purpose. Even the troublesome voice — her constant companion — had all but disappeared. It would mutter a few sullen words every now and then, but she could easily ignore it or drown it out. There was now a cacophony of happiness and life in her ears.

Even Aidan's meddling couldn't bring her down. He had tried earlier that week to talk to her about Teddy's offer to buy Harbor Hill, arguing it might be a smart move to consider. He insisted that when she got older, she wouldn't be able to live in such a big house all alone.

"You're no spring chicken, Dee," he'd said.

*Spring chicken,* she now thought, sucking her teeth.

He should worry more about himself and his life than her own. Besides, it wasn't like she was on the verge of infirmity or going senile. Aidan knew good and well she still had all her faculties about her. She still took her morning walks around the property, and though she was occasionally forgetful, she could spout her name, address, and what year it was in a matter of seconds.

Delilah had dismissed Aidan's advice outright, just as she had dismissed Teddy's many offers. Harbor Hill was her home and her burden. She was connected to this house, just as her hand was connected to her wrist and her wrist was connected to her arm. She would not . . . *could not* detach herself from it even if she wanted to. Delilah would only leave Harbor Hill behind on the day she died, and even then, she certainly wasn't going to put it in the hands of a total stranger like Teddy.

"What are you doing, Dee?" he now called to her.

"What does it look like I'm doing?" she said as she placed a stack of towels in one of the linen closets. She shut the door. "I'm getting ready for Tracey and the children."

As she walked around Aidan to make her way back down the hall, he slowly shook his head.

"I don't like this. I don't like it at all."

"You'll get used to her and the children, Aidan," she called over her shoulder as she walked down the stairs with him only a few steps behind her. "It'll just take some —"

"No, I mean I don't like a family moving in here when you're the . . . well, the way that you are. I think you should see a doctor."

"For what?" she snapped, hopping off the last riser.

"What do you mean 'For what?' You remember what happened two weeks ago, don't you?" he asked as he followed her into the living room. He trailed her like a shadow.

Delilah grabbed one of her books from the shelves and sat in her chair. She began to read — or at least pretended to — then huffed in exasperation when Aidan continued to loom over her.

"Do you remember how you were screaming, Dee? How you —"

"Yes, I remember! I'm not *that* loose in the head, honey!" She tapped her temple before flopping back into her recliner. "We were both there! I just got scared and confused. That's all it was! You're making a big fuss over nothing."

"*Over nothing?* You were hysterical! You didn't even recognize who the hell I was!"

Delilah pretended to ignore him and flipped to another page.

"Damnit, Dee, I'm not kidding! If you don't go to the doctor . . . if you don't let me take you to see someone, I'm . . ." He paused. His shoulders rose, then fell as he took a deep breath. "I'm not letting that woman move in here with those kids. I'm not doing it! You hear me?"

At those words, she sat her book aside and frowned up at him. Aidan stood in front of her recliner, looking as strong and immovable as a mountain, but she wasn't intimidated. She remembered him when his voice still squeaked, when he had proudly showed her his first razor.

"What do you mean you won't *let* them move in here? This is my house, not yours! Or have you forgotten?"

"Of course I haven't."

"You just don't want her to move in here! You're scared those children are going to remind you of —"

"It's the kids I'm worried about! What if you start ranting again and do it in front of them? What if you forget where you are and —"

"It's not going to happen! I told you that I just got a . . . a little confused, but . . ."

"You *weren't* confused!"

". . . but I'm not anymore!" she continued, shouting over him. "I know who I am and where I am!"

"I'll tell her what happened," he blurted out, and her pulse stuttered. "I'll tell her what you said . . . how you acted that day. She's not going to bring little kids into this house . . . into a situation like that! You know she won't. No decent mother would!"

The living room fell silent. The silence stretched for a full minute before Delilah regained her voice.

"You would . . . you would really do that, Aidan? You would make her think I'd endanger those babies?"

She watched as he closed his eyes and lowered his head. He wouldn't answer her, and that was all the response she needed.

Delilah pursed her lips and swallowed. She turned her head to stare at the lamp, blinking back tears.

She never thought the day would come when Aidan would turn on her like the other people around Camden Beach. She remembered the old days when women would cross to the other side of the street, yanking their children to their side when she passed. She remembered when one of the old-timers had spat at her feet, mumbling, "You murdering nigger bitch! You should still be in jail for what you did!"

It had taken every part of her to continue to hold her head high and not go running back to the house and cower in her bedroom.

Aidan knew her heart. She had practically raised him, and yet he could do this to her.

"Are you going to tell her she should be afraid of me?" she persisted, facing him again.

He opened his eyes, scratched the back of his head, and sighed. "I'm not trying to hurt you, Dee. I just need to make sure you're okay. That's all. I need someone to say you'll be okay."

One tear fell down her cheek — but only one. She would allow herself that solace, but no more.

"Okay," she whispered. "I'll go to the doctor."

It wasn't like she had any other choice.

Delilah pushed the ugly memory of her confrontation with Aidan a week ago to the back of her mind and instead focused on the squeals she now heard and the thump of footsteps on her wooden stairs. It was a siren call she couldn't resist. She set down the ladle she was holding and walked out of the kitchen into the foyer. The front door swung open, and a small figure came racing through — a blur of color and sound, energy and joy.

"How many times do I have to tell you to slow down?" Tracey shouted to the boy as he galloped across the hardwood. He ran straight to Delilah, barreling into her and wrapping his arms around her waist. He knocked her back a step, making her laugh and drop her dish towel to the floor.

"Is my room upstairs?" he asked Delilah almost breathlessly. His face was flushed. His eyes were wide and bright, and Delilah couldn't help but clasp his freckled cheeks in her hands.

"Yep," Delilah said with a grin, "right up the stairs to your left . . . three doors down."

"My *own* room! Woo-hoo!" Caleb cried before letting go of Delilah and charging to the staircase. He thudded to the second floor.

"Caleb, didn't you hear me?" Tracey shouted, stepping through the entryway. "I said stop running!"

But he ignored her and instead headed down the hall to the upstairs bedrooms. Delilah heard more squeals and shouting before the noise finally died down. She chuckled quietly to herself.

Tracey lowered Maggie to the floor, and the little girl toddled off toward the living room to explore. Curious about the new little human, Bruce trailed into the living room behind Maggie.

"There's a lot of nice stuff in there," Tracey said, staring into the living room, furrowing her brows with concern. "You know, I can get Maggie's playpen and put her in there so she doesn't do too much damage. I do it at home all the time when —"

"Oh, it's fine!" Delilah waved her hand. "I baby-proofed everything."

Delilah had gone to the local Target a few days before to fill her shopping cart with more than a hundred dollars' worth of supplies. Now every electrical outlet was covered, every table and shelf was padded with a rubber bumper, and every door had a safety lock.

Her home was better fortified than the Alamo.

"I prepared. The little one can only cause but so much mischief in there," Delilah said.

"Oh, trust me. You'd be surprised!" Tracey laughed awkwardly as she stood in the foyer, gazing around her. She peered up at the exposed beam ceilings and the wainscoting along the walls. She slowly lowered her suitcase to the floor. "Thank you so much for doing this, Delilah."

"Oh, just call me Dee, and no thanks needed. It's a pleasure, honey," she whispered, and she meant it. She cleared her throat. "Why don't you go upstairs and get settled into your room," Delilah suggested to Tracey, who still looked as if she didn't quite know what to do with herself. The young woman had an air of nervous energy Delilah hoped would disappear the longer she lived at Harbor Hill. Whatever was making her anxious would not find her here.

"Dinner should be ready in less than an hour, honey."

"Oh?" Tracey asked, looking hopeful. "Well, if there's anything you need help with, I can —"

"Nope, I've got it covered. Everything's already done."

Tracey's face fell.

"I'll cook on the first night to give y'all a chance to get situated," Delilah quickly added. "But if you want to handle dinner tomorrow —"

"I'd be happy to!"

A silence fell between them again.

"Well, I'll just . . . I'll just grab Maggie and settle in, I guess." Tracey started to walk toward the living room but paused to turn back and look at the opened front door. She pointed toward her minivan parked in the driveway. Aidan was currently unloading boxes from the rear. "Do you think he needs help with some of that stuff?"

"Even if he did, he wouldn't let you help him," Delilah said, reaching down to retrieve the dish towel Caleb had knocked out of her hands when he greeted her. "Don't worry about it. Just go on and get yourself freshened up and set up your room the way you want it."

Tracey nodded absently before finally breaking her gaze from the driveway. She headed into the living room to retrieve Maggie.

Delilah walked across the foyer and through the opened door. Aidan had just picked up one of the boxes from the asphalt. He started to walk toward the stairs.

"Make sure to be careful with her things," she admonished, making him roll his eyes heavenward as he carefully balanced the box in his arms.

"I *know* what I'm doing. Do you know how many times I've had to move in boxes in the past four years?" he asked between huffs of breath as he climbed the last step. "More times than I can count! I could do this in my sleep."

She stepped aside to let him through the doorway.

"Have you taken your pill today?" he asked, keeping his tone nonchalant, though he knew the very question went over her like sandpaper.

He was referring to the pills the psychiatrist had prescribed for her. She'd explained to the doctor — a middle-aged woman with short gray hair and an indulgent smile — what had happened in the pantry and how she occasionally heard a voice that made her uneasy. The psychiatrist had nodded and listened patiently for a half an hour before prescribing Klonopin for Delilah's "panic attacks." Delilah had been taking the medication for about a week, but she didn't like it. It made her dizzy when she climbed the stairs and made her want to take more naps than Bruce.

"I'll take it later," she mumbled, turning back around to head to the kitchen to put her yeast biscuits in the oven.

He stopped in his tracks in front of the stairs leading to the second floor.

"Dee, you need to take your pill. There was no point in the doctor prescribing it for you if —"

"Don't talk to me like I'm some child, Aidan."

"Then don't act like one!" he ordered, dropping the box to the floor.

"You better not have broken anything in there," she said, pointing at the box. She watched as Aidan closed his eyes, took a deep breath like he was counting to ten, then opened his eyes again.

"*Please* just take the damn pill. I don't want to have to worry about you. All right?"

Delilah didn't respond.

"You remember our deal, don't you?"

"Yes, I remember. I went there just like you asked me too, didn't I?"

"And you also have to follow the doctor's orders! Don't pretend like that wasn't part of the deal too."

She crossed her arms over her chest.

"I can still tell her the truth, Dee."

Delilah clenched her jaw. She pushed her way past him and walked up the stairs, pausing at the top and holding onto the newel post when the dizzy spell struck her. She waited a few seconds for it to wane to the point where it was at least bearable, then placed one shaky foot in front of the other as she headed down the hall to her bedroom. She walked past her four-poster bed and into the en suite bathroom with its high ceiling and sunken tub. She paused in front of the bathroom mirror and watched as her reflection spun around like a slow-moving carousel and then, finally, mercifully settled.

*There I am.*

She gazed at the constellation of moles along her cheeks, chin, and neck, the wrinkles framing her mouth, and her big dark eyes. She was sixty-seven, and yet she felt and looked much older. She could remember her face when she was a young woman of seventeen. She had once thought of herself as pretty. Many men had too — but not anymore.

*A hard life will do that to you,* she told herself. *Besides, it's not like you're entering the Miss America Pageant anytime soon! What judge's eye are you trying to catch?*

She opened the mirror, revealing the shelves of her medicine cabinet. She removed the bottle of Klonopin and shook one pill into her hand. It was blue and circular and stood out against the pale skin of her palm. She remembered a similar pill from long ago, but that one hadn't made her dizzy.

Delilah sighed.

Maybe she could lie to Aidan and tell him she took it. It's not like he would know the difference. And it's not like she really needed the damn thing. She was fine. He was just overreacting, that's all.

She stared at the pill again.

"Just go on and take it," a voice ordered, startling her and making her almost drop the pill into the sink.

This voice didn't sound like the one she was used to hearing. It sounded very different — female, almost playful.

"What?" she whispered.

"Oh, go on, Dee! It ain't gonna hurt you!" the voice assured.

*"Agnes?"* Delilah breathed. "Is that . . . is that you?"

The voice didn't answer.

Delilah hesitated for a second longer before she closed her eyes, popped the pill into her mouth, and swallowed.

■ ■ ■ ■

# PART II

■ ■ ■ ■

*Chevy Chase, Maryland*
*May 1968*

# CHAPTER 12

"Just go on and take it," Agnes whispers, stopping me just before we step into the kitchen, pinching a little blue pill between her fingers.

I squint down at it and frown. "What is that?"

"Oh, go on, Dee! It ain't gonna hurt you!" she says, then drops her voice to a whisper. "Miss Mindy takes them all the time. I take it sometimes too when she's driving me up a wall!" She winks and presses the pill into the palm of my hand before closing my fingers over it.

"You *stole* this? You stole it from Miss Mindy?"

Agnes waves off my worry.

"She's got plenty more where that came from. Just take it, girl! It'll calm you down, and the way you're actin' right now, you'll need all the help you can get! You're never gonna make it through this dinner, and I can't do it all by myself. Take it! It's good for you. It's like vitamins."

Vitamins?

I hesitate a few more seconds before I raise the pill to my mouth. I drop it on my tongue, close my eyes, and swallow. I feel the muscles working along my throat as it slides its way down. As soon as it does, I regret what I've done. I want to spit the chalky taste out of my mouth.

Lord, what did I let her talk me into?

"Give it about thirty minutes to work. You'll be all right."

Agnes tightens the ribbon of her stiff white apron, then pushes the kitchen door open. She steps inside, and I trail in behind her. Agnes beelines to one of the counters, where a line of sparkling serving trays covered with lace are arranged. They look as pretty as wrapped presents under a Christmas tree.

"Now when you walk in there, you hold the tray like this. *See?*" Agnes says, lifting one of the sterling silver trays and holding it in front of her, clutching it in both hands about half a foot away from her chest and midway down her body.

I nod — though I'm still a little confused.

I thought I would be holding the tray like the waitresses at the Woolworth's Downtown I sometimes see through the windows on 14th Street — or even like the waiters in picture shows who wear tuxedoes and bow ties. Those waiters always balance the tray in the air over their heads like they're performing a circus act.

But I don't tell her that. The question sounds silly before it even comes out of my mouth. Plus, I figure Agnes has to know what she's talking about. Agnes has been serving white folks a lot longer than me — since she'd left school at fourteen to become a maid and help her mama take care of a family of eight. Those days of scrubbing someone else's toilet, ironing their clothes, and changing their children's soiled diapers seem to have aged Agnes beyond her twenty-six years, filling her head with fifty years' worth of knowing. But I just turned seventeen two months ago and have been serving as a maid in the Williams household for only two weeks. Tonight is the first time I'll be helping with one of their cocktail parties, and I feel like I'm about to pee my pants.

"You listening, Dee?" Agnes barks at me.

I nod. I nod so hard my eyes almost roll. "Y-y-yes, I'm listening."

I'm also trying not to be so scared of all the new things around me: the feel of the cardboard-like collar of my dress uniform pressing into my neck, the opening and slamming shut of the oven door over and over again, and the laughter and music just beyond the kitchen. But I can't keep the fear pushed down for long. It is all too much. My fear is like one of the pots on the oven whose lid clatters rhythmically; it's threatening to boil over. "Like I said . . . when you wanna offer them something to drink, you don't say, 'Excuse me. Would you like some refreshments?' or 'Would you like something to drink, sir?' " Agnes says in an exaggerated British accent, waving her hand in the air like a queen greeting her peasants.

Her dark eyes go earnest again as she loads glass after glass onto one of the silver trays. She reaches for the opened bottle of champagne. "You don't say a damn thing! You just stand there and wait for them to look at you. They'll shake their head or nod. Then when they done, you move on to the next."

"B-but what if they're blind?" I ask.

Agnes stops pouring the champagne and eyes me. "What?"

"What if they're blind? What if they can't see you?"

The cook — a broad-backed woman ornerier than the devil himself, named

184

Roberta — pauses midway in opening the oven yet again to turn and shake her head at me.

I can tell she's been half listening to our conversation this whole time.

"Lord, that chile got all the book learnin' in the world and don't have a lick of sense!" Roberta says.

By "book learnin'," Roberta means my high school diploma and the books I keep tucked in my apron pocket to read whenever I have downtime or when I get bored. Tonight, I've got a beat-up copy of *Great Expectations.*

But "all the book learnin' " hasn't done me a bit of good. I'm still in the same place as Agnes and Roberta. I'm still a servant just like they are — though I had hoped . . . had once *dreamed* of being a lot more than that. But here I am.

"What do you mean what if they're blind?" Agnes asks. "What if *who's* blind?"

"Th-the party guest," I say, feeling even more flustered by Agnes and Roberta's re-action, by the expressions on their faces. "What if they can't see me and my tray because they're blind? Should I say some-thing then?"

Agnes purses her lips and cocks an eye-brow. "Well, I ain't never run across a blind party guest! I don't think you got anything to worry about."

Roberta shakes her head, then lets out a rumbling laugh, making her bosom jiggle behind her pale blue uniform.

"Agnes!" a voice suddenly booms from the doorway.

Agnes, Roberta, and I turn to find Miss Mindy standing there. We instantly fall quiet and go still.

Miss Mindy's red hair is up tonight. It looks like a copper helmet. You could throw a plate at that thing and it wouldn't move. She's wearing an ice-blue cocktail dress with a diamond broach at the waist. The cocktail dress seems a size too big on her reed-thin frame, bagging at the bust, but I've heard that's what white women like to look like nowadays — like they're starving.

I've always thought it peculiar that people who have so much money want to look like they can't afford to buy food. And the Williamses have more money than most. Whereas many of the families in their neighborhood are lucky to have one housekeeper and maybe a driver, the Williamses have a driver, two maids, and a cook.

"Everyone thinks it's because Mr. Williams got a lot of money," Agnes whispered to me one day as we were folding laundry.

"But the one who really got all the money is his wife. She come from it, was born with it, and took it with her when she got married. That man wouldn't have a pot to pee in if it weren't for Miss Mindy!"

"Our guests are starting to arrive, Agnes," Miss Mindy says through pinched, frosted-pink lips. "Are you bringing out the drinks soon?"

I watch as Agnes and Roberta shrink into themselves in Miss Mindy's presence. Both shift their eyes away from her. Agnes even lowers her head.

They are like the pages of one of my books fanned wide open, and then suddenly the covers are slapped closed by Miss Mindy's pale, freckled hand.

"Yes, Miss Mindy. We'll be out there in just a minute," Agnes answers in a small voice, losing all her boldness from earlier.

Miss Mindy nods before giving a scant glance at me, seeing me for the first time since she came into the kitchen. "You make sure to follow Agnes's lead. She knows the proper way to conduct herself on these occasions."

"Yes, ma'am," I answer, lowering my gaze too and feeling myself shrinking.

Miss Mindy steps through the doorway, letting the wooden door swing behind her.

Agnes watches the door a second longer. When it closes, she lifts one of the trays and shoves it at me. "You heard what she said. Now go on and get out there! And remember everything I told you now!" she whispers shrilly.

I grab the tray and head toward the kitchen door, nudging the door open with the tip of my borrowed shoes. They are already pinching my feet. Through the crack, I can see all the people standing around the Williamses' living room — sitting on the sofa, hanging around the polished baby grand, and lingering near the windows. The champagne glasses on my tray start to rattle. I look down and realize my hands are shaking.

"Go on!" Agnes hisses.

She looks like she's about to shove me through the door.

"Chile, what are you waiting for?" Roberta calls to me.

I take a deep breath and step through the door, holding my tray midway down my chest like Agnes showed me, praying I won't mess up.

And for the rest of the night, I try to remember everything Agnes told me. I whisper her words of warning to myself as I walk around the room with the tray.

*Don't look them in the eye.*

*Don't walk by anyone with an empty glass and not offer to take it from them.*

*And — for the love of the good Lord above — keep quiet, and speak only when they speak to you first!*

I do all right, I guess. Then one of the guests picks up a glass and sips some of the champagne and says, "Nice! Hey, what vintage is this anyway?"

I look up and realize he's talking to me. He nods and smacks his lip, taking another sip. He's staring at me as though he expects me to say something back.

He is a short man with thick black glasses, a bald head, and a big beaky nose. He has an accent from farther up north. He sounds an awful lot like the late President Kennedy — God rest his soul!

I remember seeing the gold label on the champagne bottle as Agnes was pouring the glasses. It was a Champagne Grande Cuvée Grand Siècle 1965.

I can't pronounce the French words too well. I tried to teach myself some French after I read a few books with French phrases in them, but I haven't gotten far. Still, he asked me a question. I could try to say the name of the champagne. I open my mouth to answer him, but then a woman beside

189

him wearing white elbow gloves and thick eyeliner begins to laugh.

"Like *she* would know!" the woman squeals before I can answer, slapping his shoulder. " 'What vintage is this?' Phil, you're such a hoot!"

The man, Phil, turns and seems to blink at the woman in confusion before erupting into laughter too, like he knows what she's been laughing at all along.

"Sorry," he says. "Guess I've already had too much hooch tonight!"

I close my mouth. My cheeks and my neck feel hot — so hot I want to run into the kitchen, grab one of Roberta's washcloths, douse it with cold water, and lay it on my face. I feel foolish . . . foolish for wanting to answer the man's question, foolish for even bothering to try to learn French. When would I ever have to speak French? I am a maid and probably will always be one. Who was I fooling?

The man and the woman stop laughing and return to whatever conversation they were having before I came along. Watching them, I feel my eyes start to sting. I slowly back away from the couple. As I get farther away, I can feel the pain in my chest expand like the distance from me to them. I stop walking when I bump into someone, brushing my shoulder against an arm.

I turn around to find Miss Mindy glaring at me. She's standing with a group of her friends, women who look a lot like her. They all have hair helmets of different shapes and sizes, dresses too baggy for their frames, and shrewd, scornful faces.

"I'm so sorry, Miss Mindy," I blurt out. "I was just heading to the kitchen to —"

My words taper off when I realize Miss Mindy is staring at me like I've just lost my mind.

I've broken the first commandment; I spoke to one of the white folks without being spoken to first.

Ashamed yet again, I rush toward the kitchen door, the glasses rattling on my tray louder than the steel wheels of a roller coaster.

"She's new. She came recommended, but it's so hard to find good help nowadays," I can hear Miss Mindy say before a few of her friends murmur in agreement.

I shove the kitchen door open and see Agnes walking toward me with a tray of deviled eggs. Roberta is putting the finishing touches on the tiny sandwiches I'm supposed to take out next.

"Just what do you think you doing?" Agnes asks me, her voice full of accusation.

"Hey, there's still full glasses on that tray. Get back out there!"

I don't answer her. Instead, I rush past her, almost tossing the champagne tray onto the counter. I run toward the door on the opposite side of the kitchen.

"Did you hear her talking to you, gal?" Roberta shouts after me.

My eyes are closed when I step through the door into the laundry room. The tears come by the time I reach the sink basin where I scrubbed off the bottom of Mr. Williams's golf cleats yesterday.

The ache in my chest is worse now. It is a sharp pain, like someone has stabbed a knife inside me and is twisting it. I can barely breathe. I'm gulping for air as I choke back my sobs.

"Where's the fire, honey? The party isn't that bad, is it?" a deep voice drawls behind me.

I whip around. I can't see well because the lights are off, and only moonlight filters through the opened window blind. I squint and find a shadowy figure sitting on the counter along the adjoining wall where we usually fold laundry.

"I'm sorry," I say, quickly wiping the tears off my cheeks and the snot from my nose with the back of my hand. "I didn't know anyone w-was in here, sir."

The figure reaches up and pulls the dangling cord to the overhead light, making the room go bright.

I squint as my eyes adjust to the light. Now I can see the shadowy figure is a man wearing a tuxedo like the other men at the party, except he isn't wearing a tie and the first three buttons of his shirt are open, revealing a mat of brown chest hair that grows thinner as it climbs from his chest to this throat. He is leaning against an empty laundry basket. A lit cigarette hangs from his lips. On the windowsill of the open window beside him, sits a silver flask that glints in the light. The letter C is stamped on the front.

"I'm sorry! I didn't mean to disturb you, sir." I turn around and head back toward the door.

"Hey, hold on there! You weren't disturbing me."

I stop.

"You look like you need this room more than I do anyway."

He laughs, and I hesitate, unsure what to do next. I know I shouldn't stay in here, alone with this strange white man. I should go back into the kitchen and get the silver tray covered with small sandwiches with the crusts cut off. But I don't want to leave yet. My eyes and my nose are red now, and everyone will see I've been crying. The ache in my chest hasn't gone away either.

I look at him again.

"You look like you could use a smoke too."

He hops off the counter, strolls toward me, and smiles, with his cigarette still hanging from the side of his mouth. The edges of his bright green eyes crinkle up, and I see one of his front teeth overlap the other. His auburn hair is a bit too long and a little greasy. It hangs limply into one of his eyes, and he pushes it aside. And his black tuxedo is wrinkled, like he threw it on in a hurry. But aside from those imperfections, he is a handsome man — very handsome. He slaps the pack of Newports against the heel of his hand, and one of the cigarettes pops up. He holds the pack toward me.

I stare at the cigarette: the white filter and the gold wrapping paper at the tip.

"What are you waiting for? Take one!"

"I'm . . . I'm sorry, sir, but I don't smoke."

"Oh?" He laughs again and opens his jacket, tucking the pack into one of the inner pockets. "She doesn't smoke," he mutters before raising his brows. "So what do you do . . . uh, what's your name anyway?"

"Delilah, sir."

"Delilah," he repeats, then nods thoughtfully and tugs the cigarette out of his mouth. "What do you do, Delilah, besides crying in laundry rooms? Though I'm sure anyone would be brought to tears working for my darlin' sister!"

His sister? Miss Mindy is his sister?

I look again at his green eyes and the auburn hair — now I can see the resemblance, though I didn't know Miss Mindy had a brother. Agnes certainly never mentioned it.

"I'm sorry. I don't know what you mean, sir," I say, playing stupid.

He taps ashes of his cigarette onto the tiled floor. I furrow my brows and stare at those specs of gray beneath the shadow of his wingtips. I'll have to sweep it up later or Miss Mindy will have a fit.

"Stop saying you're sorry and stop calling me 'sir.' My name is Chauncey . . . though most people call me Cee. You can call me that too, if you'd like. And you know damn well what I'm talking about. I'm talking about working for my sister, Melinda . . . the lady of the house! That woman could drive a saint to drink. I admire anybody who could work *with* her, let alone be her maid."

"She treats me nice, Mr. Cee," I lie.

"It's Cee, not *Mr. Cee.* Now say it with

195

me on the count of three. One . . . two . . . three!"

He sucks in a deep breath, and I giggle at his dramatics. I clamp a hand over my mouth with embarrassment for laughing.

I wonder if Miss Mindy's pilfered blue pill is finally starting to kick in.

"Cee," he says.

"Cee," I repeat and give a small smile.

"There! That wasn't so hard, was it? And you've got a pretty smile, Delilah. You should use it more often."

He takes several steps toward me, and I can smell him now. He's a mix of tobacco, a spicy cologne, and rum. That's what must be in the flask.

"So if my sister didn't run you off, why are you crying?"

"I was just . . . sad, sir . . . I-I mean, Cee."

"Sad about what?"

I hesitate again.

"Don't worry. Your secret's safe with me."

His friendliness is making me wary. I'm not sure if I'm stepping into some trap. Why is he being so nice? Why is he asking so many questions, and can I know for sure that he won't tell Miss Mindy what I say?

"People just feel . . . blue sometimes," I mumble with a shrug. "Sometimes, you don't know what's wrong. You just know things aren't right . . . that things aren't the way they should be."

He takes another step toward me so that there is only a small space between us. He stares at me, eye to eye. I can't hold his gaze. I don't want to, so I look away.

"And how should things be, Delilah?"

I force myself to raise my eyes again to look at him. Yes, the pill is definitely kicking in, making me bolder. I could tell another lie, but I don't want to do that either.

"I don't know how they should be — but I shouldn't be here," I whisper.

"Dee, where are you?" Agnes shouts as she shoves open the laundry room door. "I've only got two hands! I can't hand out all this stuff by my —"

She stops when she sees Cee is also in the room. She does what she did with Miss Mindy the instant she sees him. Her face changes. Her shoulders hunch, and she lowers her head. I wonder how many times she does it during the day, shutting the door on her real self for white folks. I haven't been around them as much as she has. I know the rules, but sometimes — like tonight — I forget them.

"I'm sorry, sir," she says in a teeny voice. "I didn't know you were in here."

"It's fine," Cee replies. He reaches back

and grabs the flask perched on the window-sill. He then digs out his tie from the laundry basket. We watch as he tosses his cigarette to the floor and takes a sip from his flask before tucking it into his suit's inner pocket. "I was just leaving. I'd better get out there or Mindy's gonna wonder where I've disappeared to."

He then glances down at the silver tie in his hand. It is so shiny, it gleams like aluminum foil. "I'm horrible at putting on these things. Can you help me, Delilah?"

I stare at him in shock and glance with uncertainty at Agnes. She gives me no clue on what to do. Her mask is still on.

Cee holds out the tie to me as he buttons his shirt. The tie dangles like a fish on a hook.

"Well?" he asks, raising his brows.

I step forward and take the tie before looping it around his neck. My hands start to shake again as I raise his collar and begin to put on his tie, trying to remember the right knot, trying not to touch him but just the tie and the shirt. He stares at me as I do it, almost smirking. He is amused by my discomfort. Agnes stares at me too as I do it, boring a hole into my back. My fingers accidentally graze the skin along his neck and jawline. His skin is warm and covered

198

with a prickly stubble. It makes the tips of my fingers tingle. When I finish with his tie, I lower his collar and ball my fists to my sides.

"Thanks." He gives me a wink. "You have a good night now."

Agnes and I both watch as he strolls toward the door. She quickly steps aside to let him pass her. When the door swings closed behind him, she whips around to face me.

"*What* were y'all doin in here?" she asks. Her voice is tainted with anger, like I've done something wrong.

"N-nothing!" I shake my head. "Nothing at all! We were just . . . just talking."

She eyes me warily. I can tell she doesn't believe me. Agnes looks back toward the closed door. She stares at it for a long time. "You best be careful 'round him, Delilah."

"*Be careful?* Why?"

"Never mind," Agnes mutters, shifting her apron at her waist. "We've got work to do. Come on!"

# CHAPTER 13

It's been three months since that night at the party, and now Cee always seems to be at the Williamses' house. He's as permanent as the oil painting of the fruit basket and urn on the wall in their living room — the ugly one Agnes said Miss Mindy must have gotten from a yard sale. Cee stops by for dinner at least twice a week. Even Miss Mindy has noticed how often he's around.

"Cee," I heard her say at dinner two nights ago when she'd drunk a little too much, "is Mama not feeding you at home? We might as well charge you rent, with how much you're here!"

"We could certainly use the money," Mr. Williams muttered, and Miss Mindy laughed and laughed like it was the funniest joke in the world.

But not everyone's happy to see him hanging around the Williams residence.

"Mmm-hmm, here comes the fox sniffin'

'round the henhouse," Agnes mutters whenever Cee's cherry-red Pontiac GTO convertible glides into the driveway, all glistening steel and black leather seats. "If he had a job, he'd have other things to do than loafin' 'round here all day," she says.

I always laugh and shake my head at her, then return to my ironing or whatever else I'm doing.

Though I'm flattered at the notion, it's hard for me to believe Miss Mindy's brother is stopping by her home just for me. For one, he hasn't spoken to me again like he had that night in the laundry room. When he sees me, he nods and says, "Hey there!" or "Hello," and I do the same to be polite, but that's all. And second, Cee already has a girl — some bottle blonde with a big bust and long legs who kind of looks like Marilyn Monroe but not as comely. He started bringing her around in June. When she first came to the house, I could hear her high, squeaky voice scratching through the wall plaster.

*Oh, Cee, you're so funny.*

*Oh, Cee, you're so smart.*

*Oh, Cee, not here! Someone might come in!*

I even saw him kiss her once while they were sitting in his GTO with the top down, and I swear no man has ever kissed me like

201

that. Only one has ever tried — Benjamin Spencer from Sunday school back in Virginia. He called himself French kissing me behind our church one day, but all he did was dart his tongue in and out of my mouth like some lizard. I'd had to push him away.

But that girl didn't push Cee away. She nearly climbed over the armrest and onto his lap and probably would have done a lot more if it wasn't for the steering wheel. He slid his hand up her gingham shirt, and the kiss deepened like they were trying to swallow each other whole. They were acting like they were alone in a bedroom and not sitting in the middle of the Williamses' driveway, where practically the whole neighborhood could see them.

I watched them while I washed the front windows, feeling the soapy suds from my rag ooze down my wrist and bare arm and soak the short sleeves of my uniform. After a while, I had to turn away, and not just because I was watching something that seemed too intimate for anyone to witness, but because it made me feel funny to watch it. It was like I was falling ill. My stomach started to cramp. My face felt hot and sweaty. To make it stop, I had to close the curtain. I grabbed my soap bucket and left the living room and the last windowpane unwashed.

Now I stay away from the front of the house when he drives up with his girlfriend or plays in the yard with his niece and nephew. When he comes to dinner, I make an excuse to help Roberta in the kitchen with scrubbing the dishes and pots and pans so only Agnes serves the dinner table.

Of course, I can't avoid Cee all together. I catch a glimpse of him every now and then or hear his voice. My stomach used to twist into knots when that happened, but after a while, even that stopped. It is only a dull ache now that I've gotten used to. I know it is a silly infatuation that will pass, a school-girl crush that will be forgotten in a month or two.

I distract myself with my routine: the laundry, mending torn seams, and mopping the floors. The upside of all this is that I am doing my job so well Miss Mindy told me today I can stay on at the house. Up until now, my employment had been conditional. She tells me that at least once a week.

"You are on probation, Delilah. Behave accordingly," she says through pinched lips.

But now I'm not on probation anymore. I'm finally getting paid the same as Agnes — a whole two dollars an hour — and maybe I'll be able to stow away a little extra money outside of what I have to pay my Auntie Mary for my room and what I send back home to Mama.

I am thinking about that extra money and what I will do with it as I walk to the bus stop where I always wait for the 6:35 bus to take me back to Auntie Mary's.

I already know what book I will read as I wait for the bus: *Age of Innocence* by Edith Wharton. I am already at the part where Newland is riding alone in the carriage with Ellen, and I know something is about to happen, something that is exciting but that they will both regret later.

It is July, and the air is thick and sticky with heat and exhaust fumes. Sweat pours from my pores like my skin is crying. It pools between my thighs as I walk, making my cotton underwear soggy. It seeps below my breasts and above my bra. I fan my face, though it does me no good. I pray for a stray breeze. As I'm about to cross the street, I hear a horn honk, stabbing the soft quiet of the evening. I jump back onto the sidewalk, worried I've stepped into oncoming traffic and I'm about to get hit by a car until I look to my right and realize Cee is staring up at me from the driver's seat of his GTO.

"I've been calling you, Delilah! You didn't hear me?" he asks with a smile.

I blink and look around as if he's talking to another Delilah who must be standing next to me. When I realize I am the only one there, I turn back to him. "Sorry, sir, I didn't hear you."

"I told you, enough of that 'sir' nonsense. Call me Cee! You headed home? You need a ride?"

"No, sir . . . I-I mean Cee. I don't need a ride. The bus stop is right over there." I point into the distance where an empty bench sits near the sidewalk. "I'm fine."

"But I'm closer," he drawls, leaning out his window to gaze up at me. "Hop in!"

I hesitate.

Everything is telling me not to get in that car — propriety for one, and convention for another. I do not know Cee well enough to ride alone in a car with him, and how would it look for me to roll into my auntie's neighborhood, sitting beside some rich white boy in his shiny GTO?

But then I see that traffic on the street has come to a standstill because Cee is sitting at the intersection with his engine rumbling, waiting for me to climb inside his car. A man in a fedora leans out the window of his powder blue Ford Fairlane. He taps his horn. Two more cars are behind him, and all the drivers' eyes are on me. I look back at Cee's face — those green eyes and upturned nose that are much like Miss Mindy's.

Will she be angry if she finds out I refused her brother's offer for a ride home?

"Much obliged," I say with great reluctance as the driver of the Ford Fairlane beeps his horn again. I scramble to the other side of the GTO and yank open the door, almost dropping my paperback to the ground as I do it. Cee pats the front passenger seat, urging me to sit down, but I push up the back rest and climb into the back seat. As I settle, Cee leans over to look at me in the rearview mirror. I can see laughter in his eyes again.

The driver of the Ford Fairlane beeps his horn a third time. It is a long, loud blast.

Cee finally pulls off with a rumble, and I feel the whoosh of cool air hitting me in the face as he drives down the street.

"Mind if I smoke?" he calls over his shoulder as he digs out a pack of Newports from the glove compartment.

*It's your car. Do what you want,* I think but instead say, "No."

He lights a cigarette as he drives. It dangles from the side of this mouth. "So where to?"

"Uh, Tenth Street Northeast please," I

shout back over the wind.

He nods as he turns the wheel, making a left onto the next street. He pulls the cigarette from his mouth and blows smoke into the air. "So you're a city girl?"

"No."

"But you live in the city, right?"

"Yes, but I just moved there. I grew up in Virginia on a . . . a farm."

"*A farm?* So what brought you up here?"

"Work," I answer honestly.

If I had stayed back in Lynchburg, Mama would've married me off to one of the boys who lived nearby, like she had done with my eldest sister, Tammy. Tammy had dropped out of school in eighth grade and married Richard Bolton, a gap-toothed son of a tobacco farmer who lived six miles up the road. Now she had a house full of children and a husband who worked her like a dog all day and then climbed on top of her at night to make more babies.

If I thought my brain was in danger of rotting while I served the Williamses, it would have certainly disappeared like a rabbit in a hole if I had stayed back home. Luckily, I convinced Mama to let me finish school so I could head up north, make money, and send some back for her and my six brothers and sisters. She hadn't liked the idea, but she had seen how desperate I was to escape Lynchburg, to escape my fate.

"Go on and go," she said one night when I showed her the mason jar filled with money I had saved for a bus ticket and the letter from Auntie Mary that said I could take her daughter Lucille's old room if I came to town. "You're so fired up that you'd probably run away in the middle of the night to head up there anyway, even if I told you no!"

She was right. I probably would've.

I had thought . . . *hoped* that maybe I could work in a secretarial pool or as a shop girl once I got to D.C., but the only thing I could find was work as a maid or housekeeper.

*Working for the Williams family isn't the best job, but it's just a start,* I tell myself every night before I lay my head on my pillow and drift off to sleep. I tell myself I am meant for better, and one day I will get it.

"You know," Cee says, tapping his cigarette into the car's metal ashtray, "if you need a ride home from now on, I can take you. You don't have to catch the bus."

I frown and shake my head. "That's not necessary, sir . . . I mean, Cee. The bus is just fine, and I wouldn't want to impose."

"You're not imposing!" he shouts as the

lanes go from one to three. The traffic begins to pick up speed, and the wind rushes by now, filling my ears with thunder. "I'm offering. It's no big deal!"

"Don't you have to take your friend home?"

The question is out before I have a chance to take it back.

"What friend?"

I purse my lips. I shouldn't have said anything. The car brakes at a stoplight.

"What friend are you talking about, Delilah?"

"The . . . the lady you bring with you sometimes."

He leans over in his seat, extinguishes his cigarette, and looks at me again in the rearview mirror. His green eyes crinkle at the edges. I can tell he's smiling, though I can't see his mouth.

"You mean Betsy? She's old news! We broke up two weeks ago!"

I feel almost happy when I hear him say this, then angry that I care at all.

"Betsy's a nice girl, but she's a little too clingy, if you get my drift. I like my girls more . . . I don't know . . . aloof, I guess. I like a girl who lets me chase her. A man wants a challenge," he says and winks at me in the mirror's reflection.

My eyes drop to my lap. I don't know what to say to this, and he bursts into laughter again.

I don't say anything else, and neither does he for the rest of the drive. When we finally arrive on the block where I live, boys are playing football in the middle of the street, and a couple of girls are playing jump rope on the sidewalk. Our neighbor is sitting on the front porch fanning herself with a folded newspaper.

The children stop their games and part like the Dead Sea to make way for Cee's GTO. They stare slack-jawed at it and then at me in the back seat. He pulls to a stop in front of Auntie Mary's house, and I am suddenly embarrassed at how shabby it looks. Only four months ago, I thought the brick row house was almost grand compared to Mama's small shack. Now I wonder how it looks to Cee's eyes.

"Thank you kindly," I murmur before pushing open the car door.

"Didn't take long to get here. I know where you live now, so it should go even faster when I bring you home tomorrow."

"You don't have to do that," I say as I climb out of the back seat. Several eyes are watching us. My neighbor has stopped fanning herself.

He chuckles again. "I told you that it's —"

"No," I say firmly as I slam the car door and throw the strap of my purse over my shoulder, stopping him short. "Thank you for the ride, but . . . no."

I rush away from the car and open the chain-link fence. I run up the concrete steps leading to the house. Before I reach the top stair, the screen door opens.

Auntie Mary takes up the width of the door frame with her wide hips and shoulders. The smell of fried chicken and collards hovers around her. She stares at Cee's GTO as he drives off. The children trail behind the car like Cee's the pied piper.

"Who was that?" Auntie Mary asks, her dark face wrinkling over as she squints at me. "Why were you riding in that car?"

"Miss Mindy asked her brother to bring me home," I lie before squeezing past her through the doorway. I set down my purse on the floor. "You need help finishing up dinner?"

Auntie Mary is still frowning, but to my relief, she doesn't ask me any more questions about Cee. Instead, she nods. "Take the biscuits out the oven for me and set up the table, will you?"

# CHAPTER 14

I can't find my book.

I look for it before I go to sleep, eager to return to nineteenth-century New York with its balls, operas, and intrigue. I check my purse, look under my bed, scavenge through my drawers, and scour the front parlor room. I look for it so long Auntie Mary shouts for me to turn out the lights and "stop making all that racket," because I'm keeping her and the children awake. I do as she asks and reluctantly climb back upstairs to my room and go to sleep.

I figure I must have left the book in the back seat of Cee's car. Now I may never find out what happened between Newland and Ellen.

When I wake up the next morning, I try to push *The Age of Innocence,* along with Cee, to the back of my mind and prepare for work.

I hop off the bus and arrive at the Williams house a little before six A.M., as streaks of blue, pink, and orange are finally painting the morning sky. I walk in through the servant's entrance, and the smell of breakfast already fills the air. When I step into the kitchen, I find Roberta hunched over the oven burners. She drops one sizzling piece of bacon onto the iron griddle, then another. Agnes is making fresh lemonade. She glances up at me as I shrug out of my sweater and set down my purse.

"I didn't hear you come in!" she says after slicing a lemon in half on the wooden cutting board. "Can you set the table while I finish this up?"

I nod and do as she says.

The rest of the morning goes by without commotion. I pack the children's lunches — cutting off the crusts of the sandwiches and peeling the grapes like the little ones like — and I stand with them on the street corner with the other housekeepers and their charges until the school bus arrives. Miss Mindy heads out at ten A.M. to meet one of her friends at a shop downtown.

"I'll be back at around three, girls! I'll likely need help carrying my bags into the house, so make sure you're ready. Don't leave me standing by the car like last time!" she calls over her shoulder while her kitten heels *click, click, click* across the driveway's cement.

We watch from the window as she climbs inside her Lincoln Continental. She waves at us, and like pups on command, Agnes and I both wave back.

" 'Don't leave me standing by the car like last time,' " Agnes mimics in a high-pitched voice. With a droll roll of the eyes, she turns away from the window. I stay to watch Miss Mindy's car pull off, then walk back into the kitchen to join Agnes and Roberta.

"Why's she always shopping anyway?" Agnes asks.

"Shoo, if I had the money she had, I'd spend it too!" Roberta says as she pulls back the lid of a can of crushed pineapple. She shakes the contents of the can into a glass bowl.

"She's not the Queen of England, Berta," Agnes says. "Miss Mindy comes from money, but it ain't *that* much money!"

"Humph, she got more than you!"

I bite my lower lip to keep from laughing. I open the pantry closet and pull out the feather duster and Lemon Pledge so I can start dusting upstairs.

"Why do you think Leroy isn't here anymore?" Agnes persists.

She's referring to Mr. Williams's old

driver, Leroy, who disappeared one day in June. He took Mr. Williams to work that morning, as usual — then we never saw him again. Mr. Williams drove himself back. Leroy didn't even come back to the house to get his pack of Marlboros or his lunch pail.

"They *had* to let him go!" Agnes shouts. "Couldn't afford him anymore! And at the rate she's spending money, they may not be able to afford us either."

At Agnes's words, I drop the duster limply to my side. I'm stunned.

"That's not . . . that's not true, is it?" I ask, my voice tight with panic.

I've just started getting my full salary, and now I may have to start looking for another job?

"Oh, chile, don't listen to that nonsense she's talkin'!" Roberta flaps a towel in Agnes's direction.

"It's not nonsense!" Agnes crosses her arms stubbornly over her chest. "It's the truth! They're spending money like it's —"

"You an accountant now? You've seen their books? You don't know for sure if that's why they let Leroy go!" Roberta argues, cutting her off. "You're trying to bring the devil on us talking all that mess! I don't wanna hear any more! Keep it to yourself!"

Agnes sucks her teeth and walks off, mumbling under her breath. I linger in the kitchen a few seconds longer before I head upstairs and dust and vacuum the rooms while Agnes does the first floor. By the time we all eat lunch together at noon, it seems the argument from earlier is forgotten. We are back to our usual selves. I wash my dishes in the sink, then return to cleaning and washing the house and doing the laundry. By the end of the day, my arms and feet are aching. I am longing for my book again and the escape it would offer.

I keep an eye out for Cee's car in the driveway, but he does not make an appearance. I wonder if my snubbing of his offer has anything to do with his absence today, and then I brush away the thought. Cee certainly wouldn't change his schedule based on something I did or said. I am of no concern to him, so he should be of no concern to me.

A little after six, I start to pack my things and wave good-bye to Agnes and Roberta.

"See you tomorrow!" I call to them.

"You have a nice evening, girl. See ya!" Agnes calls back.

Roberta only grunts her reply.

I stroll back to the bus stop. Today seems

even hotter than yesterday, and I wipe the sweat from my brow. I fantasize about the lemonade Agnes made this morning. I can almost feel the coolness of the drink against my lips and taste it as it slides down my throat. Is this what people daydream about when they are crossing the desert and have nothing to drink?

As I draw near the old wooden bench, I pause.

Cee is parked about twenty feet away. He is leaning against the hood of his GTO, smoking and holding a book in his hands — *my* book. I stare as if I am seeing a mirage, but he doesn't disappear. He's still standing there. He tosses his cigarette to the ground and crushes it under the rubber sole of his tennis shoe.

"I thought I'd find you here," he shouts to me with a grin. "You left this behind!"

"Th-thank you," I stutter as I walk toward him. I take the book from him and stare at the paperback, elated to see it again.

"*The Age of Innocence,* huh?" He lets out a low whistle. "That's some heavy stuff."

My eyes jump up from the book to his face. "You think it's too heavy for me?" I ask, unable to keep the defensiveness out of my voice.

"No! Nothing like that. I'm just . . . I'm

just saying I haven't met too many girls who read Wharton for fun. I like that you do, though!"

I lower my eyes again and scan the pale woman in repose on the cover. "You've read it?"

"Yeah, I had to read it my first year at Tulane. Freshman composition. It was a little steamier than the other stuff we had to read, but I would've liked more action, frankly. She's no Kerouac!"

"So you know how it ends?"

"I sure do!" He pushes a wayward strand out of his eyes and hooks his thumbs into the back pockets of his jeans.

I flip through the book's yellowed pages. Many are bent from bookmarks made by the paperback's previous owners before it arrived at the used bookstore where I purchased it.

"I was hoping for a happy ending . . . that Newland and Ellen would . . . you know . . . end up together."

But I can tell from the look on his face my hope is pointless.

"Not all stories are meant to have happy endings, Delilah."

I nod sadly. "You're right." I drop my book into my purse. "Thank you for bringing my book to me. It was —"

"I didn't just come here to bring you your book. That was just an excuse." He pushes his unruly hair out of his eyes again. I wonder why he doesn't just cut it, but so many men are wearing their hair long these days. "I'd still like to drive you home again."

I don't answer him right away and instead look around to see if anyone is watching us — and they are. A woman who is pushing a stroller pauses. She's pretending to adjust her baby's bottle, but I can see her squinting behind her cat's-eye glasses, staring at us across the roadway. Even a few cars seem to slow down as they pass us. The drivers' gazes linger on us a second too long.

I shake my head. "I'm sorry, but I can't do that."

"Yes, you can!" He pushes himself away from the hood and walks toward me. Only a few inches are between us. "You did it yesterday!"

"You know I can't," I whisper. "I wasn't —"

"I know no such thing." He shrugs. "It's not like it's against the law!"

"But your sister! She would —"

"Oh, Mindy doesn't care! As long as her hair and nails are done and Garfinkel's is open, she's fine! Besides, if she asks, I'll tell her the truth: I'm just driving you home."

"But why?" I plead, because I honestly don't understand.

His smile widens. "Because I like you!"

I am not relieved by his answer. Instead, I feel worse. I feel cornered.

I have brushed off boys . . . men before, but not a white man, and none have been as persistent as Cee. I am on the verge of telling him no yet again when he says, "You're special, Delilah. I saw it the moment I met you that night of the party. I just wanna get to know you. That's all!" He stares into my eyes, and I can't help but be drawn in. "We can talk about books. We can talk about movies. Whatever you want! It doesn't matter to me." He tilts his head. "Wouldn't that be nice?"

He's right. It *would* be nice to talk to someone, finally. I realize how little talking I do nowadays, how all my thoughts are pushed toward the bottom of my mind like Mr. Williams's socks, which always seem to float to the bottom of the laundry basket. What would it be like to talk about the things that are important to me? There are so many questions I have and things I want to say, but have no one to say them to. Auntie Mary wouldn't know what I was talking about, and Agnes and Roberta would probably look at me like I was crazy or think my musings were just silly nonsense. But I suspect Cee wouldn't. He wouldn't laugh at me if I talked to him about the characters in my books or Martin Luther King Jr.'s death or the Beatles. He'd listen.

"For example," Cee begins, as if reading my mind, "if you like *The Age of Innocence,* you should try *The House of Mirth* next, if you haven't read it already. I liked it better!" He steps toward the passenger door and holds it open for me. "I could tell you why I liked it more . . . while I drive you home."

I can't help but laugh at his persistence, at his guile — handsome devil that he is. And like the devil, he dangles the apple from the tree of knowledge in front of me. As much as I suspect I will regret it later, I must have a bite.

He inclines his head toward the leather passenger seat, and ever so slowly, I step forward. But instead of climbing onto the front seat, I sit in the back.

He shakes his head, shuts the door behind me, and shrugs. "Well . . . it's a start, I guess!"

# CHAPTER 15

When I'm ready to leave the Williams home for the day, I duck into the second-floor hallway bathroom and shut the door behind me. I have to turn on the bathroom light because hardly any light streams through the window nowadays. The sun is setting earlier now that it is late September. It is cooler too, so the swampy heat, which used to linger in the air at all hours and had Miss Mindy turning up the air conditioning, has now disappeared.

I check my reflection in the mirror to make sure my hair is combed and there is nothing in my teeth. I reach into my purse and spray the dime-store perfume I purchased a week ago on my neck and my wrists so the stench of bleach and sweat are no longer on me.

I want to smell nice for Cee. I hope I look pretty too.

"Of course you do, beautiful," I can hear

Cee whisper to me like he did last week when we went driving to the waterfront.

At the memory, I smile so much my cheeks hurt.

I open the door, step out of the bathroom, and head down the hall. I'm humming as I walk, but I stop near the stairs when I hear something slam behind me. I look over my shoulder, in the direction of Miss Mindy and Mr. Williams's bedroom. The door is ajar. A shaft of orange light shoots into the hallway. I can hear hushed voices seeping out, then Mr. Williams shouts, "*Really? Another goddamn party, Melinda?*"

I take a few steps back and peek through the crack in the door to find Mr. Williams pacing back and forth in front of their bed. He's frowning too.

Agnes told me they were set to go out to dinner tonight at some supper club in the city. That's why Mr. Williams is wearing an evening jacket and tie, but he roughly yanks off his tie and tosses it to the floor.

Miss Mindy acts like she can't see the tie splayed on the carpet or her husband's pacing. She stays perched at her makeup table, smoothing the edges of her bouffant hairdo as she gazes in the mirror.

"There's no need to get angry, honey." She reaches for a pair of diamond studs on the mahogany tabletop. She places one of the studs in her earlobe.

"What do you mean there's no need to get angry?" he yells. "The last thing I need right now is to have to foot the bill for another goddamn party! Two hundred bucks for booze! A hundred bucks for hors d'oeuvres! All because a bunch of tight-assed —"

"It's our turn to host again," she says calmly, putting in her other earring. "Suzy did it last month. When you live in a neighborhood like ours, you're expected to have parties . . . to be social. You don't want us to become pariahs, do you? What do you expect me to do?"

"I expect you to tell them no, dammit!" He finally stops pacing and grits his teeth. His skin is flushed. I can see the blue vein bulging along his temple even from where I'm standing. "Look, I explained to you that things aren't good at the firm. We're losing clients, Mindy! It's getting really bad, and I'm . . . I'm . . ." He lowers his head. He takes a deep breath. "I'm worried that they're going to let me go. They think I'm washed up!"

She slowly rises to her feet and turns to face him. She's wearing another one of her cocktail dresses. This one is black and off the shoulder.

"You're always worried, sweetheart. In fact, you worry too much! But that's why I'm here." She traces a finger along his pockmarked cheek and grins. "Come on, let Mindy get those frown lines off your face." She giggles and loops her arms around his neck. She starts to kiss him, but stops when he roughly shoves her away. Her smile disappears. Frosted pink lipstick is now smeared along her mouth.

"You think this is funny?" he snarls, and she takes another step back. "I just told you I could lose my job! That doesn't just mean no more parties! It means no more god-damn servants . . . no more big house and cars! I'm on the edge of desperation, and meanwhile you're living the high life like it doesn't —"

"*I'm* living the high-life?" she shouts back, pointing at her chest. "Like I'm all by myself in this, Jake? Like you don't like the parties and the cars and the house too? I guess I made you buy those things?"

"Well, you never said no, did you?"

"And neither did you! You were more than happy to spend money too — as long as *someone else* was footing the bill. You forget that half of the clients you wined and dined to get their business, you did it with the cash my mother gave us . . . that she gave *you*! You try to pretend that it was just me wasting money when you didn't mind playing Mr. Big Shot yourself!"

"That's bullshit!"

"No, it isn't. Admit it, Jake! The real reason you're mad is because she's cut us off! The real reason is because I can't beg my twenty-two-year-old brother for more money! The real reason is because you're not enough of a man to stand on your own two —"

She's stopped short by a hard smack across the cheek that sends her stumbling back and bumping into her makeup table. It knocks her bouffant hairdo askew. A perfume bottle clatters to the floor. Instead of bursting into tears, her eyes go bright with anger.

When he hits her, I clap my hand over my mouth to stifle my cry of surprise, but I must not have done it fast enough. Mr. Williams suddenly whips around to face the doorway, and for a brief moment, we lock eyes. I'm frozen in place.

"You son of a bitch," Miss Mindy hisses, clutching her cheek. She pushes herself upright and rushes toward him but stops short and looks in the direction that he's looking. Seconds pass in silence — with them staring at me and me staring right back at them. Finally, she begins to walk toward the bedroom door, like she's about to shut it. It takes all the will I can muster to turn away and rush down the hall. I'm almost tripping over my own feet as I fly down the stairs to the floor below.

*"Dee?"* Agnes calls after me as I race through the kitchen, grabbing my coat from the closet. I head to the back door. "What's wrong?"

My heart is racing as I rush into the night. I realize I'm running, and I have to slow down. I stop on the sidewalk and take several deep breaths to get my heartbeat back under control.

Mr. Williams saw me. He saw me watch him hit Miss Mindy, and he may want to fire me now. What am I going to do?

A cold breeze lifts my hair from my shoulders and licks my skin, causing goose bumps to sprout on my arms and legs. I throw on my coat. It is almost dark, but I can still see Cee's GTO waiting in the dim light at the end of the block. The cloth roof of the convertible stands out like a white sail under one of the street lamps. As I draw near it, his headlights flash on. He waves at me through the windshield, and I tug the passenger door open and hop into the seat.

"So where . . . Hey, what's up?" he asks, squinting at me and tugging the cigarette from his mouth. "What's wrong?"

I shake my head. "Nothing."

"Doesn't look like nothing." He stares at me more closely. "You look like you've just seen a ghost. What happened?"

"It's nothing! Please just . . . just drive somewhere. Anywhere!" I say, wringing the strap of my purse in my hands.

He looks at me a few seconds longer, then tosses his cigarette out the open window and blows out a cloud of smoke from the side of his mouth. "Okay, then. Where do you want to go?"

"I'll let you decide," I say, gazing out the windshield at the dark and mostly deserted neighborhood street. "But I have to be back by seven thirty at the latest," I quickly add. "Auntie Mary will get mad if I'm not home by then."

He nods, and we pull off, not talking. The music from the radio takes over where the conversation left off.

I usually like our drives in the evening. I even look forward to them now. He used to drive me straight home, but after a few weeks, Cee started to take the long way to my neighborhood, asking if he could stop by Gino's to pick up a hamburger and fries, or the local park because it was nice outside and he wanted to walk around barefoot in the grass. I knew it was just an excuse to extend our time together, but I didn't mind, and Auntie Mary has gotten used to me arriving home after dinner is done. I told her Miss Mindy sometimes needs me to stay later, and now I can because I don't have to take the bus home anymore. I can tell Auntie Mary is suspicious, but she doesn't voice her qualms.

I've gotten used to these fun little excursions Cee and I have, and normally I would be excited, wondering where he will take me tonight, but I am distracted. I keep replaying what I saw and heard back at the Williamses' house. I close my eyes, and I can see Mr. Williams's slap from all angles.

Cee notices the change in me, how quiet and pensive I am this evening.

"Something happened, but you're not telling me what it is. Is my sister being as sweet as usual?" he asks with a smirk. "Roberta still bossing you around?"

During our drives, I've told him the truth about what my day is like working for his sister. I could only keep up the façade of politeness for so long. Cee knows I find Miss Mindy haughty and rude. He knows

Roberta is motherly but bad-tempered and Agnes is my only confidante.

I've also learned things about him and his friends, like how his old classmate Hank from Tulane wants him to invest and go into business in some start-up, as they call it, that deals with computers. I know he meets his old high school friends Bill and Robert for tennis twice a week and they go out for drinks afterward, but he's starting to get bored with the whole routine. I know the infamous Betsy is now engaged to another fellow, a balding lawyer from Biloxi who she had been dating while she was with Cee but hadn't told him.

I don't mind telling Cee my secrets anymore. He will never talk to Roberta or Agnes and has no interest in telling his sister. I will keep his secrets too. He knows I will never meet any of his friends. I won't accidentally blurt out something at one of the cocktail parties he's always forced to go to. Cee and I have crossed paths, but our lives never will truly meet, which is why tonight is so awful. I've intruded in a world I shouldn't have. It could mean Miss Mindy will fire me and I can no longer pay the rent for my room like I promised Auntie Mary I would. It could mean Cee and I may never see each other again.

"Are you going to tell me what's wrong or not?" he asks.

"Can I . . . have a sip from your flask first?"

His eyes widen in surprise.

When we first began our evening rides, he always used to offer me a drink, but I'd always declined. After a while, he stopped offering.

When we brake at another stoplight, he flips open his glove compartment and removes his silver flask. He uncorks the lid and offers it to me. I bring it to my lips and take one long drink. I make a face as the alcohol burns its way down my throat. I cough into my fist.

"This must be good if you need a drink first. What the hell happened?"

I close my eyes and take a deep breath. I open my eyes again. "I think . . . I think I'm going to have to go home, Cee."

"You mean you want me to take you straight home tonight after all?"

"No, I mean, I'm going to have to go home to Virginia."

"What?" His thick brows knit together. "Why?"

"I can't tell you, but it's . . . it's bad. It could mean I'll have to pack my things, and I —"

"Wait," Cee says, holding up his hand from the steering wheel, "let me pull over because I have no idea what you're talking about."

A minute later, he pulls into a vacant storage lot. Empty tractor trailers and wooden crates sit several feet away. The light from a loading dock shines on our faces as he turns off the headlights and shifts in the front seat. He places a hand on my shoulder and squeezes it. I can feel his strong fingers through the cloth fabric of my coat and uniform, and my breath catches in my throat. He's never touched me like this before.

"You've gotta tell me what happened, Delilah. What do you mean you may have to go back to Virginia?"

I want to tell somebody. I want to tell him especially, but Miss Mindy is his sister. What happened to her would be hard for any brother to hear, and I can't find the right words to explain it.

"It's too embarrassing, Cee. I'm sorry but I . . . I can't tell you. I want to, but I can't! All I can say is that if I . . . I do have to go back home, I want to thank you."

"Thank me for what?"

He lets go of my shoulder, and I lower my eyes again. I'm about to cry.

"Thank you for everything you've done for me."

The tears are on my cheeks before I have a chance to wipe them away. I sniff so at least I don't have snot running down my nose. I remember Leroy and how he disappeared from the house without a trace, and the tears come even harder. I remember how they didn't even let him come back to get his things. Miss Mindy and Mr. Williams will do the same to me, I'm sure.

"You've been . . . been good and . . . and kind to me and —"

I stop short when he cups my cheek. I look up at him just as he leans forward and his lips touch mine. It takes me a few seconds to realize Cee is kissing me, that his tongue is trying to find its way inside my mouth. I panic and start to pull away, but then I stop myself. This could be our last moment together. Tentatively, I kiss him back.

I am not Betsy. I am not coy or practiced at this. I do not know where my tongue goes or how to keep our teeth from clicking together. I don't know where to put my hands or how to angle myself so the gear shift isn't jabbing into my hip, but Cee doesn't seem to mind. A few minutes later, he eases back. He is smiling. He traces a finger along my eyebrow and the curve of my cheek.

"I think you'll be all right, Dee."

I am too dazed to disagree. I nod, and he gives me a quick peck on my cheek, then turns to face the windshield.

"Let's get you home," he says as he shifts the car into drive and I ease back into the passenger seat. When we pull off, he reaches for my hand. I link my fingers through his, and they stay that way the entire ride home.

# Chapter 16

"Girl, why are you late? What happened to you yesterday?" Agnes asks as soon as I step out of the cold, crisp outdoors into the warm kitchen. Roberta is stirring grits, and Agnes is gathering dishes from the overhead cabinet for breakfast. Both stop what they're doing to stare at me. "Why'd you rush out like that?"

I take my time before I answer her, slowly unwinding my scarf from around my neck and shrugging out of my wool coat while they wait for me to respond.

I had considered not coming back today. Though I had wrapped Cee's words of comfort and the memory of his kiss around me like a warm blanket all last night as I slept, by morning my anxiety was back, and it wouldn't go away. I dallied for an hour, debating about what to do. Finally, I figured the risks of getting fired if I didn't show up for work were greater than if I did show. I made it out the door in just enough time to catch the 6:15 bus.

"You know Miss Mindy came down here looking for you," Agnes says, and I stop mid-motion with my coat dangling off my arm and shoulder.

"She did?"

"Uh-huh. Right after you left yesterday. She came into the kitchen asking where you went. We said you'd left for the day." Agnes takes another step toward me and narrows her eyes. "Dee, what happened? Why was she asking after you?"

I muddle over how I'm going to answer her question when the kitchen door suddenly swings open.

"Delilah, there you are!" Miss Mindy calls out to me from the doorway, and my heart stops. It literally stops beating, and I think I might collapse dead on the kitchen floor and have to be rushed to the hospital in an ambulance with sirens and all, but then my heartbeat picks back up again a second later. I am still alive, unfortunately, and Miss Mindy is staring at me with her cool green eyes.

"Can I speak with you?" she asks.

"Ye-yes, ma'am."

I neatly fold my coat and scarf over one of the kitchenette chairs. I can feel Agnes and

Roberta's gazes on my back and bowed head as I shuffle out of the kitchen with my hands linked in front of me. I hear their whispered conversation even before the door closes all the way behind me.

"Lord, what did that chile do?" Roberta mumbles.

"I don't know, but it must be bad if she wants to talk to her," Agnes whispers back.

I silently follow Miss Mindy down the hall, and we stop in front of her husband's home office door. When we step inside, she shuts the door behind me, and I wonder if this is how prisoners feel when they hear the clink of a cell's metal bars slam close.

"Have a seat, Delilah," she orders, gesturing to one of the leather chairs facing her husband's desk.

I sit down and watch as she pets her hair, smoothing an invisible strand back into place. "I wanted to talk to you about . . . well . . . about what happened yesterday," she begins, walking around my chair to face me.

"I am so sorry, Miss Mindy!" I rush out, wringing the hem of my uniform. "I wasn't trying to —"

"Be quiet," she snaps, and I shut my mouth like a steel trap. I bite down on my bottom lip so hard I worry it might bleed.

She is going to fire me. I am certain of it. But will she let me finish out the day, or will she make me pack up my things — as meager as they are — and leave right now? Will she give me a chance to say good-bye to Agnes and Roberta, or will I get escorted out the door with haste as though I did something shameful, as though they caught me stealing from the silverware drawer?

"You know, Delilah," she begins, sitting on the edge of her husband's desk, crossing her skinny legs at the ankles. "My mother always taught me to be very particular with the help I hire. She said be careful of who you let into your home . . . who you let around your children. 'A maid is more than just a maid, Mindy. A nanny is more than just a nanny.' You trust them with so many things that are precious to you, things that can't be replaced. Why, they become almost like . . . like family!" Her face goes somber. "So when they break that trust, you feel violated. Do you know what that word means, Delilah? *Violated?*" she enunciates slowly.

I nod, too scared to be offended that she's talking to me like I'm wearing a dunce hat.

"I don't like sneaks in my house. I will not tolerate it."

"But I'm not a sneak, ma'am! I swear! I

238

was only trying to —"

She holds up a finger to silence me. The nail is painted a soft pink. "Don't interrupt."

I close my mouth again.

"As I said, I don't like sneaks," she continues, "and I don't like liars." Miss Mindy tilts her head. "I don't think you've been very honest with me, Delilah. I don't think you've been honest about your intentions in working here."

I furrow my brow. "I'm sorry, Miss Mindy?"

"I'm sorry, Miss Mindy?" she repeats back to me in a comically high-pitched voice, batting her false eyelashes. She then barks out a brittle laugh. "Oh, you Negro gals are always pretending to be deaf and dumb! You think I don't know what you're really doing? I grew up around maids and nannies my whole life! I've heard all the gossip, all the whispering — and the scheming. I know what you're up to, Delilah Grey, even if my little brother doesn't."

I'm at a loss for words now, because I don't understand what she means.

"When I went after you yesterday, I saw you run out the door. I followed you down the steps, and imagine my surprise to find you running not to catch the bus, but to my brother's waiting car. You didn't hesitate before throwing open the door and hopping inside — like you've done it hundreds of times before." She purses her lips and pushes herself away from her desk so that she's standing over me. "So just how many rides has my brother given you, Delilah?"

I don't like the look on her face, the tone of her voice, or the insinuation in her question. Why is she asking me about Cee when I thought we were talking about what I saw happen between her and her husband yesterday?

"A . . . a few. Your brother was nice enough to offer to drive me home at the end of the day so I wouldn't have to take the bus."

"*Really?* And that's all you've been doing? Riding around in the car with him?"

My cheeks and neck flush at her question, at the memory of the kiss in the deserted parking lot last night, and the bold-faced lie I'm about to tell. But I force myself to nod anyway. "Yes, ma'am. That's all."

She laughs again. "I know my brother, and he doesn't do things out of the sheer kindness of his heart. If he agreed to let you ride around in his car, he expected something in return. And like I said, you Negro girls aren't stupid! I bet you expected something in return too. So what did he give you in exchange, Delilah? *Gifts?* Maybe a bracelet or two? Or did he give you spending money?"

My fear from earlier has now transformed into anger and disgust. Just who does Miss Mindy think I am? *What* does she think I am if she believes I would agree to be with a man for a bracelet and spending money?

"He hasn't given me anything. And I haven't given him anything either!"

"Oh, sure," she says dryly.

"I haven't!" I yell, then catch myself when I realize I'm shouting.

This woman has made me so mad that I have forgotten who I am, who she is, and where I am. But I have to remember quickly. I am a black woman and a maid in her employ. She holds all the cards — and she knows it.

"So you're still dangling him on the hook then, are you?" Miss Mindy shrugs. "Well, he'll get tired of that eventually. But before he does, I want you to do something for me."

She pauses, making me uneasy again.

"I know you overheard my conversation with my husband. We've been trying to get a small loan from Chauncey to help keep our household afloat, to help pay *your* salaries. He's refused to give it to me. So I want you to ask him for the money for me."

"What?" My mouth starts flapping open and closed like a dying catfish, gasping for air. "I-I don't . . . I don't know if . . . Miss Mindy, I can't —"

"Before you tell me that you can't do what I've asked, consider this, Delilah. I am willing to share some of the money with you if you can convince my darling brother to give you the cash. A small sum, but still, it's better than nothing! Also consider that you already have a strike against you for your underhanded behavior. Mr. Williams told me that we should've fired you on the spot, but I argued that we should give you a chance to redeem yourself first . . . to regain our confidence."

And this is how she wants me to redeem myself? By begging her brother for money?

"The decision is yours, but if you can't do this one little favor for me," she says, crossing her arms over her chest, "I don't see why I should convince Jake to let you stay here."

I stare at Miss Mindy, trying to reconcile the woman standing in front of me with the vulnerable one I saw yesterday. This woman isn't the least bit like her — she is too cool, cunning, and mean.

"How much money?" I whisper.

"Not much. A thousand dollars will do."

*"A thousand dollars?"* I nearly choke on the words. "You . . . you want me to ask him for a . . . a *thousand dollars*?"

"That's what I said."

A thousand dollars. Why not ask for ten thousand or a million at this rate? This woman is insane if she believes Cee will just hand over that much money to me. But insane or not, I can tell from the look on her face that she is serious. And I think about the money I had planned to save while working here, and how Mama and my brothers and sisters back home in Lynchburg are waiting for the envelope filled with cash that I will mail later this month. That money could mean the difference between an empty table and full bellies during the upcoming winter. I think about my dream of a better life I had planned for myself.

"So what will it be, Delilah?" Miss Mindy persists.

I know what my answer must be.

"Where to, gorgeous?" Cee asks me as I climb into the passenger seat that evening. He leans over and kisses me on the cheek. He then takes a nip from his flask, like he always does, and offers it to me. I shake my head at his offer and whisper, "Wherever you wanna go. Just have me home by seven-thirty."

He flips open the door to his glove compartment, tucks the flask inside, then pulls off, eying me the whole time.

"You're frowning again," he shouts over the girlish chants of "Soul Finger" squealing on the radio. "I can't have that! You were smiling when I left you yesterday. What changed?"

"I've just . . . I've just got a lot on my mind, Cee," I say, staring down at my hands under the dim roadway light coming through the car windows. He shifts beside me, grumbling as he drives.

"I gathered as much. But you wouldn't tell me yesterday what it was. Are you finally ready to tell me today?"

I have two choices: tell Cee the truth or lie. I can tell him that his sister caught me spying on her and her husband and I witnessed something that can now get me fired. To keep from getting fired, she is forcing me to beg Cee for money — an insane amount of money. Or I can make up a story that will get Miss Mindy the thousand dollars she wants. Neither is appealing. Both make my stomach twist into knots and make me chew my lower lip.

He throws back his head in exasperation. "For God's sake, Dee, just tell me! Maybe you'll feel better if you get it off your chest!"

"I . . . I need money," I say before I can stop myself. The lies start seeping out one after another. One pops up, then the next, and I can't stop the deluge.

"My . . . my mother . . . she called yesterday and told me that . . . that the harvest wasn't good again this season. We were already in arrears with the bank on a loan. I was sending her money, but it isn't enough, and now the bank is calling in the loan. They want to collect and . . . and she's scared we're gonna lose everything if she doesn't give them their money, but we don't have it."

I look up at him. I have never been good at lying. Even as a little girl, my mother told me she could always tell when I was fibbing. I expect to find Cee chuckling at me, ridiculing my feeble story. Instead, he's squinting. His expression is serious.

"How much money do you need?"

I swallow the lump in my throat. I can no longer meet his eyes. "A . . . a thousand dollars. A thousand dollars will pay off the loan, I . . . I think."

He brakes at a stoplight and turns back around to face the windshield. He doesn't say anything else for what feels like forever.

Cee's silence unnerves me. I've played the wrong hand. I realize that now. I can't believe I let Miss Mindy talk me into doing something so stupid. What made her think I could convince Cee to give me a thousand dollars?

I open my mouth to tell him I really don't need the money and to forget everything I just said, but then he murmurs, "I can give it to you by the end of next week."

"What?"

"I said you can have it by the end of next week. Do you need it sooner?" he asks, glancing at me.

"No, no . . . next week is fine," I whisper, still stunned. "Th-thank you, Cee. Thank you so much!"

He nods. His gaze lingers on me a few seconds longer, and then he returns his attention to the roadway. We say nothing else about it for the rest of the drive.

# CHAPTER 17

I told Miss Mindy last week Cee agreed to give me the money she needed, and now she won't stop pestering me about it.

"What do you mean he hasn't given it to you yet?" she hissed behind me just yesterday as I carried a basket of dirty laundry from the children's room. She was at my heels, almost tripping over me as we both made our way down the stairs to the floor below.

"He said by the end of this week," I whispered back to her over my shoulder, but I stopped short when she grabbed my arm. She squeezed it so tight I could almost feel her nails digging into the flesh.

"Don't make a fool out of me, Delilah. I told my husband we would have the money soon. You aren't lying to me, are you?" she asked between clenched teeth. "Because if you are, I'll —"

"N-n-no, ma'am," I stuttered, and she

gave one last long look before finally releasing me and walking away.

Her desperation makes me regret lying to Cee all over again. I wish I hadn't done it, that I hadn't ever turned back to look at what was happening in the Williamses' bedroom that evening. Who knew ninety seconds worth of watching would land me in this much trouble?

I am in the laundry room, hand-scrubbing a tablecloth when I hear a knock behind me. I turn to find Cee leaning against the door frame with a smile on his face and his hands tucked in his pockets. His long, auburn hair is parted down the middle and catches in the light, making it look almost as shiny as a new copper penny.

"Hey, beautiful!" he calls out to me.

"Hi, Mr. Buford," I say in my best formal tone before peeking over his shoulder to make sure neither Agnes nor Roberta are lingering in the kitchen and can hear us. When I realize neither are in sight and hopefully not in earshot, I wipe the water and soap from my hands on a nearby towel, rush across the room, and give him a hug. "What are you doing here?" I whisper with a grin.

He pulls his hands out of his pockets. In one is a thick roll of bills held together by a rubber band.

"I came to give you the money you asked for," he says, holding it out to me, "that you said your mother needed."

"Oh, Cee!" I grab the money from him and feel its heavy weight in the palm of my hand. I stare down at it in awe. "You really did it!"

"Of course I did. I said I would."

"That you did. Thank you, Cee." I then stand on the balls of my feet and timidly peck him on the cheek, surprising even myself. I can feel his beard stubble against my lips. "You're wonderful."

His brows knit together. "That's it? That's all I get?"

"What do you mean?"

"I mean I want a kiss . . . a *real* kiss, Delilah!"

I laugh and playfully smack his shoulder. "Oh, Cee . . ."

I tuck the money into my apron pocket next to my battered paperback of *The Red Badge of Courage,* turn, and grab the tablecloth I was scrubbing earlier. I dunk it back into the soapy water and start scrubbing it again. "Are you going to stay for a bit or head back out? Miss Mindy won't be back for another few hours. I wasn't sure if . . ."

My words fade when I realize he is no

longer standing in the doorway but only a few inches behind me. He rests his hands on my hips and pulls me back so he is pressed against me, so his groin rubs against my behind. My throat goes dry.

"I'm not leaving until I get my kiss," Cee whispers, and I tingle at the warmth of his words and the feel of his breath against my ear and neck. My mind harkens back to us on the leather seat of his GTO and me in his arms under the moonlit sky, but I push the memory aside. We are in his sister's laundry room. I am handwashing a stubborn stain from one of the chenille tablecloths. There is no reason why he should be in here with me.

Miss Mindy and Mr. Williams are having lunch at the country club today, but Roberta, Agnes, or one of the children can walk into the room at any moment and see us. It is a risk I cannot take.

"No," I whisper back, drawing up my will and getting back to my work. I stare down into the foam and continue to scrub. I try to ignore him and his body up against mine. I don't dare look over my shoulder because if I look into his eyes, I'm lost. He grabs my wet, soapy hands, and I stop again. Startled, I drop the tablecloth into the hot water.

"Kiss me, Dee," he orders.

His voice is deeper when he says it, and there is a hard edge to it, making me almost frightened to disobey his command. As soon as I turn to him, his lips meet mine. My eyes drift closed, and just like that, I'm gone — I've handed myself over to him.

The kiss is long and slow, and I have finally figured out what to do with my tongue and my teeth, how to tilt my head in just the right way. He pulls me closer, almost crushing me in his embrace. I link my arms around his neck, and his hand slides from my waist to my bottom. He tastes like rum, peppermint gum, and smoke. I'm finding it hard to think, to *breathe.* That's when I hear the laundry room door squeak.

I open my eyes and see Agnes standing in the doorway. She is carrying another basket of laundry. When she sees us, her eyes widen. Her mouth gapes. I start to push Cee away as she backs out of the room, letting the door swing wildly behind her.

"What's wrong?" he asks, frowning and taking a step back from me.

"A-Agnes saw us," I stutter, unable to hide my panic. I wring the front of my apron in my wet hands. "We shouldn't have done that in here! I told you we shouldn't!"

He laughs and rolls his eyes. He rubs my

arms like he's trying to warm me. "Oh, who cares!"

"*Who cares?* She *saw* us, Cee! She —"

"So what?" He shrugs. "So what if she saw us! All that matters is us two. Who cares what they say."

I bite down hard on my bottom lip. It is still swollen from his kisses.

He is right. So what if Agnes saw us? Miss Mindy already knows Cee and I are together. She thinks we're doing a lot more than kissing, but this was something I did not want Agnes to see, for her to know. I feel embarrassed and ashamed that she witnessed us together.

"Look," he whispers, realizing I'm still upset, "if she tells anyone, I'll say she's lying. I'll say it never happened — and so will you. It'll be our word against hers!"

I know he really means *his* word. I could swear on the Bible and no one would care what I had to say, but they'll certainly believe Cee over Agnes, and knowing this is unsettling, not comforting to me.

"It's all right," he assures me, raising a hand to my cheek. "Don't worry about it."

After Cee leaves, I find Agnes sitting alone at the kitchenette table where she, Roberta, and I usually eat our breakfast and lunch together. A wicker sewing basket and a spool of blue thread are on the tabletop. A rumpled pair of Mr. Williams's pants are in her lap as she carefully stitches the hem of one of the pants legs. The light from the kitchen window plays on her face — her broad nose, high cheekbones, and cleft chin — and I can see she's frowning with concentration.

I don't know what to say to her. She does not like Cee and warned me against him, but she does not know the man that I know. I don't want to argue with her, but I prepare myself to defend him against her harsh words.

I clear my throat to get her attention, and she glances in my direction but doesn't face me. "You finish the tablecloths?"

I nod. "I'll get to the napkins next."

"Good. We'll start on the silver tomorrow," she says, not looking up from her work. The needle and thread make a high arc in the air, then dip down again.

"If you're busy with that, I can finish up vacuuming the rest of the house later. I just have to —"

"No, this won't take too long. I can vacuum."

The needle goes up and then comes down again.

I pivot anxiously from one foot to the

other. I fight the urge to wring my hands. Why hasn't she mentioned what she saw in the laundry room? Why hasn't she asked me about Cee?

"Well," I say after the silence in the kitchen seems to stretch for a full minute, "I guess I'll get back to the washing."

I wait for her to respond, but she says nothing. I purse my lips and start to turn back toward the doorway.

"You know how all of this ends, don't you?" she says out of nowhere, and I pause. "You think you're the first Colored gal those white boys have come sniffing after? You think you're the first one who's gotten caught up by one of them or their nonsense?" She sucks her teeth and continues to sew. "You ain't the first, Dee, and you ain't gonna be the last either! But it always ends the same way, and you're a fool if you think any different."

I'm mute with shock. I knew she would have nothing nice to say about Cee, but I'm surprised and hurt by the venom she's spitting at me. Slowly but surely, I regain myself.

"I'm . . . I'm not a . . . a fool. I know what —"

"Yes, you are." The needle and thread finally fall to rest in her hand. She pivots in

254

her chair and glares up at me. "Any gal who thinks one of them wants anything more from you than to get in her pants, is a straight-up fool! He just wants a piece of that black tail, Dee! Don't you get it?"

I shake my head. "That's not true!"

"Roberta was right! All that book learnin' hasn't done you a bit of good if you can't see what's right in front of your face . . . if you're gonna be deaf and dumb to the ways of the world! Dee, you're just any ol' cow . . . just any ol' cow being led to the slaughter-house, and you're —"

"You don't know as much as you think you know! I'm not dumb or a 'cow'! And he knows it. He thinks I'm smart and beautiful. We talk. We talk about books and life and . . ."

My words trail off when she coughs out a laugh that makes her shoulders go up and down, that makes her lean forward. "Lord, would you listen to this nonsense?" she mumbles. Her eyes level me with so much contempt that I have to fight the urge to look away. "If you can't hear how stupid you sound right now, Dee, I feel sorry for you."

I raise my chin and glare right back at her. "You know what? I don't think you're try-ing to warn me off of him because you're

255

worried about me. I think . . . I think you're jealous."

Her cold smile fades. *"Jealous?"*

"Yes!" I take another step toward her. "I think you're jealous that he likes me and not you! That . . . that he can see I'm not like you and Roberta, and I'm . . . I'm meant for more than just . . . just washing dishes and cleaning shit out of toilets!"

I am smiling because I can spit venom too.

"I'm meant for more than frying chicken and scrubbing floors! And it eats you up inside that he knows it, and you know it too! So it's *you* I would feel sorry for, Agnes. Not me! You're just a maid. Just a stupid maid, and that's all you'll ever be," I snarl before turning around and marching out of the kitchen.

# CHAPTER 18

Now when I kiss Cee, I do it with a vengeance. In the back seat of his GTO at night as the car sits idle in deserted parking lots, in the laundry room midday unbeknownst to anyone except maybe Agnes, he and I kiss with a fierceness and passion I did not know was possible. His mouth and tongue against my bare skin, his body pressed against mine — I must have it, and I don't know why.

"I'd love to keep going, but we're going to have to slow down, sweetheart," Cee told me breathlessly just last night. He pulled his mouth from mine, licked his lips, and sat upright in the seat. "I didn't bring a raincoat."

I pushed myself up to my elbows, closing my top and squinting up at him. "But it's not raining outside."

He burst into laughter, confusing me even more.

I tell myself all this fervor is because Cee has awakened something inside me I hadn't known was there before, but that is only partly true. I also know that with each kiss, caress, and moan, I am proving something to myself: that Agnes doesn't know what she's talking about. I'm not "just another colored girl" who will get tossed aside as soon as Cee gets what he wants out of me. What Cee and I have is lasting and real, I tell myself.

And Cee must believe it too — that what we have is real — because he trusts me now. When Miss Mindy whispered to me two weeks ago that she needed money again, "Only three hundred this time," and I asked Cee for the cash, he handed it over without question. He did it again on Tuesday after Miss Mindy told me she needed a hundred dollars to cover a bill. He tucked the folded money into my apron pocket before nuzzling my neck and nipping my earlobe.

We are in love, and we are happy. I just wish Agnes could be happy for me.

Agnes and I haven't really spoken to one another since that day in the kitchen. When we do speak, it's always a stilted conversation, like we're strangers meeting for the first time on the street. Even Roberta has noticed the difference between us.

"Why y'all two acting so funny?" she asked a few days ago while we were all eating lunch at the kitchenette table.

We both shrugged in response. I returned my attention to my tuna sandwich and my paperback. Agnes continued to eat her slice of leftover meatloaf and green beans while watching her "stories" on the mini RCA that sits on the fridge.

I miss Agnes — our easy conversations, our whispered gossip, and our laughter. I wonder if we will ever be like that again.

"Oh, I'm sorry. I didn't know you were in here," I say when I walk into the living room and see her crouched on the rug on all fours with a scrub brush in her hand.

She glances over her shoulder at me and wipes her brow with the back of her hand. "You don't have to apologize. I'm almost done anyway." She points down at a spot in the carpet. "I think somebody spilled some wine in here. Have to get it out before the party next week."

She gradually rises to her feet and drops the scrub brush into a water-filled bucket with a loud plunk. "Go ahead and vacuum," she says, gesturing to the vacuum cleaner at my side and the cord looped in my hand. "Just be careful of the wet spot."

I nod and watch as Agnes walks across

the room. When she brushes past me, I blurt out, "I'm sorry!"

Agnes frowns and squints up at me. "Girl, what you apologizing for now?"

"I'm sorry for what I said to you about . . . about you being nothing but a stupid maid. I didn't mean that."

She sighs and nods. "I'm sorry too." She gives a small smile and nudges me with her elbow. "And I don't think you're a dumb cow."

I laugh, relieved we are joking with one another again.

"But I *do* think you're making a mistake, Dee," Agnes continues on, dropping her voice down to a whisper. "I wouldn't be a good friend if I didn't warn you."

My shoulders slump. "There's nothing to warn me against! We haven't . . ."

She drops her bucket to the floor and raises a finger to her lips, motioning for me to be quiet. She then grabs my hand and tugs me into the adjoining kitchen, which is empty.

"We haven't done anything but kiss," I insist, picking up where I left off. "Well, maybe some kissing and rubbing, but I swear that's it! He's not —"

"You haven't done anything but kiss — *now,* but that's how it starts. I know. I've been there."

"You've been there?" I frown. "What do you mean?"

She sighs again, long and deep. I can see her rib cage go in and out under the cotton fabric of her uniform. "A . . . a long time ago, at my first job, I . . . I had something like this happen to me. I was fourteen, fresh outta the South Carolina backwater, and my mama got me a job at one of the big houses in Charleston. The Stanleys were old money, had a big staff. I was one of four maids, and sometimes I would help the nanny with the children since I was so young and I liked kids back then. That's how I met Jimmy." Her face suddenly changed. Her wistful smile disappeared. "He was their oldest. He was home from West Point that summer, and he flirted with me all the time! I didn't know what to say or do. I knew it wasn't right, but he was funny . . . charming. Pretty soon the flirting led to more and more and . . . the next thing I knew," she shrugged her shoulders, "I was caught up."

I frown. "*Caught up?* You mean . . . you mean you were . . ."

She nods so I don't have to say the words.

"I was so scared, Dee. Scared of what he would say. I told him I was in the family

261

way. He said it wasn't his. I told him it couldn't be anyone else's baby, but he wouldn't believe me. He went back to West Point in September, and I heard he proposed to some gal who he'd been messin' around with the whole time he was smiling up in my face. Some bucktoothed Louisiana debutante with a lot of money." She sucked her teeth. "He acted like what happened between us never happened, and I . . . I tried to do the same thing, but of course, pretty soon I couldn't pretend anymore. Everybody could see I was with child, and the Stanleys fired me."

My stomach drops.

"I went back home to have my baby, but I couldn't keep her," she says, blinking back tears. One falls onto her cheek, and I can't help but reach up and wipe it away for her. "I couldn't afford no baby, and my mama already had plenty of other mouths to feed. So . . . I gave her away. I gave her away to a reverend and his wife who always wanted a girl." She sniffs and finally looks at me. "And now they have one . . . with pretty ivory skin and chestnut curls."

I take a step back, almost bumping into the stove, because it feels like Agnes's story has knocked me off-kilter. But she grabs my hand to keep me upright. She holds it tight.

"I'm trying to warn you, Dee. I'm trying to warn you as a *friend*. They don't think like us. They don't act like us. Don't let them use you like they used me. Don't let them fool you!"

# CHAPTER 19

I can't get Agnes's words out of my head.
They echo throughout the afternoon as I
work and well into the evening. I find myself
lingering over them, picking at them like
leftover meat from a chicken bone even as I
climb into Cee's car.

"Hey, beautiful," he whispers to me before
leaning over to give me a kiss. His hand
snakes inside my wool coat, and he fondles
my breast through my uniform. I can smell
the rum on his hot breath, and I recoil, shifting my head aside so his lips graze my
cheek, not my mouth. I shove his hand away.

"What the hell was that about?" he asks.
He looks and sounds wounded, but I can't
work up the energy to care.

"Nothin'," I murmur, turning to look out
the passenger-side window. "I'm just tired
and want to go home, please."

He doesn't reply. Instead, he turns up the
volume of the radio. I see in the reflection

how his green eyes narrow and his lips tighten. He doesn't look as handsome or mannish to me anymore. He looks more like a sullen little boy who can't get his way.

He sits there like he's waiting for something, maybe for me to apologize for how I'm treating him tonight, but I don't. When I continue to ignore him, Cee turns and glares out the windshield. He pulls off, flooring the accelerator and making me slam back into my seat.

We arrive at Auntie Mary's house thirty minutes later, and I pause before I climb out of the car, listening to the idling engine.

"Well? You getting out or what?" Cee asks, taking a puff from his cigarette.

"I think . . . I think we need to take a break from each other," I say in one exhalation.

His cigarette goes limp. "Huh?"

"I said I think we need to take a break from each other. We need to think things through, Cee."

Because I am confused. Everything I thought I knew about us doesn't seem certain anymore. Agnes and her story have made me question everything.

"What the hell are you talking about? Think *what* through?" he shouts as I climb out of the car. "Wait! Wait! Damnit, Delilah, answer me!"

"I said what I had to say!" I lean down so I am facing him eye to eye, so that he knows I am serious and will not budge. "We need a break. I need some air to . . . to breathe . . . to think. Just give me that — please? That's all I'm asking!"

I watch as his face goes from pale white to crimson. Even the tips of his ears burn bright. His green eyes narrow into slits like a viper's. He bares his teeth.

"I thought you were different, but you're like every other stupid bitch I've ever wasted my time on!" he barks, stunning me into silence. He tosses his cigarette at me, making me flinch back from the car door. "You want a 'break'? I'll give you a goddamn break! I'll break your goddamn nose for doing this shit to me! You *owe* me, Delilah!" He points at his chest. "And you're out of your fuckin' mind if you think I'm going to let you just —"

I don't wait for him to finish. I've heard enough. I slam the car door, turn, and keep walking even though I can hear him bellowing my name behind me, screaming for me to turn back around and look at him. I walk until I'm up the concrete stairs and the screen door closes behind me. I don't look back.

The next day, I tell Miss Mindy I'm not feeling well and ask to leave early.

"You can't finish out the day?" she asks, raising an eyebrow.

"No, ma'am. I feel too bad." I say, rubbing my stomach, making a face.

She blinks. Her face drains of all color. She points at my aproned waist.

"You're not . . . are you?"

When I realize what she's asking me, I grit my teeth.

"No, ma'am. I got my menses yesterday, and they hurt awful bad. That's all."

"Oh," she says. Her shoulders sink with relief. She waves me away. "Well, if that's the case, go ahead."

I take the bus home, though I know Cee will probably arrive at 5:40 on the nose to ferry me wherever I want to go despite what I told him last night and the horrible things he said to me. But it is not Cee fruitlessly waiting in the dark that I am thinking of as I stare out the bus window at the passing scenery of trees, buildings, and cars, at the people strolling by on the sidewalk.

I'm thinking about Agnes's little baby and the terrified four-teen-year-old girl Agnes must have been back then. That man had treated her like she didn't matter, like she was a trifling plaything he'd gotten bored with. Agnes had been innocent and blind to the ways of the world when that happened to her. I am older and supposedly wiser but had wandered into the same trap. And it wasn't just Cee who had ensnared me. Even Miss Mindy had latched her hooks into my back, dragging me along in whatever direction she wanted. But not anymore. I'm done with being pulled like a rag doll by them both.

I manage to avoid Cee the next day and the day after that. When I spot his GTO waiting for me by my old bus stop, I turn around and walk to the stop six blocks away. I make sure I am busy with Agnes or Roberta whenever he comes to the house, seeking me out. I think Agnes senses what I'm doing and — bless her heart — tries to act as a buffer, as my interference.

"Dee, can you help me take the clean laundry upstairs?" she asks cheerfully when Cee bursts into the laundry room on Wednesday, demanding to speak with me.

"Dee, I think Miss Mindy is calling you," she says when he tries to corner me in the living room on Friday while I am scrubbing the bay windows.

When he stomps away, looking like steam will come out of his ears, Agnes shakes her head ruefully. "That boy looked mad enough to spit nails."

"Well, he can stay mad," I mutter in reply, staring after him uneasily. "It's over between us."

"You better be careful, Dee. I told you. Those white folks ain't nothing but trouble!"

But it doesn't matter how careful you are. Trouble lies in wait; it will not leave you alone. I know this because when I leave for the day, Cee is parked at the end of the block. He's perched on the hood of his GTO with a cigarette dangling from the side of his mouth and his hands shoved into the pockets of his blue peacoat.

"Delilah!" he calls out eagerly, waving when he spots me. He tosses his cigarette to the ground and crushes it under his heel.

Oddly enough, he's smiling. He doesn't look angry anymore like he did earlier today. Instead of making me relieved, his smile makes me nervous. Like I'm staring at a waiting trap.

"Cee," I whisper, walking toward him, "what are you doin' here?"

"What do you mean what am I doing here?"

"I mean *why* are you here?" I say tiredly, because I am tired. I'm damn near exhausted. He's wearing me out. "I told you, we're done."

"I just wanted to talk to you, Dee, and . . . and to apologize."

I stop short. I hadn't expected to hear that. I watch as he shoves his hands into his pockets again and his eyes drift to the asphalt. He kicks aside a rock, and his lips form into a thin white line. There are bags under his eyes. He looks tired too.

"I acted like an ass," he says, scratching at the scruff along his chin. "I said those things to you, and I didn't mean to. I wanted to apologize for that."

"Th-thank you."

"No thanks necessary. It needed to be said." He finally raises his eyes to look at me again. He pushes himself away from the hood and takes halting steps toward me. "Look, Dee, I just . . . I just want to talk to you. I'm not asking you to do anything but talk."

Everything in my head says no. *Tell him no, Dee!*

"Just so I understand," he pleads, "because . . . because I don't. I don't understand why we were good one day and then the next day we weren't."

Alarm bells are sounding, but the ache in his voice tears at me. It is even louder than the bells.

"O-Okay," I hear myself say, "we can talk . . . just for a bit."

There's no harm in talking, is there? I look over my shoulder again at the Williams house and the light coming through the open windows. I expect to find Agnes shaking her head in disappointment, but thankfully she isn't there.

"We can't do it here, though. We can drive around or go to —"

"No, let me pick where we go. I want to take you somewhere nice. Somewhere special."

I frown at him apprehensively, and he holds up his hand, stopping me before I can voice any arguments. "Look, this may be the last time I get to do this. I've wanted to take you there before but never had the chance. Let me do it tonight. *Please?*"

I sigh. "All right, Cee."

Though he said he wanted to talk, for most of the ride, Cee doesn't say anything. The radio announcer's voice fills the void along with song after song, some of the saddest love tunes I swear I've heard in my entire life. His silence means I'm left with nothing else to do but stare out the car window and wonder where he's taking me. At first, the streets zipping by us are ones I've seen every day for the past year. I would know what these streets look like — from every fence post to every mailbox — even if my eyes were closed. But gradually, the streets start to become less familiar, and I start getting anxious. We end up on a stretch of roadway where the houses become fewer in number, then disappear completely. Dense trees take up both sides of the road and start to cast shadows in the GTO's headlights. I turn to Cee, peering at his face in the darkened car.

"How much longer?" I ask.

"Don't worry. We're almost there," he says in an almost trance-like voice, like he's half dreaming.

That's when I start to worry Cee is taking me to a place where we will do more than talk. A few minutes later, I swear I can hear water in the distance, a low rumble that grows louder. It sounds like the surf hitting against a rock wall.

"Cee, where are we going?" I ask, no longer able to keep the panic out of my voice.

"I told you," he mutters, not looking at me, "it's a surprise."

"No!" I shout. "I wanna know where you're taking me!"

That's when it finally comes into view.

"We're here," he says as we pull to a stop

on a gravel road leading to a house — the biggest house I've ever seen, even bigger than the Williams home. In the gauzy light of the full moon, I can see the peaked roof, six dormers, and cedar shingles. Rosebushes are planted near a wooden wraparound porch, and an extinguished gas lamp hangs near the screen door.

At the sight of the house, all my anxiety disappears. I have never seen anything so lovely.

"Where are we?" I ask breathlessly as he removes his car keys and throws the driver's-side door open.

"My beach house," he says, then shrugs. "Well, it's really my *family's* beach house, but Mama said I inherited it when I turned twenty-one. It's what Dad wanted. You should see it in the daylight. It's even more beautiful than this." I open my car door, and Cee offers me his hand. I take it and follow him down a winding stone path bordered by flowers and shrubs leading to the wooden stairs. As we walk, a light drizzle begins to fall. A lightning bolt etches its way across the heavens, and the entire sky is bright for a few seconds. I can see the entire yard and the vast water in the distance before a loud boom fills my ears and the world is only moonlight again.

"We better get inside," he says, and we climb the steps, taking them two at a time.

When we reach the porch, he pulls back the screen, inserts a key, and shoves the front door open. He gestures for me to step in front of him, and I walk inside the beach house and gaze around me.

The inside of the house is as nice as the outside, with exposed beam ceilings and cream-colored walls. But it is also empty. For the first time, I realize what folks mean when they say "quiet as a tomb" because the house is that. The creak of our feet against the floorboards sounds as loud as the thunder outside.

There are a few pieces of furniture in each of the rooms, but they are all covered in drop cloth, cloaking the house in gray and white, giving it an otherworldly feel.

"We usually keep the house closed after September. You really can't take advantage of the beach after that because it's so cold," he says, walking across the living room to remove one of the cloths, revealing a tweed sofa. "But I come up here on my own every now and then . . . for the peace and quiet."

I am standing in the center of the living room with my arms crossed over my chest, clutching my elbows, when he turns to me.

"If you're chilly, I could start a fire," he

says, gesturing to the fireplace on the other side of the room.

"Thank you. That would be nice."

I wander from room to room, exploring the house, taking it all in as Cee builds the fire. I have not been here before, but everything feels right about this place. It feels welcoming, almost like home. I wonder if Cee anticipated this. Is that why he brought me here?

When I return to the living room, Cee is sitting on the rug in front of the fireplace, nudging the logs with a poker, stoking the flames. The room feels considerably warmer, and I remove my coat as I walk toward him. I set it next to his peacoat, which he has thrown over the arm of the sofa.

"This . . . this house . . . ," I begin but can't find the right words to describe it.

He chuckles. "I know. I figured you'd see Harbor Hill the way I do."

So I was right. He knew.

"Harbor Hill. Why do you call it that?"

"More than a hundred years ago, there was a harbor here. The sailors didn't have a lighthouse to guide the way, but a farmer lived on this hilltop. He'd leave a fire burning, and that's what they would look for. They knew when they saw the hill that they were near the harbor, that they were almost home."

I nod and drop to my knees, taking a spot on the rug beside him. We both stare into the fire.

Cee sets down the poker, turns, and rifles through his jacket pocket. He pulls out his flask, removes the lid, and takes a sip. He offers it to me, and I consider it for a few seconds before taking the flask and taking a sip too.

"So I guess we should talk now," he says.

I nod and hand the flask back to him. "I'm ready whenever you are."

He takes another sip, exhales, and bows his head. He ruffles his hair, pushing it back from his face. "I've just got one question, Delilah, and it's a simple one: What did I do wrong?"

"You didn't do anything wrong."

"So then why'd you end it? Why'd you walk away? There *has* to be a reason!"

I open my mouth, then close it. I purse my lips. He raises his head and glares at me.

"I mean . . . dammit, Dee! Just be honest with me! Don't bullshit me! Is it just because you were . . . were ready to move on? You used me and got what you wanted, so you were done with me? Is that it?"

"I didn't use you, Cee."

"Yes, you did! You used me for my money! A thousand here. Three hundred there! I wondered if the story you told me about your mama and the bank was just bullshit. That's what it was all along, right?"

I want to lie to abate his anger and hurt, but I can't. I lower my eyes instead.

"You think you're the first girl who's done this? You think you're the first one who was only interested in what she could get out of me? Well, you're not! I've had plenty — and I could spot them coming from a mile away. But I let down my guard with you! I thought you were different. I bought all that horseshit about your books and your dreams and your —"

"It wasn't horseshit. I meant every word. And I wasn't using you for your money. I really liked you. I *still* like you, Cee, but I just can't . . ."

My words drift off. The room starts to blur, and I realize it's because my eyes are flooding with tears.

"You can't what, Delilah?"

"Miss Mindy . . . she knows what's going on between us," I say, and his face changes. "She knows, and Agnes knows too. She said it never should've happened."

"So? Why the hell should we care?"

277

"Because Agnes has been through this! She knows how it will end — and I do too!" I yell through my tears. I wipe them away with the backs of my hands. "This isn't going to work, Cee. This was never meant to go anywhere! We should just end it . . . end this foolishness before someone gets —"

"Before someone gets hurt?" He raises his brows. "Well, too goddamn late! Because I love you! I'm in love you, and this is hurting the hell out of me. You're destroying me! Don't you get that?"

I slowly shake my head.

He won't be destroyed, not really. He will be hurt, but not broken like I will be if this continues on, the way Agnes was broken all those years ago. I will never be the same, and I can already feel some part of me sliding away the longer he and I are together.

But Cee doesn't see that. All he can see is what *he* needs and wants.

"Look at me! Look at me, dammit!" he orders, roughly grabbing my face. His eyes are bright again, and that's when I know he's not himself anymore. He's the Cee who throws cigarettes at me and cusses. This is the Cee who makes me nervous, the one I must get away from. "It's true. I love you, and I'm not going to let you get away from me! I'm not!"

I try to pull my face away and to rise to my feet. "Just find someone else! Take me home, and find —"

That's when he clamps his hand over my mouth and my nose to silence me. It happens so fast I don't realize what he's done until he shoves me to the floor, and I can feel the hardwood and the rug against my back. He holds me down, and I claw at his hands. He yells like he's the one being smothered as I fight for air, trying to wrench his hand away. I can hear Agnes in my head along with my own screams.

*You're just any ol' cow . . . just any ol' cow being led to the slaughterhouse, Dee.*

Agnes was right: I am just any ol' cow being led to the slaughter. I am going to die tonight.

I see pinpricks of light in my line of vision. Air fills my throat, screaming to get out. My head aches, and the world starts to dim. Just when I feel myself going limp, Cee removes his hands, and I gasp for air. He drags me up from the floor toward him, kissing my cheek, my neck, and my mouth like he hadn't been smothering me just ten seconds ago.

"I can give you everything. Everything you ever wanted," he murmurs against my lips. He rips open the buttons of my uniform jumper, sending them flying. His hands are shaking as he pushes the jumper and my bra straps off my shoulders.

He shoves me back to the floor again, and I try to push him away — but I can't. I am too weak, too frightened. I try to scream "No!" and "Stop, Cee!" but my throat is burning, and no sound comes out. He lowers his zipper and pushes his jeans down his hips. I watch the lightning flash, playing on the planes of his face. I hear the thunder as he raises my skirt, shimmies my panties over my knees, and pries open my legs. I hear the sound of his panting breath against my ear and the rain pounding against the roof when he climbs on top of me.

"You're meant for more. You said it yourself. I can give it to you, beautiful. I can! Just let me. You're meant for me," he whispers as he pushes himself into me, like I am something to possess, not to love.

After it's over, he kisses me in a soft, sweet way. I flinch and turn my mouth away as he does it, and his lips land on my wet cheek.

"That was lovely, sweetheart," he gushes, then climbs off of me. He stands and begins to dress. He does it casually, like what just happened was perfectly normal, like he didn't just rape me on the hardwood floor of his family's empty house. "But we better get you back home. I bet your aunt is wondering where you are."

I slowly rise from the floor to a sitting position, feeling numb all over except for the painful throbbing and sticky wetness between my legs. My brain is sluggish. I am still in shock. I watch dully as Cee tucks his shirt hem into his pants and raises his zipper. He gestures at me.

"You definitely have to keep your coat closed though. Can't have her seeing that."

I look down at myself. The front of my jumper is splayed open and one of my bra straps has been ripped, revealing my left breast. I raise my hands to cover my nakedness, but it is of no use. He tosses my coat to me after he shrugs into his.

"Put it on," he orders, and I do as he says, almost automatically.

Later, Cee drives me home. We don't talk as he drives. He smokes and listens to the radio while I stare out the window. In the car windows' reflection, I can see his face in profile. He seems serene, almost happy.

Meanwhile, I feel like I've been cleaved from true myself, like my body and my mind are in two different places. I sit calmly, but inside, I am sobbing. I am screaming. I want to bolt from the car and run, but I don't make a move. I adjust my position in my seat, holding my purse in my lap, and continue to stare out the window.

When we arrive at Auntie Mary's house, I climb out of the GTO on shaky legs. I just want to go upstairs to my bedroom and curl into a tight ball on my bed. I want to forget about tonight, about everything. I want to forget I ever met Chauncey Buford.

"Hey, Dee!" he calls out, making me halt in my steps. I slowly turn to find him leaning toward the open window. "I'm glad we put that behind us, that we're back together."

I stare at him, at a loss for words.

"I'll see you tomorrow, beautiful," he calls to me with a smile, then turns around, guns the engine, and pulls off.

I watch as he drives down the block until he turns the corner and his taillights disappear.

That's when I know for sure he has me trapped.

■ ■ ■ ■

# Part III

■ ■ ■ ■

*Camden Beach, Maryland*
*November 2016*

# CHAPTER 20

Aidan tried to avoid her.

He stayed out of the hallway when he heard the children clamoring in the morning — the boy screaming for his book bag and the little girl babbling her baby talk. He had set up the swing and play set in the backyard for them, as Delilah had asked him to, but now he avoided having a beer by the shed in the evenings to relax. That space was the children's domain; he had relinquished it without a complaint, as long as he didn't have to look at her. Aidan had even stopped eating breakfast and dinner in the dining room. Every night, Delilah would call upstairs, asking if he would come down. He would make an excuse for why he couldn't have dinner with the entire brood. He would say anything to avoid having those magnetic blue eyes peering at him from across the table.

But, of course, he couldn't ignore her

completely. He could still hear her toddling through the house — the rhythmic *thump, thump, thump* of tiny feet over hardwood. Or he'd see her playing in the front yard, squealing and laughing as she and her brother tossed around the newly fallen leaves, her cheeks red from the blustery wind. Aidan had caught a glimpse of her and her older brother making "leaf angels" in a pile of leaves Aidan had raked only an hour earlier. He'd tried to pretend to be annoyed that he had to rake the pile again, but he had smiled at their play and shenanigans despite himself.

And today . . . today she was unavoidable. The little girl was right in front of him — or more accurately, right in front of his door.

Aidan had just loaded one of his old CDs into his stereo — Stevie Wonder's greatest hits — and was humming along to the music while getting settled for the night when he turned around and saw her standing there in zebra-striped onesie pajamas. They froze simultaneously, staring at one another.

The little girl was the first to break the spell. Her cherubic face broke into a grin, revealing four teeth and two bright pink gums. She raised her arms over her head and started to do a little shimmy, clomping her feet and dancing in his doorway to "Sign, Sealed, Delivered."

Watching her, Aidan couldn't hold back his laugh. It burst from his mouth before he had a chance to control the volume. He started laughing so hard at her little dance routine, he had to hold on to the edge of the mattress to stay upright. Tears sprung to his eyes. Seeing him, she started to laugh too. Her girlish, high-pitched giggles filled his room and the entire corridor.

"Maggie! There you are!" her mother called out, rushing to the little girl's side. She scooped her up into her arms, kissed her plump cheek, and turned to face Aidan. "I'm sorry if she was bothering you!" she shouted over the music. "I didn't know she had wandered down here!"

He quickly shook his head and grabbed the remote to lower the stereo volume. "No, she wasn't bothering me. Not at all. She was just dancing. I thought it was . . . cute."

But she didn't look convinced. Instead, she eyed him anxiously and pasted on one of the fakest smiles he had seen in quite a while. It was a smile he had used himself while working at the law firm years ago.

"Well, anyway, we'll get out of your hair." She grabbed the doorknob. "Come on, Maggie! Time to go to night-night."

"That's okay, really. You can leave it . . ."

The door slammed shut with a thud.

"Open," he finished and then sighed and reached for the beer on his night table. He shook his head in exasperation and took a long, slow pull from the bottle.

The children seemed to be simple creatures. They went to school. They slept. They played. They ate. But the woman, Tracey — *she* was an enigmatic figure. He didn't know what to think of her or what the hell her deal was.

Though Aidan had tried to avoid the children, he at least remained reasonably polite to everyone, including Tracey, offering to help her move her furniture around the room in whatever configuration she wanted or washing her car when he washed Delilah's. But it didn't seem to matter to her. Instead, the longer she lived at Harbor Hill, the more aloof she became. Well, that wasn't true. She and Delilah seemed to have bonded quickly, cooking meals together and sitting on the couch to watch television with the children. But she continually gave Aidan the cold shoulder, like she'd rather not be in his presence.

He supposed it was to be expected. He was polite to her, but he wasn't particularly warm or overly welcoming. And to be honest, a few women who had come to Harbor Hill had also been gunshy of him in the beginning, which made sense considering the two tons of emotional baggage they often carried with them through the front door. He had heard all the horror stories of past abusive relationships: drunken husbands who pushed you when you got too lippy, or boyfriends quick to slap a girl if his steak came to the table well done instead of medium rare. He went out of his way to make them feel comfortable. If these women were recovering from trauma doled out by his own sex, the last thing he wanted was to be yet another man to make them wary — or worse, outright scared. Luckily, after the first month or so, all the women would warm to Aidan. They would see he wasn't one of *those* guys. But Tracey was different.

He didn't know how to make her feel at ease around him and wasn't sure if it was even worth trying.

By morning, Aidan's thoughts were less on Tracey Walters and more on fixing the trim around the oversized French doors leading to the back porch.

The temperature had dropped considerably last night and had been hovering just below thirty degrees for most of the morning. The wind had kicked up, and there was a sharp bite in the air that made Aidan's fingers go numb from the chill when he wasn't wearing gloves. It made the work cumbersome, and it was taking longer than he would have liked, but he forged ahead. He had just glued the painted trim on top and was about to nail it into place when he heard over his shoulder, "What are you doing?"

Aidan turned and looked down from his perch on the ladder to find the boy staring up at him quizzically from the foot of the porch stairs. He had on a blue puffy winter coat and a wool hat pulled so low on his head that only his eyes, cheeks, mouth, and nose were visible.

"Oh, uh, hey, Caleb. I'm just hanging up some trim," Aidan said, picking up his hammer.

The boy wiped his nose on the back of his mitten. "Why?"

"Well, because . . . because the old trim is rotted." He pointed down to the discarded trim on the porch. "I've got to replace it."

"Oh," Caleb said, still gazing up at Aidan. He lingered near the stairs.

Feeling conspicuous now, Aidan took one of the nails and positioned it in place.

"Can I do it?" Caleb called out, making

Aidan turn around to face him again. "Can I help?"

He considered the boy's request for a few seconds, then shrugged. At the rate he was going, the kid couldn't slow him down. "Sure, I guess."

Smiling, Caleb ran up the stairs as Aidan hopped off the ladder.

"Climb up," he said, motioning to the ladder, "and I'll hold the nail while you swing. Can I trust you not to break my fingers? You ever nailed something with your dad before?"

Caleb lowered his eyes. He bowed his head, looking embarrassed. "I'm . . . I'm not supposed to talk about my dad."

Growing up with a father who was married and had another family only thirty miles away, Aidan had had his fair share of awkward questions about his dad. He should've known better than to do the same to Caleb.

"No problem," Aidan said with a shrug, making Caleb raise his head. "Don't worry about it. Just forget I asked. How about this? We'll take it slow." He patted one of the metal rungs, gesturing for him to climb.

"Can you hold this, though?" Caleb asked, offering a well-worn Incredible Hulk action figure to him. "I can't fit him in my coat pocket."

Aidan reached out and took the doll. "You like the Hulk, huh?"

Caleb nodded eagerly. "I want to be strong just like him one day."

"Don't we all, kid." He then inserted the Hulk into his jacket pocket. "Come on and hop up here."

Caleb followed his command, taking one unsteady step, then the next, exercising so much intense focus to climb a mere two and half feet that Aidan almost burst into laughter, but he bit it back. He didn't want to spook Caleb or make him self-conscious. When the boy was finally high enough, Aidan handed him the hammer.

"I'll steady you," he said, holding his hand between the boy's shoulder blades, feeling the thick cotton against his palm.

"Okay," Caleb said uneasily, holding the hammer and sticking his tongue out the side of his mouth. He squinted in concentration.

Aidan often wondered whether, if things had been different, if he and Trish would have had more kids. Would he have had a son, and would Aidan be doing projects like this around his own house in Chicago with him? Would his son be timid like Caleb, or would he be brash and go charging up the ladder?

"All right! Let her rip," he said, and Caleb hauled back the hammer so far over his head, Aidan was worried he'd fall off the ladder.

He swung, banging a few times, and the nail went in. The head was a little warped, but it wasn't a bad job.

"I did it!" Caleb exclaimed, grinning. "I did it!"

"Yep, you did it!"

They both jumped, startled, at the loud pounding against a nearby window. The boy dropped the hammer and teetered back from the ladder with his arms windmilling wildly. Aidan caught him just before he lost his balance and crashed to the porch.

"Caleb!" Tracey screamed, yanking open one of the French doors. She had the little girl perched on her hip. "What were you doing up there?"

"I was . . . I w-was fixing the t-t-trim," Caleb stuttered as Aidan lowered him to the porch.

*"What?"* she screeched, looking and sounding hysterical.

Caleb's eyes went bright with tears. He sniffed. "I-I-I was just —"

"You know you're not supposed to do that! You're never supposed to climb ladders. You know better, Caleb! You almost

293

fell. I saw you!"

"He almost fell because you scared the hell out of him," Aidan said with a chuckle, patting Caleb's shoulder. He handed him back the Hulk and watched as Caleb clutched the doll in front of him like it was a talisman, like it could protect him. "He was doing just fine before that. We had it covered."

Tracey shifted her gaze from Caleb to Aidan. She pursed her lips before lowering the little girl to the porch.

"Cabe, take your sister inside, please? I'll be a minute."

Caleb wiped his nose with his mitten again and nodded. He grabbed the little girl's hand, and they went back in the house. When they did, Tracey shut the door behind them and whipped back around to face Aidan. She was wearing only a turtle-neck and jeans and was shivering, but Aidan wasn't sure if it was from the cold or her anger.

"Aidan," she began, "my son isn't allowed to climb ladders. He knows that."

"But it wasn't like he was climbing just for the hell of it!" Aidan pointed to the trim. "He told you he was —"

"And I don't appreciate you challenging the instructions that I've given to my son," she continued tightly, ignoring him. "I especially don't appreciate you doing it in front of him!"

"Hey, I wasn't trying to 'challenge' anything! He asked me if he could —"

"Yes, you were!" She took another step toward him. "Look, I understand that you don't particularly want me and my family here, but *while* we're living here, I ask that you respect me."

He frowned. How had she gotten the impression he didn't want them living there?

*Well, you don't,* a voice in his head mocked.

Maybe, but that was beside the point. He had been cordial to her and her two kids. He had even let the boy help him with the trim, and she was acting like he had popped the kid in the mouth.

"Lady, I wasn't disrespecting you! If anyone was doing any disrespecting, it was you, yelling at the kid like some . . . some lunatic. He was fine! He didn't need you embarrassing him like that!"

She crossed her arms over her chest. "I'm sorry, but do you have kids?"

Aidan's firmly set mouth softened. His throat went dry. He took a steadying breath, sending a mist into the cold air. "No. No, I don't."

*Not anymore,* he wanted to add.

"Well, then I'd appreciate it if you'd let me raise mine." She then yanked open one of the French doors and slammed it shut behind her, leaving him standing alone on the porch.

# CHAPTER 21

"Girl, *what* are you doing?" Delilah called out, making Tracey raise her head from her yoga mat.

She saw the upside-down image of Delilah standing in the doorway of the living room, wiping her hands on a dish towel and staring at her in amazement.

Tracey gave a tired smile, rolled upright, and pushed the sweaty hair that had escaped her ponytail out of her eyes. "Kapotasana."

Delilah frowned. "Kapo-what?"

"Kapotasana. I'm doing the pigeon pose . . . or at least a vague attempt at it." She fell back to her shins and wiggled out her arms. "I'm a bit rusty, though."

She had taken up yoga again, something she hadn't done in a year, not since leaving Paul. In the old days, she used to go to yoga class twice a week with the other stay-at-home moms, all preening in their Lululemon leggings and tanks, stretching their way through handstands and the lotus position and then meeting up for wheatgrass and acai berry smoothies after class. But that wasn't her life anymore. Paying the bills and the rent and eluding her husband became her constant worry and main focus. She couldn't afford yoga class, and breaking out the mat for thirty minutes of exercise and meditation had been the least of her concerns. But she was allowing herself the luxury now that she was living at Harbor Hill. Her worries hadn't disappeared completely, but she could feel them peeling away slowly, like onion skin. It felt refreshing to focus on herself, to be aware of her own body.

"Why were you rolling into a pretzel like that?" Delilah asked, stepping into the living room.

"Maggie is down for a midday nap, and Caleb is engrossed in one of his games. I thought I'd get a little yoga in. It helps me center myself, to . . . to find peace."

Though to be honest, when she did yoga while she was still with Paul, she hadn't found the practice very peaceful. Maybe because she was always glancing at her watch, wondering if she had enough time after class to get home and make dinner before he arrived from work. There would be hell to pay if dinner wasn't waiting for him on the table. Or maybe it was because the silence of the yoga studio had been too overwhelming. Silence was when her voices of panic shouted the loudest.

Delilah inclined her head. "Well, whatever works, I guess. To each his own! So how long do you think you'll be doing that?"

"Maybe fifteen more minutes. Did you need anything?"

Delilah nodded. "I forgot a few things when I went to the grocery store last week. I need them to finish making dinner. I was wondering if you could get what's on the list for me? I told the children they can help me with the pumpkin and sweet potato pies for dessert tonight. We can work on that while you're at the store."

"Sure!" Tracey pushed herself to her feet. "I'll get to it right —"

"No, finish your yoga," Delilah said, waving her hand. "There's no rush, honey. I'll have the list waiting for you when you're done." She then turned and walked back into the kitchen, humming to herself.

But as soon as she turned around, Tracey began to roll up her yoga mat. She ran out of the living room and into the foyer so she could race upstairs, take a quick shower, and dress.

She wasn't going to make Delilah wait for anything, not when she had done so much for her.

If Tracey had had any doubts about moving into Harbor Hill when she first arrived, they had disappeared within days of settling into her new home. It was a serene place that was spacious and open — unlike the shabby, confined quarters they had been living in for the past year. The children loved it, and they loved Delilah, who was warm and giving and watched over Tracey and the kids like they were her own kin.

"You should meet her," Tracey had told Jessica when she stopped by the Chesapeake Cupcakery last month to tell her friend she had moved out of the old rambler. "She really is sweet, Jess. You'd like her!"

"Yeah, I'll take your word for it," Jessica had said, putting the finishing touches on one of her confections. "I just hope you're right, though. I hope you know what you're doing moving in with someone with her . . . well, her background."

Yes, Delilah had been convicted of murder, but the circumstances leading to the crime made Tracey sympathetic, not fearful. It clearly had been an accident based on all the evidence. Delilah had been a young African American woman railroaded by the racist judicial system of the time. Even the appeals judge admitted the odds had been stacked against Delilah and had reversed the guilty verdict. Tracey would never hold what had happened to Delilah against her. One serious look at the woman she was today would easily convince someone it was impossible for Delilah to be a cold-blooded killer. It just wasn't in her nature.

Tracey returned downstairs thirty minutes later, washed and dressed in a sweater and jeans. Maggie was awake from her nap and perched on Tracey's hip, playing with her mother's wet hair, which now hung in thick clumps around Tracey's shoulders. Tracey spotted Delilah at the foot of the stairs.

"Here she is!" Delilah exclaimed. "See, Aidan, I told you that you wouldn't have to wait long."

At those words, Tracey stumbled on the last step and would have dropped Maggie and face-planted on the cherrywood floor if she hadn't caught herself. But even with her best efforts, she couldn't hide the look of distaste on her face. She watched as Aidan shrugged into his wool jacket, then reached for a scarf dangling from one of the brass hooks near the door. She hadn't known he was going to the grocery store with her.

She did not like Aidan Dominguez, and she knew he didn't like her either. Why else would he go out of his way to not be around her or her children by hiding in his room or leaving the house whenever they were around? Perhaps that's why she had been so shocked to find Caleb not only standing on a ladder, but also standing there *with* Aidan. What did this man want with her son? And Aidan had had the gall to call her hysterical, to tell her she was embarrassing Caleb. Aidan must be insane to think she would take parenting advice from a childless bachelor, and a standoffish one at that.

"Here's the list," Delilah said, handing her a folded sheet of paper. "Some of that stuff will be pretty heavy. Aidan can carry it for you, though. Meanwhile, I need to get back in that kitchen. Better get started!"

"B-but . . ."

Tracey didn't get to finish. Delilah scooped Maggie out of her arms and began to walk toward the kitchen. "Come on, honey. Your brother is already in there. We've been waiting for you!"

In Delilah's absence, Aidan and Tracey stared awkwardly at one another, like two dancers forced together in a crowded ballroom. They listened to Delilah and the children's conversation filtering through the kitchen wall, waiting for who would make the first move. After almost a full minute, Tracey relented. She finally walked toward the coat hooks and removed her jacket.

"You know, if you have other things to do today, I can take care of this myself. You don't have to come — really."

"No, I *do* have to come — really," he replied, snapping closed the buttons of his jacket and rolling his eyes. "Dee will have my ass if I don't." He unlocked the front door, opened it, and gestured for her to step outside first. "Come on. Let's go."

They didn't speak for the entire ride to the store. Tracey noted that he didn't even attempt to make polite conversation as they sat in the cab of his Toyota pickup. Instead, he turned up the volume on the radio, filling the car with annoying sports commentator banter, as if to ward off the possibility of talking. Tracey could take the hint. Rather than engage him, she stared out the passenger-side window at the passing scenery of Camden Beach, taking in the mostly deserted streets.

The sweaty beach bums, oil-slathered sunbathers, and summer-vacationing families had left the town by the last week of September, and the frenetic up tempo of Camden Beach had died down to a tired lull. She had even noticed it at the hotel and resort where she worked. The customers barely filled the dining room, even at the height of lunchtime, and tips left under perspiring glasses and saucers were smaller than before or nonexistent. But Tracey didn't resent the calm and quiet. In some ways, she may have been yearning for it all along.

When she and Aidan reached the Milton's Grocer parking lot, he hopped out first and headed to the store's automatic doors — not looking to see if she was following, like she wasn't there at all. Mumbling to herself, Tracey climbed out and slammed the door behind her. When she reached the store, she found him standing by a display of soda bottles stacked in a pyramid. He leaned against a grocery cart. At least he had waited for her, though she suspected that was only because she had the shopping list, which he immediately asked for.

"Where's the list?"

"I have it right here," she said, pulling it out of her coat pocket.

"Let me see it." He held out his hand to her.

"No, that's all right. I've got it."

"Trust me. You should give it to me. I'm used to Dee's chicken scratch. Been staring at it for years. You'd probably need a Rosetta Stone to translate it."

Tracey bit the inside of her cheek, trying her best not to look annoyed. She handed him the sheet of paper. He scanned the list and nodded.

"Right. Let's head to produce."

They slowly made their way up and down the aisles as Aidan continued to be a list hog.

He bore little resemblance to her husband; Aidan was dark-haired with olive-toned skin, while Paul was blond and could get a sunburn after fifteen minutes of direct sunlight. But Aidan still reminded her of him. Paul hated grocery shopping but insisted on barking out the list to her, rather than let her read it on her own. She was always secretly relieved when Paul decided to skip their trips to Whole Foods. She desperately wished Aidan had decided to skip today — or maybe *she* should have stayed home. As the minutes wore on, Tracey pondered why she was here at all since Aidan obviously could do it all on his own. Half the time he behaved as if she wasn't standing next to him.

When they reached the diary aisle, she watched, confused, as Aidan grabbed a giant tub of margarine and lowered it into the cart, shoving items aside to make room.

Tracey squinted at the list in his hand. "Margarine isn't on here. She asked for butter."

He shrugged and started to steer the cart away from the diary freezers. "She means margarine."

"No," Tracey stood in front of the cart, blocking his path. "If she meant margarine, she would have written margarine, wouldn't she? She clearly asked for butter!"

She watched as he leaned against the cart's plastic handrail. He leveled her with a gaze that conveyed not only fatigue but contempt. It also reminded her of Paul, the way he would look at her when he thought she had said something stupid or when he thought she was wasting his time.

"Trust me," Aidan began infuriating her even more. "She meant margarine. I've known her long enough that I —"

"I get it!"

She held up her hand, no longer hiding her annoyance. Aidan wasn't Paul, and she was no longer the timid little housewife who had been married to Paul. She wasn't going to bite her tongue anymore.

"I get that you've known her for decades. You told me that already, but what was the point of her writing her list if we're just going to disregard what she wrote? Maybe she needs butter for one of her recipes. You don't know!"

"No, but I *do* know that Delilah has high blood pressure, and her cholesterol levels have been elevated for the past two and a half years. She doesn't *need* butter, and she knows she shouldn't eat butter! That's why I chose the brand I always buy for her because —"

"Are you always like this?" Tracey asked, crossing her arms over her chest.

"Always like what?"

"Do you always presume to know what's best for other people? First, you lecture me about how to raise my son, and now you're —"

"Wait, wait, wait!" He shook his head, sending his dark, shaggy hair flying. He pushed himself away from the cart. Now even *he* looked annoyed. "I wasn't trying to lecture you about how to raise your son. I was showing the kid how to hammer a nail — and you came out there screaming at the top of your lungs!"

"I was not 'screaming at the top of my lungs'! I was . . . was speaking firmly to my son because I was concerned about his safety, because he was doing something he knew he shouldn't be doing. That's how conscientious parents behave! If you were a parent too, you would know that!"

"Lady, I may not be a parent —"

"Please stop calling me lady! It's incredibly patronizing!"

"And it's *incredibly patronizing* for you to keep pointing out that I don't have kids like that makes you the authority on everything and I'm some kind of idiot."

She clenched her fists at her sides. "I never said I —"

"Besides, I may not be a parent, but I've been a little boy before," he continued, ignoring her, "and I know what it feels like when your mother is talking to you like you're an infant . . . when she's not listening to you!"

"You don't know anything about me or my son, so don't try to —"

She stopped her tirade when she glanced over Aidan's shoulder and saw who was standing behind him at the far end of the dairy aisle, next to the shredded cheeses and yogurt.

"Paul?" Tracey whispered.

She went numb. All the blood seemed to drain from her head and fall straight to her toes, and the world around her started to tilt and swirl. She felt faint. Tracey took a shaky step back from the cart, then another.

Her sneakers felt like they had transformed from fabric, foam, and rubber to solid lead. Her legs felt like liquid.

"What's wrong?" Aidan asked, furrowing his brows at her, taking in her ashen face and slack jaw. He looked in the direction she was now staring.

*Paul found me,* she thought dazedly, feeling an equal mix of shock and horror. *He found me!*

She turned, prepared to bolt. Instead, she ran smack-dab into a display of glazed and frosted donuts. Several boxes tumbled to the tiled floor, spilling in all directions. Tracey would have fallen with them if Aidan hadn't grabbed her hand and tugged her back.

"Whoa!" He pulled her back upright. "Slow down! Okay?"

She began to shove out of his grasp but halted when she looked over his shoulder again and saw the man she was trying to escape was a mere five feet behind them. She could see him more closely now.

"Th-that's not P-Paul," she stuttered.

*"What?"*

"That's not Paul!"

The man who stood in front of her could pass for a leaner version of her husband, but it wasn't him.

Tracey closed her eyes and took several deep breaths, dropping her trembling hand to her stomach. She wanted to break into tears. All the worry from seconds ago rushed out of her like air from a deflating balloon.

"Who's Paul?"

Her eyes stayed focused on the man as he passed them. She studied his every feature, even the glint of his blond hair under the track lighting. He stared back at her uneasily, like she was a skittish dog who could nip him.

"Who is Paul, Tracey?" Aidan repeated, finally releasing her shoulders.

She hesitated before she answered him. She couldn't believe she had said her husband's name aloud. She had told Delilah about Paul, about why she was running from him, because after she moved in she'd felt she had to. She felt she owed Delilah that. But for everyone else she had schooled herself to never mention his name — and if she did talk about him, to give only superficial details. And here she was, raving about him in the middle of a grocery store, creating a scene.

Aidan continued to stare at her, waiting for an answer. Finally, she caved.

"Paul is my . . . my husband. I thought

that guy was . . . that he was Paul."

Aidan's face changed. His furrowed brows disappeared.

She threaded her fingers through her damp hair, lifting it from her shoulders. "Look, Aidan, I'm sorry I —"

"There's no need to apologize. I get it." He dropped to a knee and began to pick up the doughnut boxes, adding them back to the stack she had partly knocked down. Tracey quickly dropped to her knees to help him.

"You get what?"

"Every woman who comes to Harbor Hill comes for a reason, Tracey," he said gently, gathering the last of the boxes. She watched as he rose to his feet and placed the ones he held on the stack. She stood up too. "I guess he's your reason then?"

She didn't nod right away. The admission felt like it was being physically pried out of her. "We . . . we haven't seen him in about a year," she finally said. "We had a close call ten months ago, not too long after I'd left him. I'd moved out of the house but hadn't moved far enough, I guess. I hadn't covered my tracks. I tripped up, and he almost caught us."

It had been her neighbor in the apartment building where she once lived who had

311

given her the heads up. The old woman had told her a man whose description sounded eerily like Paul's had shown up in the lobby and had been asking if they knew of a woman named Tracey who lived in the building. He'd even shown a few of the tenants her picture.

Tracey had moved out of her apartment that very night. She'd meandered her way from hotel to hotel and then finally to Camden Beach.

"But he doesn't know we live at Harbor Hill now — and I want it to stay that way."

"Yeah, Caleb mentioned that he's not allowed to talk about his dad. I figured there was a good reason why."

She did a double take. She squinted up at him. "Cabe said that to you?"

He nodded.

"Wow!" She let out a low, mirthless laugh. "You guys really bonded, didn't you?"

"I wouldn't call it 'bonding,' though I got a sense that's kind of what the kid may have wanted, even if he couldn't put it into words. If it's just you and his sis, he probably longs for some male bonding. I know I did at his age when it was just me, Mom, and Dee."

"Your mother left your father too?" she asked tentatively, wondering if it was intrusive to ask. She slowly placed the boxes she held on the stack.

"It's hard to leave a man who's still married and living with someone else."

"Oh," she whispered, unsure of how else to respond.

"But I still secretly would've liked having my dad around," he confessed. "Or if not him . . . a guy who could've taken his place."

She grimaced. "I wonder sometimes if Cabe misses his father, but he never talks about it."

"Are you really surprised, though? I bet he knows how you feel about his father. Why would he talk about him?"

Tracey felt prickles of irritation at his statement, but she quickly patted them down. It was obvious Aidan wasn't needling her anymore or being passive-aggressive. He seemed earnest. He also was offering an insight she hadn't considered.

"Look, I know that the way I've . . . I've handled this may not be the best, but it's not like they give you an instruction manual for this type of thing!" she said.

She looked again at Paul's doppelgänger, who was closing the glass door to the freezer after taking out two canisters of gelato — peppermint bark and chocolate hazelnut. He didn't seem wary of Tracey anymore; he was back to ignoring her. He strolled to the end of the aisle, then disappeared behind a line of shelves. She returned her gaze to Aidan.

"I'm just winging it," she said.

"Hey, I get it! And I'm sure you're doing fine. They seem like good kids, and considering everything, they seem well-adjusted too."

"You think so?"

"Yeah. And . . . uh . . . if you want me to hang out with Caleb a little . . . give him some of that male bonding he may be yearning for, I wouldn't mind."

"*Really?*" For the first time since she had been around Aidan, she smiled at him. It was a real smile, not a forced one. "You would . . . you would do that?"

"Sure. Why not?"

"Well, you didn't seem to want to be around them . . . around *us* when we moved in. I thought maybe you just didn't like kids."

He stared at her. A change washed over his face, an expression she couldn't quite pin down because it flashed so quickly. But within seconds, he was smiling again, and the smile looked genuine. "I like kids, Tracey. I just hate the bratty ones. I wasn't sure what brand you were bringing with you to Harbor Hill, but like I said, now I know for sure they aren't brats. If you need me to help with Caleb, I'm willing."

She stared at him in shock, momentarily struck speechless. Suddenly, Aidan had transformed from a man she loathed to one she could see herself considering as a friend.

"Thank you, Aidan," she whispered, feeling a thaw set in. "Thank you so much!"

"No problem." He held the grocery list aloft. "Now let's get back to shopping."

# CHAPTER 22

"All right," Delilah said as she placed two tin pans filled with sweet potato and pumpkin pie on one of the oven's metal shelves, sending a blast of hot air into her face, filling her nose with a whiff of cinnamon, nutmeg, and sugar.

The children sat at the kitchen island as she did it — Caleb on one of the wooden stools and Maggie in her high chair.

"Now we let them bake for a little more than an hour," she said, closing the oven, setting the digital timer, and turning to them.

"Then what do we do?" Caleb asked.

He and Maggie were licking the remaining bits of pie filling from their fingers and spatulas. It was their reward for helping Delilah make the desserts.

"We reheat them after dinner, and we eat them."

"But what else do we do?"

"What do you mean, honey?"

"I mean what do we do now . . . so we don't get bored?"

"Well . . . I don't know!" Delilah chuckled. "I guess Miss Dee didn't plan that far ahead. I thought your mama would be back by now and she'd keep you occupied," she said as she glanced at the digital clock on the microwave.

It was almost two-thirty. Aidan and Tracey had been gone for more than an hour. Why hadn't they returned from the store yet? She hoped they were finally getting along.

Delilah had sent the two on an errand under the guise of buying groceries she had forgotten, but that wasn't the real reason. She'd done it so they would finally interact with one another, since the two seemed to go out of their way to pretend the other didn't exist. She refused to sit with them at the table tonight with either Aidan conspicuously absent or having to endure a stilted, unsatisfying meal while Aidan and Tracey looked through each other like they were windowpanes. She'd had enough of that childish nonsense.

Delilah guessed that, in some small way, she should be relieved Tracey was the first woman who'd lived at Harbor Hill whom Aidan hadn't tried to bed in quite a while.

Oh, he'd thought Delilah hadn't heard him tiptoeing down the hall to the women's rooms late at night, only to creep back to his room in the wee hours of the morning, but she had. The walls in the bedrooms weren't that thick. At least, he'd had good enough sense and the decency to keep his distance from the more tenderhearted girls. She would've snatched him by the ear and given him a verbal blistering if he'd hadn't, but thankfully, such lectures hadn't been necessary.

Delilah suspected Aidan was sticking his ding-a-ling in just about everything and anything because he wanted to bury his heartache and forget the pain he had left behind in Chicago — but he was a grown man, as he often told her. It wasn't her place to question what he did with his life. Fortunately, Aidan wasn't her concern right now. The children were, and they were staring at her expectantly, waiting for her to give them something to do.

She went over the list in her head of the things she had left to cook, clean, and prepare. All of it was too complicated for the children to assist her.

"I'm sorry. I don't really have anything for you."

"Maybe we can play a game!" Caleb

piped, still sucking his fingers. "Do you have a game we can play, Miss Dee? Toys we could play with?"

"Toys," Maggie echoed before shoving the plastic spatula back into her mouth.

Delilah's brow wrinkled. "You don't want to play with your own toys?"

"We play with those all the time!"

"Well, Miss Dee doesn't really keep toys around the house." She walked toward the island. "But maybe I could —"

"Come on now, Dee! That's not true," Cee whispered, halting her in her steps. "You shouldn't lie to the kiddies. It's not nice to lie, beautiful!"

That's when she remembered it: the chest. The chest with the broken lock in the corner of one of the upstairs bedroom closets. It had been there for more than forty years.

Soon after she'd arrived home to Harbor Hill from prison, Delilah had gone to great lengths to exorcise the house of all symbols of her tortured past. She had given away furniture that had been in the Buford family for decades. She had repainted all the walls herself. She had tossed out everything Cee had owned, with the exception of his old silver flask; she had never found it and therefore couldn't throw it away. The chest was the one thing she hadn't taken to the county dump or given to the local Salvation Army.

"Did you forget what you were about to say, Miss Dee?" Caleb asked.

Delilah blinked at him, abruptly yanked back to the present. "I'm sorry, honey. What did you say?"

"I asked you if you were about to say something and forgot it." He dropped his spatula into a glass bowl, then rested his elbows on the butcher block. "Mommy does that all the time! She said sometimes there's so much going on in her head that she can't think straight."

Delilah laughed again. "No, I didn't forget what I was going to say. I just remembered something I'd forgotten."

Caleb stared at her quizzically. "Huh?"

"Come on," she said, reaching around the island to rub his shoulder. "I'll show you."

Delilah flicked on the light switch on the wall, revealing a plain white, ten-by-ten-foot room with two small, shuttered windows. The room was filled with three-foot-tall towers of cardboard boxes and one solitary wooden desk covered with stacks of yellowing paper and an old Smith Corona typewriter.

While they stood in the doorway, survey-
ing their new surroundings, Bruce strolled
inside the room, sniffing his way through
the maze of boxes.

"Eww! It stinks in here!" Caleb exclaimed,
pinching his nose.

Caleb was right. The guest room did have
a distinct smell — a stale stench born of
dust and cobwebs, of confined spaces that
hadn't been aired out in years.

"Don't let the smell scare you off!" Delilah gave a conspiratorial smile as she carried Maggie inside and beckoned for Caleb
to follow her. "We're here to find hidden
treasure."

Caleb squinted up at her, releasing his
fingers from his nose. "*Hidden treasure?* You
mean like pirates?"

"Yep, and the treasure is in a *real* pirate
chest."

His face lit up.

Delilah hoped the chest wouldn't be too
hard to find, though she knew it was buried
under decades' worth of junk. She hoped
its contents were still in reasonably good
condition too and weren't just measly
remains left behind by moths and dust
mites.

"Stand over there and hold your sister's
hand," Delilah said as she walked toward

the bedroom closet's door. "Miss Dee hasn't opened this closet in who knows how long! There's no telling what might tumble out."

"Okay." Caleb drew Maggie to his side.

Delilah twisted the gold knob and gave the door a hard tug. When it popped open, she jumped back, barely missing getting hit in the head by an old tennis racket and an album cover. The racket caught Bruce on the tail, however, sending him scampering from the room.

"I guess scaredy cat's out," she murmured, before glancing over her shoulder at the remaining duo behind her. "Should we keep going?"

"Yeah," Caleb said, nodding.

She dropped to her knees, listening to her joints crack. Delilah began to dig, fighting her way through the dark closet, through piles of clothes, boxes, and old shopping bags, sneezing and blinking her watery eyes from all the accumulated dust.

"Do you need any help?" Caleb called to her.

She glanced over her shoulder at him, noticing his look of concern.

"No, honey, I'm doing just fine!" she lied as she gulped for air, then winced at the taste of mothballs on her tongue. "I'm almost done anyway."

She finally spotted the chest under a pile of old coats. After several grunts and tugs, she managed to get it out of the closet.

"It *is* a real pirate chest!" Caleb shouted, rushing across the room toward her.

Maggie toddled after him.

Delilah knelt in front of chest, reverently running her hand over the brown leather, gold studs, and latch.

"Let's open it, Miss Dee!" Caleb said, rubbing his hands together eagerly.

Despite his keenness to dig in, Delilah hesitated. Would opening the lid be like opening a time capsule or, worse, Pandora's box? Would a rush of memories and emotions, both good and bad, overwhelm her? Would they be recollections she would cling to forever or ones she would be more than happy to forget? But she had promised the children they could have what was inside the chest. She took a deep breath, bracing herself for the onslaught of whatever she might encounter. She slowly raised the lid.

Delilah noticed the plush yellow bunny first — the one with the button eyes she had purchased from Macy's in New York City during her and Cee's brief honeymoon. Then she saw a stack of lace-trimmed bibs, a mobile that would have hung over her baby's crib, and a Fisher-Price Barky the Dog.

Delilah sniffed. Her eyes began to water again, and this time not because of the dust.

Aidan thought he was the only one who had endured a loss that seemed almost impossible to bounce back from. But she had experienced one too when she lost her baby. To her relief, she felt sadness now, but not the awful pain she had experienced the day the doctor had broken the news to her.

"Wow, look at all the toys!" Caleb yelled.

Delilah eased back, blinking through her tears as Caleb and Maggie dove almost headfirst into the chest.

She watched their pure joy at discovering the new toys, how they marveled at them like they were objects from some alien planet. Soon her sadness shifted to laughter as she watched Maggie wrap a baby blanket around her waist and pretend to do the hula.

"Thank you, Miss Dee!" Caleb said, kissing her cheek, catching her off guard and making her grin. He then grabbed Barky the Dog and began to tug him around the room by the string, making yips and barks. "This is cool!"

That's when something in her broke. She couldn't hold back the tears anymore, but at least they were happy ones.

■ ■ ■ ■

By the time Tracey and Aidan finally arrived home from the grocery store, the children were in the living room, and the toys were strewn everywhere. The kids were lost in play, having erected a multicolor dream coat of a tent from all of Delilah's old knitted blankets and quilts. Caleb had proclaimed that the stuffed bunny and a few of the other toys were now at war, and the tent was their fort.

"Where'd you guys get all this stuff?" Tracey called out, snatching Delilah's attention. She stood in the doorway, watching the chaos with amused interest.

Delilah pushed herself up from her wing chair. "I found it upstairs. They were a few old things that I had. I handed them over to the children, and well" — she gestured to the cluttered room — "they ran with it."

"I can see!" Tracey said, stepping into the living room. "Well, thank you for watching them. I'm sorry we were gone for so long, but we wanted to make sure we got everything on your list."

"Oh, no worries, honey! Thank you for going. So everything went okay?"

Still smiling at the children, Tracey nodded absently. "Sure! It went fine."

Delilah continued to eye her, trying to decide if the young woman was only putting on a façade and pretending the shopping trip had gone smoothly. Tracey must have heard her silent question. She shrugged.

"Well, we had a little hiccup, but Aidan and I . . . we worked it out."

"*Hiccup?* What hiccup?"

Tracey shook her head. "Don't worry about it. Like I said . . . we worked it out." She strolled toward the tent and stooped down so that she could see through the parted, makeshift curtain. She rested her hands on her knees. "Can I come in?" she sang.

"What's the password?" Caleb's muffled voice asked through the curtain.

"Mommy is awesome?"

"Wrong!" Caleb replied.

"Is it . . . Mommy is the best mommy ever?" Tracey asked, yanking open the curtain, revealing her children, who were doubled over with giggles.

"No!" Caleb squealed.

"Well, I'm coming in anyway!" Tracey yelled, making monster sounds and crouching on all fours as she barged inside their tent. The children laughed even harder.

Delilah gazed at them, taking it all in. She wondered if Tracey realized how radiant she looked with the children in her arms. She wished she could take a picture and show it to her later.

"Whenever you're frightened . . . whenever you're sad, remember this moment," she would tell her, handing her the photo.

But instead, Delilah walked out of the living room in search of Aidan — her other concern. As she neared the front of the house, she heard the sound of his truck door slamming shut. She found him walking up the porch steps, carrying the last of the plastic grocery bags in both hands.

"You two had a hiccup?"

He frowned, stopping in his tracks. "Huh?"

"Tracey said you had a hiccup but 'worked it out.' What hiccup? What happened?"

Aidan rolled his eyes. "Nothing happened, Dee. Everything is fine! Stop worrying."

She dropped her hands to her hips. "I'm not worrying! I'm just —"

"Yes, you are. You worry about everything and everyone. You wouldn't know what to do with yourself if you weren't worrying." He paused in the doorway. "But everything is fine — I promise."

She stared up at him, hearing a tone in

his voice and a look in his hazel eyes she hadn't witnessed in quite a while. He actually looked . . . happy. She guessed the shopping trip had gone better than she'd thought.

"I'll set these in the kitchen and then get started on the stuff in the garage," he said, brushing her shoulder as he walked into the house. "Let me know if you need me to do anything else."

Delilah stared after him, then turned to face the driveway. She rubbed her arms against the chill and squinted into the sunshine.

Could things really be taking a turn for the better? After all these years, could she finally put her mind at rest, be at peace?

*Everything is fine,* she thought.

She then repeated the words aloud.

"Everything is fine. There is nothing to worry about."

Delilah tried to let the sense of peace wash over her, to let it sink in and fill her up, but a niggling sense of apprehension lingered. She just couldn't relax. She chuckled.

"Maybe I should take up that yoga like Tracey. Maybe that would help me."

She turned back to head inside the house, but paused when something caught her eye at the foot of the stairs. It looked like a small, white sheet of paper. It was probably the receipt from Milton's Grocer that had tumbled from one of the bags, she speculated.

Delilah could never stomach littering and, even worse, trash on her pristine lawn. She sauntered down the wooden stairs, leaned down with a grunt, and grabbed the sheet of paper. She began to shove it into the pocket of her sweater, but stopped short when she noticed the words scribbled in black ink:

This house is NOT YOURS. You DO NOT belong here! GET OUT, MURDERER!!!

# CHAPTER 23

In the course of six weeks, Aidan found four letters around the Harbor Hill property. Today, he found another.

The letters were rotten Easter eggs hidden in the most random of places — taped to the underside of the lid of a recyclables bin or stuffed inside the bird feeder in the center of the driveway. He had even found one on the kid's play set about a month ago, on Christmas day, sitting at the top of the yellow slide under a rock, like a present left behind by Santa Claus. Thankfully, he had discovered it before the children had come out to play that day. He had kept it in his jeans pocket as he tossed a football to Caleb and pushed Maggie on the swing.

His initial reaction to the letters was annoyance. Aidan had known about Delilah's criminal past for most of his life. It was impossible to have lived in Camden Beach and not heard some whispers about it. She had never hidden it from him or his mother, and they had accepted her tear-filled explanation when they had questioned her about it.

"You judge people for what they do . . . how they treat you, *mijo*!" Aidan's mother had told him. "Not for what they've done." And Delilah had always been kind and protective of him.

But he knew not everyone felt the same way. That was evident from the content of these letters. And with the discovery of each new note, he felt an ominous foreboding. His stomach would drop, and his lips would form into a grim line. He wondered who the culprit was. Was it an angry neighbor or a stranger in town? Why were they doing this? Why now?

Delilah was content to pretend the letters didn't exist.

When he'd shown her the first set, she'd gotten a look on her face like she was going to be sick and upchuck right there on the kitchen's terra-cotta-tiled floor. He had instantly regretted showing them to her, wondering if, despite the medication she was taking, she would freak out again and start raving like that time in the pantry closet. But instead, she had regained her composure. She'd pushed back her shoulders and taken a deep breath.

"I found one too about a month ago," she'd announced, making him stare at her in amazement.

"Wait. You found one too? Well, why didn't you say anything, Dee?"

"There was nothing to say. It's all nonsense! Just rip them up and throw them in the trash." She'd shoved the paper back at him and turned away, refusing to look at the letter again.

"We can't rip them up! We have to show them to the police or . . . or someone. It's evidence!"

"Evidence of what?"

"Evidence of systematic harassment, Dee. Someone is obviously stalking you!"

She'd sucked her teeth in response. "The cops don't care! You think this is the first time this has happened? I used to get letters like that all the time . . . *worse* than that, calling me all kinds of things! Nigger . . . coon . . . bitch . . . You name it! I told the police, and you know what they did? Absolutely nothing! It comes and it goes, Aidan. It'll stop — eventually. Besides, if I tell the police, what if it gets back to Tracey? The poor girl has enough on her plate. She came here for peace and quiet! I won't have her worrying about whether some wacko is creeping around the house at night while the babies are asleep!"

He'd stood in front of her, staring at the letters in his hands and thinking about those angry words. He'd wanted to dismiss them like Delilah, but something didn't feel right. He'd slowly shaken his head. "This could be serious, Dee. What if —"

"Enough, Aidan! I'm done talking about it! Just get rid of them!" she'd snapped before leaving him alone in the kitchen.

After that, Aidan stopped showing Delilah the letters, but the lawyer in him wouldn't allow him to throw them away like she'd said. He sealed them in a plastic bag that he stuffed in the bottom of a dresser drawer. He added each new note to the growing stack. Every now and then, he would examine them, rereading each word. He'd felt the urge to talk about the letters with Tracey, to ask her what she thought about all this, but so far he hadn't done that.

He and Tracey talked a lot nowadays — over cups of coffee in the morning, in the living room after the children went to bed, or standing on the back porch, watching the children as they played. Their conversations weren't like the ones he'd had with the other women who lived at Harbor Hill. With them, it felt less like a chat and more like a therapy session, with Aidan playing the therapist, patiently listening and interjecting a few words while they rambled. But Tracey wasn't comfortable with his extended silences. She constantly asked him questions.

At first, it had felt as if she was prodding at a sore tooth, and he'd wince before beginning a story about himself, but after a while, he became more loquacious. Some stories he still wasn't brave enough to tell. Whenever they wandered onto the topic of his life in Chicago and his marriage to Trish, he would steer the conversation in another direction. But he still told her a lot; he told her more than he told most people.

And once again, he felt the urge to confess to her. He read the note in his hand, "GET OUT, you LYING MURDERER!" and exhaled.

Aidan wondered if it would it escalate past letters, whether this was benign or if he really should be concerned. Would a rock come crashing through the living room bay window one morning? Would they find tires slashed or a burning bag of dog poop on the front porch?

"Hey! What are you up to?" Tracey said from behind him, startling him.

He quickly shoved the letter into this coat pocket and turned to face her. He painted on a smile. "Nothing. Just . . . uh . . .

daydreaming. What's up?"

"Delilah is keeping the kids occupied with a craft project to give me a breather. I came out to ask you if you wanted to go for a walk."

"Sure! Lead the way." He gestured toward the yard and the path they usually took.

She nodded and stepped forward, raising the zipper of her coat and pushing her hair out of her eyes. Aidan tried his best not to stare at her.

He had predicted Harbor Hill would physically transform Tracey. Aidan had seen it enough times — the way the women looked so much better after the weight of the world was lifted from their shoulders. Their hair would take on a luster and a bounce. Their skin would glisten. Skinny frames and hollow cheeks would fill out, and hefty bodies would become strong and lean. But Tracey wasn't just pretty now — she was downright beautiful. She also smiled and laughed readily, enhancing that beauty even more. She'd taken on an almost ethereal glow.

"So," she began over the sound of frozen grass and strewn leaves crunching underfoot and the rumble of the bay in the distance, "I wanted to get your opinion on something."

"Shoot."

"I was . . . I was thinking of signing up for courses at the local community college in Prince Frederick."

She cut her eyes at him after that, like she was waiting for him to voice an argument against it. He didn't.

"I was a few credits shy of my degree when I left school to have Cabe, and I figured that now might be a good time to finally take those classes. I'm saving money living here, and Delilah watches the kids for me. The semester started last week, but I wouldn't be that far behind if I started now. I could take one or two classes, if they still have spots available, and see how it goes." She glanced at him again. "What do you think?"

"I think it's a good idea! You'll never know when you'll get an opportunity to do something like this again. Living at Harbor Hill comes with its advantages. I'd seize them if I were you."

"Famous last words!" She pushed the strands of hair blowing into her face out of her eyes and nudged him playfully with her shoulder. It was an innocent gesture, but even through the wool of his jacket he felt the tingle of her touch. "You may not be so eager for me to take classes in the evenings when Caleb is bored and bugging you for attention. Maggie too."

"I can take it," he said — and he truly meant it.

It hadn't taken him long to become attached to the kids. He still felt a slight ache when he looked at Maggie, a tug of remembrances, but it was nothing compared to what he had experienced when the trio first arrived at Harbor Hill. He liked Maggie and her silly little ways. He enjoyed his time with Caleb.

"Maybe I'll take them out one evening when you need to study. He's been begging me to take him to a basketball game."

"I don't know how well Maggie would do at an arena."

He shrugged as they walked and squinted at the setting sun that filled the sky with broad strokes of orange, red, purple, and blue. The bright colors refracted off the bay's choppy water. "Okay, well, maybe we'll just make the basketball game a guys' thing. I'll have to figure out something else for Maggie."

"That's sweet of you."

He shrugged again. "It's no problem."

"No, really." She grabbed his arm, halting him in his steps. "Thank you, Aidan! I know I've said thank you before, but I mean it.

You've been so kind to the kids — Cabe especially. You're one of the reasons he's so happy here. I think he likes you almost as much as the Incredible Hulk."

Aidan chuckled. "Well, that's quite an honor."

"I think he always wanted to do the sort of things he does with you, with his dad. He wanted Paul to take him to basketball games. He wanted to build things with him, to play football, and Paul did it sometimes, but it wasn't really his . . . his thing, you know?" She pursed her lips. "He was the provider. I was the nurturer. I thought that's how it worked. I thought it was what our family needed."

Aidan grimaced, not at her words, but at the memory of the dynamics in his own marriage. He and Trish had played similar roles. She had her job and he had his, and he thought they were doing their jobs well — until it all fell apart.

He watched as Tracey let go of his arm. She started to walk again, so he followed suit, watching as the wind made her dark hair whip around her shoulders. Her lower lip trembled before she caught it between her teeth.

"When I think about all the . . . all the shit that I put up with . . ." She squeezed her eyes shut so tightly that the pale lids started to jitter. "When I think about . . . about the days I felt like utter hell and how I let myself become a punching bag! I used to fantasize about hanging myself just so I could make it all stop. I put myself through agony because I thought Paul was giving me, giving *us* what we needed . . . the life we wanted. I thought it was worth the sacrifice, and now I realize I was all wrong!" She opened her eyes and looked off into the distance, at the roiling sea. It and the sun were reflected in her big, dark eyes. "I wasn't happy. The kids weren't happy. Why didn't I realize it back then? Why did I stay so long?"

"Hey," he said, grabbing her hand, forcing her to turn to look at him again, "you did the best that you could, okay? Not everyone could've survived what you went through, let alone find the courage to finally leave. Don't beat yourself up about it!"

"Who else should I beat up?"

"Your husband, maybe. Or all male kind! We're pretty shitty creatures, to be honest."

She squeezed his hand back. "*You're* not."

"You're giving me too much credit. You should've seen who I was five years ago."

"Were you hitting your wife? Were you covering her with bruises? If not, you were still miles ahead of Paul."

"No, I never would've done that to Trish. Never! But . . ."

He lowered his head, no longer able to meet her gaze. They were talking about the past again. They were treading onto ice that was so thin he feared he might fall through.

"But what?"

"But I was . . . selfish, driven . . . emotionally stunted; at least that's what Trish told our counselor. You wouldn't have liked me."

"Now who's beating themselves up?" she whispered.

"No, Trish was right. That's who I was, and she deserved better. She needed me, and I wasn't . . . I wasn't ready to put her first. To put our family first. I wish I could've . . ." His words drifted off. He gazed at the grass beneath their feet.

"You wish you could've what?"

"I wish I could've been better to her, better for her."

*Every day, forever and ever,* he thought. He knew now it was the wishes that could never be fulfilled that you longed for the most.

Maybe that's why he tried so hard with all the other women at Harbor Hill. He didn't just want them to feel comfortable around him; he'd wanted to embody their every hope, every desire. He would mold himself into whatever they needed at that point in their lives — from a passionate impresario to a tender boyfriend — because he had fallen so pitifully short of what Trish had needed. All he had done was disappoint her.

Tracey placed a gloved hand on his cheek, catching him off guard. "If being the guy you were then helped you become the man you are now, I'd think it was worth the journey if I were you, Aidan."

He was struck mute by her words, too overwhelmed by emotion to speak.

Aidan had never hugged Tracey before, let alone tried to kiss her. He often wondered why he was so reserved with her. He had never been like this with the others. It certainly wasn't because of lack of desire for Tracey, because that is what he felt as she trailed her thumb over his beard stubble, as she looked into his eyes. Something was holding him back.

He knew that, unlike the others, Tracey wasn't just looking for a respite. She wouldn't lie with a man one night and then pretend nothing had happened the next day. If he started something with her, it would be different than what he had done with the other women. This would be something more — a real romantic relationship, some-

thing he hadn't experienced since Trish —
and the idea terrified him.

After all this time, could he take that leap?

She dropped her hand from his face and
glanced in the direction of the house. "We
should head back. I bet Delilah is waiting
for us. Are you ready?"

He slowly nodded. "I think I am," he said,
lowering his mouth to hers for their first
kiss.

# CHAPTER 24

Could someone subsist on panic and desperation? Could they eat it like bread or drink it like water? Could they breathe it like air?

Tracey had inwardly posed this question before, and had decided the answer was yes. Fortunately, she wasn't on that diet anymore.

"Hot fudge or whipped cream, big guy?" she asked Caleb as they all stood around the kitchen island, laughing and making sundaes.

It had been Delilah's idea: sundaes for a Sunday evening treat.

"I want both!" Caleb shouted gleefully, bouncing on the balls of his feet, slapping his palms on the granite. "Both!"

"Someone's greedy," Aidan said with a smirk, licking melted strawberry ice cream from his spoon.

Tracey gazed up at him from the other

side of the island, meeting his eyes and giving a knowing smile. "Nothing's wrong with being a little greedy."

She certainly was. She was gobbling freedom and happiness by the forkful. Even the folks she worked with at the hotel and resort noticed the difference in her. One of the grizzled old waitresses had eyed her only yesterday, asking her why she was "humming like some Disney princess."

When Tracey had told she was just in a good mood, the old woman had smiled knowingly.

"Could've fooled me, kid," she'd said. "Could've sworn you were in love!"

Tracey hadn't responded at the time, but she thought about that comment for the rest of the day, pondering over it during her drive home yesterday. She'd pulled into the driveway at Harbor Hill and seen Aidan standing on the front porch, changing the motion detection light. He'd lifted his hand and waved at her. He'd grinned, and a heat spread across her chest. A flush had risen to her cheeks and along her neck.

She'd wondered, *Am I in love?*

Tracey certainly had all the symptoms. She thought about Aidan constantly and couldn't wait for the end of the workday when she would see him again. During their walks, they would talk and talk, about big things and little things, about their hopes and fears. She would lean into him as he looped his arm around her waist. She would rest her head on his shoulder and gaze dreamily into his eyes. Then they would kiss, and she would flash back to the moment when he had first kissed her a month ago, and everything would explode on the inside.

She hadn't felt this way in years, not since the early days when she and Paul started going out. It made her happy but wary, excited yet scared. Was she ready to fall in love again?

She guessed it didn't matter. It wasn't like she had a choice.

"All right. Let's clean up," Tracey said, grabbing one of the sponges. "Miss Dee was nice enough to let us make sundaes. We don't want to leave a mess."

"But I'm tired!" Caleb whined, stomping his foot.

She opened her mouth to argue with him, but Aidan interceded before she could.

"You heard your mother, Cabe. Clean up. We're all doing it together."

Caleb started to pout, and Tracey prepared herself for more whining and maybe even tears, but she watched in surprise as he grudgingly reached for one of the sponges and started to wipe smears of ice cream and caramel from the island's butcher block surface.

"Good job," Aidan said, ruffling his hair.

By nine o'clock, the children were washed and tucked in their beds, slumbering blissfully in sugar comas. Tracey, however, was wide awake. She pattered down the hall in bare feet and gently knocked on Aidan's door. He opened it a few seconds later. She could see he was already bedding down for the night: The lights were off, but the television was still on. He was wearing only a tank top and sweatpants that hung low on his hips.

She smiled shyly up at him.

"I just wanted to say good night," she whispered.

Then, before she lost her nerve, she stood on the balls of her feet, intending to give him a quick peck.

She was hesitant to kiss him with Delilah and the children nearby. Neither had told anyone about their budding relationship, and Tracey still wasn't sure when would be the best time to do it.

But Aidan didn't seem content with a peck. He wrapped his arms around her and drew her close. He teased her lips so that she opened her mouth and the kiss deepened. They were both panting by the time she finally pulled away.

"We have to stop," she whispered.

"You're right." He kissed her brow. "Good night, Trace." He then stepped back into his bedroom and shut the door behind him.

Tracey walked back down the hall to her room with her fingers pressed to her lips. She sat down on her bed, still trying to regain her breath. She closed her eyes, replaying the kiss in her mind. The truth was she hadn't wanted to stop. She yearned for more — more kissing, more touching. She wondered what it would be like to have sex with Aidan. Would he be a tender lover or rough and commanding? Would he help her remember the woman she used to be before the slaps and the name calling, before Paul?

She sat awake in bed past midnight mulling over it. She tossed and turned. Her body seemed to vibrate with unspent need and desire. She couldn't get comfortable. She couldn't sleep.

At about one o'clock, she eased from her bed and rose to her feet. She opened her door, wincing at the creaking hinges. She peered into the hallway and found it empty, which was no surprise. Only ghostly moonlight pierced the blinds of the windows along the corridor.

Her heart was pounding so fast she could hear the blood whistling in her ears. The floorboards creaked beneath her feet as she walked. With each step, Tracey battled dueling voices: one that told her to go back to bed and not make a fool of herself, and another that told her to seek what she wanted. Finally, she reached Aidan's door. She stared at the wooden slab, drawing up her courage.

"Do it on the count of ten," she whispered and then began counting in her head.

When she reached ten, she raised her fist to knock. She closed her eyes, hoping it would be easier if she didn't have to watch herself do it.

"Mommy?" a sleepy voice called to her in the dark.

Her eyes flashed opened, and she looked down to find Caleb standing in his doorway in his pajamas. He was rubbing his eyes.

"What is it, honey?" she asked, quickly lowering her raised fist, hoping she didn't look guilty.

"Mommy, I had a bad dream," he moaned. His round face crumbled. He looked close to tears.

She rushed toward him and rubbed his shoulders reassuringly. "It's okay. You know it was just a dream, sweetheart. Go back to sleep. You'll be fine."

"Will you sit with me until I fall to sleep?" he asked, yawning and rubbing his eyes.

"Sure, honey," she whispered, before ushering him back into his bedroom and giving one last wistful glance at Aidan's closed door.

# CHAPTER 25

Though she would find out later that Aidan had shouted her name a few times before she woke up, it was a rough shake to the shoulder that finally did it. Delilah slowly opened her eyes, squinting against the morning light streaming through her plantation shutters. She yawned and smacked her lips. When she rolled over, she found Aidan looming at the edge of the bed, wearing a hoodie and jeans. He hadn't shaved. His face was gaunt and pale. His skin looked almost ashen against the gray of his pullover.

"I'm sorry for waking you up like this, Dee, but you have to see it."

"See what?" she croaked, rubbing her eyes. "What's wrong?"

He lowered his gaze to the hardwood floor and shoved his hands into his pockets.

"What is it?" she asked, pushing herself up to her elbows and shoving off her comforter. Her skin prickled with goose bumps at the cold air and the fright he was giving her. "Good Lord, just tell me, Aidan!"

His shoulders rose then fell as he exhaled. He turned away from her and headed to her bedroom door. "It's outside. Throw on your robe and your coat. It's cold out there. I'll wait for you in the hall."

She watched, confused, as he softly closed the door behind him. Delilah turned to Bruce, who was perched on one of her decorative pillows, licking between his claws.

"Do you know what he's talking about?" she asked.

Bruce paused from his grooming to stare at her quizzically, then returned his attention to his paw.

"Well, you'll never find out until you go see, now will you?" her dead husband prodded.

When Delilah walked out the front door five minutes later, raising the collar of her coat against the chill and tightening her belt around her waist, she found Aidan, Tracey, and the children standing in the driveway. Aidan's arms were crossed over his chest. Tracey was holding Maggie, who was wearing rubber duckie PJs underneath her coat, in one arm; the other arm was wrapped around Caleb's shoulders. They were all staring at the garage.

"Who did this, Mommy?" Caleb asked, glancing up at his mother.

Tracey didn't answer him but instead continued to frown.

Delilah rushed down the front porch steps, nearly stumbling in her slippers. She turned around to see what they were looking at. When she did, she gaped.

The word was written on the garage door in two-foot-tall letters: MURDERER.

"Well, well, well," Cee whispered, then chuckled. "Whoever did this certainly has a flare for the dramatic, wouldn't you say?"

It was painted in a garish red, and some of the paint had oozed and dripped down the garage panels so it looked like it had been written in blood. Seeing it, Delilah quickly went from shock to confusion, then finally she felt real anger. She was angry that someone had done this to her home and, more importantly, had left it behind for all the world to see, including Maggie and Caleb. Innocent children shouldn't witness something like this.

She quickly turned to Tracey, wincing at the kids' bewildered expressions.

"I'm so sorry, honey," she whispered.

"What? Why are *you* sorry?" Tracey asked, squinting at her. "You didn't ask for this, Dee. Some . . . some horrible person did

352

this to you!"

"I told you we should've called the cops when we first got those letters," Aidan said, stepping toward them, gesturing to the garage door. "Now look what's happened! This is insane!"

"Wait . . . letters. What letters?" Tracey asked, her frown deepening

"Nothing." Delilah shook her head. "It's nothing."

"No, it's not nothing! Tell her the truth, Dee!"

"Aidan," she began warningly, glaring up at him.

He rolled his eyes, ignoring her. "In almost two months, Dee has gotten five or six letters from some . . . I don't know . . . psycho who obviously is not letting up," he explained to Tracey, whose expression changed. She now looked scared, something Delilah had been trying to avoid. "It's just gonna get worse if we continue to sit around pretending like what's happening here isn't happening!"

"You don't know that for sure!" Delilah argued.

"No, I don't. But I do know that it's time to finally get the police involved. Look at what they did, Dee! We can't keep . . ."

His words trailed off when they heard the

sound of a car engine, then the crunching of gravel under tires. They turned around simultaneously as a silver BMW sailed up the driveway. When Delilah saw who was in the driver's seat, she grumbled.

"Oh, not now," she muttered under her breath.

She watched as the BMW lurched to a stop a few feet away from where they stood. The door flew open, even though the engine was still running. Teddy leapt out, shoving his RayBans to the crown of his head. He staggered toward them, gawking like some five-year-old seeing a high-wire act for the first time.

She hadn't seen him in several months, not since they had spoken at the grocery store. Teddy had called the house a few times since then, inquiring over voice mail whether she had given any further thought to his offer to buy Harbor Hill. But each time, she would delete his message. There was no point in responding when her answer was still the same. She guessed he had gotten tired of being ignored.

"What on earth!" Teddy shouted, pointing at the words on the garage door. "What is that?"

"What does it look like?" Delilah answered dryly, wishing he would just climb back into his car and go home.

"Why would someone do this? Oh, Ms. Grey!" He pitched forward and grabbed Delilah's hand in his leather-clad one. Before she had a chance to respond, he yanked her into a bear hug, almost smothering her against the shearling wool of his coat lapel and overwhelming her with his heavy cologne. "I'm so sorry this has happened to you! Is there anything I can do?"

It didn't take her long to regain her bearings. She quickly shoved herself out of his grasp and tugged her hand back.

"Thank you for your offer but no, we don't need your help. We have it covered." She pushed back her shoulders and turned to Aidan, who still had a bleak expression on his face, like he was attending a funeral. "Do we have enough paint thinner in the shed to take it all off?"

"*Take it all off?* Dee, I'm not taking it off! We're showing this to the cops! I told you that already."

"I'm friendly with the sheriff," Teddy piped. "He and I are golfing buddies. If you want me to reach out to him, I can —"

"No," she said firmly, shaking her head. "No, I do not."

"Dee, come on!" Aidan groaned. "This is getting ridiculous! We have to —"

"I said, no! Didn't you hear me? *No,* dammit!" she screamed.

Her voice echoed in all directions, bouncing off the side of the house, the trees, and even — it seemed — off the canopy of the sky up above. It sounded like a thousand Delilahs shouting at the same time.

At her outburst, Teddy and Aidan fell silent, staring at her uneasily. Tracey winced, and Caleb cowered against his mother's side, burying his face in her coat. A startled Maggie began to cry, letting out strangled sobs.

"Shsssh! It's okay, honey," Tracey cooed to Maggie, kissing her cheek.

Seeing their faces, Delilah felt a wave of regret and shame. She hadn't wanted to scare anyone. She didn't want to look crazy. But in their eyes, she saw the judgment that had haunted her for decades. They reflected every frightened glance, every person who shrank back from her when she passed by them on the street. This is exactly what she'd wanted to avoid.

"You can run, but you can't hide, Dee," Cee whispered. "They all know what you really are."

"I'm . . . I'm sorry," she said shakily, clearing her throat, feeling her eyes burn with tears. "I'm so sorry. I'm just . . ."

She didn't finish. Instead, she turned and fled to the sanctuary of the house, running up the wooden stairs and not looking back as the screen door slammed shut behind her.

A few hours later, Delilah heard a knock at her bedroom door.

She was reclining on her bed with the shutters drawn. The only light in her room came from the television, whose flickering images danced across her face. Despite his protests, she knew Aidan was trying his best to remove the paint from the garage door as she'd asked. She'd heard him clomping to and from the shed in the backyard. Even now, she could hear a rhythmic scraping against the side of the house.

"Dee, it's me," Tracey called out, knocking on her door again. "Are you busy?"

Delilah tiredly closed her eyes, which were puffy from the tears she had shed in a fit of frustration. She opened them and pushed herself upright, adjusting the pillows behind her. "No, I'm not busy. You can come in."

The door slowly creaked open, and Tracey stepped inside, shutting the door behind her. She bent down to pet Bruce, who rubbed himself against her pants leg, purring softly.

"You didn't come down for breakfast or lunch," she said as she sat on the edge of Delilah's bed and gazed at her. Worry marred her pretty face. "The kids missed you."

"I wasn't hungry, honey," Delilah whispered.

Tracey nodded. "After what happened this morning, I can imagine."

Delilah didn't respond.

"Dee, can I ask you something?"

"Go ahead."

"Is there a reason why you don't want Aidan to call the police, that you don't want them to figure out who's doing this to you?"

"It's too hard to explain, honey."

How could she explain that she had learned not to trust cops back in the old days, when many in Camden Beach knew Cee was abusing her, but did nothing? How could she explain that the only time the police had come to her home to put anyone in handcuffs, it was her, after she had discovered Cee's dead body? And during those years after she was released, the local cops had known she was being harassed and threatened, but had turned a blind eye to it all — how could she explain this?

She didn't trust the police. She didn't want to have anything to do with them and would rather they had nothing to do with her.

"I just . . . I just want to put that part of my past behind me," she said weakly, hoping her answer would soothe the young woman. "I hate that this nonsense is dredging it back up."

"Look, Dee, I want you to know that I'm incredibly thankful for everything you've done for me, Cabe, and Maggie. When I was getting kicked out of my home, you gave us a place to stay. You didn't ask any questions or for anything in return. You've supported me and been like a second grandmother to my kids . . . in fact, you're better than their actual grandmother! So I don't care what anyone else says about you. I . . . I know who you are." She reached out and grabbed Delilah's wrinkled hand and squeezed it. "You're a kind, giving, wonderful woman."

Delilah closed her eyes again. She wanted to believe her. For many years, Delilah had certainly tried to prove to herself and to the world that she was all those things. But life still seemed hellbent on punishing her. If she was such a kind, giving, wonderful person, why did she still feel like she was in prison, even though she had been released more than forty years ago? When would she finally atone for her sins?

"I know you're not a murderer," Tracey whispered, leaning toward Delilah.

Delilah's eyes snapped opened when she heard that ugly word. She stared at Tracey, shocked to hear it on the young woman's lips.

"I have a confession to make." Tracey's dark eyes drifted to the velvet comforter. "Before I moved in, I . . . I read a few old newspaper articles. I'd heard about what happened to you . . . and . . . and your husband. I had to make sure the kids would be safe here." She started to gnaw her lower lip. "I feel so stupid now . . . stupid that I doubted you. But the articles explained everything." She looked at Delilah again. "I looked at your picture from the trial, and I saw you with your bowed head and that lost look in your eyes. I saw you and I knew. I knew it *had* to have been an accident."

Again, Delilah didn't respond. Instead, she stared at their interlocked fingers.

"I was right, wasn't I? It *was* an accident . . . wasn't it, Dee?"

It was a simple question that warranted a simple answer, but Delilah couldn't give one. She couldn't answer "Yes, it was an accident" or "No, I meant to kill him." Not anymore — though she had been sure of her answer way back when.

"I didn't do it!" she had shouted to the officers, even as they had placed her in handcuffs and dragged her across the foyer to her opened door. They hadn't even let her put on shoes. The cruiser had been waiting, with the back door open, only a few feet away from Harbor Hill's porch steps. "It had to be an accident!" she'd screamed. "He fell! I didn't do it!"

But Delilah wasn't so sure of that now. Time hadn't sharpened the focus of her memory but made it blurrier. She could no longer divorce intentions from actions, what she had wished for versus what had really happened. Her memories were made no longer of concrete, but of the same gauzy filament as dreams.

The truth was she'd secretly wanted Cee dead. She had wanted to be rid of the man she had once cared for and maybe even loved after enduring his countless beatings and constant berating. That night back in 1969, when she had woken up at the top of the stairs and found his crumpled body at the bottom, she could no longer recall if she had accidentally shoved him, or if she had stood at the top of the staircase, watching as he tumbled below. Had she fallen, tripped, and knocked herself out running away from him, or had she done that only after she had shoved him and heard the crunch signaling that his spine was severed?

"I don't . . . I don't know," she finally answered, making Tracey blink. The younger woman released her hand. "I just don't know anymore. But I *do* know that I will regret what happened for the rest of my life."

# CHAPTER 26

The word painted on the garage door was the first sign that things had changed at Harbor Hill for Tracey. The second was Emma Lynn's arrival.

The busty bottle blonde showed up at the house on a day that Tracey was already struggling to stay afloat. Maggie had developed a bad cough that had kept both the toddler and Tracey up for most of the night. Tracey was also two days into her period, and no amount of chocolate and ice cream seemed to appease her bad mood. She was sleep-deprived and ill-tempered when Emma Lynn came clomping up Harbor Hill's front porch, toting a duffel bag, a suitcase, and a 100-watt smile.

"Hi, I'm Emma Lynn . . . . Emma Lynn Rose," she gushed when Tracey answered the door. She yanked off her sunglasses and adjusted the straps of the purse and the bag on her shoulder. "Is *Miss Dee* around?"

Tracey nodded weakly, taking in the woman in front of her wearing the garish orange jacket, skintight jeans, and pink cowboy boots.

"Uh, y-yes. She's in the kitchen. Let me get her for you and tell her that you're —"

"Oh, no need for that, hon," Emma Lynn said before barging past her into the foyer. "Miss Dee knows me. I'll just see myself in. Miss Dee!" she shouted before dropping her duffel bag and suitcase to the floor. "Miss Dee! It's Emma Lynn! I've come to visit!"

That night, Emma Lynn revealed that she had been one of many women to stay at Harbor Hill over the years. Two years ago, she had spent six months there after a brief stint in prison for embezzling money from the funeral home where she worked. Her prison term had left her without a job and a home, and disowned by her family. Delilah had been the only one willing to take her in. Emma Lynn professed she was now on the straight and narrow and had a good job as a waitress in Baton Rouge, a cute little apartment, and a boyfriend who stayed on an oil rig out in the Gulf for half the year. She said she was on her way to visit an old high school friend in New Jersey and decided to stop by Harbor Hill to see Delilah.

"I'd just thought I'd stick around a day or two, if you wouldn't mind, Miss Dee," Emma Lynn said over dinner before shoving a forkful of mashed potatoes into her mouth. "I've just missed you so much!"

"Of course you can stay, honey!" Delilah assured before taking the chair beside her and giving her a hug. "Stay as long as you like!"

But "one to two days" soon turned to three . . . then four . . . then *five.* After a while, Tracey started to wonder just how long Emma Lynn intended to stay at Harbor Hill, though she knew it wasn't her place to ask. It was Delilah's home, not Tracey's.

Tracey also started to wonder if it was really Delilah whom Emma Lynn had missed — or Aidan. She noticed how Emma Lynn made a habit of visiting him when he worked in the shed. She'd trot out there with hips swinging and two cold beers in hand. She would linger by the shed for more than an hour. Tracey had caught Emma Lynn hanging out in the doorway of Aidan's bedroom at night, laughing and joking with him.

"She's flirting with you," Tracey said to Aidan during one of their walks.

"That's just Emma Lynn." He drew her close, and she sank into his warmth and inhaled his smell — a mix of aftershave, wool, and sawdust. He rubbed her shoulder reassuringly. "She's just a flirt. She does it with every guy."

"So you two were never . . . you know . . . together? You were never a couple?"

He paused mid-stride and stared down at her, narrowing his hazel eyes. "Why are you asking?"

She shrugged casually, trying to mask emotions that left her anxious and confused.

She had known Aidan for only a few months, and they had been secretly dating for just a few weeks. And she was married. Despite all that, Tracey's heart still believed she had some claim to Aidan. She couldn't help but feel a prickle of jealousy and anger when she saw Emma Lynn standing in his bedroom doorway in a tank top and pink yoga pants with the word JUICY stenciled across her butt, giggling like some schoolgirl. She'd wanted to tell her to back off, to yell that Aidan was hers and hers only, but the impulse had felt ridiculous. She knew she would look like a fool.

"I just . . . I just wanted to know," she whispered, her cheeks coloring with embarrassment. "If you and she were a couple, it's not a big —"

"No, we were never like that. We were just

buddies — good buddies. That's all," he said before leaning down to brush his lips across hers. "Nothing for you to worry about."

"Who said I was worried?" she asked with a forced smile before he gave her one searing kiss, then another, making her forget her doubts and unease.

Finally, after a full week, Emma Lynn announced she was leaving Harbor Hill. She said she would be on the road by noon. Delilah made a big farewell breakfast in Emma Lynn's honor — waffles, pancakes, omelets, bacon, sausage, and eggs. Tracey was in a surprisingly good mood, doling out food with a grin on her face.

Of course, Emma Lynn wasn't on the road by noon, like she'd promised, but her bags were packed and sitting in the foyer, and by five o'clock, the bags finally made their way to her car.

When Delilah pulled dinner out of the oven, Tracey heard Emma Lynn's car engine, signifying that she was finally leaving.

"Caleb, can you help me set the table, honey?" Delilah asked as she stood on the balls of her feet, revealing worn, cracked soles over the heels of her slippers. She opened one of the overhead cabinets and began to remove plates from the shelves.

Caleb rushed around the kitchen island to

stand next to her, almost ramming into her thigh as he hurried to be by her side.

"Caleb, slow down and be careful," Tracey admonished. "You don't want to drop anything."

"Oh, he's fine, honey! We've got this down to a science now, don't we, Cabe?"

Caleb nodded as he held up his arms and took the stoneware she handed to him. He walked out of the kitchen and placed each plate on a linen mat in the dining room.

Tracey followed him and lowered Maggie into her high chair at the table, sweeping aside old cookie crumbs on the plastic tray before securing the straps in place. She then admired the duo that was setting the dining table, examining them like a poignant painting on a museum wall: a study of a woman and a boy.

Caleb had practically become Delilah's shadow in these past months. His affinity for Delilah wasn't surprising. Despite what people in town thought about her, Delilah was a woman who emanated warmth and light. Caleb was drawn to her — the proverbial moth to a flame. But in some ways, Tracey was wary of Caleb getting so close to this kind, enigmatic woman who claimed she couldn't remember if she had intentionally or accidentally killed her husband forty-eight years ago. If he drew too close to Delilah, he might get singed.

"I can help too," Tracey said. "Want me to get the glasses?"

"No, we've got it covered, sweetheart," Delilah said with a smile, waving her away. She then furrowed her brows and glanced around her. "You can find Aidan, though. I know he helped Emma Lynn carry that stuff to her car before she left, but he should be back by now. You can tell him to get his hind parts in here. We're about to eat!"

Tracey hesitated and glanced at Maggie, who was banging her plastic spoon and spork against the tray like she was doing an epic drum solo.

"Don't worry about the kids," Delilah said, reading her mind. "They'll be fine. Go ahead and find Aidan so that we can try this quiche. It's a new recipe, and I'm eager to see if it's good or a bust."

Tracey nodded and reluctantly left the kitchen in search of Aidan.

"Aidan!" Tracey called as she finished climbing the staircase. She walked down the darkened hallway, watching as particles of dust danced in the sparse shafts of evening light coming through opened window blinds along the corridor.

She glanced out the line of windows at

369

the front yard. In the driveway, Emma Lynn's Nissan sedan sat with the trunk yawning open, casting a long shadow on the asphalt.

Tracey frowned. So Emma Lynn hadn't left yet. For some reason, Tracey felt a hint of unease.

Her footsteps down the corridor were muffled by ghostly soul music emanating from Aidan's opened door. She passed his room but found it empty. Tracey lingered in the doorway, noticing for the first time how neat his room was but also how sparsely decorated. There was a bed, dresser, and night table — nothing else. No pictures or knickknacks. Nothing that let you know anything about the man who lived here. The only hint was the music. She listened as the trumpets whined and Otis Redding pleaded for someone to not make him stop loving her. The music was so torturous, she winced. She could almost feel it physically. She had to turn away.

"Stop!" she heard Aidan say, farther down the hall. "Damnit, I said stop! All right?"

"Aidan!" Tracey called again as she walked, her voice growing weaker instead of stronger when she realized his voice was coming from the room where Emma Lynn had stayed. The door was closed. Tracey raised her hand to knock but paused when she heard laughter — Emma Lynn's laughter.

"Oh, come on!" Emma Lynn cooed. "I'm about to hit the road. Just one more for old time's sake!"

"I said no," he repeated firmly. "Get the last of your stuff and come on! Or you can finish loading the car yourself."

"Aidan, don't be like that! You've never turned me down before. Why now?" Emma Lynn asked. Her tone was deeper now, almost husky. "Didn't you miss me, baby?"

Tracey stilled, feeling a sharp stab at Emma Lynn's words.

*You've never turned me down before.*

Aidan had lied to her.

Tracey knew what was inside this room would mire her in a sea of disillusionment and disappointment. But she had to hear it, *see* it; some part of her insisted. So she closed her eyes, took a deep breath, and pushed the door open, just a smidge, just enough.

First, she saw Emma Lynn sitting on the edge of the bed. Tracey couldn't see her face clearly because her back was to her, but she could see her pale hands and how she was trying to unbutton Aidan's jeans and lower his fly. Emma Lynn had a fervent nimbleness, like she had done this many, *many* times before.

Aidan wasn't quite as eager. He shoved her hands away. "Jesus Christ, will you fucking stop! I said no!"

"*What?* Can't handle two women at one time?" She flopped back onto the mattress, resting on her elbows.

Aidan squinted down at her, pulling up his zipper. "What are you talking about?"

"I get that you've moved on to the next girl in line, but I bet she wouldn't mind sharing you — just for a little bit."

"Stop talking shit and let's go!" he repeated louder.

"*Why?* Worried Little Miss J. Crew downstairs might hear us?" He didn't respond, and Emma Lynn started to laugh. "She's staying at Harbor Hill now, so I figured she's the one you've been heating up the sheets with. She looks like she'd be a bore in bed, but," she shrugged, "people can surprise you, I guess."

Tracey knew that she should turn away then. She certainly had seen more than enough to convince herself that whatever feelings she had harbored for Aidan had been wasted, had been foolish. But her feet seemed to be rooted in place; she couldn't turn away. Instead, she watched Aidan shake his head.

"I don't have time for this," he muttered, walking around the bed toward the door. "Grab your stuff and come on."

Despite his order, Emma Lynn stayed, reclining, on the bed. She laughed again.

"Yeah, you're definitely screwing her — since you've got a fire under your ass to get rid of me. Weren't in such a hurry to see me leave a year ago when I was sucking you off every night, though, were you? But I know how it goes. I ran into Candy Myers. You remember her? She stayed here back in 2013. She asked about Delilah — and *you.* She told me how you like to make the girls who stay here feel 'right at home.' " She giggled and nudged his leg with her booted foot. He shoved it away. " 'Whatever gal moves in there is next in line for a jump in the sack with Aidan Dominguez,' she told me. Guess I had my go, and now I've lost my turn."

"Are you done?" he barked.

"Yeah, I'm done." She pushed herself up from the bed and slowly shook her head. "You men are so goddamn predictable. You more than most!"

Tracey quietly shut the door and turned to head back down the hall.

Those memories of their strolls hand and

hand, of the few kisses they had stolen in Delilah's backyard, seemed sophomoric, almost laughable now. Aidan had done all of that and more with Emma Lynn and maybe all the other women who had come to Harbor Hill while he lived here, like Emma Lynn claimed.

How could Tracey have harbored any fantasies about this man, any hopes for a future with him? How could she have been so naïve, so dumb?

When Tracey reached the stairs, she was almost shaking. She fought back the tears that welled in her eyes and needed the handrail for guidance as her vision blurred.

By the time she arrived in the dining room, the table was set. The quiche sat cooling in an orange ceramic dish at the center of the table. Delilah was draping a bib around Maggie's shoulders while Caleb sat in his chair, reaching for a pitcher of lemonade.

"Where's Aidan?" Delilah asked, a frown marring her wrinkled face.

"Couldn't find him," Tracey said while pulling out a chair next to Caleb. "Guess he'll come down later."

"You couldn't find him?"

"No."

Delilah stared at her quizzically, and

Tracey lowered her reddened eyes, unable to meet the older woman's gaze. The quiet between them stretched, filled with unasked questions.

"Eat! Eat!" Maggie shouted, banging her spoon, breaking the uneasy silence that had fallen over the dining room.

"All right," Delilah said resignedly. "Let's start without him."

# CHAPTER 27

Aidan walked into the living room, covered in dirt and dust, and smelling faintly of bug spray, thanks to cleaning out the tool shed to prep for the upcoming spring. Now exhausted, he hung up his coat and wearily made his way toward the staircase to head to his room, but he paused when he glanced over his shoulder and saw Delilah sitting on one of the twill sofas with Maggie on her lap and Caleb at her side, resting in the crook of her arm.

"Now let's flip the page and see what happens next," Delilah said. Maggie giggled and clapped her tiny, chubby hands eagerly. The trio flipped to the next page in the oversized children's book, and Delilah began to read aloud. "And then the horse went clip clop up the hill, and he saw a —"

"Hey!" he said, waving. "Just finished out back." He glanced around. "Where's Tracey?"

Delilah seemed to hesitate before she looked up from the page. She shrugged. "I don't know." She then gazed at the book again. "And then the horse saw a turtle and said, 'What are you —' "

"You don't know?"

She pursed her lips, seemingly perturbed at being disturbed again from her reading. "She said she needed a break. She asked me to watch the children for her for a bit."

He took a step toward the sofa, wiping his damp hands on the front of his T-shirt, smearing the cotton fabric with twin tracks of dirt. "Well, where'd she go?"

Delilah loudly huffed. "I don't know, Aidan. She's a grown woman! She doesn't have to check in with me."

"You're telling me she didn't tell you where she went?"

"No, I'm saying that she doesn't have to —"

"Mommy went for a walk," Caleb piped, and Delilah gave him a censoring look.

At Delilah's reaction, Caleb furrowed his brows. "*What?* Mommy didn't say it was a secret."

"Your mom went for a walk?" Aidan persisted, surprising even himself with the urgency in his voice. "Where'd she go? How long ago?"

Caleb gnawed his bottom lip and glanced at Delilah before he answered. "She said me and Maggie were giving her a headache, so she wanted to clear her head. She just left."

"But she'll be back soon," Delilah quickly added, closing the children's book. "She said she'd be back in a bit. She just needed a little bit of alone time. That's all."

Aidan vaguely nodded, though he was barely listening now. He turned back around, his fatigue now forgotten.

Tracey had gone for a walk without him. She hadn't asked him to come with her like she had every time in the past. But she had been acting strange lately. Almost like she was avoiding him. He had felt some tension between them while Emma Lynn had stayed at Harbor Hill, but it had been almost a week since she'd left, and yet the tension lingered.

"She doesn't need you following her, Aidan," Delilah called across the living room.

*Mind your own business,* he snapped inwardly then chided himself for the misplaced anger.

It wasn't Delilah he was furious at or even Tracey, but the disoriented feeling that had plagued him for the past couple of days. Something between him and Tracey had shifted. He wasn't sure what it was or why it had happened, but he was about find out.

He headed out of the living room. As he stepped into the foyer and grabbed his coat again, he felt a cool hand clamp around his wrist. He whipped around to face Delilah, who was glaring up at him.

"Aidan," she whispered harshly through clenched teeth, "leave her be!"

"Stay out of it," he warned, yanking his wrist out of her grasp.

"I don't know what went on between you two, but I can tell it was something. I thought you would've had good enough sense not to try something with her," she said, pointing her finger up at him. "She's not like the other ones, Aidan, and you know it! Don't try to make her into —"

He didn't let Delilah finish. Instead, he yanked open the front door and strode across the porch. He shrugged into his coat as he headed down the steps at a near run, hoping to catch up with Tracey along the path they usually took to the waterfront.

He found her a minute or two later, hearing her first — the sound of gravel crunching under the soles of her shoes. Then he saw her shadowy silhouette set against the orange flame of the setting sun. She was walking on the dirt path. Her head was bowed slightly, and her hands were shoved into her coat pockets.

"Hey, Trace!" he called, startling her.

She jumped and turned. When she saw him, her face changed. He would have accepted surprise . . . maybe even anger. But instead, she greeted him with marked disappointment, like he was the last person she wanted to see walking behind her at that moment.

"I didn't know you were out here," she said as he drew close.

"I wasn't. Caleb told me you went for a walk, so I followed you."

She didn't comment.

"Why didn't you tell me you were headed for a walk? I could've come with you."

"I don't know. I guess I thought you were busy out back. I didn't want to disturb you."

"You wouldn't have disturbed me. You could *never* disturb me," he said warmly, reaching up to touch a lock of hair near her brow that had fallen into her face. But she tilted her head, pulling out of his reach.

"Or maybe I just wanted to walk alone."

Her tone was flat and cool.

Aidan's jaw tightened. He knew he should turn around then, head back to the house with his tail between his legs. But he stayed and continued to walk by her side.

"Why? Is something on your mind?"

"Things are always on my mind, Aidan." She stared at the view of the bay in front of her, squinting against the light. "I'm a mother of two with no money and —"

"You *know* what I mean. Something else is bothering you. Is it me?"

She loudly sighed and adjusted the scarf around her throat. "Look, it's been a long day, and I'm not up to this conversation right now. I came out here to get some peace. All the tables today were filled with assholes, and Maggie and Caleb have been at each other's throats for most of the afternoon. I just want to —"

"You've been avoiding me for the past five days! I try to talk to you, and you pretend like you're busy. I walk into the room, and you make an excuse to leave!"

"I do not, Aidan."

"Yes, you do! Goddammit, you do! Something's wrong, but I don't know what it is. So solve the mystery for me and tell me what's going on."

She halted but didn't answer him.

"Jesus Christ, Tracey, just tell me! Put a man out of his misery," he said, only half joking.

She stood silent for a bit longer, and for a second he wondered if she still would keep whatever secrets she harbored. "I saw you," she said, making him frown.

"You saw me? You saw me what?"

"I *saw* you, Aidan. I saw you with her . . . with Emma Lynn the day that she left. You were . . . you were in her bedroom, and I saw you. I heard you."

And suddenly, it all made sense: her inability to look at him and not wanting to be alone with him anymore. He remembered his conversation with Emma Lynn. He remembered the way she had groped at his fly, like she owned his dick — like she owned *him.*

"I wasn't trying to spy on you. I came upstairs to find you for dinner, but I should've knocked. I know I should have knocked, but I didn't. I opened the door, and I saw you two." She finally looked up at him then. She had traded her look of disappointment for a look of pain. "I asked you, Aidan. I asked if you were ever with her and you told me no. You should have been honest with me!"

"Trace, you asked if we were a couple, and we weren't. We never had been! We were just —"

"Buddies," she finished for him. "Buddies who happened to have sex with each other."

He roughly shoved his fingers through his

hair, blowing air through his clenched teeth. He knew how ridiculous it sounded at the time. It sounded even worse now coming from her lips.

"And were all the other women who came to Harbor Hill who you had sex with just 'buddies' too, Aidan? Did you plan to add me to your little friend list?"

"It wasn't like that," he said, shaking his head.

*I shouldn't have gone back upstairs with Emma Lynn,* he thought. He was mentally kicking himself for it now. None of this would have happened if he hadn't. He should have escorted her to her car, kissed her cheek, shut the door, and walked away. Why had he let her talk him into going back? Why had Tracey stumbled upon them at the worst possible time?

"Then what was it like? Explain it to me, Aidan. What am I not understanding?" she persisted, staring up at him with tears in her eyes. "Because it looks like you were taking advantage of vulnerable, broken women . . . that you *used* them for sex!"

He continued to shake his head. "That's not what happened."

"Did you plan to take advantage of me too? Make me think you really cared when you didn't? Was I supposed to be some —"

"No! No, of course not! Look, I never took advantage of anyone. Every woman I ever slept with knew what was happening. I never made any promises I couldn't keep, and I didn't lie. I didn't make them think I could give any more than what I could give! I was always up front! I —"

"But you weren't up front with me," she said softly. "You weren't up front with *me.*"

He lowered his head. "No. No, I wasn't, and I should've been. I was just . . . just worried about how you'd react if I told you everything. If I told you the truth. I know how bad it looks."

He took a step toward her and, after much uncertainty, reached out and held her shoulders. He wanted touch her more — hug her, kiss her — but knew he'd be pushing his luck if he did.

"I didn't want to hurt you, Tracey, because I care about you. I have feelings for you that I haven't had for . . . for *anybody* in a long time! What we have —"

"We don't have anything, Aidan," she said calmly, pulling away from him, taking a step back. "You said before that your wife left you because you weren't ready to put her first. Well, you're still not ready. That's pretty evident."

Her words sliced into him, tiny paper cuts

made with inflection and syllables.

"You're still selfish," she continued, slicing again. "You're still emotionally stunted. It's why you did what you did. It's why you lied to me. I'm glad I finally realized that. Besides," she crossed her arms over her chest, "I need to focus. I have two children to worry about. I have classes to finish and a degree to complete if I want to make a better life for them and myself. I can't live with Delilah forever, and I have to make plans for when I leave here. This *thing* — whatever it is, whatever it *was* — has distracted me. I needed to wake up. What you did woke me up."

She was masking cruelty with honesty, but it was her honesty that wounded him the most. He had no right to be hurt or angry. He had done this to himself, shot himself in the foot, as he had so many times in the past. But he was hurt all the same.

Aidan fought to control his features, to keep the blandness in his voice. "Well, I'm glad my screwup helped you focus."

She nodded half-heartedly, then turned back toward the waterfront, looking longingly at the trail beyond the tall grass. "I better keep going before I lose the light and end up walking back in the dark," she said softly. "Will you tell Delilah I should be back in about a half an hour, maybe forty-five minutes at most?"

"Sure," he said, because there was nothing else he could say.

He watched as she strode alone down the path with her ponytail swaying listlessly behind her. He then turned on his heels and headed in the opposite direction, feeling the burden of missed opportunity and loss weigh him down as he walked.

Aidan didn't head toward the house but walked to his pickup truck. He climbed in the cab with no idea where he was going or how long he would drive. He just needed to get away from here.

He drove around Camden Beach, through downtown and along the waterfront. He drove into neighboring towns and then the entire length of the county, passing houses and strip malls, office buildings and fast food joints. He turned on his headlights when it got dark, all the while listening to his CDs, letting the music fill the car compartment. He turned up the volume to drown out his thoughts but didn't succeed.

He thought about Tracey and that look of disappointment on her face and the hurt in her eyes. He remembered how she had turned her back on him and walked away. He couldn't blame her. He was a man riddled with weaknesses and mistakes. She should stay as far away from him as possible.

He thought about Trish, their marriage, and their baby girl. He remembered the counseling sessions in which Trish had made tear-filled admissions while he'd fought the urge not to check the clock on the wall to see when the session would be over or his BlackBerry for messages from clients. He recalled with vividness the day his father-in-law had carried her suitcases out of their condo while Trish toted a wailing Annabelle in her arms.

"I'm sorry, Aidan, but I have to do this. I can't stay," she had whispered.

It was after 11 o'clock when Aidan crossed the Camden Beach border and the gas tank needle hovered dangerously close to E. Aidan had no choice but to stop driving. He spotted a blazing white and red sign of a Stop 'n' Go in the distance and made his way to the gas station. He pulled up to one of the vacant pumps, hopped out of the cab, and strolled inside the small convenience store.

When Aidan walked back to his truck a few minutes later after paying the sales clerk, he saw a BMW come to a screeching halt at the pump behind him. He raised the gas nozzle and turned to fill his truck with unleaded but paused when he heard someone shout out.

"Aidan! Aidan Dominguez, fancy running into you here!"

He glanced to his left and saw Teddy Williams striding toward him. He nodded politely. "Hey, Teddy, how you doin'?"

"Good! Good! Just leaving a late night dinner with the wife." He gestured over his shoulder to the BMW's tinted windshield. Aidan could see a plump brunette in the passenger seat who was staring down at her cell phone, tapping at the screen.

"It's our twenty-five-year anniversary," Teddy elaborated with a grin.

"Congratulations." Aidan then returned his attention to the gas nozzle and the readout on the digital screen behind him, hoping Teddy would take the hint that he wasn't in the mood for conversation. Besides, the man's cologne was almost as overwhelming as the smell of gasoline filling Aidan's nose.

"I've been thinking about you guys, you know . . . about how things are going at Harbor Hill." Teddy took a step closer to him. "Did you call the police, by the way? Did they find out who were the bastards that vandalized poor Ms. Grey's house?"

Aidan shook his head. "No, we didn't call the police. She insisted that we didn't and I . . . well . . . I had to respect her wishes."

*No matter how crazy they are,* he thought but didn't add.

"Well, that's a shame. That is a shame." He inclined his head. "So Ms. Grey isn't worried that things will only get worse? I mean . . . if someone paints that on your garage, you have to wonder what else they'll do!"

Aidan rolled his eyes. "I've had this conversation with her already. She says she's not worried."

"*She's* not — but *you* know better!" Teddy thumped him on the shoulder. "Look, Aidan, I can tell you're a rational, practical man. You know that house will get to be too much for her eventually, and all these shenanigans will only make it worse for her. She's an old woman who should be enjoying her later years in life, not dealing with this nuisance!"

Aidan pursed his lips.

"And you're a single young man with your own life, your own aspirations! You've done a fine job of taking care of her and Harbor Hill, but don't you want something for yourself? If I were your age, I'd be eager to get out! You're not an old married guy like me with a wife and three kids. I envy you, fellow!"

Aidan lowered his eyes, not feeling particularly worthy of Teddy's envy at that moment.

"I know you and I have both tried to convince her to sell Harbor Hill, but maybe a better tactic is to get her to come to my office instead."

He laid a hand on Aidan's shoulder when Aidan started to mount an argument.

"Just hear me out! Bring her by my office, and I'll give her the full dog and pony show. I'll pull everything out of my salesman's hat. I'll show her what I would do with Harbor Hill so that she'll know it would be in good hands. Maybe that will finally do the trick!"

Aidan considered his offer for several seconds before he finally nodded. "I'll talk to her. I'll try my best."

# CHAPTER 28

"What do you mean you're moving out?" Delilah asked. Her eyes went wide. Her mouth fell open.

"I'm not moving out right away," Aidan said, taking the armchair facing her. He ran his hands over his jeans-clad legs. "It probably won't be for a few months. But I want to be gone by June at the latest."

"So another bird leaves the nest," Cee whispered in her mind with a chuckle, though she told him to hush up.

She set her opened paperback of *The Color Purple* aside on the footstool, making Bruce narrow his eyes. Now, having had his sleep disrupted and unwilling to share his space with Alice Walker, the tabby cat rose to his feet and hopped down from the stool. He then walked out of the living room, leaving Delilah and Aidan alone.

"But why?" Delilah asked. "Why *now*?"

She had anticipated this day would come

eventually. To be honest, Delilah hadn't planned for Aidan to stay at Harbor Hill for the four years that he had lived there, but this revelation felt like it had come out of nowhere. She felt blindsided, as she had so many times these past few weeks. She'd thought things settled down the older you got, that life became more predictable. Instead, she was finding the opposite.

"You said I would never leave, and I told you I would. Now is . . . well . . . it's just the right time." He shrugged. "I don't know what else to tell you."

She frowned, taking in his facial expression and his body language. He was trying his best to convey nonchalance, but she could see what was lurking beneath. She knew him too well.

"This decision . . . is it because of her?"

He squinted. "*Her?* Her who?"

"You know who I'm talking about, Aidan. Is it because of Tracey . . . because of whatever happened between you two? Is that why you're leaving?"

He paused for a beat. She saw his Adam's apple bob over the collar of his shirt as he swallowed. "No, this has nothing to do with her."

He was lying. She *knew* that he was lying. Delilah was now even more at a loss for words. She had worried that Tracey would get hurt if something romantic developed between her and Aidan and it inevitably fell apart. She hadn't considered that *he* would suffer any emotional blows. But here he was, putting on a brave front when she could see the wounds and the bruises as clearly as if they were on his face.

Staring at him, she recalled the young Aidan, the quiet boy with the lanky limbs and the sad eyes who also tried to mask his hurt and disappointment with nonchalance, with a casual teenage bravado that didn't fool her even then.

*Like mother like son,* Delilah thought.

He had inherited Rosario's depression, carrying it around with him like the stacks of old CDs she used to play, which he now played all the time. But while Rosario wallowed in her pain, taking laps in the cesspool of torment and gloom, Aidan would deny he'd ever set foot in the water.

"You're not ready," Delilah said, sadly shaking her head. "I've seen this enough times to know when someone is better after being here. I can see when they've healed, and you haven't, honey."

"Well, that's not up to you to decide, now is it? If I decide it's time to go, I'm going."

She pursed her lips. "You're a grown man.

I know that. But, Aidan, I'm just trying to —"

"I didn't come down here to start an argument," he said, holding up his hand. "I told you this because you need to know. Because when I do leave, I want to make sure that you're okay . . . that I'm not leaving you alone to fend for yourself."

"I won't be alone. I'll have the girls to help me take care of Harbor Hill."

"What girls, Dee? Tracey will leave too one day. You have no idea how long it will be before the next woman lives here — *if* one lives here. And how long will she stay? You can't do this forever."

She raised her chin. "Says who? *You?*"

"Life says so, Dee. The writing is on the wall — literally! You have some crazy person harassing you and writing offensive messages on your garage door. Add that to the fact that you're sixty-seven years old, with diabetes, arthritis in the knees, and high blood pressure. You're getting older and —"

"I wish you'd stop talking about me like I'm near death's door. My grandmother lived well into her nineties! She still picked apples and tended her own chickens to the day she died. I could have more than twenty years ahead of me!"

"Again," he said, exhaling as he leaned

forward and braced his elbows on his knees, "I'm not here to argue with you. But I do think it's time to seriously consider moving on from Harbor Hill. You should —"

"No," she said, shaking her head again. "No, Aidan!"

"Just hear me out."

"There is nothing to hear! I've told you a *thousand times* I'm not leaving this place! It's my home. My . . ."

*My burden,* she wanted to say but didn't.

"My responsibility," she said instead.

"Dee, you've taken care of countless people your entire life. You've done it selflessly, and most have never given anything back in return. Isn't it finally time for you to do something for yourself . . . to live for yourself?"

She turned away from him then, unable to meet his earnest gaze any longer.

Delilah would never be able to explain to him that what she did for him, his mother, and the many other women who came into her home was a penance she felt she owed. She had taken a life, and she would strive for the rest of her life to make up for that sin, to make amends to God for what she'd done.

"Teddy wants to buy the house," he said. "And —"

"And turn it into another ugly hotel, I bet! Like we don't have enough of those around here! Or maybe he'll make it into a casino."

"Dee, I don't think he wants to do that. And frankly, I don't think he *can* do that. Harbor Hill isn't zoned for —"

"If you have enough money, you can do anything. Trust me! I know." She had come up against money and power before. She'd seen how often people won when they had the dollars to back up their motives.

Aidan sighed and scrubbed his hand over his face. "Look, you're making assumptions . . . blind assumptions. The only way to find out what Teddy really wants to do with this place is to ask him. He wants to have a meeting with you at his office in the city. I'll go with you, if you want."

She opened her mouth again to say that if Teddy Williams disappeared out of her life, she'd be perfectly happy, but Aidan spoke before she could.

"You don't have to commit to it. But I really, *really* want you to hear him out, to seriously consider what he has to say."

She gnawed the inside of her cheek.

"If you do this for me, Dee, I won't bring it up again. I promise! Just . . . go there with me. Give him thirty minutes, and see what he has to say."

She closed her eyes, took a deep breath, then slowly opened her eyes again.

"Fine, Aidan. I'll go. I'll go if we never have to talk about this again. You hear me?"

Teddy's waiting area at his real estate office was as sterile and banal as Delilah expected it to be, with lots of chrome, glass, and bright lights that made her feel like she was on a theater stage. A pretty redhead sat behind the receptionist desk, clicking away at her computer and chirping perkily into her headset. She had offered Delilah and Aidan coffee, tea, or bottled water when they'd arrived.

Aidan had accepted the coffee. Delilah had said she didn't want anything, thank you very much.

"If you will wait here, Mr. Williams will be with you shortly," the young woman had said nearly fifteen minutes ago.

"Does he expect us to wait for him all day?" Delilah now whispered none too softly to Aidan, who sat in one of the leather club chairs beside her.

She watched as he glanced up from the magazine he held, an old issue of *People* with a smiling actress on the cover. "We got here early, Dee. We haven't been waiting that long."

As if on cue, one of the glass doors at the end of the hall swung open, and Teddy strode out. He was decked out in a pin-striped suit and periwinkle shirt today, with a gold tie clip and cufflinks — looking every bit the smooth-talking salesman she expected him to be.

"Ah, so you made it!" he said as though he was surprised to see them, as if the receptionist hadn't told him fifteen minutes ago that Delilah and Aidan were here waiting for him in the lobby.

Aidan rose to his feet first. Delilah reluctantly followed suit.

When Teddy reached them, he embraced Delilah in the customary hug she was starting to loathe, crushing her purse between them. He shook Aidan's hand.

"How are you today, Delilah?" he asked, turning back to her. "You look lovely, as usual!"

No, she didn't. She looked tired after getting only a few snatches of sleep since Aidan had told her a few days ago he'd be moving out soon. She shrugged. "I've been better."

"Well, hopefully, I can make you happier. Hopefully, you'll let me make you a very rich woman too! Let's head back to my office," he said, gesturing down the hall. "Follow me."

The three made their way down the with Teddy yapping the whole time, poi ing to plaques and pictures on the wall, telling some inane story. Delilah chose not to pay attention. All the polite conversation between him and Aidan was background noise for her. She wasn't going to sell Harbor Hill — not today, not ever. In fact, she planned to will it to Aidan — though she hadn't told him so. After her death, he could do with the property whatever he wished. He could even sell it to Teddy if he was still so fired up to do that.

But she wouldn't complicate things by telling him the truth. Instead, she would do what Aidan had asked her to do — or at least pantomime it.

"You can have a seat right there," Teddy said, opening his door, revealing an expansive office with twelve-foot ceilings and large windows facing a series of office buildings with glass exteriors and a parking lot. He gestured to two chairs facing a large desk that took up a third of the width of the room. Behind the desk was a series of shelves covered with photos and knick-knacks. "Make yourselves comfortable."

Aidan and Delilah took the seats he offered. She set her purse on her lap, and Aidan reclined back in his chair, raising his ankle to his knee.

"First, I want to thank you for coming here today," Teddy began, not taking the chair behind his desk but sitting on the tabletop's edge.

It gave him a two-foot height advantage over them so that they had to peer up into his blue eyes, into his smug face.

"I'm happy to see that you're finally willing to hear what I have to say, Delilah. I know you've been . . . uh . . . hesitant, shall we say, to move forward with a deal. I'm glad you've changed your mind."

"I haven't changed my mind. I just promised Aidan that I would hear you out. That's what I'm here to do."

"All the same. It gives me the chance to show you with visuals what I've had a hard time conveying with words."

He then rose to his feet and walked behind his desk, where he typed a few keys on his opened laptop keyboard and turned the screen toward them with a flourish. "Now take a gander at this!"

On the screen was a three-dimensional rendering of Harbor Hill, though it had undergone a massive makeover compared to the house she lived in now. The colors were more vibrant. It looked nearly twice as big, with east and west wings. The front porch had been removed and replaced with a grand veranda. Windows, doors, and posts had been added, along with other details that would raise the value of the house by a good hundred thousand dollars by themselves.

"She's a beauty, isn't she?" he asked with a chuckle, mistaking her shock for awe. "I had one of the best architects in the region do a mock-up. The improvements wouldn't just stop with the house itself. We'd improve the rest of the property too. Add a negative-edge pool," he said, tapping his laptop mouse. Suddenly, a pool bordered by lawn chairs, cabanas, and women in bikinis appeared on screen. "We could even add a guest house." He tapped the mouse again. "We'd stay with the beach house aesthetic throughout, of course, but it would all be amazing, without a doubt. From what I've shown you, you have to agree!"

"Yes . . . uh . . . it all looks great . . . I mean amazing, Teddy," Aidan began, "but Delilah's biggest concern isn't how you would renovate the property, but what you would do with it once it's been renovated. It's been her home for many years, and she'd hope that whoever gets the house would have the same vision for Harbor Hill.

Did you have plans to make it into a hotel or —"

"No!" Teddy insisted, frowning for the first time. "No, nothing of the sort! Harbor Hill would become a vacation home for my family, and it would stay in my family. I can promise you that!"

"Well, that sounds positive, doesn't it, Dee?" Aidan asked, raising his brows and glancing at her.

"People make plenty of promises when they're standing in front of you. It could be a different story if he got the place," she said obstinately. "He could do with it whatever he wanted then!"

Teddy raised his hand like he was making the Boy Scouts pledge. "Delilah, you have my solemn promise that I would never, *ever* turn Harbor Hill into a commercial property. And if my word isn't good enough, I'll write a contract to prove it to you."

Aidan laughed and shook his head. "Teddy, that isn't necessary."

"No, no, no!" Teddy reached for a notepad on his desk. "Anything to put Ms. Grey's mind at ease. It's not a problem, Aidan."

He then grabbed a pen and began to write on the notepad.

Delilah resisted the urge to roll her eyes at

his theatrics. While he scribbled and prattled, she scanned his office. Her eyes landed on the glass shelves behind his desk. She saw several pictures, all of which were of Teddy.

Teddy posing with his family.

Teddy with his arm slung around the shoulder of other golfers with tanned faces and paunches.

Teddy posing with a rod and reel off the back of some powerboat.

He also seemed well traveled. The shelves showed several tchotchkes he must have picked up from flea markets or bazaars around the world: a small woven basket, a porcelain doll, and a chipped ceramic pot. When her eyes landed on a silver flask near the end of one of the shelves, she squinted. For some reason, it looked vaguely familiar. She leaned forward in her chair to see it more closely.

The flask had a lid attached to it by a small chain. On the front was the engraved letter "C" in a gothic font.

Delilah's heart stuttered to a stop, then started up again.

*It can't be,* she thought, staring at the flask.

But there it was. Even the dent near the mouth looked familiar.

It was her dead husband Cee's flask.

*But how did Teddy get it?*

The last time she had seen the flask was the night of Cee's murder. She hadn't laid eyes on it since — that is, not until today.

"Here is a solemn promise *in writing,* signed by yours truly, that says I will not convert Harbor Hill into a hotel, resort, bed and breakfast, casino, condominium, or any commercial property of the sort," he said, handing her the sheet of paper. "Go ahead. Read it!"

She dazedly reached for the paper, still in disbelief.

Watching her, Aidan's eyebrows knitted together. "Are you okay, Dee?"

She nodded, then shook her head, then nodded again. She struggled to make sense of her thoughts but couldn't. She looked at the sheet of paper in her hand, at the emblem stamped at the top in embossed letters.

"Theodore Williams Properties . . . Theodore Williams," she whispered. "Williams. Williams."

She hadn't made the connection before. It was such a common name she hadn't given it a second thought, but now it seemed so obvious. It had been staring her in the face this whole time. Delilah let the paper flutter from her hand. She slowly raised her hand to her forehead, feeling disoriented. The office seemed to spin around her, and she had to grip the arm of the chair to steady herself.

"Dee, what's wrong?" Aidan asked, snatching the paper out of her lap and staring down at the sheet. "What are you looking at?"

She looked up at Teddy as Aidan scrutinized the note. "Williams . . . as in Melinda and Jake Williams. Your mama and daddy."

At her words, Teddy's eager smile disappeared.

Miss Mindy had had a baby while Delilah was in jail — her last child, the one who was supposed to save her marriage. Delilah had never learned the name of the boy.

"You're their son, aren't you?" she pointed up at him. "You're . . . you're Cee's nephew."

She was about to ask, "How in the world did you get his flask?" when Aidan suddenly exploded, "What the fuck!" making her jump in her chair. "You mean it was you this whole time?"

Teddy broke her gaze. His eyes snapped toward Aidan.

"You wrote all those fucking letters, didn't you? You're the one who left those notes around her house!"

Teddy stepped from behind his desk,

straightening his shoulders. "I don't know what you're talking about."

Neither did Delilah. Her eyes danced between the two men, not knowing where to land. What was happening? Aidan had shot to his feet and was jabbing at the paper in his hand. Teddy had stepped back behind his desk, as if to use it as protection from Aidan.

"Yes, you do! I kept all of those letters — every single one! I've stared at them a hundred times. It's the *same* handwriting!" He brandished the note in Teddy's face, making the older man take another step back. "Did you paint 'murderer' on the garage too or have someone else do it?"

"You better be careful with allegations like that and the name calling, Mr. Grounds-keeper, or you'll find yourself in court!" Teddy yelled back. His face was red now. Perspiration was on his brow. "I'll have my lawyers sue you for —"

"I was a lawyer before I was a grounds-keeper, asshole! You don't intimidate me. You're the one who should be intimidated . . . no, *terrified,* because you fucked up! You got caught!"

"They must have taken it," she said, making Aidan whip around to face her.

"What?" he asked, blinking in confusion

and frowning down at her.

"Miss Mindy and Mr. Williams . . . they must have taken it with them," she repeated, staring at Cee's flask, remembering everything all at once. "They had to have been there that night."

The wonky carousel she had been riding for decades had finally slowed, and she could clearly see the world around her. More importantly, she could fill in the blanks from her past, those missing pieces that had confused her for so long. After forty-eight years of doubt and confusion, it all started to make sense. Delilah suspected she finally knew the truth.

She turned to Aidan, wanting to explain everything, but it was all too much. The words piled up on each other, clogging in her throat; no sound would come out. Aidan gave her a worried glance before returning his glare to Teddy.

"We're leaving! And I'm taking this note with me. I'm showing it and the rest of the letters to the police. You're going to jail, you son of a bitch!" He reached for Delilah. "Come on, Dee."

Dazedly, she took the hand he held out to her, still confused as to why they were leaving. What exactly was he ranting about?

Her thoughts were still lost in the past.

"I'm not going to jail!" Teddy bellowed and then pointed to Delilah. "*She's* the one who should be in jail. She murdered my uncle and stole Harbor Hill from my family. By rights, *I* should own that house." He pointed at his chest. "I was doing her a favor by offering her money for it."

"You're delusional," Aidan spat over his shoulder. "Let's go, Dee."

She slowly rose to her feet, feeling wobbly. Aidan grabbed her purse from the floor and handed it to her. She stared at it for a few seconds like it was a foreign object before finally figuring out what it was. She looped the straps onto her shoulder. She and Aidan then began to walk toward Teddy's office door, and Aidan wrapped an arm around her, like he was protecting her from something. Delilah took once last glance at Cee's flask. She felt the strong urge to rush across the room and take it, to say she was owed it for what she had been through.

"She should've been smart and taken the money! But she didn't, and now it'll crumble to the ground. It'll —"

Aidan slammed the office door behind him, ending Teddy's rant mid-tirade.

They rushed down the corridor toward the elevators, and the red-headed receptionist looked up at them quizzically.

"Leaving so soon? Do you need your parking validated?" she called out as Aidan pressed the elevator's DOWN button. He didn't respond. Instead, he silently stepped onto the elevator when the doors opened, dragging a bewildered Delilah behind him.

They didn't speak again until they arrived at his truck and Aidan stuck his key in the ignition. She watched as he shifted the car into reverse, but instead of pulling out of the parking space, he gritted his teeth. He thumped his fists against the steering wheel, making her jump in the passenger seat.

"Shit! Shit!" he yelled over the sound of the car radio. He closed his eyes, then opened them. He sighed. "I feel like a fool, Dee. I should've realized he was behind it. He gave me bad vibes the moment I met him, and I should've followed my instinct. I've known assholes like that. I know what they're capable of. I'm . . . I'm so sorry I brought you here," Aidan whispered. "I'm so sorry."

He then lowered his forehead to the steering wheel and closed his eyes again. After some seconds, she placed a hand on his shoulder.

"Aidan," she said, and he slowly raised his head. He turned to look at her. "Don't apologize, honey. You've got nothing to apologize about. If I hadn't come here today, I never would've found out the truth."

Aidan pursed his lips. He nodded. "You mean the truth about Teddy, that he was the one harassing you. That's what you mean?"

She inclined her head and stared. "No, honey. I mean, the truth about what happened all those years ago. I don't think I was the one who killed my husband."

■ ■ ■ ■

# PART IV

■ ■ ■ ■

*Chevy Chase, Maryland*
*November 1968*

# CHAPTER 29

"So you got caught up, huh?" Agnes says, and I lower my hand.

I am showing off my three-carat diamond wedding ring to her after not seeing her in a couple of weeks. I am hoping she will "ooh and ahh" over how the diamond catches the light and sparkles. But I should've known Agnes would see past the ring, the expensive coat, and my newly pressed and styled hair. Of course, she'd get straight to the point.

"When you due?" she asks, peering over the diner's tabletop, eyeing my waist through my wool coat.

"In May," I whisper sheepishly, pulling back my hand.

Agnes exhales and shrugs. She grabs her fork and slices into her pie. "Well, if he asked you to marry him, he's done more than most." She chews and wipes her mouth with a paper napkin. "At least there's that. Because a white man marrying a Negro gal ain't no little thing. People used to get hung for something like that. Y'all don't have the noose to worry about no more, but it ain't gonna be easy, Dee!"

"We know. We want to get married any-way."

Well, by *we,* I really mean Cee. But Cee never cares about anything but what *he* wants.

I can't tell Agnes that Cee didn't ask me to marry him; he *told* me we were getting married. One day, I told him I was in the family way, which was no surprise consider-ing how many times he had climbed on top of me in the back of his GTO — whether I wanted him to or not. A few days later, we were on our way to the city to exchange wedding vows at the courthouse. We left for our honeymoon in New York City that night.

Cee insisted we do all that before we told anybody else.

Of course, that wasn't the plan *I* had. I didn't want to get married. I was going to quit working for Miss Mindy as soon as I started showing. I'd already called Mama and given her the news. I was going to head down to Lynchburg to have my baby, but I wouldn't give it away like Agnes did hers. The baby would stay with my Mama until the child was old enough for me to send for it to live with me up north. But Cee had dismissed the idea before I had the chance to explain.

"There's no goddamn way I'd have my kid growing up on some dingy colored tobacco farm in the middle of nowhere Virginia," he told me. "No, you'll stay here. We'll get married. It's legal now."

I knew not to argue with him. I would never win. I was caught up in more ways than one.

When I obey Cee, he's nice to me. He talks sweet; he calls me "gorgeous" and tells me how special I am, how I'm unlike any woman he's ever met. He gives me things — gifts and more money I can send home to my family. But when I disobey or talk back, he yells at me. When I walk away, he grabs me, shoves me down, or slaps me.

"Why do you keep testing my love for you, Dee?" he said as he wrapped his hand around my throat and squeezed when I tried yet again to end it with him. "I wanna make you happy, but don't piss me off!"

Every night I hope and pray that it will get better, that the man who wooed me with conversations about books and life will stay and the mean Cee will finally disappear forever.

But then a voice whispers to me, "Honey,

if you believe that, you're as crazy as he is."

"So where are you two living now?" Agnes asks, snapping me out of my thoughts. "I know you can't be still living with your auntie."

"No, we're living at his beach house, Harbor Hill." I smile for the first time. "It's a beautiful place, Agnes. You should see it! It's got all these rooms and windows. You can see the water. I love it."

It is one of the few things in my life with Cee that truly makes me happy. Sometimes, I walk up and down the halls and look at the rooms, and I am in disbelief. I never thought I would live in a home like Harbor Hill, that I could ever call such a place my own. It's like something out of one of the novels I read.

"Well, look at you, Mrs. Buford! The lady of a big ol' house now!"

She chuckles softly and takes another bite of her pie. I ordered some apple pie too but haven't taken a bite yet. Now that I'm pregnant, smells overwhelm me so easily. The greasy onion smell of the hamburger the man nearby is eating is making me sick to my stomach.

"It's what you always wanted though, right?" Agnes continues, and I frown.

"What have I always wanted?"

"To be the lady of the house . . . to be in charge. You didn't want to be just any dumb maid like the rest of us, having to bow down to the likes of Miss Mindy. Remember?"

I lower my eyes to my pie and stare at the sugary filling because I can't meet her eyes anymore. "I didn't mean that, Agnes. I just said it when I was mad."

"You *did* mean it. You didn't mean it in a mean way, but you still meant every word you said." She reaches across the table and gently raises my chin so I have to look at her. "And I could see it in you. I could see it in the way you carried yourself, in the books you toted around with you and how you always seemed like you just wanted to run away, to not be there." She drops her hand from my chin. "Well, you got out, Dee! I don't know if I would've done it your way, but your way worked. You wanted better, and you got better! That's all that counts."

But is it? I wonder if she would still think so if saw the bruise on my hip from when Cee knocked me down to the floor a week ago.

"How is Miss Mindy, by the way?" I ask, and Agnes rolls her eyes to the ceiling.

"Mad enough to spit nails. No, mad enough to *spit fire*! She's not too happy about her baby brother marrying the help

— let alone *Negro* help! She talks about it all the time with Mr. Williams and with her mama. The Buford women both just beside themselves, chile!"

Agnes pauses to take another bite.

"Nothing me or Roberta does makes her happy anymore. Just the other day, she tried to accuse me of stealing a pair of her earrings. Can you believe that?" Agnes sucks her teeth. "Like I'd want the ugly things she wears. She found them later behind her bureau but didn't apologize. Just acted like it never happened and started fussing about something else. She threatens all the time that she's gonna let me and Roberta go." Agnes leans forward and drops her voice down to a whisper. "Personally, I think they're running out of money. Roberta tells me that Miss Mindy's been cutting back on the groceries and telling her to stretch out whatever she buys. They usually go away on vacation for Christmas, but they're staying right here this year. Maybe it is just a matter of time before they let us go."

I open my mouth to tell Agnes the truth — that the Williams family *is* running out of money and Miss Mindy had been blackmailing me for months to convince Cee to give me money that I would then give to Miss Mindy. But I close my mouth. I can't tell her. I'm still ashamed of what I did, of what I let Miss Mindy talk me into doing.

Agnes's shoulders slump as she finishes the last of her pie. "Lord, I wonder if I should start looking for a job again! I've worked for that woman for almost six years now. Miss Mindy ain't the best lady to work for but, like they say, 'The devil you know is better than the devil you don't.' Who knows what kinda woman I'll have to work for the next time around." She chuckles again. "If you're looking for a maid at that big ol' house on Harbor Hill, let me know!"

An hour later, I pull up to Harbor Hill. The drive from the city doesn't usually take that long, but when I'm in the car that Cee gave me as a wedding gift — a tan 1968 Plymouth Fury — I love to drive. Sometimes I fantasize about driving straight out of Maryland and going for miles and miles. I dream about not coming back. Before I know it, I'm on I-95, and I'm in the center lane headed to a place unknown. But then I remember that I'm eighteen years old and pregnant. I remember that I'm married to a man who owns the car I'm driving and he could track me down. If I ran and he found me, there will be hell to pay. So I look for the first exit and take it. Even though every part of me screams "keep driving," I always head back home.

When I pull up to the house today after my time with Agnes, I find Cee sitting on the front porch in one of the rocking chairs. His flask is in one hand and a burning cigarette dangles from the other. He's slumped so low in the chair any regular person would think he was fast asleep, but I can see that his eyes are open. He's glaring at me as I open the car door and step onto the gravel.

"Where the hell were you?" he barks as I walk toward the stairs. "What took you so long?"

"I was only a couple of hours, honey," I say, trying to keep my voice gentle. "Agnes and me had a lot of catching up to do."

"Agnes *and I*," he corrects with an air of exasperation, then pushes himself to his feet. "Well, I'm tired of waiting for you. If you came back any later, we were going to be late."

"Late for what?" I ask, climbing the porch stairs.

"Late for the party! Jesus Christ, can't you remember anything?" He flicks his cigarette toward the rosebushes.

I don't know what to say. If I say the wrong thing, like telling him that he never

420

mentioned any damn party, it could earn me a slap to my cheek. So instead I stare at him.

"They're having the annual cocktail party at the country club. We've gotta make an appearance." He tucks his flask into his coat pocket. "My family goes every year."

"You . . . you want me to go with you?"

"That's what I said, didn't I? You're my wife now. It wouldn't look right if you weren't there with me."

Yes, I am his wife, but I am also a Colored woman, and I don't think they let folks like me in his family's country club who aren't carrying a tray or toting a broom. But I can tell from the firm set of Cee's jaw that he doesn't want to hear reason. He certainly doesn't want to hear it from me. I don't know what he'll do if they turn us away at the door, but I guess I'll deal with it when the time comes.

"Okay," I say, painting on a smile, "I'll find something pretty to wear."

# CHAPTER 30

When we arrive at the country club, I can hear the band playing inside. The music floats through the opened glass doors, where men in tuxedos and women in cocktail dresses huddle at the entrance, laughing and talking. Seeing them, I feel light-headed and sick to my stomach again. I'm not sure if it's because of the corset I'm wearing or the baby or my nerves. Maybe it's all three.

I don't want to get out of the car, but Cee is already climbing out of his GTO and handing off the keys to a colored boy in a red jacket and black slacks who looks to be my age. The boy's mouth falls open as he watches Cee walk around the car hood and hold out his hand to me. I take it and rise to my feet. When I do, I try not to fidget with my dress and my jewelry, but it's hard not to. I feel weighed down by it — the mink shawl, the diamond and emerald necklace around my throat, and the diamond cuffs around my wrists. Even I know it's too much for a party, and I didn't want to wear them, but Cee made me do it anyway. I wonder if he thinks no one will notice my brown skin under all the fur and jewels.

But they do notice. As soon as I link my arm through Cee's and we climb the short flight of stairs, the conversations stop. The men and women standing near the doors turn to stare at us. One woman lowers a cigarette from her red lips. Another just blinks her false eyelashes, like she can't believe what she's seeing. One of the men raises his hand in a half-hearted wave.

"H-hey, Cee," he stutters, and Cee nods at him and grins, like he can't see their slacked jaws.

"Hey, Bill, how you doing?" Cee says, and we keep walking.

I can feel their eyes on our backs as we make our way down the grand hall toward the ballroom. The light seems brighter under the crystal chandeliers. The music and voices are louder now too — and so are the whispers. The people lining the halls aren't just staring at us. Some lean their heads toward one another and point. Others frown. I can tell Cee notices, but unlike me, he seems to take pleasure in all the attention. His smile goes wider. He holds his head up higher. He waves and says hello to a few people, but they either give him a vague "hey" back or just look at him, confused.

I'm not having as good a time as he is. I want to get out of here, to run back to the car. I'm not wanted here, and I can feel it. I start to tug my arm out of Cee's grasp, but he stops me. He holds on to my hand even tighter, and I know I'm trapped.

"Smile, Dee," he orders between clenched teeth, glancing down at me.

I paint on a smile though my legs feel like taffy. I worry I might faint.

We enter the ballroom, where couples are doing the twist on the dance floor. I feel a little less conspicuous in here with the crushing mass of people, but now the heat from all their bodies overwhelms me instead. I follow him through the sea of dancers and lingerers to one of the tables near the stage. I can see a few people are already sitting there. When we draw closer, I recognize the red bouffant, and I stop in my tracks.

"Come on," he says, tugging me forward, and I shake my head.

"I can't, Cee. Don't make me do this," I whisper desperately.

He narrows his eyes at me and yanks again, and I almost fly out of my high heels. We walk to the table, and Miss Mindy turns away from a gray-haired woman with sallow skin and a willowy frame sitting to her right. Mr. Williams lowers his cigarette from his mouth and stares up at us.

"Mama, Mindy, Jake . . . how are y'all doing tonight? Sorry, we're a little late." He laughs. "Delilah had to put her face on. You know how women can be."

He pulls out a chair at the table for me — next to his mother — and I glance at it, unsure whether I should sit down.

"Go on." He slaps the back of the chair. "Take a load off your feet, gorgeous. A woman in your condition shouldn't be standing around all the time."

I slowly sit down. His mother scowls at me, eying me over the top of her eyeglasses. Her eyes then land on Cee.

"If your father could see you now," she whispers through wrinkled lips, then gravely shakes her head, "he would be so ashamed, Chauncey!"

I clamp my mouth shut and close my eyes, feeling the bile rise in the back of my throat.

"Ashamed that I knocked up a colored gal — or that I married one?" Cee asks, removing his flask from the inside of his tuxedo jacket and raising an eyebrow. "You're going to have to be specific, Mama."

I open my eyes and stare at him in disgust.

"Not here, please," Jake says, tapping the ashes of his cigarette onto an empty bread plate. But Cee ignores him.

"Come on! Why are we all pretending? We've all heard the rumors. Even my dear Daddy sowed his share of pickaninnies in his day. At least I'm owning up to it."

"Cee!" Miss Mindy snarls. "You stop this right now! You hear me?"

Cee laughs even harder as he twists off the lid to his flask and raises it to his lips. I realize then that he hasn't brought me here because I'm his wife and he felt I should be at his side, like he said. He did it just for the spectacle. It's like he enjoys torturing his family as much as he does bullying me. He likes watching them squirm and their faces go red. But I don't. I can't stand it anymore. I shoot to my feet and push back my chair.

"Where do you think you're going?" he snarls.

"To the ladies' room," I mumble before rushing from the table and heading across the ballroom, not giving him a chance to stop me.

I ignore the eyes that follow me as I run

to the ballroom doors. I look up and down the hall, searching for the women's bathroom, clutching my gloved hand over my mouth. I finally spot the gold sign and run toward it, excusing myself as I push my way past a group of women. I fly into one of the stalls, drop to my knees on the marble tile, and throw up right there in the country club toilet. I throw up until my stomach feels empty, until I can't do it anymore. When I'm done, I stagger to my feet and wipe my mouth with some toilet tissue. I open the door and find a woman standing at one of seashell-shaped sinks, applying lipstick.

I slink to the sink next to her with my head bowed.

"Not feeling too well, huh?" the woman asks. "I hope it wasn't the shrimp."

I shake my head and fill my cupped hands with water. I lean down and lightly douse my face. "It wasn't the shrimp," I whisper. "I haven't eaten anything."

"Did you tell Cee you didn't feel well?" she asks, and my head shoots up. I blink water out of my eyes and see her smiling at me in the mirror's reflection. "I bet he made you come to the party anyway. He can be stubborn about those sorts of things."

I didn't recognize her when I ran into the bathroom. I was more concerned with finding a toilet. But I recognize her now.

"Just look at me, jabbering like we're old friends," she says with a chuckle. "I saw you walk in with Chauncey. I'm Betsy, by the way."

"I know. We've met before. I'm Delilah."

*"We have?"* Her upturned nose wrinkles. "Why, I didn't know we've made prior acquaintance. I'm embarrassed to say I can't remember! When did we meet?"

"I worked for Miss M— . . . I worked for Cee's sister, Melinda. We met when you visited her home."

"Oh," Betsy says.

There still isn't any recognition on her face. I doled out meatloaf and mashed potatoes to her at the Williamses' dinner table and stood inches from her for hours, but she still doesn't know me from Adam. I could've been one of Miss Mindy's table lamps or potted plants as far as Betsy is concerned. But then again, back then she only had eyes for Cee — or so I thought. She must not have only had eyes for him since she was dating that lawyer from Alabama at the same time she was dating Cee.

"Well, it's a pleasure to run into you again." She grins, opens the clasp of her purse, and drops her tube of lipstick inside.

"I heard Cee had gotten married, and I wanted to meet the gal who was brave enough to become Mrs. Chauncey Buford. I wasn't expecting a colored gal, but . . . Cee's always had . . . well . . . *interesting* tastes!"

"Brave enough?"

She nods. "Cee is quite the handful. Always has been! The other girls warned me that going out with a man like him isn't for the faint of heart. But I didn't listen. He was so charming and funny in the beginning, I thought, 'What are they talking about?' I finally figured it out, and I had to throw in the towel after a few months. I had no choice but to break it off with him. He was just too intense for me and, frankly, too possessive," she says with widened eyes.

"You . . . you broke it off with him?"

She nods.

"He . . . Cee told me he broke up with you."

She drops a hand to her hip. Her smile disappears. "Did he now?" She tosses her blond hair over her shoulder. "Well, that's news to me, considering that he refused to accept the fact that we had broken up for more than a month. He kept calling my apartment. Sometimes a dozen times a day. He terrified the hell out of my roommate!

He even showed up one night when I was headed out on a date and threatened the poor fellow. He cornered me on my way to campus a few days later, threatened to kill me *and* kill himself. Then one day, all the calls and the threats stopped. It was so strange. It was like he just . . . disappeared. I wondered why." Her blue eyes scan over me. "I guess you're the reason."

When she says that, a chill goes down my spine.

Betsy closes the clasp on her purse, then tosses the strap over her shoulder. "Like I said, you're a braver woman than me." She exhales gravely. "Good luck to you, Delilah."

She then turns away and walks out of the ladies' room.

# CHAPTER 31

After that night, I don't look at Cee the same way anymore. I knew before, but I can finally admit it to myself now — he isn't going to change back into the man I first met. That man wasn't real. Cee was just wearing a mask to win me over — and it was so well-crafted you couldn't even tell it was there. Now the mask has been removed, and it's staying off.

I was wary of him before, but I'm even more wary of him now. In the morning as he brushes his teeth, over dinner as he eats, and at night while he sleeps, I watch him like he's a coiled snake that can snap at me if I handle him wrong, or if he just takes the notion. And Cee seems to watch me too, judging my every move and every word, picking over them with a fine-toothed comb. He has more chances to do it now since he is almost always at the house.

After the party at the country club more

than a month ago, his social calendar seems to have winnowed down. I suspect Cee may have crossed some line with his friends by taking me to the country club that night, one that he shouldn't have crossed. Now they've distanced themselves from him.

He still goes out sometimes, though I don't know with whom. I watch from the bedroom window as he hops into his cherry red GTO and disappears for hours and comes back smelling like a distillery. But most of the time, he lounges around Harbor Hill, drinking, smoking, and staring sullenly at the television. He mutters to himself or yells at me, calling me lazy and stupid, disrespectful and ungrateful. I try my best to ignore him, to focus on decorating the nursery and getting ready for the baby who will arrive in four months — but it isn't easy.

I stay because of the baby. Living with Cee, I can still offer our child more than I ever could alone. If it wasn't for the baby, I would leave, I tell myself.

Today is one of the rare days that Cee is away from Harbor Hill, and I am enjoying my freedom. This morning, I sit at the kitchen table in my nightgown and bare feet, eating toast smothered in marmalade without a plate, which he hates. I turn up the volume on the radio — something else he doesn't like — so I can hear the Hit Parade in every room. I make hot cocoa for myself and give a mug to our grounds-keeper, Tobias, a Georgia boy whose wife and kids are still down south, though he hopes he can save enough money to bring them up here with him soon.

It is December and too cold to go to the beach. Heavy clouds have been hanging low on the horizon since dawn, hinting that snow is probably in the offing, but I take a walk around the property anyway. I look at the bay, picturing the ships that must have docked there centuries ago with their sails high and puffed with wind, and their bows pointed toward shore. As I stand staring at the frigid water, I imagine that this is my life — peaceful and quiet, without the tension and fury that Cee brings.

I arrive back at the house an hour later, sniffing and shoving my gloved hands into the pockets of my wool coat. I discover a familiar car parked in our driveway, and I pause. The door to the Lincoln Continental flies open, and Miss Mindy climbs out. She is covered head to toe in pink wool and brown fur.

"There you are!" she says, looking annoyed. "I saw your car and thought you were home, but no one answered the door when I rang, so I was starting to wonder." She holds up a key ring, then shakes it, making the keys jingle like brass bells. "I tried to open the door myself, but my key doesn't seem to work anymore."

"Cee changed the locks."

She drops the keys into her purse. "Of course my darling brother did. Where is he anyway?"

"He isn't here," I explain. "He won't be back for a couple more hours. If you want to come back later or wait until —"

"I didn't come to speak to him." She takes a step toward me, narrowing her green eyes. "I was asking if he was here because I came to speak to you alone, Delilah."

"Why do you want to speak to me?"

She doesn't answer my question but instead turns and stares at the front door. "Can we do this inside? It's cold out here, and frankly," she adjusts the rabbit fur collar of her coat, "I'm starting to feel a little chilly."

I hesitate, then nod.

When Miss Mindy enters Harbor Hill, she does it with the familiarity of one who has not only been here before but also once owned the place. She takes off her coat and hat and wordlessly shoves it at me to hang them up, like I'm still her maid, like I'm not the lady of the house. She then walks into the living room and sits down before I have a chance to offer her a seat.

"I'll have Earl Grey," she says, adjusting her skirt as she fluffs one of the sofa pillows beside her. "No sugar — just honey."

I hang her coat and hat on the coatrack near the door, along with my own, then reluctantly head to the kitchen to make her tea. When I return, I set the teacup and saucer in front of her. She reaches for the cup and clutches it in her pale hand, but instead of taking a sip, she stares at me over the lip as I lower myself into the armchair facing her.

Under Miss Mindy's gaze, I clutch my hand over the lump at my waist, over my baby. Her eyes seem almost predatory.

"I want you to know that I am here strictly at my mother's request," she says, raising her nose into the air. "I told her that trying to talk to Cee would be like trying to have a conversation with a brick wall. I said I might have more luck reasoning with you. I know you're more . . . well . . . practical than my brother is about these things."

My blank face sinks into a frown. I'm confused by the course this conversation is taking. I watch as she drinks some of her tea.

"This whole thing with Cee has taken its toll on Mama. It pains her to see her son like this — just throwing his life away!"

I wasn't aware that being married to me was the same as "throwing his life away," but I don't comment.

"Frankly, I've given up on him, but now that Mama is ill, I'm willing to put forth the effort to try to give her some reconciliation. She should get some sense of peace before she takes her last breath."

I wasn't aware that their mother was sick. Cee certainly hadn't mentioned it, but then I remember the yellow hue to his mother's skin and her skeletal frame that night at the country club. She hadn't looked well.

"So," Miss Mindy says, pausing to take another sip of tea, "in order to reunite mother and son while there's still time, I need your help — and I'm willing to pay you handsomely for it."

My frown deepens. My confusion is being replaced with annoyance.

"Well . . ." She inclines her head. "*My mother* is willing to pay you handsomely. She wants to offer you twenty-five-thousand dollars to file for divorce from Cee. That should be more than enough money to take care of you and your baby . . . for you to start all over again. All we ask is that you remove yourself from his life gracefully, that you go your separate ways."

"You mean you want me to go away . . . to disappear."

"Exactly!" She smiles for the first time. "Now I know my brother isn't easy to live with. I love him, but I'm aware that he can be a bit . . . trying. The men in our family are very . . . very passionate," she says diplomatically while glancing at my forearm, where a purple bruise has already bloomed from where Cee grabbed me in a viselike grip last week when I made the soup too salty for dinner. Now that she sees it, I cover the bruise with my hand. "They aren't good at holding in their emotions. My father had quite the temper, and so does my brother."

*And your husband,* I want to add but don't.

"It can be challenging for those who aren't used to it," she says. "I'm sure you could use a break from his tantrums. This is your chance to do it. We'll even help you move out of Harbor Hill. Get you set up in a nice, cozy place for you and your baby. You won't have to worry about a thing, Delilah."

I clench my hands in my lap, feeling my baby squirm in my belly and something else squirm inside of me: anger.

I try my best to ignore her patronizing and her pretense of looking out for my welfare

437

when I know deep down she really doesn't give a damn what Cee does to me. I try to get my anger under control, but it is a struggle — one that I am quickly losing. While I worked for Miss Mindy and she handed out her put downs and threats, I bowed my head, looked meek, and didn't talk back. Even Agnes and Roberta — two women more outspoken than me — did the same. We did it because we knew she had all the power and control. But I'm not Miss Mindy's maid anymore. I am her brother's wife, and this is my home. Even the sofa that she's sitting on and the cup she's drinking from is mine. She does not hold all the power, I realize. I don't have to be meek anymore.

"Well, aren't you thoughtful," I mutter. "You've just thought of everything."

Her smile disappears. She slowly lowers her tea cup to the coffee table. *"Excuse me?"*

"One moment you're blackmailing me into *giving* you money," I begin, meeting her eyes, "the next moment you're trying to bribe me into *taking* money from you." I push back my shoulders. "You think you can just . . . just throw money at anything to get what you want? Y-you think you can . . . can just play with me like I'm some puppet. You pull my strings and make me do a little dance, then toss me aside when you're done?" I furiously shake my head. "Well, you can't! I'm not your puppet, and I'm not gonna just disappear because your mother's shaking twenty-five thousand dollars in my face! If she wants to reconcile with Cee, I'm not keeping her from doing it. It has nothing to do with me!"

Her lips tighten. "It has *everything* to do with you. You've made him and her, by extension, a laughingstock . . . *social pariahs*! She can barely hold her head up among her friends, and our family has worked hard for the reputation we have in our community. My mother is being kind by offering to take care of you financially. Not everyone would be so generous, Delilah!"

"And not everyone is as desperate for cash as you are!"

Even I'm shocked by my words. I guess the fury finally got to me. Miss Mindy's face reddens. Her pert nostrils flare.

"Well, I guess I gave you too much credit. I thought you were smarter and knew when you were getting a good deal, but I guess I should've known better." She gave a cold laugh. "Every colored girl I've ever met has been cunning, but when it comes to basic smarts, they were dumber than a sack of bricks. I guess you're no different."

At that, I push myself to my feet. "I'll tell Cee that you stopped by. Let me show you to the door."

She blinks in shock as I turn toward the foyer. Her mouth falls open. "Are you . . . are you kicking me out?"

"I didn't think you wanted to stay in a place you weren't wanted. I know Cee doesn't want you here, and frankly," I shrug, "I don't either. I'm not kicking you out, but I *am* asking you politely to leave."

She shoots to her feet, sending her purse tumbling from the sofa cushion to the rug. Her eyes seem to catch fire. "Why, you little nigger bitch!" she hisses. "You can't throw me out of my own house! The Bufords have owned this home since —"

"The only Buford who owns this home is Chauncey Buford, and he changed the locks for a reason — to keep you out! Again, I am asking you politely to leave. I don't know if he will do the same."

She narrows her eyes at me before bending down to pick up her purse from the floor. She stomps toward the front door in her kitten heels. I watch as she grabs her coat and hat from the wooden rack, sending the entire rack and the rest of the coats toppling to the ground.

"You're going to regret this, Delilah," she says over her shoulder. "I'll make sure you regret what you did today for as long as you live. Mark my words!"

She then tugs open the front door, steps into the cold, and slams the door.

# CHAPTER 32

Cee is asleep with his head buried in his pillow, filling our bedroom with his snores, when a call comes in the middle of a snowy February night. Bleary-eyed and yawning, I struggle to roll onto my side with my ever-growing belly and reach for the old-fashioned, gold princess phone on my night table.

"Hello?" I whisper, careful not to wake him. He hates to be woken up by anything or anyone that isn't an alarm clock.

"Put my brother on the phone," the voice on the other end of the line orders. It takes me a few seconds to realize that it's Miss Mindy.

I frown and am about to tell her that Cee is snoring louder than a bear and to call back after the sun is up, but then I hear her sniff and whimper. I know something is wrong.

I set down the phone and turn around to

face Cee. I nudge his shoulder, but he doesn't budge. The snores continue. He drank half a quart of bourbon before he passed out, so I know it won't be easy to wake him up, but I can tell from the desperate sounds on the other end of the line that I should. I nudge his shoulder, shoving it a little harder.

"Cee!" I shout into his ear. "Cee, wake up! Your sis —"

"What? What is it?" he yells, snapping awake. Instead of looking serene or confused, he looks furious. "What did I tell you about doing that?"

"But your sister is on the —"

My words are cut off when he flops onto his other side, balls his fist, and punches me squarely in the mouth. I scream and grab my face. The pain radiates across my jawline and stings my cheek. It feels like a hornet has attacked me and a prizefighter has hit me at the same time. I pull my hands away, and even in the darkness, I can see the glint of blood on my fingers. My eyes flood with tears.

"Goddammit, Dee," he says tiredly, pushing himself up to his elbows. He shoves his hand through his hair and closes his eyes. He takes a deep breath, opens his eyes, and flexes the fingers of the hand he just used to punch me. "I didn't mean to hit you like that, honey, but I told you about waking me up from a dead sleep. Didn't I?"

I slowly nod, now shaking.

"I hate it. You *know* I hate it, Dee. Why'd you wake me up?"

"Your . . . your sister is on th-the phone," I garble between sobs, cupping my hand in front of my face to catch the blood pooling in my mouth. He'd have a fit if I got the blood on the sheets. "Sh-she said she n-n-needed to speak with you."

"Mindy's on the phone?" He frowns, then shrugs. He shoots out his hand, and I flinch. He doesn't hit me again. He just snaps his fingers. "Hand the phone to me, will you, sweetheart? If she's calling this early, it's gotta be important."

I give him the phone, then climb off the bed to walk to the bathroom. As I step onto the cool tile, turn on the vanity light, and stare at my reflection — with blood dribbling down my mouth and chin, puffy eyes, and a swollen lip and cheek that will probably be purple by the afternoon — I listen to Cee's end of the conversation.

"What is it, Mindy?" he says as I spit blood into the sink and turn on the faucet, watching as the red liquid swirls its way down the drain.

"Uh-huh . . . What? . . . Oh, God," he breathes.

I grab one of the washcloths and begin to wipe my mouth.

"Oh God . . . Mindy, when did it happen? . . . Okay. Okay . . . Of course, I'll come! Just tell me when it is . . . Yeah. I'm sorry too, Mindy . . . Whatever you may think, I loved her. I loved her as much as you . . . Okay . . . Yes. Good-bye."

When all the blood is gone from my face, I return to the bedroom and find Cee sitting on the edge of the bed with his head bowed. I hesitantly walk toward him. When I am less than 1 foot away from him he raises his head. I can see there are tears in his eyes.

"What happened?" I whisper.

He loudly swallows and rubs his bare legs. "Mama died an hour ago. She died in her sleep," he answers softly. He lowers his head again and begins to weep.

I don't know how to respond. He is my husband, and I know I should hold him, touch him, and comfort him. I should console him — but I can't work up the urge to do it. I'm as moved by his tears as he is by mine. He has punched and slapped the feelings out of me. Instead, I stare at him as he cries. I watch him as he mourns his dead mother.

I stay home the day of the funeral. Cee thought it better that I do, and I don't care one way or the other, frankly.

I am sitting in the living room, watching *Gilligan's Island* and knitting a blue, yellow, and pink blanket for the baby and making a mess of it, when the front door flings open. It slams against the side of the foyer wall, and I jump in my chair, dropping my knitting needles to the floor. Cee stumbles through the door, laughing. He is being held up by a man I've never seen before — tall, blond, lanky, and dressed in a black suit just like Cee.

"Hey, where can I put him?" the man asks dispassionately. He looks annoyed.

I point toward the staircase. "You can take him to the bedroom upstairs."

He nods, and I set aside my blanket and follow them up to the second floor. The whole time Cee has his arm slung around the man's shoulder, laughing and talking like he's just come from a bar, not a funeral.

"Do you remember the time when we played that prank our sophomore year at Tulane, Henry? Huh? Do you remember, buddy?" he slurs drunkenly to his friend, tapping his chest too hard.

"Yeah, I remember," Henry mutters as he grunts and staggers under Cee's weight. He still manages to carry him up the flight of stairs and down the hall, huffing and puffing along the way. I open the bedroom door for him, and he drops Cee onto the bed.

He glances at me. "You got it from here?"

I nod. "I'll take care of him."

His gaze drops to my protruding belly, then rises to my face. The bottom right half is swollen and bruised thanks to the punch earlier that week. He squints. "Are you sure? He's not in a good place, kid. I'd call someone to help with him if you can."

I am not a "kid," and there is no one else to call, I want to say but don't. "We'll be fine."

After Henry leaves, Cee's laughter dies down, and he becomes sullen. It's only three-thirty, so I head downstairs to make him a cup of coffee to sober him up.

"I don't want any goddamn coffee!" he says, spitting the liquid onto me and himself, shoving the cup away. "Not unless you put some Irish whiskey in there!"

"I don't think you need anything more to drink," I whisper.

"Don't tell me what I need, goddammit!"

"Why don't you just go to sleep, Cee? You'll feel better when you wake up."

I try to undress him, starting with his suit jacket and tie, but he roughly shoves me away.

"I don't *need* your fuckin' help," he barks, and I take a step back from the bed.

"Fine." I hold up my hands in surrender and turn toward the door. "I'll leave you alone. I'll be downstairs."

"Would it have killed you to come to the funeral?" he shouts at me, out of nowhere. "Would it have killed you to show my mother a little respect?"

I pause and face him again. "I thought . . . I thought you didn't want me to come. You said it would upset your sister and the rest of the family."

"I said no such thing, you lying bitch! You just didn't want to go. Admit it! You don't care about me! You just want my money. You always have!"

His eyes are bright, and his face is red. He is in his wild state again, beyond logic and reason. The alarm bells sing in my ears. I want out of this bedroom.

I start backing toward the door. I don't want to turn my back to him. He might grab my hair or my clothes and pull me. I keep my eye on him like he's a rabid dog.

"Melinda told me all about you," he snarls. "I didn't believe her at first, but I'm

448

starting to wonder now. She said you set this whole thing up! Girls like you know how to do it. You wanted to trap me with some nigger baby so you could get all my money!"

"I didn't trap you, Cee. I didn't want to get married. You *told* me that we had to. I —"

"That's what you wanted me to think!" His lips tighten as he lurches to his feet. "Mindy said that you've . . . you've messed with my head. That you turned me against my family, against Mama! She said you'll only stick around long enough to divorce me and then take everything! Well, it's not gonna happen. You hear me? No fucking way!"

I take another step toward the door, then another.

"Don't you walk away from me, you lyin' cunt!" And he grabs for me.

I turn and run. I'm not that fast to begin with, and I am slowed down even more by the baby who is shifting around in my belly, kicking at my ribs as my heart thuds in my chest at a breakneck speed. But the alcohol has made Cee's gait unsteady and his feet unsure. He stumbles a few times and hits the wall hard. He struggles to keep up with me.

I run down the stairs, and I can hear him cussing and shouting my name. His voice sounds dry and hoarse. I glance over my shoulder and see his face. Its contorted by rage. He doesn't look human anymore but like some picture show monster — a were-wolf in a wrinkled funeral suit or maybe Mr. Hyde himself.

I trip on the floor runner and land splayed on the hardwood. The pain shoots up my abdomen and down my legs, and I scream out. But I can hear Cee not far behind me. I push myself to my knees and then my feet and start running again.

He lunges for me as I round the staircase. I whip open the pantry door and run inside, closing the sliding lock behind me.

When I moved into Harbor Hill, I was confused when I saw the lock on the door. *Why would a pantry need a lock on the inside?* But Cee explained that the pantry had once been the maid's quarters in the early days of Harbor Hill. A twin bed and petite dresser had once been where shelves are now.

The lock afforded the maid some privacy, Cee explained.

I was eternally grateful for that lock today.

"Damnit, Dee, you better come outta there!" he yells, slamming against the door over and over again, making it rattle on its frame. "You open this door right now!"

I step away from the door, clutching my belly, biting back my sobs. I bump into one of the shelves, sending a canister of Cream of Wheat tumbling to the floor and rolling across the pantry.

"Open the damn door!" he screams, and I clap my hands over my ears.

There is more banging and yelling. I squeeze my eyes shut, feeling the wooden shelves pressing against my back and shoulders. I sink to my knees, then crouch on the floor. I wrap my arms around myself, rocking back and forth, singing the Lord's Prayer. I pray that if Cee exerts himself, his anger will eventually be spent and he will walk away. I pray the liquor will finally take its toll and he'll pass out.

"Fine, Dee!" he shouts. "Fine! You don't wanna come out? You don't wanna open the door, then you can damn well stay in there!"

I hear his shuffling footsteps, then the sound of something being dragged across the floor. There is a heavy thump. After that, the noises stop.

I wait. I count to one hundred twenty times before I finally press my ear against the door. I can hear nothing but the settling of the house.

Maybe Cee is asleep.

Ever so slowly, I slide back the lock. The click as it opens makes me whimper.

What if he heard it? What if he comes back?

But nothing happens. The silence and stillness remain.

I take a deep breath, drawing up my courage, and push against the door to open it — but it doesn't budge. I try again, but nothing happens. I try over and over again, forcing my weight and muscles against the wooden slab until I'm gritting my teeth, until I'm panting — but it's useless. I realize now what I heard minutes before. I know now what he meant when he said I could "damn well stay in there."

Cee has propped a chair against the door so I can't get out.

I whimper again, ease back against the shelves, and slump to the floor.

The hours stretch. My eyes grow heavy. I fall asleep in the cold, damp pantry. I am jolted awake by the sound of Cee's footsteps near the door. The pain in my abdomen is worse now. I suck in deep breaths and fight back moans.

I squint against the bright light coming from the overhead bulb. Is it still afternoon, or is it night? Is it the next day? How long have I been in here?

"Cee? Cee? Open up! I'm hurt. Open up, please," I call out, but he doesn't answer me. The thud of his footsteps recedes, then disappears.

More hours pass, though I don't know how many. I can feel my bladder growing heavy.

I call again to be let out.

I cry.

I count the cans and jars on the shelves until I reach forty-three, then start over again, anything to distract me from the pain that feels like someone is running a knife across my stomach.

I open a jar of preserved peaches and gobble them up, letting the juice slide down my chin. I pee in the same jar.

The hours stretch. I don't know if it's still Wednesday or if it's Thursday now.

I fall asleep again and wake up. The pain is still there, and it is scaring me. The baby isn't moving as much. I jiggle my tummy. I whisper to it, "Baby, wake up. Wake up for Mommy." Still no kicks. Maybe it is exhausted like I am.

I eat a jar of pickles and half a box of Frosted Flakes.

I pee in two more jars and set them in a line on the other side of the pantry, trying my best to ignore the smell of urine that fills the air.

The sounds of Harbor Hill become the symphony of my lonely space, marking the time with a rhythm.

Footsteps . . .

Radio . . .

The ringing of the phone . . .

The sound of flushing water . . .

Footsteps . . .

A door creaking open, then slamming shut . . .

The ringing of the phone . . .

Footsteps . . .

The monotony is broken when I feel a wetness between my thighs. Oh, dear. I've peed myself. But when I look down at the puddle on the floor, I see that it's red, not yellow. A moan rises in my throat. It doesn't sound like its coming from me. It sounds like an animal. It sounds horrible.

"Cee!" I scream, scrambling toward the door, banging my fists against it. "Chauncey, let me out! Something is wrong with the baby! I'm bleeding. Cee, please!"

And finally, the door swings open.

# CHAPTER 33

It was a boy. The doctor breaks the news to me in my hospital room as the nurse tends to my bruises and I'm treated for blood loss and acute dehydration after the three days I spent stuck in the pantry closet.

They took the baby out by emergency C-section while I was under anesthesia. They said he was already dead by the time I'd arrived at the emergency room. They said the trauma from my accidental fall at the foot of the stairs (I told them it was an accident because it was; I didn't need to tell them I was running from my husband) is likely what killed him.

I am too tired and numb with grief to cry. I am glad I wasn't awake in the operating room when they pulled out my boy, who still held the warmth of my body but was silent and unmoving in the doctor's pale hands. I wouldn't have wanted to see that or hear it.

When Cee walks into my hospital room with a bouquet of more than two dozen roses in his arms, I can tell from the look on his face that he already knows our son is dead. His eyes are red. His face is pale and gaunt. He hasn't shaved. He rushes to my bed and collapses into the chair beside it, almost flinging the bouquet onto my thighs. He wraps his arms around me.

"I'm so sorry, honey," he sobs. "I'm so sorry!"

I'm not sure what he's sorry about — that our baby boy is dead, or how he kept me locked in a closet for three days while I screamed in pain and our baby slowly died. I don't ask, and I don't hug him back. I sit stiffly in the bed as he cries, wetting my hospital gown with his tears.

He finally pulls back a minute later and looks up at me. He wipes his runny nose on the back of his hand.

"I know you're angry at me. And . . . and you have every right to be. What I said, what I . . . I *did* was unforgivable. You . . . you probably want to leave me now. You're ready to pack your bags and move out." He grabs one of my hands, which are folded in my lap. He kisses it, then squeezes it gently. "But please give me another chance, Dee. I can't lose my mother, the baby, *and* you in

456

a matter of weeks! I would never make it!"

Again, I don't respond. Instead, I marvel that even at a moment like this, Cee manages to make it about himself.

I want to tell him how selfish he is, how he claimed I lied to him but really he lied to me, spouting beautiful words and false dreams that ensnared me like a fly in a spiderweb. He stole my hopes. He killed my baby. I will not absolve him of my pain. I open my mouth to tell him all of this when he reaches into his coat pocket and pulls out a sheet of paper. I watch as he unfolds it.

"It's all yours, baby," he says, holding out the paper to me. "Harbor Hill . . . everything that I have. I don't give a shit what my sister says. You're my wife, and I love you. I want to finally show you that I do. I called my lawyer this morning and had him draw up the paperwork. I signed my intent. I'm adding you to the deed. I'm changing my will, Dee. My mother and my sister were my beneficiaries, but now it's just you. When I die, everything . . . *everything* goes to you."

I slowly take the sheet of paper and read it. Exactly what he said is typed on the page. I am co-owner of Harbor Hill. I will inherit everything upon Cee's death.

"Will you stay, Dee?" he asks, taking my

free hand again and clutching it for dear life. "Baby, if you leave me . . . I'll kill myself. A bullet to the head. I mean it!"

I stare down at the paper and then into his desperate eyes. I am still numb, still exhausted. I can't answer. I can't work up the energy, so I nod instead, and he begins to weep again.

When I arrive back home from the hospital a few days later, I expect Harbor Hill to look different for some reason. I expect my loss and misery to be painted on the walls, to hang from the windows like a shroud. But I am greeted by cheery yellow wallpaper and hardwood that smells of lemon. The air inside is light, and sun streams through the windows.

"I'll be back later tonight, sweetheart," Cee says to me after he deposits me on our bed. He kisses my cheek. "Rest. Put your feet up. Okay?"

I nod limply.

After I hear the front door shut, I slowly rise from the bed and walk down the hall to the nursery. Part of me doesn't want to go in there, but I know I will have to make this journey eventually. I push open the door and look at the walls, which are covered with a painted motif of bunnies and chicks.

A crib is nestled in the center of the room, and I walk over to it. I stare down at the empty bed and drop my hand down to my waist, which isn't quite flat but no longer full and round like it used to be. I wait for the tears to sting my eyes, but they don't. Instead, I turn away from the crib and walk back into our bedroom. I grab the princess phone on my night table and turn the rotary wheel to start dialing.

"Hello?" Agnes answers.

"Hey, it's Dee." I twirl the phone cord around my finger. "I know today is your day off and you may have plans, but . . . I need your help."

Agnes arrives at the house a couple of hours later. When I greet her at the door, I am all smiles and wearing one of my maternity dresses, but she looks me up and down and squints, sensing instantly that something is wrong

"What happened?" she asks, stepping through the door, frowning.

"Nothing!" I answer nervously. "Why do you think something happened?"

"Because you look strange, girl! Where did you get that?" she asks, pointing to the bruise on the side of my face that still hasn't healed completely from the punch Cee gave me more than a week ago.

"Oh," my smile widens as I raise my hand to my chin, "I was being clumsy when I did that. It was just an accident. It looks worse than it feels." I beckon her forward. "Come on. Let me show you the place. I'll take your coat."

I told Agnes on the phone that I needed her help cleaning up a room, but I didn't tell her which room. I promised her a nice lunch in a big house — a day all to ourselves.

I give her the grand tour of Harbor Hill since she has never been here before. She goes wide-eyed at all the rooms, the big windows, and the expensive fixtures. I make her a lunch of pork chops, mashed potatoes, and biscuits, and we eat and gossip. She tells me that the Williams family aren't tightening their purse strings anymore now that Mama Buford died, leaving Miss Mindy some money. She tells me that she's met an MP from Nashville and they've gone out on a few dates.

All the while, I can feel her discerning eyes on me. The wrinkle of concern doesn't leave her brow. She asks me again what's wrong, and I shrug it off. I tell her it's time to clean the room.

We head upstairs, laughing and talking all the way. I push open the nursery door, and she steps inside. The wrinkle in her brow deepens. She turns to me.

"Why are we in here?"

I take a deep breath. "I have to pack up the nursery."

"What for?" She leans toward me and whispers, "You leaving him?"

"No . . . nothing like that." I run my hand over my stomach to show how flat it is now. "I lost the baby."

*"What?"* Agnes cries. She grabs my shoulders and yanks me toward her and envelopes me in a hug. "Oh, honey! Sweetheart! Lord, I knew something was wrong. I could see it on your face!" She leans back and stares into my eyes. Tears are on her cheeks. "Here we were talking and eating pork chops like some fools! Why didn't you say something?"

"I didn't want to tell you over the phone. I didn't know how to say it, so . . . I thought it was just best to . . . well . . . show you."

"When did it happen? *How* did it happen?"

"I tripped and fell on the stairs. I landed on my stomach. It was an —"

*"Accident?"* she finishes for me. "You seem to have a lot of those."

"I'm just clumsy," I say weakly.

"Delilah, tell the truth! Is that man beating on you? Did he push you down the stairs and make you lose your baby?"

I shake my head. "No! He didn't push me . . . I-I fell. I did!"

"So how did you get that thing on your face? Did you fall then too?"

I lower my eyes to my feet.

"Girl, you can't stay here! You have to get out of this house and away from him!"

"He feels bad for . . . for what happened. He knows he's wrong. He wouldn't admit it before, but I think he . . . he finally realizes it now."

Agnes purses her lips.

"He's giving the house to me! He's putting my name on it. He showed me! He made me the beneficiary in his will. He wants to make up for everything he's done, and —"

"Delilah Grey, shut up! Just shut up and listen to me — and you listen to me good!" She points her finger up at me. "You didn't listen before, and look where it got you. That man *beats* you! And I don't believe for one damn minute he isn't behind you losing that baby! What difference does it make if you have his name or get this house or get his money when he dies. You ain't gonna live long enough to see that goddamn money! Those daydreams of yours are gonna get you killed!"

I open my mouth to argue, to tell her that she's wrong, but then she grabs my shoulders again and shakes me. She shakes me hard. The look on her face is frantic, like she sees me sinking into the ocean and she's throwing me the last life preserver.

"Dee, you either need to leave this house — or kill him. You hear me?" she says in a harsh whisper. "Because if you don't, he'll kill you first."

# CHAPTER 34

I think about Agnes's words for the next week. From one moment to the next, my resolve shifts. One minute, I agree with her and start to gather my things, to pile my clothes on the bed so I can pack them in a suitcase. A few minutes later I return my clothes to their drawers and the closet. I decide Agnes has the right to be worried, but I have things under control now.

Cee is still full of apologies, and this time, he's not just pretending to be sorry. He finally realizes what he's done wrong, and he wants to be better. I can see it. He isn't as quick to anger. He hasn't hit me since I've come back from the hospital or shouted at me. He *seems* better.

Another week passes, then another. Nothing happens. Cee and I settle into a routine that I expect normal married people would follow. I finally start to feel like things may have changed permanently between us.

Agnes's warning begins to fade into the back of my mind.

I come home from grocery shopping Monday evening to find Cee sitting in the living room, staring at the television. I can hear the *Bonanza* soundtrack.

"Hey! How was your day?" I ask, juggling my paper bags and closing the front door with my foot.

He doesn't look at me or answer. Instead, he continues to smoke his cigarette. I can see that his flask is in his other hand.

"I'm making meatloaf and mashed potatoes," I call out to him. "Your favorite."

He still doesn't answer, and I walk down the hall toward the kitchen. I take off my coat and throw it over a chair. I begin to unload the groceries, opening the refrigerator and putting the butter and milk on the shelf. When I close the door, Cee is standing a foot away from me. I jump in surprise.

"Honey, you scared me!" I say, dropping my hand to my chest. "I didn't hear you walk in here."

"They kicked me out," he says with a frown.

"*What?* Who kicked you out?"

"Those sons of bitches at the country club! Now that Mama's gone and they don't

465

have to kiss her ass anymore, they kicked me out. Revoked my membership!" he pauses to bring his flask to his lips. He takes a swig. "They actually put it to a board vote. Said my behavior wasn't becoming and in proper representation of the club. They tried to say it was because I've been drunk a few times at the clubhouse, but I know why they really did it." He squints at me. "They did it because of *you.*"

I don't comment. Instead, I return to the groceries. I grab a loaf of bread from the bag and walk across the room to put it away.

"Do you even care how much I've sacrificed for you, Delilah?" he says to my back. "Do you know what I've put up with? I've lost my friends . . . my family. My mother's dead and my sister's disowned me. I've ruined my name. No one wants to be around me anymore because I married a Colored gal!"

"No, no one wants to be around you anymore because you're always drunk," I mutter.

"What did you say?" he asks between clenched teeth. "What the hell did you just say to me?"

He stomps across the kitchen and grabs a chunk of my hair. I shout out in pain. He pulls and whips me around to face him.

"Stop it, Cee! You said you weren't gonna do this anymore!"

"You think you can just say whatever the fuck you want to me, you ungrateful little bitch!" he shouts, spitting into my face. I can smell the alcohol on his breath, and I cringe. "You think I'm just gonna take it!"

I don't know what came over me — instinct or just being fed up with all of this, all of his broken promises and anger — but I grab one of the knives from a butcher block on the counter. I do it with my free hand, lightning fast. I point it up at him.

*You need to leave this house — or kill him.* Those were Agnes's very words, and I tremble at the idea that she was right again. I have no other choice.

He releases me and squints down at the steak knife in my hand. "What the hell are you doing? You're gonna stab me, Dee?"

I don't answer him. I continue to point the knife up at him.

"You goddamn cunt! You fucking bitch!" He drops his flask to the counter and grins. Mr. Hyde is back. He begins to unbutton the cuffs of his shirt, to roll up the sleeves like he's preparing for heavy labor. "Well, you better kill me or kill yourself, because once I get my hands on you, you're gonna

467

wish you were dead."

I take one hesitant step back, then another. He follows each step.

"Stay away from me, Cee!" I scream through my tears that are blurring my vision. The trembling of my hand increases, and I look like I'm waving the knife instead of pointing it at him. "Leave me alone!"

"Do it! Do it, Dee!"

I try to work up the will to stab him, to force my hand to plunge forward — but I can't. Even after all that he's done to me, I can't kill him. Instead, I turn and rush down the hall. I run toward the stairs, and he comes chasing after me. The steak knife falls from my hand in my haste, but at least this time, I don't trip on the runner. I rush straight up the stairs to head to the bedroom.

"I'm gonna kill you, you bitch!"

When I reach the bedroom, even if he locks me in, this time I will call the police. He will not harm me anymore. I will not die tonight.

I start to reach the top step but feel myself being yanked back. He's grabbed onto the belt of my dress. He pulls again, and I lose my footing. I try to regain my balance, but I can't. My forehead goes crashing onto the newel post.

I don't have the chance to scream before

everything goes black.

When I wake up near the top of the staircase, the sun is up. It floods through the opened front door, and the bright light blinds me for a bit. I can feel the cold air from outside rush over me, lighting goose bumps on my arms. I squint and look around me dazedly, wondering what happened. Why is the door open?

"Cee?" I call out and then look at the bottom of the staircase, where he seems to be sleeping for some reason. "C-Cee?"

He doesn't move, and for the first time I realize that his head is at an odd angle. It's facing the wrong way from the rest of his body, away from me, though his torso is turned toward me.

I let out a shrill cry and scramble to my feet. When I do, I instantly feel a pounding in my head. My vision blurs a little. "Cee! Cee, oh, my God!"

I rush down the stairs to him and see that his eyes are wide open, staring out the door. No, not out the door. He's staring at a place that even I can't see.

"Oh, my God! Oh, my God! Oh, my God!" I keep repeating as I peer down at him.

I don't know what else to say.

■ ■ ■ ■

# PART V

■ ■ ■ ■

*Camden Beach, Maryland*
*April 2017*

# CHAPTER 35

The sun hadn't made its way past the horizon before the storm clouds chased it away, covering the sky with a dull gray blanket no light could pierce. From the moment Aidan opened his eyes, even before he raised his head from his pillow, he could hear the torrential rain beating against his window and Harbor Hill's roof like someone was taking a fire hose to the brick and siding. With the rain came an unholy stench, a toxic mix of rotting fish and boiled shit thanks to the bay coming ashore and the town's sewer mains overflowing. The smell would make most of the inhabitants of Camden Beach frown and hold their noses as they crossed the street, as they walked along the town's sidewalks.

Aidan knew it would be inescapable, much like the realization of what today was, of what had happened on this day exactly five years ago. He could not ignore it or forget it, even if he wanted to.

Delilah, who was well aware of the date and the effect it had on Aidan, mercifully kept her distance. When he didn't come down for breakfast, she knocked on his door and told him that a plate of scrambled eggs and toast waited for him in the fridge.

He looked up from the last of the boxes he was packing and nodded at her. "Thanks, Dee."

He made his way downstairs to the kitchen an hour later, ignoring the plate of breakfast on the top shelf. Instead, he grabbed the six-pack on the bottom shelf and took it with him back to his room.

Delilah knocked again at around noon to ask him if he wanted lunch. He told her no and turned up the music on his stereo, letting the mournful tunes drown out the sound of the rain.

Caleb didn't know what today was and didn't understand why his buddy refused to leave his room.

"Aidan? Aidan?" Aidan heard along with a knock after he had finished his third beer and smoothed the masking tape over one of the cardboard boxes at the foot of his bed.

It would join the other boxes he would load in his truck to take to his new place — a condo he was renting in the new waterfront complex. He had already signed the lease and gotten the keys last week. All he had to do was move in.

"Aidan?" Caleb shouted again, knocking louder.

Aidan sighed. He guessed he couldn't continue to pretend like he hadn't heard the kid. He glanced at his opened six-pack. He couldn't let Caleb see it, to get any inkling that Aidan was slowly drinking himself into a stupor during daylight hours, so he quickly hid the empty bottles, along with the six-pack, in the bottom drawer of his night table. He crossed his bedroom, cracked open the door, and found Caleb peering up with him, holding two wooden paddles.

"It's raining, and Mom won't let me play outside. Will you play Ping-Pong with me downstairs?" Caleb asked.

Aidan leaned against the door frame and shook his head. "Sorry, not today."

"But I'll let you win a few games. Please?"

"I'm a little busy, Cabe. Not today."

Caleb peered around Aidan's shoulder into the bedroom, as if inspecting it for some evidence of a project he was working on. "Busy doin' what?" Caleb asked, sounding skeptical.

"Adult stuff."

Caleb lowered the paddles to his side, looking dejected. "That's just what grown-ups say when they want you to go away," he mumbled before turning around with his head bowed and shoulders slumped. He began to walk back down the hall toward the staircase.

"Shit," Aidan muttered under his breath, watching Caleb's retreating back. He opened his mouth to shout for Caleb to stop, to tell him he would play Ping-Pong with him after all — but he held back. Instead, he closed his bedroom door and opened another beer.

"It's not my fucking problem," Aidan whispered before taking a swig.

He was tired of the guilt trips everyone in this damn house had been dumping on him lately, tired of feeling like he had disappointed them.

He knew he had disappointed Tracey. She had stated it plainly, and she'd practically radiated the message ever since — in her body language, in how she would no longer look him in the eyes. She was never mean to him. She hadn't uttered one unkind word in his presence. But that stilted politeness from someone you had sincerely cared for, and maybe even grown to love, seemed crueler.

He had disappointed Delilah too. Not only was he moving out and leaving her alone to fend for herself at Harbor Hill in a week, he had almost talked her into selling her house to that psycho Teddy — to the very man who had been harassing her for months. Aidan would never forgive himself for that. He had tried to make amends by going to the police, filing a report, and telling them what the pompous Theodore Williams had done. He had gotten a half-hearted promise from the investigating detective at the sheriff's office, who said they would "look into it," but it was almost a month later, and nothing had come of it.

Delilah had warned Aidan that it would be pointless to go to the cops for help, and he hadn't listened. Now she had been proven right.

Aidan slumped back onto his bed, exhaling as he landed.

He didn't need this. He felt bad enough as it was. But he couldn't help feeling like he was being buried under an ever increasing pile of sadness and regret. It made it hard to think. It made it hard to breathe. He was drowning.

A little before midnight, Aidan finally emerged from his bedroom. Everyone else in Harbor Hill was fast asleep, judging from the silence and darkness that permeated the house. Only his footsteps and the squeak of the floorboards under his weight filled the void.

"Good," Aidan muttered as he walked down the hall.

He'd finished his six-pack and was in search of more to drink. He didn't want to run into Tracey or, worse, Delilah, with their questioning gazes. They'd take one look at him with his heavy-lidded eyes, his wrinkled clothes, and the smell of alcohol on his breath and start judging him.

*To hell with that shit,* he thought before letting out a rumbling belch.

He was going to fall asleep drunk, and he planned to do so without a lecture. Six beers on an empty stomach was getting him well on his way there.

Aidan steadied himself as he descended to the first floor by grabbing the handrail to keep his balance. When he stepped onto the hardwood, he noticed a light was on in the kitchen. Delilah must have left it on. She always did things like that. She had gotten used to him following behind her, turning off lights and the television whenever she forgot. But he wouldn't be here to do that anymore.

He stepped into the kitchen, expecting to find an empty room. He was surprised to see Tracey sitting on one of the stools at the island.

A stack of textbooks sat in front of her, one with its pages fanned opened. She was scribbling into a spiral notebook, pausing to grab a highlighter and draw a bright yellow line across a few sentences. When Aidan stepped into the kitchen entryway, she looked up.

"Burning the midnight oil, huh?" he asked.

"I have an econ test in a couple of days."

"You couldn't study in the office upstairs?"

"I prefer the kitchen. I knew I wouldn't keep getting up and leaving the office for a snack or coffee if it's all right next to me and I could spread out." She gestured to all the books. "I've fallen a little behind on one of the chapters, so I'm crunching to try to catch up."

"Well, crunch away! I'll be out of your hair soon. Just came down for a little . . . uh . . . snack too," he said with a drunken smile as he strolled toward the refrigerator, bumping into the island edge as he did it. He tugged open one of the stainless steel doors, gripping the handle for balance as he leaned down.

"I haven't seen you all day."

"Oh?" he said, scanning the shelves, shifting aside a jar of preserved peaches and a container filled with leftover mac and cheese.

"Yeah, I thought you weren't home until Caleb told me you were in your room."

"I'm honored that you cared."

All the beer was gone, unfortunately, but he spotted a Smirnoff ice malt toward the back. It wasn't an ideal choice, but he guessed it would have to do. Aidan tugged it out, turned, and found Tracey staring at him and restlessly tapping her pen against her notebook.

He narrowed his eyes at her, feeling the tingle of a female judgment wriggle down his spine.

*"What?"* he snapped. "What is it?"

She stopped tapping her pen and shifted on the stool. She cleared her throat. "Look, Aidan, I-I know that things have been a little . . . tense between us."

He choked back a laugh and twisted open the lid of the bottle. The metal lid fell to the tiled floor with a clink. He raised the bottle to his lips and took a drink.

"I was hurt by what happened. I admit

that. But just because we didn't work out doesn't mean I've stopped caring. I *still* care about you, and I'll be honest, you're starting to worry me."

He slammed the stainless steel door shut. "Why the hell would you be worried about me?"

"For starters . . . you've been distant lately."

He tipped the bottle to his lips again, muffling his grumble of exasperation. She had told him she wanted nothing to do with him, and now she was wondering why he was being so distant?

*Jesus Christ!*

"And it's not just me who's noticed," she continued. "Delilah has too. Even Caleb has asked about what's going on with you."

He snorted. "Considering that I'm going to be out of all your hair in six days, I'm not sure why you're expending that much energy on little ol' me."

"I'm serious! It didn't help that you made the announcement out of nowhere that you were moving out. Caleb was really disappointed when he heard that —"

"Do me favor," he said, cutting her off. He set his bottle on the island and braced his hands along the edge. "Stop fucking hiding behind your kids."

She blinked. "I wasn't hiding behind him. I just know you guys have developed a relationship — a friendship. He would never say it himself, so I was telling you how hurt he —"

" 'I'm just worried about Caleb . . . I have to think of my children now, Aidan,' " he said, imitating her. He rolled his eyes. "If you feel some kind of way about me, just say it, goddammit!"

The kitchen fell silent. She shook her head. "I'm sorry I brought it up. It was a bad idea to do this now. Obviously, this conversation is going nowhere."

"Fuck!" he yelled. "Don't do that shit either!"

"Don't do what, Aidan?"

"Don't start in on me and then retreat like I came at you first. Like I've done something wrong!" He walked around the island, pointing at her. "Trish used to do that shit all the time: pick a fight, then act all wounded when I came back at her! It pisses me off!"

She began to close her textbooks and notebook, to grab her pen and highlighter. "I'm not doing this," she said, shaking her head again. She rose from her stool. "It's the middle of the night. Everyone else is asleep, and I just don't have the energy for it. I'm going to bed. Good night."

"No! No, don't fucking walk off! Finish what you started!" He banged his fist on the tabletop. "This shit is so typical! I should've known —"

"I'm not Trish!" She gathered her books in her arms. "I'm not your wife!"

"You think I don't fucking know that?"

"You must not because you keep comparing me to her. You keep blaming me, and I don't have to put up with this!" She then turned around and headed to the kitchen entrance.

"Because you keep dumping the same guilt trip on me that she always did!" he shouted at the back of her head. "It must be genetic . . . like it's on the X chromosome to make a guy feel like shit. Yes, I fucked up! I know that! But let's be honest, I could never really please you, could I? A guy like me will never be good enough!"

She whipped back around. "*That's* what you've been telling yourself? That my standards are too high?" She shook her head again, looking disgusted. Her cheeks burned bright. "You've got some nerve, Aidan Dominguez! If you were this stubborn and dense with your wife, no wonder your marriage fell apart! No wonder she kicked you out and you had to come running here!"

At that, his face drained of all color. He took an unsteady step back, bumping into one of the kitchen stools. Seeing his reaction, realizing what she'd said, Tracey instantly looked remorseful. She dropped her books back to the countertop. She closed her eyes.

"I'm . . . I'm sorry, Aidan. I didn't mean that."

"Yes, you did." He grabbed his bottle and walked around her with his head lowered, no longer able to look at her. He made his way across the kitchen.

"Aidan? Aidan, come on!" she said, reaching out to him, placing a hand on his arm. "I didn't mean it. Don't leave like —"

"I didn't fucking come here because my marriage fell apart or my wife kicked me out!" he yelled, snatching his arm out of her grasp. "I came here because I couldn't stand to live in the same town where my wife and my kid died! All right? I wanted to get as far away from fucking Chicago as possible."

"W-what?"

"They died in a car crash! The accident was five years ago today. Trish got hit by a fucking eighteen-wheeler while she was driving through an intersection. Our baby, Annabelle, died instantly. Trish stayed on life support for about three days before she died too."

Tracey continued to gape.

"She hated driving," he rambled. "I did most of it because I knew how much she hated being behind the wheel. She never should've been on the road that night, but we were separated, so I . . . I couldn't drive for her anymore. I wish she'd just gotten a fucking Uber." He let out a chuckle, and Tracey cringed. "Yeah, I know what you're thinking. 'How can he laugh about something like this? He must be a real son of a bitch.' Well, you're right. I am. And I'm an even bigger son of a bitch than you think — I skipped the funeral. I stayed home and got drunk. I pissed off her parents, but I didn't care. There was no way I was going. There was no way I was going to see her and our little girl in those boxes."

Tracey's face crumpled. She actually looked on the verge of crying. "Oh, Aidan, I'm so —"

"Sorry?" He sneered, furious that she had made him talk about something so painful, something he had refused to say out loud for years. "Yeah, you said that already."

"What in the world?" Delilah called out.

They both turned to find the older woman standing in the kitchen entryway in her pink terry-cloth robe and pajamas. Her face and eyelids were puffy with sleep. A black cap was on her head.

"Why are y'all shouting? What if you woke up the children with that noise? Don't you know it's past midnight?"

"I'm sorry we woke you, Dee," Tracey answered softly. "We were talking, and things got a little . . . heated. We're done now, though." She reached for her books again. "I was leaving."

"No, I'm the one leaving," Aidan said, stomping out of kitchen, brushing past a bewildered Delilah as he did it. "I'll be out of here tomorrow."

# CHAPTER 36

Aidan made good on his promise. He left Harbor Hill the next day.

Tracey was at a loss for what to say to him after his outburst, so she didn't say anything. Instead, she pretended she didn't notice him loading the last of his things into his truck. She behaved as if the day was just like any other. Aidan seemed to be diligently doing the same. He went about the task of moving out with a mundaneness that was almost unnerving.

She served the children their breakfast and got them ready for school, not looking up when she heard his footsteps thudding on the stairs. When she returned home from work, she helped Caleb with his homework and played with Maggie, ignoring Aidan's grunts as he lifted each cardboard box. After the children went to bed, she kept her head in her textbook and her eyes on its pages.

Tracey broke her casual façade only when

she heard Aidan's engine rumble a little after eight o'clock. She closed her book, rose from her bed, and walked into the hall. She watched through a window as Aidan stood next to his truck with Delilah. Both were silhouetted by the dying light. They seemed to be talking about something, though she couldn't hear what they were saying from her bedroom. She watched as Delilah stood on the balls of her feet, looped her arms around him, and gave him a motherly hug. Aidan hugged her back. The two stood like that for what seemed like a full minute before Aidan stepped back, kissed her cheek, and climbed into the truck's cab. Delilah waved good-bye, then walked back toward the porch with her head bowed.

Tracey stared at the rear lights of his Toyota as he pulled out of the driveway and took the gravel road that led off the property. She then walked down the hall and the stairs in just enough time to see Delilah step back through the front door and close it behind her.

"He's all set then?" Tracey called out to her.

Delilah sniffed then nodded. Her eyes were pink, and her nose was red. She looked like she had been crying. "I guess so."

"At least he isn't moving that far away.

He's still in Camden Beach."

"He won't be here for long though. I can tell," Delilah said, glancing back at the closed front door forlornly. "I bet he won't even stay at that condo until the lease is up. He'll move on to somewhere else, but who knows where. He'll keep going."

Tracey lowered her eyes to her bare feet. "I hope . . . I hope I'm not the one who drove him away from here. I hope he didn't feel like he had to leave Harbor Hill because of me."

Delilah gave a sad smile. "Oh, it's not your fault, honey." She walked toward her and rubbed her arm. "Aidan's never been very good with facing his problems. He ran away from Chicago after his wife, Patricia, and their baby, Annabelle, died. Now he's running away from here too. But he doesn't realize that your pain and heartache follow you wherever you go. He's gotta face the pain and the grief. He's gotta face all those demons or he'll never be settled."

"It's so much easier to run, though. *I* did."

She raised her eyes to find Delilah squinting at her. "You ran for survival, honey. He runs because he refuses to face the truth. Those are two very different things."

"Same outcome, though."

Delilah wrapped an arm around her and

drew her close. Tracey closed her eyes, surprised to find her lashes dampening with tears. She clung to the older woman.

"You'll be strong enough to face your demons too one day," Delilah whispered, patting her on the back. "Until you are, you're welcome to stay here."

Tracey lay awake in bed for entire the night, tossing and turning, considering Delilah's words. She knew she and Aidan were both running from something, even if they had different motivations. But he would never admit that to himself. He was numb to his emotions, and no amount of arguing or cajoling could make him feel what he had no desire to feel. It sounded like Delilah had been trying for years to make him do it with no success. So why was Tracey still agonizing over him? Why did she worry so much about this man when she had enough problems of her own?

*Because I care about you,* she could remember Aidan saying. And she cared about him too. She couldn't turn off affection like it was a faucet. It poured forth regardless of her wants or reservations.

Tracey sighed and glanced at her alarm clock. It was a little after five o'clock. The sun would be up soon.

"Might as well get up," she whispered, rubbing her puffy eyes and throwing back the bedsheets. She pushed herself up from the mattress, stretching as she did it.

Tracey didn't have to be at the hotel and resort today until nine, so she would be able to stick around to make breakfast for the kids and see them off to school and day care, but first she needed a cup of coffee — maybe two.

"Or I'll be a zombie," she mumbled.

She grabbed her robe, shoved her arms into the sleeves, and made her way to the bedroom door. She opened it slowly and tiptoed down the hall so as to not wake the children or Delilah. She walked down the staircase and across the foyer, yawning as she did so. When she reached the kitchen, she dug up a packet of French roast from one of the overhead cabinets and then removed a clean coffee mug from the dishwasher. She poured in the ground coffee beans and let them percolate before walking across the room, leaning against the kitchen entryway frame, and gazing into the foyer, watching it brighten with filtered light as the sun slowly climbed across the horizon.

The coffee maker began to beep. Just as she started to turn around and turn it off, she saw a dark figure walk past one of the windows near the front door. Tracey squinted and walked out of the kitchen, wondering if she had made a mistake, if her tired eyes were playing tricks on her. But there it was again, a figure passing the window. Thanks to the closed curtains, the figure was nothing more than a looming silhouette. This time it was headed in the opposite direction, like it was pacing the front porch.

"Aidan?" Tracey whispered. She closed the panels of her robe and knotted her belt.

Had Aidan come back to the house to get something he had forgotten last night?

She took a few steps across the foyer, watching as the figure passed the window a third time. The figure paused, and she heard the windowpane rattle. This time, an icy sensation washed over her. Tracey slowly shook her head, now wary. That wariness was verging on alarm.

No, it wasn't Aidan. He still had a key to the house. He wouldn't be walking back and forth like that. He wouldn't be fiddling with the window either, like someone who was trying to find their way in.

So who could it be?

A thought dawned in Tracey's head.

That son of a bitch Teddy was back. It was bad enough that he had sent those letters and had painted that message on Delilah's garage. Now he was trying to break into the house. Perhaps he had seen Aidan's truck leave, laden down with boxes, and thought this would be the best time to do it, when two defenseless women were alone with children in the house.

"He's in for a rude awakening," Tracey mumbled as she raced across the foyer and grabbed the cordless phone from its perch on the oak console table. She began to dial, pressing the number 9 on the key pad. She was prepared to dial 1 twice if Teddy didn't leave — and she planned to tell him as much.

She marched toward the front door, filled with indignation. She unlocked the door and threw it open.

"Look, you son of a bitch!" she shouted, charging onto the porch. "You know you're not supposed to —"

Her words died on her lips and sank into her throat when the figure turned away from the window, which he had been trying to jimmy open with a screwdriver. He faced her, and she did a sharp intake of breath. The cordless phone fell from her hands and clattered to the porch.

It had been more than a year, but he still looked the same.

When their eyes met, Paul pushed back the brim of his baseball cap. A smile spread across his face. "So there you are!"

# CHAPTER 37

Delilah heard the scream first, roughly yanking her out of her sleep. Then she heard the crash, making her shove herself up from her bed.

For a second, she'd thought she was still locked in one of her old nightmares, the dreams she'd had in prison and for quite a few years after Cee's murder. In the dream, she'd replay that deadly night in vivid detail — from the smell of bourbon on Cee's breath to the chill in the air that had lit her bare arms with goose bumps. Sometimes in the dreams, she would watch him tumble down the stairs, his hands flailing wildly for one of newel posts or the handrail to stop or slow his momentum. She'd reach out and try to stop him, but it never worked. She'd watch him as he tumbled and hear the *thump, thump, crunch* when he landed.

Each time, she would wake from the dream with a lurch. Perspiration would be on her brow, and a shout would burst from her parched lips. It angered her to know she kept having the same dream, even though she hadn't killed him — and she suspected she knew who had.

"Oh, God!" Delilah screamed, jolting upright.

She looked around her bedroom with her heart thudding like a snare drum against her rib cage, making her wonder if it would burst from her chest. She slowly exhaled, and her heartbeat decelerated. She realized she wasn't standing at the top of her staircase but was safely in bed. She wasn't the young Delilah Buford waking up to the lurid scene of her dead husband, but an older Delilah Grey with that past far behind her.

But then she heard the scream again. It sounded like Tracey's voice, not her own.

"Let go of me! I said let go!" Tracey screeched.

Delilah leapt from her bed, almost getting tangled in the sheets and nearly tripping over Bruce, who went scurrying underneath the bed frame. She ran across the room, threw open her door, and peered down the hall.

"You ran out on me!" a male voice yelled back, and Tracey cried out again. She sounded like she was in pain. "You stole my children from me, and you thought I was just going to sit on my hands forever? I gave you the chance to come back. Now I'm taking you home!"

"Please, just let me go!" Tracey sobbed. "I'll do whatever you want. Just don't —"

"You're goddamn right you'll do what I want! You will if you know what's good for you! Where the fuck are my kids?"

"Paul, stop! Stop it!" she screamed.

"Mommy?" Caleb said.

Delilah whipped around to find the little boy standing in his bedroom doorway. His face was stark white. His blue eyes had gone so wide that they seemed to take up almost half his face. He was shaking so much that he looked like he was doing a little dance.

"It's all right, honey. It's okay," Delilah whispered, rushing toward him. "Come with me."

"I want my mommy," he cried, running toward the stairs, but she grabbed his arm and stopped him.

"No!" she whispered, wrestling with him as he twisted in her arms, as he kicked his feet and hit her shin, making her wince. "No, honey, we can't go down there yet! Your mama wouldn't want you to do that."

"I have to help my mommy!" he cried. Plump tears fell onto his cheeks.

"Caleb . . . Caleb, look at me! Look at me!"

Finally, he stilled. He started to cry in her arms.

"We will help her, honey. But we've got to call the police first, all right? Let's call the police."

He looked up at her and slowly nodded.

Delilah ushered him into her bedroom, hoping that ruckus Tracey's husband was making had covered up the sound of their voices upstairs.

"Sit right here," she said to him, after closing her bedroom door. She motioned to her bed, and he climbed on top of the disheveled sheets. "Don't you go anywhere! You hear me?"

He bit his lower lip and nodded.

Delilah rushed to her night table and removed the cordless phone. She didn't usually trust the police, but under the circumstances, she would make an exception. She pressed the green button to turn it on and start dialing but winced when she heard the line beep, like the phone had been taken off the hook.

"Damnit," she spat, before dropping the cordless handset back into its cradle in defeat.

The only other phone she could possibly

use was her cell phone. She ran toward her purse and began to dig through it.

"What are you doing, Miss Dee?" Caleb asked.

She didn't answer him. Instead, she up-ended her purse over the bed —

watching her wallet, sunglasses, keys, and everything else tumble onto the mattress. She searched desperately for her cell phone, her hands shaking as she did it. All the while she could hear Tracey's screams of despera-tion and Tracey's husband bellowing at her.

"Where did I put it?" Delilah said, turn-ing away from the pile, raising her hand to her head. She tried to recall the last time she had seen it, sifting through her cluttered mind much like she had the contents of her purse. Then she remembered.

She had left it sitting on one of the foot-stools in the living room last night after she had gone out to say good-bye to Aidan. How could she retrieve it without being seen by Tracey's husband?

She closed her eyes and sighed.

"I thought you were calling the police," Caleb said, making her eyes flash open. She turned to find him gazing at her expectantly.

"We will, sweetheart. I just have to go downstairs to get my phone. This one isn't working."

"Can I come with you?"

She shook her head. "No, honey, you stay right here."

Despite her words, he hopped off the bed. "I want to come with you!"

"Caleb, I said no!" she shouted, making him shrink back.

She hadn't meant for it to come out so harsh, but she didn't have the patience or the best nerves at that moment. She took a deep breath and rubbed his shoulders. "I need you to . . . to stay up here and watch over your sister. What if she wakes up and no one is up here? She'll get scared in her room all alone. I need you to watch over her, honey."

She could tell from the look on his face that she had finally gotten through to him. She knew the kind of boy Caleb was — eager for responsibility, yearning for approval. He would not turn down the weighty duty of protecting his little sister.

Ever so slowly, Caleb nodded.

A minute later, Delilah began to creep toward the staircase. As she rounded the newel post and saw the foyer below, she almost froze in place, shocked by what was in front of her. She had heard the chaos upstairs but was not prepared for it visually.

The front door sat ajar, and Delilah could spot the house phone sitting abandoned on the front porch. The foyer console table was overturned. Two of the flower vases that had been sitting on top of it now lay shattered on the hardwood floor. The roses and freesias they had once contained were strewn everywhere in the pooling water, like someone had tossed them there as an offering to a bride or a fertility goddess. One of the curtain panels of the bay windows had been ripped down, and the torn cotton fabric and its tassels blew gently in the breeze coming from the outdoors.

Delilah remembered the last time the house had looked like this, how the light had streamed through the window and the door had been left open. The only exception now was that a body wasn't crumpled at the bottom of the stairs.

Tracey's scream shook Delilah out of her stupor. She jumped and started walking again, finally descending the stairs. The creak of each step sounded like a thunderclap in her ears, but it was nothing compared to the shouting in the kitchen, the clanging and the banging. A real struggle was happening in there, and Delilah's sense of urgency fought with the need for stealth.

"Get up! Get up, goddammit! Now where

*are* they? Are they upstairs?"

"Th-they're . . . they're sleeping if they haven't woken up already," Tracey stuttered between sobs. "Please, Paul, just —"

Her words were abruptly cut off by a sharp slapping sound, then a thump. Tracey cried out.

"I haven't seen my kids in more than a fucking year! I'm not waiting any longer. You hear me? Take me to them. I want to see my kids! I said get up!"

As Delilah rushed across the foyer, carefully dodging the debris, she caught a glimpse of Tracey and her husband. Tracey lay on the floor, her face bloodied and streaked with tears. Her legs were twisted underneath her as her hands pried at Paul's fingers, which were currently entangled in her long dark curls. The hulking man was dragging her across the kitchen tile like heavy luggage.

Though Tracey had once described her husband as handsome, he didn't look it at that moment. His face was red and distorted with so much fury and malevolence that he barely seemed human anymore.

Delilah ran the remaining distance to the living room, hoping that he hadn't seen her as she did it. She spotted her cell phone instantly. It still sat on the footstool next to one of her opened books, just as she remembered.

She reached for the phone and stared down at the glass screen. She almost dropped it because her palms were so sweaty and her hands trembled so much. The screen showed that only eight percent of the battery's charge was left — just enough to make one phone call. She began to dial.

"Hello, this is the Camden Beach Police Department," the voice answered on the other end of the line. "Please state your emergency?"

Delilah hesitated. Again, she felt like she was being transported back in time.

"Camden Beach Police Department, please state your emergency."

Delilah took a shaky breath. She could feel herself being transported back forty-plus years. She could remember standing at the console table in the foyer long ago with a phone headset against her ear. She'd fought the urge to hang up the phone back then.

*I could run,* she'd thought at the time. *I could pack my bags and disappear before they even found his body. I could be far, far away!*

And now, she wanted to run all over again.

But then she could hear Tracey in the kitchen, beaten and screaming. She remembered Caleb sitting on her bed upstairs, ready to protect his little sister and diligently fighting the urge to come to his mother's rescue. He was willing to be brave.

"Camden Beach Police Department. I can hear breathing. Is someone there?"

Delilah closed her eyes, blotting out the vision of her terrified eighteen-year-old self. "H-hello?" she finally answered.

"Yes, ma'am? What's your emergency?"

"Yes, a man has broken into my house," she whispered, cupping her hand over the receiver. "He's . . . he's . . . uh . . . violent and beating up his wife. I think he might kill her. You . . . you have to send someone right way!"

"I understand, ma'am. I'll send officers there. What's your address?"

"It's —"

She stopped when the phone was yanked out of her hand.

Delilah whipped around to find Paul standing behind her, holding the tip of one of her Wüsthof knives only inches away from her button nose, catching a glint of the morning sun on the cool steel. Tracey stood at his side, hunched over with her head bowed, looking almost ashamed. Delilah

504

watched as Paul pressed the button to hang up her phone, stopping the dispatcher mid-question.

"So this is your house?" he asked. His lips were so tight they were almost white. His blue eyes were dilated and rimmed in red.

Delilah gradually nodded. "Y-yes."

"Pleased to meet you." He grinned then dropped the knife down to her neck, letting the tip hover a mere centimeter away from her jugular. "Now take me to my fucking kids."

# CHAPTER 38

Aidan raised his head from the sofa cushion, squinting at the bright light coming through the floor-to-ceiling windows. He pushed himself up to his elbows, almost feeling a sense of vertigo as he did it. He closed his eyes and waited for the world around him to settle, then opened his eyes again.

For a few seconds, he couldn't recall where he was. He wondered why he wasn't lying in his bed back at Harbor Hill and was, instead, sprawled on a rickety futon, surrounded by a sea of cardboard boxes with no other furniture. Then he remembered he had moved out last night. He'd arrived at his new condo and drunk himself into a stupor. He must have blacked out because he didn't remember lying down, let alone falling asleep here.

With a tired groan, Aidan sat up. He rubbed his eyes, then shoved his hand into his hair, cupping his throbbing forehead.

He made several failed attempts to rise to his feet before finally staggering into his eat-in kitchen. The cabinets were still bare, but he had managed to pick up a few items during his stop at the gas station last night and load them into the fridge.

"Breakfast of champions," he said, bypassing the shrink-wrapped club sandwich and the carton of OJ and going straight to the six-pack on the bottom shelf. He tugged out a beer and twisted off the lid. He took several gulps, enjoying the sensation of the cold liquid sliding down his parched throat and sloshing around his empty stomach. He then slammed the refrigerator door shut and headed back down the hall to the bathroom to take a shower.

Aidan was well aware that drinking a beer didn't qualify as breakfast. It certainly hadn't a month ago. But today, he didn't care. He hadn't drunk this much in years — in almost five years, to be exact. But he didn't care about that either. Time had taken him full circle; he was back where he started — inebriated, unencumbered, and nestled in a cushion of apathy.

Aidan had once believed that life was a straight line from start to finish, but now he knew it was cyclical. You experienced the same cycles of love and hope, heartbreak and disappointment again and again. New losses reminded you of old ones. Old wounds could be reopened.

"You still haven't healed yet," Delilah had told him. But the truth was he never would, and he wouldn't keep deluding himself otherwise.

He took a quick shower, then stumbled into his bedroom naked, in full view of the open window. He didn't reach for a towel but instead, let himself air dry, admiring the view.

Luckily, the only ones in danger of seeing the naked man on the eleventh floor of Bayside Condominiums were the seagulls hovering over the bay, darting their heads beneath the waves to retrieve flounder and striped sea bass. Aidan's windows faced the open water, giving him the illusion of a man alone on an island. It's certainly how he felt.

After he finished his beer, he threw on some underwear and one of the clean T-shirts and a pair of jeans that he'd packed in a spare duffel bag. He walked barefoot into his new living room to begin unpacking.

The first thing Aidan had done last night when he'd arrived at his new place was to plug in his stereo system and assemble his stack of CDs in an alphabetized row next to it on the bamboo floors. Now, as he arrived in the living room, he beelined toward it, loading a few of the CDs and turning up the volume. The soothing soul music surged from the speakers, and Aidan nodded in appreciation before walking into the kitchen and grabbing another beer. He then sauntered to the tower of boxes in one of the living room corners. He hadn't bothered to label anything, so it would be a grab bag of random findings: books buried under gym socks, picture frames crammed in with his electric iron and a desktop lamp.

For about a half hour, he set about his task, listening to one song, then the next. He opened a fourth box, then paused when he saw what was sitting on top of his old basketball jerseys. He squinted as he reached inside and pulled out the object. It was the Incredible Hulk action figure.

Aidan stared at it in amazement, wondering how Caleb's toy had made it into one of his boxes. He hadn't accidentally taken it, had he? And then he realized that the little boy must have put it in there himself, left it there for Aidan to find. The toy that Caleb had carried around like a talisman, he had given away to Aidan.

"I want to be strong like the Hulk," he could remember Caleb saying that day on the back porch.

"Don't we all, kid," Aidan had replied.

Aidan gripped the plastic tighter, blinking as his vision began to blur. He felt one hot tear slide onto his cheek and then another after another. He heard a loud groan and realized that it had come from his own lips. He slowly sank to his knees, still holding the action figure, and began to sob openly.

He hadn't cried like this in years, not since he had gotten the phone call from the police about the car crash. He could remember sitting at Trish's bedside, listening as the heart monitor went flat and the nurses quietly turned off all the machines and left the room. Even her parents hadn't stayed for that part. Instead, they had walked into the hallway to hold each other and weep softly. But he had stayed until the last moment, until all went silent. He had sobbed and sobbed, more than he thought any human being could. And Aidan hadn't just cried because his wife was dead, but because his daughter was dead too, and the one person in the world who could understand that pain had been taken from him.

When he'd left the hospital room, his mother-in-law had tried to embrace him, but he had shaken his head and walked away. The tears hadn't come again; it was like he'd used them all up. He'd felt alone — utterly alone. He was on his own little island.

But he realized now that he had been wrong, in more ways than one.

Aidan continued to cry until his stomach ached, until his eyes were puffy and he could barely see. When he was done, he felt better, strangely enough, like some toxin had been washed out of his system. He staggered to his feet, still clutching the toy. Through blurry eyes, he glanced at the digital clock on the stereo. It was a little after eight A.M. He wiped his nose with the back of his hand. He would drive back to Harbor Hill and return this wonderful gift, explaining to Caleb that he didn't need it anymore.

# CHAPTER 39

Tracey opened the bedroom closet, shaking as her husband loomed behind her.

"Just grab a suitcase — *only one* suitcase . . . that's all you'll need," his voice boomed, making her quivering worse. "You can leave the rest of this shit here."

Tracey blinked through her tears as she reached inside her closet and pulled out one of her suitcases — a tweed, rolling duffel bag with a leather handle — as he had ordered. She carried it to the bed, unzipped the lid, and flipped it open, realizing almost with a bemused remoteness that it was the same suitcase she had packed when she'd left Paul more than a year ago. It seemed almost ironic to be packing it again to go back to him, though she wasn't doing so willingly this time around. But it wasn't like she had much of a choice. If she wanted for her, the children, and Delilah to survive this, she had to do it.

At least Paul hadn't hurt Delilah too badly. Tracey had begged him not to. He hadn't hit or punched her like he had Tracey but had dragged the old woman by the arm up the stairs, making her cry out in pain and Tracey scream for him to stop. That, along with the punch to the arm she had given him after tossing Delilah into the upstairs closet and locking her in there, had earned Tracey a slap to the face. But she'd do it again. Aidan had told her Delilah hated confined spaces, that she was terrified of them, and Tracey could sense from the older woman's tortured sobs from behind the wooden door that he'd been telling the truth.

At the thought of Aidan, Tracey paused midway in loading her suitcase, her hand hovering near the top drawer.

Had Aidan mentioned that he was coming back to the house today to get the last of his things? Would he stumble into the horrific scene downstairs that looked like a mini hurricane had burst through the front door and made its way around the first floor? Would he make the right choice and immediately call the police, or would he come charging inside and run into Paul?

Tracey shuddered at the thought. Aidan was the same build as Paul and under normal circumstances could probably hold his own in a fight, but her husband seemed to take on an almost superhuman strength when he got angry. He could pick her up as if she was lighter than air and toss her like she was one of the T-shirts that now tumbled from her drawer to the floor as she packed her bag.

"Speed it up!" Paul barked, making her wince. "I want us out of here in less than an hour. That includes you packing the kids' things too." He paused to glance down at Caleb, who anxiously stood at his side, wringing his T-shirt. A smile suddenly came to Paul's lips, looking as out of place at that moment as the butcher knife he still clutched in his hand, and pointed at Tracey. He nudged Caleb's shoulder almost playfully. "Anything in particular you want to take with you, kiddo?"

Caleb blinked like he was holding back tears. He quickly shook his head. "No," he whispered.

Tracey had tried several times to catch Caleb's eye, to touch him and reassure him that everything would be okay, that she would protect him. But he kept evading her gaze. His big blue eyes cagily shifted around him like a cornered animal.

Tracey hesitated, then turned around to

face Paul. "Are you going to let her out when we leave?"

Paul's smile abruptly disappeared. The demented gleam was back in his eyes as he squinted at her. "Let *who* out?"

"Delilah. We can't leave her in the closet."

"Why not?"

"Because she could be in there for hours . . . or *days*! Who knows when someone could stop by here. She can't stay in there. She could die!"

He raised his brows and took several steps toward her. Instinctively, she took a step back, bumping into Maggie's playpen. The little girl began to whimper, then cry.

"If that old hag lives or dies, whose fault is that? *You* were the one who chose to come here, Tracey. I gave you a nice life, a nice home. I took care of you, of our children, and you deserted me!" He lifted the knife, jabbing it toward her, and she flinched as if it had touched her. "You stole them from me! You stole my life! I had to chase you down, to bribe your mother. I still wouldn't have found you if it hadn't been for your landlord suing you for back rent and sending that summons to the house." He chuckled, and Tracey blanched. She had wondered how he'd found her. "You changed your name, but you didn't change your Social Security number, Trace. I mean . . . come on! How stupid can you be?"

She closed her eyes as he continued to laugh, refusing to let him see her hot, angry tears.

"Your life was so much better without me, huh? It was so much better that you couldn't even afford to keep a goddamn roof over your head! Now you're living with strangers?"

She had asked him about letting Delilah out of the closet, and instead he had chosen to berate her, to humiliate her. And she'd play meek and change the subject. It was an old routine they knew well. Paul loved to be in control, and she'd give him the illusion that he was, even if she wasn't ready to hand over the reins quite yet.

"I'm sorry, Paul," she said, lowering her head. "I'm sorry I disappointed you."

He pursed his lips. "Yeah, well, don't be sorry. Just don't fuck up again!"

She nodded. "I won't." She placed the last item in the suitcase and zipped it shut. "I'm done packing my things," she said, reaching for Maggie. She placed the sobbing toddler on her hip. "Should I start packing the kids' stuff now?"

He nodded and tilted his head toward the

opened doorway. "Go ahead. Be quick, though."

"Come on, Cabe," she said, walking toward him and holding her hand out to him.

Caleb's vacant eyes slowly rose from the floor. He stared at his mother.

"Help me pack your bag, sweetheart. We don't want to forget anything."

She stared back at him, hoping to convey a silent message in her gaze, though the tips of her fingers that hovered in the air. Finally, he took her hand, and they headed out of the bedroom.

"Wait! Caleb isn't going with you. He stays here with me!" Paul rushed toward them, making Caleb cower against her side. "You think I'd let you out of my sight . . . that I'd let you out of here with the kids again? You think I'm that fucking stupid?"

She turned to him, forcing her voice and breathing to stay even. "Of course not! I thought you were coming with us."

"Oh." He blinked. The angry chords in his neck and veins along his brow disappeared. "Oh, yeah, sure."

He trailed behind them, his thudding footsteps bringing up the rear as they walked down the hall. Tracey told herself to keep her pace even and unhurried. She gave Caleb's shoulder a reassuring squeeze, though he clung to the folds of her bathrobe like it was the only thing tethering him to her, as though his father could yank him away at any second.

Caleb's room was two doors down. The closed door was adorned with a smiling half-moon, inscribed with the words, "Come back later! I'm busy dreaming." Caleb reached up to open it but stopped when Tracey suddenly said, "Let me do it, honey. I know it sticks a little."

She grabbed the door knob and pretended to twist it. She frowned. "It won't open."

"What do you mean it won't open?" Paul asked.

She pressed her shoulder against the wood and shoved, then shook her head. "It won't open!"

"Why the hell won't it open?" he shouted, and she shrugged helplessly.

"I don't know! It's an old house!" she insisted, pretending again to shove the door open. "Sometimes the doors stick. It happens a lot with this one. Maybe you can try."

"Jesus Christ," he muttered, lowering the knife. "Just move out of the way."

She and Caleb stepped aside as he reached for the door handle. She watched as Paul braced his shoulder against the door and twisted the knob. It burst open when he pushed, and he went tumbling inside with it. He caught himself before he fell to the floor.

"What the hell did —"

His words were cut off when Tracey reached out and slammed the door shut, engaging the lock — the lock she had asked Aidan to place on the exterior of the rooms to keep the children from locking themselves in. She grabbed Caleb's hand and sprinted down the hall in the direction of the locked closet.

"Tracey! Tracey, you stupid bitch! I'm going to fucking kill you!" Paul yelled.

"Mommy," Caleb whimpered as he stared down the hall at his closed bedroom door. They could hear a loud thump and rattle, like her husband was flinging himself against it. "Mommy?"

"It's okay, honey," she whispered as she unlocked the closet door and Delilah came tumbling out.

"Are you okay?" Tracey asked the older woman, wiping at the tears on her wrinkled cheeks.

Delilah gradually nodded. "I'm . . . I'm okay," she stuttered.

"We have to go!" she urged over her husband's furious screams. In addition to the thumping, there was the sound of splintering wood. The door wouldn't hold for much longer. "Do you think you can you walk?"

Delilah nodded again.

She grabbed Delilah's hand and helped hoist her to her feet. They raced toward the stairs. Delilah and Caleb were in the lead. He guided the older woman down the staircase with a care that would have made Tracey proud if she hadn't been so terrified. She adjusted Maggie on her hip and began to descend the stairs just as Caleb's bedroom door came crashing open.

"Tracey!" Paul screamed. "That's it! I'm going to fucking kill you! Do you hear me?"

She took a panicked glance over her shoulder, catching a glimpse of him as he raced down the hall, still clutching the knife. She ran down the stairs, gripping Maggie against her side.

As her feet neared the first floor, Tracey hoped that the past would repeat itself, that the curse that seemed to hang over this beautiful home would work to someone's advantage for once. Tracey prayed that Paul would take the same fatal misstep that Delilah's husband had taken forty-plus years ago. She willed the fates to make him trip, fall, and go tumbling to his death. But that didn't happen. Harbor Hill insisted on having the last laugh. Paul took the stairs two at time, but his steps were sure. As she hopped off the last riser, he caught her by the collar and yanked her back, sending Maggie flying instead. Delilah caught her, but she and the toddler went crashing to the floor, slipping in the pool of water.

"That's it!" he screamed, tugging her toward him. He yanked her head back and held the knife to her throat. She clawed at his fingers, feeling the blade against her skin. "You're not worth it! You're not worth the fucking headache! I should've —"

His words were stopped short, and his grip loosened when he went crumpling to the floor.

Tracey looked up in surprise to find Aidan standing over him with a tire iron clutched in his hands.

# CHAPTER 40

"Put the weapon down!" someone shouted, and Aidan glanced over his shoulder to find two police officers charging up the porch steps with guns drawn.

He had been staring down at Tracey's husband, crumpled on the floor, and asking everyone else in the foyer if they were all right when the officers showed up.

"I said put the weapon down right now!" the officer with the pale blond hair and blue eyes shouted again.

"But I called you!" he yelled back, lowering his tire iron to the hardwood.

He'd called them as soon as he had arrived at the property and seen the gray Mercedes parked behind a series of four-foot-high bushes only fifty yards from the house. The car was so hidden from view that it seemed almost intentional, as though the person who had driven the car didn't want it to be seen.

When he pulled up the gravel driveway, saw the front door sitting open, and heard Tracey's shouts even from the front yard, he knew all hell was breaking loose inside Harbor Hill. He'd immediately called the police. The dispatcher had told him to wait outside until the cops arrived, but every muscle and bone in his body screamed to do the opposite. That's when he grabbed the tire iron from his truck bed and went charging inside.

It had been foolish and risky in retrospect, but he had managed to take out Paul without getting so much as a bruise or a cut. Now he ran the real risk of their supposed saviors shooting him.

"Put your hands behind your head!" one of the officers shouted, rushing at him, shoving him to his knees.

"Wait! Wait!" Tracey screamed, holding up her hands. "It wasn't him. He was rescuing us! It was my husband. It was him!"

She pointed down to the unconscious man lying between them. Paul still loosely held the butcher knife in his hands.

"It was him. Please, don't arrest Aidan." She wiped the blood from her nose in a careless gesture, smearing it further on her face. "He kept him from killing me."

The officers stared at her, confused.

"That's what happened," Delilah interjected, rubbing Maggie's back gently. The little girl was crying. "It's the truth."

Aidan continued to kneel on the floor with his fingers interlocked behind his head. Sweat rolled into his eyes, but he didn't dare remove his hands to wipe it away. He gazed up at Tracey, and she smiled at him. "Thank you," she mouthed.

The two police officers exchanged a glance between them. The blond one shrugged. His shorter, darker counterpart sighed, then nodded. They finally lowered their guns.

"Okay," the blond one said, holstering his Glock, "just what exactly is going on here?"

An ambulance arrived soon after. The paramedics examined Delilah, Tracey, and the children — addressing wounds and bandaging cuts. Paul was finally awake, and he seemed to stare around him dumbly, like he didn't know how he had gotten there. His eyes finally settled on Tracey, and that's when Aidan saw the change in him. The other man no longer looked confused but now was alert. Pure hatred was in his eyes. Aidan knew that, at that moment, Paul would have killed Tracey. He would have done it in front of his own children, if Aidan hadn't arrived at the moment he did.

They led Paul out of the house in hand-cuffs with a bandage attached to the back of his head, near the neck, where Aidan had hit him. He gave one last glower over his shoulder at them all, like some menacing cartoon character, then turned around when one of the officers barked at him to keep walking.

Aidan shut the door behind them and turned back around to find Tracey sitting on the stairs, holding both her children on her lap, whispering to them. All three of their heads were bowed. They looked like they were in prayer. Delilah stepped out of the kitchen, carrying a Swiffer mop, a broom, and a dustpan.

"Really, Dee?" he asked, cocking an eye-brow. "You're going to clean up *right now*?"

"Well, I can't leave all this broken glass lying around! What if one of the children steps on it? And I can't have all this water sitting on my hardwood either. It'll damage the floors."

He watched as she began to sweep. He chuckled and rolled his eyes. "I'll help you. Just give me a sec." He then walked toward the staircase, where Tracey and the kids sat.

"Cabe," he called out.

The little boy turned away from his mother and raised his head.

"I got sidetracked because of all the . . . well, because of all that happened. But I came back here to give you this." Aidan reached into his jeans pocket. He pulled out the action figure. "It was sweet of you to give me this, but I can't take it from you."

He handed it to Caleb, and the boy slowly reached out and took it from him. He ran his hand over Hulk's plastic face.

"Did it make you feel better, though?" Caleb asked, looking up at him.

Aidan nodded and smiled. "It definitely did. I'm honored that you gave it to me," Aidan said.

Caleb puffed out his chest.

Aidan helped Delilah clean up the foyer and the kitchen, sweeping up the debris and mopping the spilled water. While they cleaned, Tracey fed the children, though neither seemed to have much of an appetite. She sat with them in the living room, drawing them close to her. At around noon, she put Maggie down for a nap. Caleb, who Tracey said hadn't taken naps in almost two years, went to sleep too. Aidan could understand why. The poor boy seemed exhausted.

Tracey strolled down the steps just as Aidan rose to his feet, holding a dustpan filled with broken pottery. She gazed at him, and he tried not to wince at the bruises and scars on her beautiful face.

*They'll go away,* he told himself.

She would heal. The wounds on both the inside and the outside would eventually lessen, even if they didn't disappear completely.

"Thank you for doing this, Aidan. For coming back," she said, walking toward him.

"It's no problem. You've got your hands full, and I know Dee would tire herself out trying to get this place back in order by herself." He surveyed the room around him. They'd finished most of the sweeping and mopping, but there were still a few knicks here and there in the wainscoting and wall trim that needed to be addressed. The same for the kitchen and porch. He'd have to go to the toolshed to dig up some spackle and paint. "Dee could use the help."

"How long are you going to stay?"

He shrugged. "As long as I'm needed, I guess."

She lowered her eyes, then looked up at him again. She exhaled. "We need you, Aidan. All of us do. Me in particular."

He fell silent.

"And I hope . . . I hope you need us too."

His throat tightened.

"Please stay."

He suddenly recalled again the day when

527

Trish had walked out on him. She'd left their house with Annabelle nestled in her arms and a pink diaper bag slung over her shoulder. He remembered her last words, "I'm sorry, Aidan, but I have to do this. I can't stay."

She then turned back around and strode out of their front door, and he had lowered his head, feeling defeated and rejected.

Now he recalled how she had lingered in the doorway a few seconds longer, like she was waiting for something. He thought she'd been fiddling with her diaper bag, looking down at Annabelle, but now he suspected she had she been waiting for him all along. She had been waiting for him to fight for them, for their family.

He lowered the dustpan to the floor and took a step toward Tracey. He held open his arms, and she almost fell into them. He held her close.

"You're right. I need you too," he said. "I'll stay as long as you guys will have me."

# CHAPTER 41

It was morning, and the sun was out, bright and intrusive, sending shafts of light into Delilah's tired eyes and across the bedroom floor. The light would not be ignored, much like the cat, who now batted at her face, purring softly. She didn't know if the sunlight was an apt metaphor for how Harbor Hill felt now, after all the chaos had finally been swept away like the broken glass and splinters in the foyer. Frankly, she didn't care. She'd take the hint and let a little sunlight into her life as well.

Delilah pushed herself from her bed and stretched, listening to the crack of her old bones and joints, groaning with each twist of the muscles. Bruce did the same from his perch on the bed, letting out a low purr as he arched his back. When he was done, he hopped off the bed and followed her into the bathroom.

Even before Delilah brushed her teeth and

turned on the shower, she knew where she was going today. She could no longer deny the magnetic force pulling her back to that place, back to her past. It was a story that needed an ending.

"Not all stories have happy endings, Delilah," Cee's voice whispered to her.

"You're right," she answered aloud.

But, all the same, she would not go another day without attempting to finish this one. It might prove pointless, but she had to try.

After she dressed, she walked down the stairs, clutching her car keys. She could hear Tracey, Aidan, and the children in the kitchen, eating breakfast. As she walked past the kitchen entrance, Aidan called to her.

"Where are you going, Dee?" he asked. Suddenly, they all turned to look at her quizzically. Even Maggie stopped chewing her Cheerios.

"Got something I've gotta do." She removed her sweater from the hook and put it on, closing the buttons with her free hand. "I'll be back soon. Don't worry. It won't take too long."

She opened the door and stepped into air, cooled with morning dew, then shut the front door behind her.

Out here the world seemed even brighter,

illuminated not just from the sun but from within. Each tree . . . each flower . . . every object seemed so luminous that she had to squint. She dug into her handbag and pulled out her shades. After lowering them over her eyes, she made her way to her PT Cruiser.

The drive didn't take as long as she thought it would, even though she felt as if she was traveling through time the closer she got to her destination. Regressing forty-eight years should have taken at least an hour, but thanks to the light weekend traffic, she was able to do it in forty-five minutes. As she drew closer, the streets started to look more familiar, even though many of the homes had changed from her memories of them. The old ranch houses had been replaced by tawny Tudors and colonials, white picket fences with wrought-iron gates, and old baseball fields with townhouse developments and lavish playgrounds. But the ghosts of those past houses and people still lingered here. She could feel their presence as if they were sitting in the passenger seat beside her.

Then she saw it. The house sat three houses from the corner.

The two-story colonial was not as grand

as she remembered. It was now dwarfed by the renovated houses on each side of it, but the exterior was the same, and so were the hedges along the front. The quarter of an acre front lawn still lazily sloped to the roadway below.

Delilah pulled the PT Cruiser to a stop at the end of the driveway. She climbed out of the car and trudged up the slight incline, wondering what she would do once she reached the front door. (Yes, she would use the front door and not the back door, as she had when she had worked here decades ago.) What would she say when she got there?

*I've come here to find out the truth.*

*Did I really kill my husband, or did someone else do it?*

*Why can't I remember what happened that night?*

Delilah practiced the words in her head over and over again. She became so engrossed in her mantra that when she rang the doorbell and the front door sprang open, she almost uttered the words instead of "Hello" but caught herself.

"G-good morning," she stuttered.

The woman who stood in the doorway in an oversized yellow sweater and linen pants did not return her greeting. Her doughy face was filled with irritation. Her plump body jittered with the anxiety of one who had forty things to do and not enough time to do them. She looked five seconds away from slamming the door in Delilah's face.

"H-hello, ma'am," Delilah continued anxiously. "I was . . . I was wondering if Ms. Melinda Williams lives here."

"Yes, she lives here, and she's been waiting for you!" the woman replied. "It certainly took you long enough. I thought you weren't coming!"

Delilah squinted. *"I'm sorry?"*

"You should be! You were supposed to be here at nine A.M." She shoved up one of her sweater sleeves and tapped the face of the gold watch on her plump wrist. The skin along her forearm jiggled. "It's almost ten o'clock! I hope you don't make a habit of this."

Delilah watched in shock as the woman abruptly turned and walked across the living room, then started up the stairs leading to the second floor. "She's up here!" she said over her shoulder, waving Delilah inside.

Delilah hesitated, unsure whether she should step over the threshold since this woman had obviously confused her with someone else.

"Mom!" the woman shouted, cupping her hands around her mouth. "The new aide is finally here!"

*Mom?*

Delilah narrowed her eyes at the woman again. She could see it now — the plump little girl whom she used to tuck in bed when Miss Mindy had drunk too much wine or had taken one of her blue pills. This was the same little girl whose leotards and tutus Delilah used to scrub, whose grapes Delilah used to peel and put in her lunch box.

*So this is the woman you've become,* Delilah thought with disappointment.

"Mom, are you awake?" The woman yelled, then faced Delilah again when she realized she wasn't following her upstairs. Her thin lips puckered into a frown. "Well, are you coming?"

Delilah waffled for a second longer. She considered whether she should tell Melinda's daughter the truth or take advantage of this unexpected luck. Not only was Miss Mindy still alive, but now Delilah had a chance to see her, to talk to her. She might not get that chance if she revealed who she really was.

Finally, she stepped inside and shuffled toward the stairs.

The interior of the house had been redecorated. In the living room, the avocado and golden wallpaper of yesteryear had been replaced with a non-intrusive gray damask pattern. The burnt orange sofa, chairs, and Barcalounger that Miss Mindy had showed off to her guests at her cocktail parties had been changed out for furniture straight out of a Pottery Barn catalog. They had even knocked down one of the walls so there was a clear view into the kitchen, taking away the privacy of the only sanctuary she, Agnes, and Roberta had had all those many years ago.

As Delilah followed Miss Mindy's daughter along the upstairs hallway, she could see that the rooms had been redecorated but were, at least structurally, the same. Near the end of the hall, one door sat ajar. Miss Mindy's daughter shoved it open, revealing a brightly lit bedroom.

"Ah, so you are awake!" she said, walking toward a modified hospital bed, where a frail old woman lay elevated with an oxygen mask over her wrinkled face. "The aide is here, Mom."

Miss Mindy's sunken eyes, which had once been a bright shade of emerald green but now resembled filmy pond water, zeroed in on Delilah. She raised a gnarled hand decorated with blue veins and liver spots to her face. She tugged down her mask and squinted.

Delilah didn't know what disease Miss Mindy had, but it was eating away at her. She was only twelve years older than Delilah, but she looked almost one hundred years old with her shrunken frame and sagging skin, and with a bald head she'd tried, but failed, to hide under a pink satin scarf.

To think how much this woman had intimidated her years ago. Now Delilah almost pitied her. Almost.

"She starts today," Miss Mindy's daughter continued, blissfully unaware of Delilah's less than flattering assessment of her mother. "I'll give her the tour in a bit, but I wanted her to introduce herself first . . . for you to meet her. Her name is . . ." She paused, then turned to face Delilah. She snapped her fingers. "I've forgotten your name already. What is it?"

"Delilah," Delilah answered softly. "It's Delilah."

"There you go! Meet Delilah. You two spend a few minutes getting acquainted, and I'll come back later to show Delilah around the house, Mom."

She then walked out of the room, leaving Delilah and Miss Mindy alone to stare at one another.

"Do you know who I am?" Delilah began, taking a step toward the foot of the bed.

"Of course I do," Miss Mindy answered in a scratchy voice. "I'm dying, but I'm not senile."

"Do you know why I'm here?"

Miss Mindy shrugged her thin shoulders. "I guess because Teddy couldn't leave well enough alone. I told him not to bother. We tried and failed to get Harbor Hill back years ago, but he insisted that he should try again since the house belongs to our family."

"The house belonged to Chauncey — and he willed it to me."

"But he shouldn't have," Miss Mindy said, raising her nose into the air, harkening back to the rich, imperious redhead she had been four decades ago. "It wasn't his to give away. That house had been in the Buford family for more than a hundred years! It should've stayed with us, but instead it went to *you.*" She sniffed. "You . . . a *maid* . . . a *nigger* who my brother had been foolish enough to knock up and even more foolish to marry. But that was Cee, wasn't it? So spoiled. So dumb," she spat. "But Mama made him that way. She coddled him, and it got even worse after Daddy died. I told her she was ruining him. I just didn't know he would ruin us too!"

"Is that why Mr. Williams killed him?" Delilah asked.

It had been her sneaking suspicion since she had seen Cee's old silver flask in Teddy's office. Cee had been carrying that flask the night of the murder, and the police had not recovered it. Delilah had never found it anywhere in the house either. For Teddy to have it, someone had to have given it to him. She suspected that either Miss Mindy or her husband had done it, and that meant they had to have been in the house the night of Cee's murder.

That also explained all the puzzling evidence that had never been considered during her trial: the position of Cee's body, indicating he had been moved, the opened door that had been unlocked from the inside.

All signs indicated that someone else *had* been there that night.

And the Williams family had inherited money after Mama Buford's death, but the way they spent it, she could see them wanting more. They stood to gain not only Cee's money but also Harbor Hill if Delilah was found guilty of his murder. While she had been in jail, they had lobbied hard for that very thing in court.

And she still remembered the hard slap Mr. Williams had given Miss Mindy, how he had sent her flying back into her makeup table. A man like that was capable of violence, maybe even murder.

All the pieces of the puzzle fit together. She just needed Miss Mindy to confirm her suspicions.

Miss Mindy laughed. It came out as a jarring cough, and she had to reach for her oxygen mask and place it back over her mouth and nose. She took several deep breaths. After a few seconds, she removed the mask again. "Is that what you think? My husband killed Cee?"

"Well . . . *did he*?" Delilah asked, taking another step toward the bed.

"No! He tried to clean up Cee's mess, not kill him! He'd even tried to sober him up by wrestling that stupid flask away. The little bastard had knocked you out cold! He called us in a panic because he'd thought he'd killed you and didn't know what to do." She sighed. "He didn't even have the brains to check for a pulse! We got there and saw you were still alive, but Cee was too drunk to care. He just kept ranting and raving, acting like the ungrateful little ass that he was . . . like he always had been! I got tired of it. I got tired of him and his selfish antics. He had been a burden on Mama, and now on us. It had to end!"

At those words, Delilah did a sharp intake of breath. "Wait. Did *you* kill him?"

Miss Mindy sank back against her pillows and sat quietly for what felt like an eternity. Finally, she said, "Hell, I'm old, and I'm dying! It's not like they would send me to prison for it now." She nodded. "Yes. Yes, I did it. I didn't go there intending to do it, but it happened. He pissed me off! He kept talking to Jake and me like we were his servants. He cussed at us. He was completely belligerent! I hit my breaking point, so when his back was turned, I gave him a hard shove and down he went."

*She did it while his back was turned,* Delilah thought. So Cee probably didn't even know his own sister had killed him.

"I don't regret it. Like I said, I couldn't take the burden anymore."

"She couldn't take the burden," Delilah repeated back in a whisper, slowly shaking her head.

She thought back to her stint in prison and the decades after, the taunts from townsfolk, and the feeling of isolation. She thought about the guilt and the grief, and how both had almost driven her to mad-ness. And this woman thought *she* had suffered a burden?

This time, Delilah was the one who laughed. It was hollow and bitter, much like she felt right now. But her bitterness quickly gave way to anger.

How dare this woman rip away her freedom? How dare she sully her name? How dare she steal years away from her life? And worse, she had justified what she did because she felt her little brother was a brat who had given away a house she'd wanted.

Delilah took yet another step toward the bed. She itched to reach out and rip the oxygen mask from the old woman's neck and slap her across her smug face. She wanted to shove her off the bed and watch her tumble to the floor. She had never wanted to physically harm someone this much in her life, but she felt an overwhelming urge to do so at the moment.

"So there," Miss Mindy said. "You got your answer. You got what you came for. I suppose you'll be leaving now?"

Delilah nodded. "Yeah, I'll leave . . . but I have something I want to do first."

She then reached for Miss Mindy. The old woman's imperious air disappeared. She looked frightened. She flinched when Delilah touched her, but then stared in surprise when Delilah didn't hit her but instead squeezed her hand.

"I'm not going to hurt you."

Oh, how she wanted to hurt her, to inflict the physical pain that reflected the emotional pain she had experienced all these years. But Delilah thought back to that night nearly fifty years ago and finding Cee's crumpled, lifeless body at the bottom of the stairs. She thought back to that night a few days ago and Tracey's bloodied face. She had seen her share of violence. She'd had enough of it.

"I'm just going to tell you something," she continued. She leaned toward her ear, tightening her grip on Miss Mindy's hand when she tried to pull away. "You may not go to jail for what you did. You may not even feel guilty about finally admitting what you did, and now he knows. He knows — and he's waiting for you. He's been whispering to me for the past forty-eight years, getting angrier and angrier. He told me that he was waiting for me so he could take revenge for what happened to him. But it wasn't *me* he should've been waiting for. It was you all along. Judging from how close to death's door you are, I'm glad Cee won't have to wait much longer to get what he wants."

She then stepped back from the bed and

stood upright. She released Miss Mindy's hand. The old woman frowned up at her.

"What nonsense are you talking about? Are you trying to say you were haunted by my brother's ghost?" She barked out a cough and gave a skeletal smile. "Am I'm supposed to be scared now?"

*Ghost* . . . it was an interesting word. Delilah couldn't say for sure that what had been chasing her for so long was a literal "ghost," in a classic sense. Sometimes, it felt like the voice she'd heard for decades was all in her head, and sometimes, the being felt as real as the bed rail now inches from her side. But that was the nature of ghosts, she supposed. They were what you allowed them to be.

"You don't have to be scared, Miss Mindy," she assured with a smile, "but know that not all ghosts are like the ones in a Charles Dickens novel. They aren't all moaning and banging shackles, floating over your head. Some are quieter than that. But it's the quiet ones that lie in wait that you really need to worry about."

"You don't . . . you don't frighten me," Miss Mindy said in a shaky voice. She didn't sound or look convincing. "I don't believe in that stuff!"

"Then don't." Delilah shrugged. "After

all, I'm just a dumb colored woman, after all. What would I know?"

"So have you two had a chance to get acquainted?" her daughter asked, bursting through the bedroom doorway. "Ready for the tour?"

"No, no tour," Delilah said, turning away from Miss Mindy. "I'll be leaving now."

*"Leaving?"* Miss Mindy's daughter blinked. Her mouth fell open. "How the hell are you leaving? I thought you were here to help my mother!"

"I'm afraid not, honey." Delilah shook her head and glanced back at Miss Mindy's stricken face. "I can't help her. No one can."

She then headed toward the bedroom door, brushing past Miss Mindy's daughter, who was still sputtering. She didn't look back as she walked down the hall and the staircase.

"It's good to finally get some peace," she whispered to Cee. "I never thought I would."

He didn't reply. She realized, almost sadly, that he would never speak to her again. He would be Miss Mindy's companion from now on.

Delilah smiled to herself and stepped through the front door into a world still illuminated from the inside out.

# ABOUT THE AUTHOR

**Shelly Stratton** is the penname of an award-nominated author who has published almost a dozen books under another pseudonym. She is married and lives in Maryland with her husband and their daughter. Visit her at her web site www.shellystratton books.com to learn more about her work.